THE LIST

J. A. JANCE

AN ALI REYNOLDS MYSTERY

THE A LIST

Pocket Books

New York   London   Toronto   Sydney   New Delhi

Pocket Books
An Imprint of Simon & Schuster, Inc.
1230 Avenue of the Americas
New York, NY 10020

This book is a work of fiction. Any references to historical events, real people, or real places are used fictitiously. Other names, characters, places, and events are products of the author's imagination, and any resemblance to actual events or places or persons, living or dead, is entirely coincidental.

Copyright © 2019 by J.A. Jance

All rights reserved, including the right to reproduce this book or portions thereof in any form whatsoever. For information, address Gallery Books Subsidiary Rights Department, 1230 Avenue of the Americas, New York, NY 10020.

First Pocket Books paperback edition February 2020

POCKET and colophon are registered trademarks of Simon & Schuster, Inc.

For information about special discounts for bulk purchases, please contact Simon & Schuster Special Sales at 1-866-506-1949 or business@simonandschuster.com.

The Simon & Schuster Speakers Bureau can bring authors to your live event. For more information or to book an event, contact the Simon & Schuster Speakers Bureau at 1-866-248-3049 or visit our website at www.simonspeakers.com.

Manufactured in the United States of America

10 9 8 7 6 5 4 3 2 1

ISBN 978-1-5011-5102-6
ISBN 978-1-5011-5103-3 (ebook)

For Loretta, my lovely friend from Lyons

Prologue

When Prisoner #74506 arrived at Folsom Prison in January of 2013, sentenced to life without parole, he came with a certain amount of celebrity. He was a highly esteemed pillar of his community as well as the scion of a wealthy founding family. His mother, a well-known area heiress with whom his relationship had been at times severely strained, would, he hoped, be able to use her considerable resources to make his time in prison less onerous.

After all, his mother's problems with him were never really with him—they were with what she called his questionable choices, first to divorce his first wife, of whom she had very much approved and loved as well, just to marry again. His mother referred to his second wife as "that bimbo," who, it turned out, managed to fleece him and then drive him into the arms of yet another piece of what his mother called "trailer trash." She considered these women beneath him intellectually, educationally, and, most important, socially and a poor reflection on herself, too. But now that neither was "in the picture," he hoped that he could become closer to his mother—and thereby closer to her seemingly unlimited funds.

Another thing on his mind, or rather in his gut, was a burning desire to avenge himself on those who'd put him away. He wanted all of them dealt with, all four of them—Leo and those three bitches as well. He wouldn't rest until they'd gotten the punishment they deserved, just as he'd been given his. Their names were etched in his brain, and he thought it would be a nice touch to etch them on his skin as well. As soon as possible, he was going to give himself a lasting and visible declaration of war—a tattoo.

Upon arrival, Prisoner #74506, a disgraced physician, soon discovered there was a thriving economy inside the prison with any number of products to buy, sell, and trade. That was especially true for inmates with salable skills, and he just happened to have some of those. By virtue of his having hired a hit man to dispose of his wife, the outside world might have stripped him of his professional credentials, but on the inside, people gave him the respect that his professional standing warranted. They also wanted to make use of his skills.

As a personal preference, the "Professor," as he came to be called, didn't smoke or do drugs, but cigarettes and drugs were highly regarded as common currency. For a package of smokes or a line of coke, he was more than happy to assist his fellow prisoners with their various health problems and issues. Thanks to his extensive knowledge, he was able to help them work their way around the system, and his ability to read people meant he could tell which guards might be bribable and which weren't, which ones might have weaknesses in the areas of gambling, drugs, alcohol, or sex that would make them suitable targets for exploitation.

Within weeks of his arrival, he was ensconced in what amounted to one of the prison's junior suites—a cell with a removable brick in the wall that allowed for keeping all kinds of contraband—hard, cold cash included.

As one of the so-called elite, he was quick to recognize others of his ilk, one of whom turned out to be a guy named Luis Ochoa, Folsom Prison's undisputed kingpin. Early on in Luis's life-without-parole sentence, he had plied his trade as a talented tattoo artist who'd transformed countless sweet-faced young kids into tough guys by covering them with walking catalogs of MS-13 tats. Over time Luis had made his way up through the ranks. His reputation as a wheeler-dealer allowed him to have a table of his own in the mess hall, where petitioners could come asking for help or favors.

When it came time for Prisoner #74506 to start on his tattoo project, he approached Luis Ochoa's table and sat down across from someone he knew to be a very dangerous man.

"What can I do for you, Prof?" Luis asked, delivering the last word in a mockingly derisive tone. Ignoring the sarcasm, Prisoner #74506 slid several packets of highly prized contraband, in this case fentanyl, across the table. He knew he was paying more than was necessary for an informal consultation, but he wanted to get Luis's attention.

"What's this?" Luis asked, while at the same time taking the packets and slipping them under his jumpsuit.

"I want some tattoos," the Professor replied. "If I'm going to do this myself, what does it take and how do I do it?"

"You're sure you don't want someone else to do the job for you?"

"Nope, I'm DIY all the way."

"All right, then," Luis told him. "You'll need india ink, needles, a candle, cotton swabs, and rubbing alcohol for sterilizing. You'll also need a guard who's willing to look the other way."

"Can you round up all of that?"

"Sure."

"How much?"

"For the supplies, three more of what you already gave me should just about cover it. To pay off the guard? That depends on the guard. Some of 'em cost more than others."

In the end the guard had cost a bundle, but he'd been happy to take his bribe in the form of a fistful of oxy. It turned out he preferred oxycodone to coke, which worked well. Pills were a hell of a lot easier to hide than cash would have been.

On the appointed night, watched over by his personally paid-for guard, the Professor did his work by candlelight, which, Luis had assured him, was unlikely to attract the attention of the cell block's security cameras. Because needles tend to grow dull with repeated use, he'd coughed up extra product for a dozen brand-new syringes, still sterile and still sealed in their original packaging. Possessing a candle or matches was also prohibited, but Luis had provided both as part of the deal.

At first the Professor thought he'd put his A List— A for "Annihilation"—on his upper thigh, but when it came time to actually do the deed, he had reconsidered. He wanted his declaration of war to be out there in the open, not only for him to see but for all the world to see as well. So rather than shaving his upper thigh, he shaved his left forearm. Then he penciled in five initials in all, in carefully printed capital letters.

First came a *D*, for the "bimbo." Dawn was already dead by then, but in terms of his kill list and for completion's sake, she had to be there right along with the others. He didn't know for sure that she would have testified against him, but he hadn't been willing to risk it. Then came *L*, for Leo, the punk gangbanger who'd taken his money and then thrown him under the bus by accepting a plea deal and turning up in court to testify against him. Next was a *K*, for Kaitlyn, his onetime lover, who was right there in court, spilling her guts to the prosecutor and pointing an accusing finger. Next was an *A*, for Alexandra, the ingrate woman who'd spent a decade trying to tear his life apart. It had worked, too. Here he was. The last letter was another *A*, for the news broad Ali Reynolds who'd aired the ungrateful bitch's charges far and wide, turning something that could have been handled quietly and discreetly into a cause célèbre.

Once the penciled list was complete, he sterilized the area with rubbing alcohol. Then he opened one syringe package, wrapped the needle in cotton thread, dipped it in the bottle of ink, and quietly went to work.

The first time he plunged the needle into his own flesh, he was surprised by how much it hurt, but every poke after that was a little less painful. Each subsequent prick wasn't quite as bad as the one that preceded it, and as the inked letters came into focus, the pain turned into a perverse kind of pleasure. He was giving himself something to remember them by, and he smiled as he went along. He wasn't sure of exactly how he'd accomplish his goal, but accomplish it he would.

He'd need worker bees to do the actual wet work, but finding hired help wouldn't be that tough, not if his mother would throw a little money his way. Much to his surprise, she'd been a brick ever since his arrest, through the trial and his subsequent conviction. If he was halfway nice to her, he was pretty sure he could charm her into helping him with this, too. And why wouldn't she? After all, the woman was in her seventies and had already survived one bout with cancer. Besides, he was her only son, her "fair-haired boy," and since she was clearly living on borrowed time, she just might enjoy the challenge.

As for the Professor himself? He was doing life without parole for first-degree murder and conspiracy to commit. So what if one of his hirelings got caught or decided to rat him out to the cops? No big deal. The death penalty was still legal in California. If he was convicted in another case, a judge and jury might hand out a death sentence, but these days no one actually received the death penalty. Odds were they'd pile on a few more life sentences, just for good measure. Well, lots of luck with that, guys! Have a ball. Knock yourselves out.

The process took most of the night. Before the doors clattered open in the morning, his contraband set of tattooing equipment was safely stowed behind the removable brick in the wall under his stainless-steel sink.

In the mess hall, Edward went straight to Luis Ochoa's table to show off his handiwork.

"Good job," Luis said, examining his forearm. "So what is this?"

"I call it my A List. It's also my kill list."

"So you've got problems with these guys?"

"With these people," the Professor corrected, "one guy and four women. Make that three females still living, that is. These are the people who put me here, and I'm planning to take them down one by one."

"How do you expect to do that from in here?" Luis asked.

"I'm not sure," the Professor replied. "I'm working on it. I'll probably need some help."

According to in-house gossip, the Professor knew that running an outside murder-for-hire network was one of the many services Luis Ochoa was able to provide—for a price, that is.

"You will need help," Luis agreed, "and help costs money. You say your mother's loaded?"

"She is," the Professor said with confidence. "Even after paying off my defense team, she's still got way more money than she'll ever need."

"And she'd be willing to pay the freight for this little project of yours?"

"If I ask her, I think she will."

Luis replied with a wolfish, gold-toothed grin. "I might just be able to help you, then, my friend," he said. "If your mother's got the money, honey, I've got the time."

They shook hands on it then and there, and that was the beginning of a beautiful and very successful alliance. From that moment on, Prisoner #74506's life in Folsom Prison improved immeasurably, because everyone—guards and inmates alike—now understood that he was one of Luis's "inner circle," and they left him the hell alone.

Two weeks later, once the original tattoos were mostly healed, he gave the guard another batch of oxy in order to do an "addition and correction" to his tat.

That night, after lights-out, he retrieved his candle and his tattooing kit. He knew how to do the job now, and it didn't take long for him to ink a black X across the face of that letter D at the top of his list.

"One down," he told himself with a confident smile, studying the deadly scorecard on his forearm. "One down and four to go."

1

Dawn Gilchrist was beautiful if not particularly bright. Back before her ex-husband divorced his first wife and before Dawn and Edward married, she'd worked as a nurse/receptionist in his fertility practice in Santa Clarita, California, just north of L.A. As a consequence, she had firsthand knowledge of Edward's secrets and lies, especially the ones she personally had helped him create.

When she'd stopped by the office to see him on a May afternoon back in 2003, her husband's relatively new blond-bombshell receptionist, a dim bulb named Kaitlyn, told her that he was with a patient but that he'd be right out. As Dawn settled in to wait, Kaitlyn chatted with her boss's wife, mentioning in passing that one of the practice's former patients, Alexandra Munsey, had come by earlier in the day asking for her records so she could be put in touch with her son's sperm donor. It seems her twenty-one-year old-son, Evan, was deathly ill and in need of a kidney transplant.

Hearing the words, Dawn—who'd once held the same position Kaitlyn now did—had felt a sudden clutch in her gut. She knew far too much about Evan Munsey's sperm donor, even if the boy's mother did not. If he was in his twenties now, that meant he'd most likely been born in the eighties. "What did you tell her?" Dawn asked, trying to hide the concern she felt.

"That those records are entirely confidential."

"Yes, they are," Dawn agreed quickly in an attempt to cover her alarm. "And they need to stay that way."

She had dropped by to let Edward know that one of her girlfriends had turned up in town and they were going out for dinner. Rather than wait around to talk to her husband in person at the end of his appointment, Dawn left him a note and then fled the office. Out in the parking lot, she sat in the car and gripped the steering wheel in hopes of quelling the shaking in her hands.

Kaitlyn had no idea that the confidential files Alexandra Munsey sought—along with those of any number of other patients—no longer required protection for the simple reason that they no longer existed. Dawn herself had personally destroyed them. It was also likely that Kaitlyn had no idea about how the clinic had operated during some very tough times back in the eighties, but Dawn did. She knew where all those bodies were buried, and she was pretty sure that if the jig wasn't up right now, it would be soon. If the fact that Alexandra Munsey's requested records had gone missing was ever leaked to the public, Edward's hugely successful fertility practice—one that had up to now supported a very lavish lifestyle for both of them as well as for his previous wife—would come crashing down around their ears.

In the years since that first divorce, Edward had developed a five-star reputation as a wizard when it came to doing fertility procedures. People from all over Southern California flocked to his door, making long pilgrimages up and down the I-5 corridor searching for answers to their complex reproductive issues. At this point Dawn was reasonably confident that sperm and egg donors were currently being handled on an up-and-up basis. Prospective donors went through an extensive screening process, and the profiles and photos in the records shown to prospective recipients were all completely legitimate. The problem for Dawn was that back in the old days, when she'd been the one running the outer office—serving as Edward's nurse, receptionist, and lover—things had been very different.

It was never quite clear how or when Jeanette, Edward's wronged first wife, had become aware of her husband's dalliance with Dawn, but once the affair came to light, all hell had broken loose. Ed's widowed mother, Hannah, who was very well-off in her own right, had been more than happy to pay her son's way through school, premed and medical school both, and once he was ready to set up a practice in his hometown of Santa Clarita, California, Hannah had been delighted to help out there as well. But when it came time to bail him out of the dire financial ramifications from a divorce settlement, she'd drawn a line in the sand and refused to lift a finger.

After all, Hannah had adored her first daughter-in-law. Any court-ordered funds due to Jeanette, from the property settlement to alimony, would be payable strictly on Edward's dime. At the time the divorce proceedings were initiated, both the office building housing the practice and the family home had been essentially free and clear. The cost of cutting Jeanette loose had been steep. Edward not only had to hand over half the value of both the office building and their home, but he'd had to pay off her half of Jeanette's interest in the net present value of the practice itself. In order to buy back his own properties, he'd had to mortgage everything to the hilt. Strapped for cash but wanting to maintain his position in the community, Edward and Dawn had started cutting corners inside the practice, corners that should never have been cut, including relying less and less on the expense of private contractors for their supply of sperm and egg donations.

During most of that time, Edward himself had functioned as the supplier of their supposedly "donated" sperm while Dawn had been more than happy to supply the occasional egg. He and Dawn both had treated it as something of a lark—their own private joke. They had worked together to create the "catalog" containing the fictional profiles of their "stable of donors"—a collection of handsome young men and stunningly beautiful young women. At Edward's direction Dawn had culled pictures of good-looking young students out of various high school and college yearbooks, mostly from institutions located on the East Coast. They had used those photos in conjunction with impressive but entirely fictional profiles to create a catalog from which prospective parents could choose the donor who would "be the best fit" for their individual families. The fictional bios always described the donors as being top-drawer students or impressive athletes, all of them purportedly in excellent health.

Dawn was one of those women who'd never wanted children of her own, so it was odd for her and her husband to be the biological parents of who knows how many living, breathing offspring. As for the parents who managed to conceive through Edward's efforts? They were always so overjoyed with the result of finally having a baby of their own that none of them bothered hanging around and asking too many questions.

But that was then—back in the mid- to late eighties. At the time DNA had been little more than an esoteric idea, a minor blip in the consciousness of the general public. Now, however, only a few years after O. J. Simpson's murder trial, DNA was familiar to everyone. And for Edward Gilchrist, that not-guilty verdict had been a wake-up call. Realizing that DNA might eventually be his undoing, he and Dawn had set out that very night to take corrective measures. They'd gone back to the office and purged the filing cabinets of all the pertinent records, including the donor catalogs. At Edward's direction Dawn had carried them back to the house and shredded every last one of them.

Since then Dawn had watched from the sidelines as DNA technology improved by leaps and bounds. Now it wasn't much of a stretch to realize that if Alexandra Munsey ever figured out that Edward Gilchrist himself had fathered her son, the clinic's ability to continue functioning would be blown out of the water.

After that visit to the office and learning that Alexandra Munsey might be on their trail and long before Edward had any idea that a financial firestorm was brewing, Dawn bailed. She didn't want to wait around long enough for grubby-handed lawyers to start filing malpractice lawsuits or for bankruptcy proceedings to turn up on their doorstep. Instead Dawn decided to grab her money and run.

She went back to the house that very afternoon, packed her bags, and moved out. She filed for divorce the next day, citing that handy-dandy catchall of irreconcilable differences. To her surprise, Edward didn't raise much of a fuss. For one thing he knew that Dawn had him dead to rights when it came to coming up with suitable grounds. Edward was a serial womanizer, after all. He'd always been one of those, his relationship with Dawn herself included. She had engaged the services of a private detective who'd managed to provide documented proof—a grainy video—showing Edward and Kaitlyn Todd, his latest sweet young thing of a nurse, going at it hot and heavy in the recliner in Edward's office. That was typical Edward, all right—ready to grab any accommodating piece of tail but too damned cheap to get a hotel room.

Several years had now passed since that fateful afternoon when Alexandra Munsey had first reappeared in their lives, and everything Dawn had feared might happen back then seemed to be coming to pass. With the aid of something called the Progeny Project, Alex Munsey had lined up a whole group of people who were intent on filing a class-action suit against Edward, claiming that he'd committed fraud while serving as his clinic's primary sperm donor by failing to disclose his late father's history of kidney disease, which had put all those resulting offspring at risk of also developing kidney disease later in life.

Dawn knew that the statute of limitations mandated that there was no longer any possibility of Edward's being charged with either fraud or malpractice. With those legal remedies off the table, the affected families had hired a hotshot trial lawyer who, working on contingency, was preparing to file a multimillion-dollar class-action suit based on the premise that by withholding and misrepresenting his own medical history, Edward had endangered the health of the progeny conceived through his sperm donations.

As the trial date approached, Dawn hoped to stay well out of it. At this point Edward was still free as a bird. His practice had remained open for business all this time, and Dawn's alimony checks continued to show up in her bank account on a regular basis. Her divorce had been final for almost five years. The generous property settlement negotiated by her attorney, and funded no doubt by her former mother-in-law, had allowed Dawn to pay cash for a relatively modest town-house-style condo right here in Santa Clarita. In the intervening years, she had dated some, but she hadn't remarried, for good reason. Had Dawn tied the knot with someone else, those alimony payments would have come to a screeching halt.

But now Dawn knew that if Alexandra Munsey and her Progeny Project allies prevailed, Edward would be out of business, bringing an end to Dawn's gravy train as well. So far she'd been able to live on that quite comfortably without having to go back to work, but depending on the outcome of the upcoming trial, that was likely to change.

Twice in the last week, two different sets of strangers had shown up on her doorstep. Some of Dawn's pals, also divorcées, had shared lessons about spotting potential process servers and avoiding same—mostly by simply not opening the door. One of Dawn's visitors had been a guy posing as a pizza deliveryman when Dawn knew damned good and well that she hadn't ordered a pizza. The next one was a pair of young men supposedly selling magazine subscriptions. Process servers or not, she didn't open the door for either of them.

But after the second set came and went, Dawn did some serious thinking. She probably wouldn't be able to dodge the process servers forever, and maybe she shouldn't. She had followed the story in the local paper and knew the name of the high-powered L.A. attorney who was handling the case. In the news he was alleging that patient files critical to the case had supposedly gone missing. As Edward's former wife, Dawn couldn't be compelled to testify against him, but considering the fact that she had donated some of her own eggs, maybe she should call up the lawyer, cut herself a deal, and offer to testify on the plaintiff's behalf. It would be fun watching Edward squirm when she told an enthralled and crowded courtroom that she knew exactly what had become of those missing files. After all, hadn't she been the one who'd spent hours on end shredding the damned things?

And if she did testify against Edward and he lost— if he and that little blond bitch of his went down in flames—wouldn't it serve both of them right? And wouldn't it be something if Dawn herself had the pleasure of pounding that final nail into their coffin?

There was a downside, of course. If Dawn's alimony ground to a halt, she'd eventually have to get a job for the first time in years, but even that might end up working to her advantage. After all, hadn't that been a hot topic of discussion during tonight's dinner—the importance of divorcées' accumulating Social Security credits in their own right?

It had been one of her customary girls' nights out with a loosely organized group of women who referred to themselves as the Seconds—divorced second wives as opposed to divorced first wives. One of them—Frannie, short for Francine—had come away from her marriage with a property settlement that required her ex to continue funding her membership fees at Santa Clarita's tony Grapevine Golf and Country Club. The group gathered there on a biweekly basis, using Frannie's membership for the reservation but going strictly dutch as far as food and drinks were concerned.

They sometimes referred to themselves as the

"Broken Babes Club" and gave each other a safe place to compare notes and vent about dickhead ex-husbands, double-dealing divorce lawyers, and missing alimony payments. And they almost always had fun, including tonight, although when the subject of ex-husbands getting their just deserts came around, Dawn Gilchrist hadn't exactly mentioned that she was pretty sure Edward was about to be run over by a Mack truck or that maybe Dawn herself would be behind the wheel.

Before driving home, Dawn had imbibed a couple of drinks—actually several more than a couple. She knew she'd had too much, so she was overly cautious on her way home. Not wanting to pick up a DUI, she was relieved to finally turn in to her own driveway and tuck her BMW into her town house's two-car garage.

After pushing the remote to close the garage door, she cracked open the car door with one hand and was reaching over to the passenger seat to collect her purse when the door was forcibly yanked open behind her. Before she could object, a small but powerfully built man, dressed all in black, reached into the car, grabbed her by the arm, and bodily dragged her out of the vehicle. Before she had time to scream, he slammed her down flat on the garage's polished concrete floor.

Momentarily unconscious, Dawn came to just in time to see the blade of a knife arcing through the air above her. She tried to scream and dodge out of the way, but before she could, the knife sliced into her throat, silencing her instantly by severing both her carotid artery and her larynx. She died without uttering a single word.

The man stood over Dawn, staring down at her as her lifeblood ebbed away. "Guess what?" he growled. "I've got a message for you from your ex. He wanted me to tell you that you won't be testifying against him anytime soon."

He walked out, leaving the garage door open and the light on. The timer kicked in a few minutes later, and the light went off, leaving the garage bathed in darkness while the clicking of the gradually cooling car engine was the only sound to be heard. Early the next morning, the guy coming to deliver Dawn's paper turned in to the driveway. Through the open door he spotted a body lying next to her black BMW. He was the one who called it in.

When the cops showed up, Dawn Gilchrist's killer was long gone. He left behind not a shred of physical evidence—no fingerprints, no DNA, and no footprints either. However, cops canvassing the neighborhood soon discovered that Dawn's next-door neighbors had recently installed a set of very high-end security cameras. Footage from one of those showed a clear image of the presumed suspect, wearing dark clothing, a hoodie, gloves, and lurking just outside Dawn's garage door. When the door opened and she drove inside, he'd entered the garage just as the door closed behind him. A few minutes later, the door opened again, and the video footage captured the suspect's hurried exit. This time, however, he was facing directly into the camera, and the resulting image came through with remarkable clarity.

There was a problem, however. No matter how clear the image was, the cops had no suspects and nothing to use as a comparison. The case stayed hot for a while, but eventually new cases came online and the homicide investigation into the death of Dawn Lorraine Gilchrist went completely cold.

2

t was a sunny Sunday afternoon in early June when Ali Reynolds came outside onto the front porch of her Sedona, Arizona, home carrying two large mugs of coffee. Her good friend, Sister Anselm Becker, was leaning back in one of the pair of Adirondack chairs that occupied most of the porch's available floor space. Ali placed one cup on the wooden surface of Sister Anselm's chair arm and then took her own cup to the other chair.

"I'm so glad you stopped by today," Ali said. "The last few weeks have been way too busy for both of us."

"Yes," Sister Anselm agreed, "way too busy. I can't tell you how much it means to me to just have a quiet moment to enjoy the view."

And the view from Ali's house on Manzanita Hills Road was indeed worthy of enjoying. Beyond a lavender valance of dripping wisteria blooms, Sedona's iconic red rocks loomed large against a cloudless blue sky. In the foreground was the lush garden Leland Brooks, Ali's former majordomo, had designed for her as a final gift before taking his retirement and returning to the UK.

Leland had wanted to create a typical English garden, but since Sedona wasn't in England, the garden couldn't be typically English either. He had been forced to substitute a variety of climate-appropriate plants, which, although not traditional, provided a lush profusion of colors that lasted from early spring to late fall. So not only were the garden's flowers not English, neither was the garden's centerpiece—a life-size statue of a bighorn sheep, a rustic piece crafted by welding together pieces of rusty sheet metal and discarded auto parts. That odd-ball combination of the rustic metal sheep presiding over a riot of colorful flowers created exactly the kind of quirky serenity that both Ali and her husband, B. Simpson, enjoyed.

"I never look at this garden without thinking of your wonderful Mr. Brooks," Sister Anselm said. "Have you heard from him recently?"

"I heard from him a week ago," Ali answered. "He called to let me know that Thomas is through with chemo and currently undergoing radiation. So far they're keeping their fingers crossed."

Thomas Blackfield and Leland had been an item back in their youth, before Leland's homophobic family had driven him to join the Royal Marines and go off to fight the Korean War. It had taken decades for Leland and Thomas to reconnect, and now that Thomas was dealing with a third-stage cancer diagnosis, Leland had gone back home to serve as his primary caregiver.

"If you speak to him again," Sister Anselm said, "please let him know I said hello and that I'm thinking of them and wishing them both good health."

"I will," Ali agreed, "but speaking of health, how's Bishop Gillespie doing?"

Francis Gillespie, the bishop of the Catholic arch-diocese in Phoenix, was the primary reason Sister Anselm was in Arizona. Sister Anselm's father, Hans, had immigrated to the States from Germany in 1934. By the time World War II rolled around, he had yet to obtain US citizenship status. As a result he was taken into custody and eventually shipped off to a multinational war-relocation center in Crystal City, Texas.

Because Hans had come down with TB and because the camp had limited medical care, Sophia, his wife, had petitioned that she be allowed to join him there to help look after him. The only way US authorities would agree to that was on the condition that she surrender both her own US citizenship as well as that of her two daughters, Rebecca and Judith. Once at the camp, while Becca and their American-born mother tended to Hans, Judith had been free as a bird. She had taken herself outside to play with the other kids in the neighborhood. An outgoing child, she'd made friends with everyone and had come away from Crystal City with the ability to speak passable Italian and Japanese in addition to her mother's English and her father's native German.

During an ill-fated "prisoner-of-war exchange" the family was supposed to be shipped "back home" to Germany, even though Sophia and her daughters had never before set foot outside the US. Hans died on board the ship and was buried at sea during the transatlantic crossing. Subsequently Sophia and her girls were offloaded in France and left to wander as displaced persons in war-torn Europe. By then Sophia, too, had developed TB. They were taken in by a Sisters of Providence convent in southern France, where the nuns cared for Sophia until her death. They tried to look after both girls as well, but Rebecca had rebelled. After running away from the convent, she got caught up in prostitution and ended up stabbed to death in an alley in Paris prior to her seventeenth birthday. Judith, on the other hand, stayed on at the convent and added three additional languages—French, Spanish, and Latin—to her growing collection.

At age eighteen Judith Becker could have returned to the US and reclaimed her American citizenship. Instead the girl who'd been raised as a good Lutheran back in Milwaukee converted to Catholicism and joined the convent, where she became Sister Anselm. At the suggestion of her first mother superior, she trained as a nurse and earned a doctorate in psychology. When an urgent call went out for translators to assist with Vatican II, Sister Anselm had been dispatched to Rome, where she came to the attention of a US-based priest named Father Gillespie.

Years later he was the one who helped arrange her eventual return to the United States. Later still, after being installed as the archbishop of the Phoenix diocese, he had brought her to Arizona and stationed her at St. Bernadette's, a small convent in Jerome. Designated as Archbishop Gillespie's special emissary, Sister Anselm traveled all over the American Southwest functioning as a patient advocate, often for undocumented and non-English-speaking immigrants who, when hospitalized, needed assistance in communicating their needs to medical personnel. That was how Ali and Sister Anselm had first met, in the hospital room of a badly injured woman at a Phoenix-area hospital.

"Oh, he's sick all right," Sister Anselm said, finally answering Ali's inquiry, "but you can bet that ornery old coot isn't going to hang up his miter until he's good and ready. In the meantime he's trying to put me out to pasture."

Ali spluttered over a sip of coffee. "He's what?"

"He says I'm too old to be driving all over hell and

gone—his words not mine—by myself. He's in the process of importing a young woman—a relatively young woman—to come 'ride shotgun' with me and 'learn the ropes,' although what he really means is for *her* to drive, with me in the passenger seat."

The visible air quotes punctuating Sister Anselm's words indicated that she wasn't at all pleased with this turn of affairs.

"He thinks he's going to replace you?" Ali demanded.

"That's the plan."

"With whom?"

"Her name's Sister Cecelia Groppa," Sister Anselm replied. "It turns out her story is a lot like mine. She was born in Argentina and was three years old during what was called Argentina's 'Dirty War' back in the mid-seventies. Her parents were dissidents, members of 'the Disappeareds'—who went missing at that time and never returned. Both Cecelia's mother and her aunt—her mother's sister—had originally emigrated from Brazil to Argentina. After Cecelia's mother and father disappeared, the aunt took care of her for a while. A few years later, when the aunt died, the child ended up in an orphanage. By then she was fluent in both Portuguese and Spanish. Eventually she joined a convent and became a nurse."

"Which is why Archbishop Gillespie wants her here?" Ali asked.

"Presumably," Sister Anselm agreed, "but I'm none too happy about having to take on a trainee at the moment."

"Still," Ali said. "You need to give her a chance." It was odd for her to be giving the nun advice, and for a time neither of them said anything.

Finally Sister Anselm shook off the silence. "Enough about me," she said. "What's going on with you? Are you tired of listening to graduation speeches yet?"

Ali smiled. "Very," she said. "All the same, I was glad to go."

For the past three weekends, she'd been on the road, attending one graduation ceremony after another—NAU, ASU, U of A, and even a completion celebration at the Cordon Bleu branch campus down in Scottsdale. As a senior in high school, Ali had been given a full-ride scholarship by the Amelia Dougherty Askins Foundation which provided help for needy girls from the Verde Valley to further their educations. Years later, when Ali finally returned to Sedona, she'd ended up being put in charge of running the very scholarship program from which she herself had once benefited.

In the years since Ali had been in charge of the program, she'd a number of successes. She had four certified teachers, three RNs, and two full-fledged pharmacists to her credit. One girl had graduated from med school and was doing her residency in pediatrics at a hospital in Tucson, while two others had embarked on premed studies at the University of Arizona. At NAU that year, she'd added in two more education graduates, one B.A. and one M.Ed. That graduation speech, otherwise boring as hell, had also brought on board a computer-science graduate as well as another four-year nursing graduate. Arizona State had yielded two more teachers, one a B.A. and another an M.Ed, along with a determined young woman who had grown up in Jerome and who'd set her sights on becoming a mining engineer.

Two years earlier, realizing that scholarships for boys were most often sports-based, Ali had added boys and trade schools to the mix. That was how a boy named Raphael Fuentes, a kid with zero athletic capabilities, had just completed a course of studies at the Cordon Bleu in Scottsdale, while another young man was now a sophomore drama major at the University of Arizona, intent on becoming a costume designer rather than an actor.

"This year's awards were handed out earlier in the spring," Ali resumed. "Without Leland there to help with the first sort, it was a lot more work than it's been in the past. Still, hard work or not, it's very rewarding. And later this summer I'm hoping to have a kind of homecoming gathering where I'll be inviting all current and past Askins scholars here to the house so they can get together, chew the fat, and compare notes."

"Agnes, too?" Sister Anselm asked.

Agnes Gray was someone Ali and Sister Anselm together had helped rescue from a polygamous cult near Colorado City. At the time Agnes left what was known as the Encampment, she'd been wise in the ways of animals but terribly lacking in formal education. Since then she had earned a GED and completed training as a veterinarian's assistant. Now, though, she had enrolled as a freshman at Northern Arizona University, intent on becoming a veterinarian. Ali had fudged the scholarship's Verde Valley resident stipulation enough that Agnes's studies were also being funded by the Askins Foundation.

"Agnes, too," Ali replied.

"I'm glad to hear it," Sister Anselm said. She put down her empty cup and glanced at her watch. "I should probably be going. Is B. around? I'd like to say hello to him before taking off."

"You missed him," Ali said. "He had meetings scheduled in Japan for Monday, which happens to be today on this side of the international date line. He's not due home until the end of the week. Lucky guy, too," Ali added. "We've got a slew of back-ordered computers that are due to be delivered sometime this week which will entail a huge installation project, a bullet he so happens to be dodging."

"That's what you've got all those energetic young people for, isn't it?" Sister Anselm said, rising to her feet.

"Exactly," Ali agreed.

Once Sister Anselm had sped away in her bright red Mini Cooper, Ali took both empty coffee cups into the house. After refilling hers, she came back outside, carrying the book she was reading and accompanied by her long-haired miniature dachshund, Bella. While Bella explored the garden at her leisure, searching for stray rodents or bunnies, Ali sat watching and thinking.

When she fled home to Sedona from California years earlier, her life had been a shambles and she'd felt totally defeated. Holed up in the double-wide mobile home she'd inherited from her Aunt Evie, Ali hadn't envisioned that any of this would come her way—not the house, the view, the garden, the dog, the statue. She hadn't anticipated having that coterie of scholarship kids in her life nor a best friend who happened to be an eighty-something Sister of Providence. As for remarrying someone who was fifteen years younger than she was? That hadn't been on Ali's radar back then either.

Bella finished her exploratory tour of the garden and came back to Ali, asking to be scooped up and held.

"That's right, girl," Ali crooned aloud to Bella. "I never saw any of this coming, but I'm glad it did."

With that, she picked up the book and located her place. She had ordered a signed copy of Alex Munsey's new book, *The Changeling*. She'd started to read it when it first came out, but her reading had been interrupted and she hadn't had time to finish it.

On that sunny afternoon, sitting and reading in the cool shade of her wisteria-lined front porch, Ali Reynolds had no idea that before the end of the week people and events from those bad old times in California were about to reach out and bite her in the butt, because, as that old saying goes, no good deed ever goes unpunished.

3

A li Reynolds kicked off her high heels, spun away from her desk, and stared out the window of her second-story corner office. As the news-anchor-in-chief of the network's Los Angeles affiliate, she had been deemed worthy of corner-office treatment. That didn't mean much today. There was a smog alert outside, and a layer of gritty brown air obscured all but the nearest lanes of traffic down below. Yes, there were mountains out there somewhere, but today they were totally invisible.

The news team had gone over the upcoming headline stories for the evening newscast, and she had a quiet hour to herself before she needed to be downstairs, where Angela, the station's go-to beauty wrangler, would see to her makeup and hair. Between the five o'clock news and the next broadcast at eleven, Ali was supposed to have a few hours off, except that wouldn't be the case tonight. Her husband, Paul Grayson, would be sending a car to pick her up and carry her off to the home of some Hollywood bigwig or other, where she and Paul were due to grace a fund-raiser for a political candidate whose name Ali didn't know and didn't care to learn. Whoever it was, he was the current darling of the network execs, and Paul and Ali had drawn the short straws of being there for the meet and greet. For Ali, however, all that meeting and greeting was starting to get her down, and that was only the start of it.

She had met Paul Grayson, a powerful network executive, when she was working for the Chicago affiliate. Theirs had been a whirlwind romance. Paul had wooed her with high-end dining, always accompanied by expensive wines, and had seen to it that fresh flowers were delivered to her dressing room on a daily basis. His marriage proposal had been accompanied by an offer to give her a lucrative promotion to the evening news anchor at the network's flagship station in L.A.

Her first husband, Dean, had died of glioblastoma while Ali was still in her twenties. His battle with cancer had been a short but terrible trip from initial diagnosis to over and out, leaving Ali a widow who was also seven months pregnant. As a single mother with a demanding career, she'd had little time or interest for the dating game. When Paul eventually came calling, Chris had been fourteen years old and a freshman in high school.

Back then she'd thought it would be good for Chris to have an adult male in his life. He was close to Ali's parents, but Edie and Bob Larson were back home in Sedona—too far away for anything but intermittent connections. Unfortunately, Ali's dream of a cozy family life for the three of them hadn't turned out the way she'd hoped. Paul had no children of his own, and he came with very limited parenting skills. At a time when Chris was an adolescent and starting to test parental limits, Paul had expected that his new stepson should hop to at every issued order. Seven years later they barely tolerated each other. Now twenty-one, Chris was about to finish his degree at UCLA. He still lived at home, but he spent most of his time in the casita down by the pool rather than in the house itself.

As for the marriage? That wasn't exactly living up to expectations either. Sure, Paul's home was magnificent—a mansion, really—and a far cry from the home she'd grown up in behind her parents' Sugarloaf Café in Sedona and a huge step up from the grim digs she and Chris had lived in on the East Coast and in the Midwest as she struggled to establish herself in the television news business. So she'd felt a bit like Cinderella when she came to live in the house on Robert Lane as a new bride, but seven years later the marriage was on the ropes. The house was Paul's house, furnished and decorated to his tastes rather than hers, and she still felt like a bit of an interloper.

As for Paul? He was glad to have her around as a visible social prop on those occasions when a spouse was called for, but he seemed to be drifting away from her. She had suggested marital counseling more than once, but he'd scoffed at the idea. Besides, his time was too valuable for him to bother wasting any of it on a shrink. Eventually Ali had come to feel at home with his indifference. It was a lot less complicated than walking on eggshells both at home and on the job.

Her work at the station wasn't exactly a bed of roses either. Because Ali was promoted from outside rather than from within and championed by the executive privilege of her spouse, she had walked into a situation where there was plenty of resentment and very little camaraderie. The longtime female reporter who had expected to take over the news-anchor position left the station in a huff a few weeks after Ali's arrival, and her abrupt departure had made things worse instead of better. Ali made friends with people at affiliates in other locations up and down the West Coast, but at her own station? Not so much.

She was often deployed as the station's standard-bearer at various charitable events around the city. Her visible participation was good for ratings. The downside was that although her PR work outside the station gave her better standing in the community as a whole, it made her even more of a pariah at work. In other words, the complications both at home and in the office left her too drained to tackle doing something about either one, so she kept her head down and did what was required—including showing up at whatever event—a wine tasting of some kind—was on the calendar for tonight. There was something terribly depressing in all that. Ali would attend and go through the motions, but her heart wouldn't be in it. She felt utterly useless—as though nothing she did really mattered.

At that point a call came through from Diane, the receptionist at the front desk downstairs. "There's someone here to see you. Her name is Alexandra Munsey. She doesn't have an appointment, but she said you chatted briefly at the Kidney Foundation luncheon a week ago. She was wondering if she could have a few minutes of your time."

Ali tried not to roll her eyes. She met a lot of people at events like that. They were usually looking for a charitable donation of some kind, or else they were searching for a speaker or a celebrity to spark interest in an upcoming event. But PR was one of Ali's primary responsibilities, and in these days of post-9/11 security precautions, stray visitors weren't allowed to wander through the station without an official escort.

"Sure," Ali said. "Tell her I'll be right down."

There was a crowd in the lobby, made up mostly of people waiting to be the live studio audience for the station's midafternoon talk show. They were an enthusiastic, excited group, gabbing energetically among themselves. None of them looked at all familiar. At last Ali picked out someone who did. A woman sat alone on one of the lobby's bright yellow love seats, staring up at the bank of high-def TV screens lining the wall. The previous week, as Ali was leaving the dais, having served as a luncheon speaker, the woman had approached her and they had exchanged a few words, none of which Ali could recall at the moment.

Seemingly unaware of the other people milling around in the room, Alexandra Munsey stared blindly at the action on the various screens, but she didn't appear to be absorbing any of it. Ali paused for a moment and studied her visitor. It was difficult to tell how old she was. From her fashionable attire and figure, Ali's initial impression was that the woman was reasonably well-off and probably somewhere in her forties or fifties, but the careworn features of her face made her appear much older.

"Ms. Munsey?" Ali asked.

The woman started as though awaking out of a sound sleep. "Yes," she said, quickly regaining her composure. "Alexandra, really, although you're welcome to call me Alex. Thank you for agreeing to see me on such short notice, Ms. Reynolds."

"No problem," Ali returned. "And please feel free to call me Ali. Since we met at the Kidney Foundation luncheon, I'm assuming your wanting to see me has something to do with that?"

"Yes and no," Alex replied. "I'm involved with the Kidney Foundation, of course, but this is primarily about my son, Evan. He's twenty-one, and he's been on dialysis for the past three years. He needs a kidney transplant, and that's why I need to talk to you."

Ali felt as though she'd been punched in the gut. Alex was probably several years older than Ali, but Evan Munsey was almost the same age as her own son, Christopher. Chris was healthy, going to school, and getting on with his life, while Alex Munsey's son was most likely dying.

"I'm so sorry to hear that," Ali said, but she was waiting for the pitch—waiting for Alex to ask if Ali would consider underwriting the cost of the operation. Ali's star presence in the room had been noted, and the people waiting to be let into the studio fell silent, listening in on their conversation with avid interest.

"Why don't you sign in?" Ali suggested. "Then we can go up to my office, where we'll have some privacy." She waited while Alex signed in on the visitors' clipboard. "If you'd like, we could stop by the break room and pick up some coffee or—"

"No, thanks," Alex interjected. "No coffee—I'm fine."

They made their way up in the elevator without exchanging another word. Wanting to put her guest at ease, Ali directed Alex to sit in one of the guest chairs before sinking down in the chair beside her rather than seating herself behind her desk. For an informal chat, side by side was better.

"Three years on dialysis," Ali said at last. "That has to be tough."

Alex nodded. "It is. Evan got sick on a trip to Mexico right after he graduated from high school. The first doctor he saw thought he'd caught some kind of bug. It wasn't until we got him home and into an ER here in the States that they finally diagnosed him. By then Evan was already in kidney failure. He nearly died. But don't feel sorry for him. He's a tough kid. He went ahead and enrolled at UCLA. He can't take a full load, but he's keeping up with the courses he's able to take, and he's getting good grades in those."

So Evan was going UCLA, too. Was there a chance that he and Chris had ever met or been in the same class together? Ali wondered.

"What's he studying?"

"He hasn't declared a major yet," Alex said with a smile, "but he's leaning toward a double major in microbiology and criminal justice. He's always loved crime dramas on TV. He's hoping for a job in forensics of some kind. He doesn't want to be a cop out on the street. He'd rather be one of the guys in the white uniforms examining evidence in some high-tech crime lab."

"Good for him," Ali said. "These days forensics are the name of the game."

"And, in a way, forensics is why I came here today to talk to you," Alex continued. "Evan has been on the organ-recipient waiting list for a long time. It's awful to have to sit around hoping for someone else to die so he can live. Recently one of his doctors suggested that maybe we could find someone, a close relative perhaps, who might be willing to give up a single kidney. I don't qualify as a match, and neither does his dad, but there might be someone out there who could be a match—a half brother or half sister, maybe."

Ali stumbled over that one. "Evan has half siblings?" she asked.

"That's the whole problem," Alex replied. "I don't know for sure. He may have half siblings, and then again he may not, and you may be my only hope for finding out."

"Wait," Ali said, holding up her hand. "You're saying your son may have half siblings that you know nothing about? How can that be?"

Alex answered Ali's questions with another of her own. "What do you know about artificial insemination?"

"I've heard the words, of course," Ali allowed, "but other than that I don't know anything about it."

"Then allow me to enlighten you," Alex Munsey said, "because that's the real crux of the matter."

4

As the two women settled in to talk, Alex Munsey launched into her story. "Jake, my husband, and I tried for years to get pregnant. Finally, with my biological clock ticking away, we went looking for a fertility clinic and were referred to a Dr. Gilchrist—Edward Gilchrist—in Santa Clarita. That's where we were living at the time, in Santa Clarita. After doing some tests, Dr. Gilchrist determined that Jake had a very low sperm count—an almost nonexistent sperm count—and suggested that we consider other options."

"In vitro, then?" Ali asked.

Alex shook her head. "The test-tube thing wasn't for us. We chose IUI instead—intrauterine insemination. It's performed as a simple in-office procedure. We were lucky, and I got pregnant on the second try. The day we brought Evan home from the hospital was the happiest day of my life, and he was a perfect baby—an easy baby and a great kid." She paused for a moment before adding regretfully, "He's already spent years on dialysis. Without a transplant he'll never have anything like a normal life."

"So who was the sperm donor?" Ali asked.

"That's the thing," Alex replied. "We never knew the donor's name, although we saw his photo. Dr. Gilchrist had a book in his office—something he called his catalog—that contained photos and detailed bios for each of the donors. As I seem to remember there were fifty or so in all."

"That's where you went shopping for your sperm donor?"

Alex nodded. "Jake and I studied the profiles and photos for a long time before settling on the guy we thought resembled Jake the most. The guy in the photo was blond and good-looking. Before Jake's hair started going gray he was blond, too."

"What about Evan?" Ali asked. "Is he blond as well?"

"No such luck," Alex replied with a sad smile. "Red hair, fair-skinned. I was so scared of melanoma that I practically smothered the poor kid with sunscreen when he was little. It turns out I should have been more worried about kidney disease."

"So you're thinking that if Evan's sperm donor fathered other children through the clinic, one of them might be a close enough match to donate a healthy kidney?"

"Exactly," Alex said. "Dr. Gilchrist is still in business, so I contacted him and asked if he would put me in touch with the sperm donor."

"How did that work out?"

"Gilchrist's office wouldn't give me the time of day. In fact, I wasn't allowed to speak to him in person. I was never able to get past his nurse. She said that sperm donors are protected by doctor-client privilege, and they wouldn't breach that under any circumstances. And that's why I'm asking for your help."

"What do you have in mind?"

"If there are other kids fathered by the same donor, chances are they're from somewhere around here. I've watched your newscasts for a long time, Ms. Reynolds, so I know that you do occasional human-interest stories. I was hoping maybe you'd agree to do an interview with Evan or with both of us. We could appeal to the public in hopes that other patients who might have utilized Dr. Gilchrist's services back in the eighties would step forward."

"Wait," Ali said. "That's like looking for a needle in a haystack. And even if you happened to locate some of Dr. Gilchrist's former patients, what are the chances that they would have used the same sperm donor?"

"Evan is dying," Alex said. "That isn't how it's supposed to work. Kids are supposed to outlive their parents, not the other way around. And I don't care how much hay there is. I only need one needle."

"And you really think this might work?"

"I do."

Ali glanced at her watch. It was time for her to head to the green room to meet that evening's guests, as well as stop for a quick hair and makeup adjustment. "I've got to get down to the studio," she said, rising to her feet. "I'll pitch the idea to my producers and let you know what they say. In the meantime how do I contact you?"

Alex reached into her purse and pulled out a business card. The address listed was in Sherman Oaks. "You don't live in Santa Clarita anymore?" Ali asked.

Alex shook her head. "We needed to be closer to the hospital," she said, a simple answer that made perfect sense.

Much to Ali's surprise, her producer jumped on the idea. So did the producer for the station's daily newsmagazine show, *L.A. Evening*. Several weeks later

Alex and her son came to the station to do not one but two interviews, a shorter one for news broadcasts, both the evening news and the eleven o'clock news, along with a longer one for *L.A. Evening*'s more expansive time frames.

Ali took to Evan Munsey immediately. He was an earnest young man and a serious one. Both interviews started with Alex relating the background regarding Evan's birth. When Ali asked him about his health issue and need for a kidney transplant, he stated his case plainly and succinctly, with no wasted words. He spoke about what it was like to be plugged into a dialysis machine for seemingly endless hours each week.

"If I do have a half brother or half sister out there," he said finally, "I'm hoping he or she might be willing to step forward and give me both a kidney and a chance to live a normal life."

End of story.

Except that wasn't the end of the story, not at all. The day after the *L.A. Evening* interview aired, Ali was in her office overlooking the day's likely lead story when her phone rang.

"Someone down here to see you," Diane said. "Her name's Cassie Davis, and she says it's urgent. It's about last night's interview."

"Okay," Ali said. "I'll be right there."

Down in the lobby, Diane nodded toward the front entry. "She's out there, smoking a cigarette. She seemed pretty upset."

Ali stepped outside, too. "Ms. Davis?" she asked tentatively. "I'm Ali Reynolds. What can I do for you?"

The community ashtray was located far enough away from the door to be legal. Without a word, Cassie Davis walked over to it and ground out her cigarette. She was a tough-looking woman, dressed in faded jeans and boots along with an equally faded western shirt. As she returned, she reached into a fringed leather purse, pulled out a photograph, and handed it to Ali. The color photo showed Cassie standing in front of the entrance to Disneyland. The lanky kid standing next to her was a much younger version of someone Ali thought she recognized.

"So you know Evan Munsey?" she asked.

"That's not Evan Munsey," Cassie answered. "He's my son, Rory."

Ali studied the photo again. "They could be twins," she said at last.

"Yes, they certainly could," Cassie observed.

There wasn't really a delicate way to ask how this spooky resemblance could have happened, so Ali dove right in.

"Is there a chance your husband was a sperm donor at one time?" she asked.

"I'm a lesbian," Cassie answered abruptly. "I don't have a husband and never have. I was in my thirties, and my partner and I wanted a kid. No one was falling all over themselves to let lesbian couples adopt back then, so we went another route."

"With Dr. Edward Gilchrist's fertility clinic up in Santa Clarita?"

Cassie nodded. "That's right," she said, "one and the same. I never watch the local newscasts, but one of my friends called and told me what was going on. She'd seen a promo for the *L.A. Evening* segment. She thought the kid scheduled to be on the program was my son but that he was going under a different name now. That made sense to me. Rory and I have been estranged for years. When Emma and I broke up, he blamed me, and he wasn't wrong. I cheated on her. A few months after that picture was taken, she packed up, moved back home to Phoenix, taking Rory along with her. As far as I know, he's still there."

"So you watched the program?"

Cassie nodded again. "Watched it and recorded it," she replied, "and I couldn't believe what I was seeing."

"Did you let him know about the program?"

Cassie shrugged. "Like I said, I'm not really sure where he lives these days."

"What about Emma?"

"Ours wasn't exactly an amicable breakup. So no, I didn't get in touch with her either, because she'd probably hang up as soon as she heard my voice, but I was able to get a current phone number from a mutual friend." With that she passed Ali a slip of paper. There were two phone numbers listed. The one on top started with a 602 area code. The second number was a 714, probably in Orange County or maybe slightly north of there.

"So is Rory aware of his . . . ?" Ali paused, not knowing quite how to phrase the awkward question. "His origins?" she finished at last.

"Emma and I were sort of at the forefront of the two-daddy/two-mommy household movement," Cassie answered, "so yes, we told him about the artificial insemination from the time he was old enough to grasp the concept."

"Did he ever indicate any interest in tracking down his sperm donor?"

"Not when I was around, but I haven't seen him for

the past eight years. He's twenty-four now, and in all that time things might have changed."

"What does Emma do for a living?"

"She teaches at Arizona State University. She's a golf instructor there and also coaches the girls' varsity golf team."

"Would you like me to give her a call?"

Cassie nodded. "Please," she said. "Rory needs to know about this. They both do."

"Thank you," Ali said. "I'll try calling right away."

"The second number on that paper is mine," Cassie added. "If you do happen to talk to Rory, would you tell him I miss him and that I'm sorry? Would you do that?"

"Of course," Ali said. "And can I keep the photo?"

Cassie nodded again. "I made a copy for you on my way here. I kept the original. It's the only one of him I have left."

With that, Cassie Davis turned and walked away, wiping her eyes on the sleeve of her shirt as she went. Ali hadn't seen any tears, but she was pretty sure Cassie Davis was crying as she stomped off. She may have looked tough as nails, but as far as her estranged son was concerned, she clearly wasn't.

Ali stood there for several long moments, staring down at the piece of paper and wondering what the right move was. During the interviews the station had posted both Alex's and Evan's contact information on the screen, but Cassie Davis hadn't taken that route or done things the easy way. Instead she'd gone to the time and trouble of making the trip to the station from OC or wherever else she lived, and she'd done so without calling ahead to make an appointment. Instead she had made that long drive on the off chance that Ali would actually be on hand and willing to see her when she arrived.

Upstairs in her office, Ali was still conflicted about what she should do—should she call or not? Finally, taking a deep breath, she picked up her phone and dialed the 602 number. She was hoping Emma herself would answer. Instead a male voice came on the line. "Hello."

"Is Emma there?" Ali asked.

"She's at work. Who's this?"

"My name is Ali Reynolds. I'm a newscaster at a television station in Los Angeles."

"What's this all about?" he asked. "Is something wrong?"

"Is this Rory?" Ali asked.

"Yes, it's Rory," he replied. "But I don't know anyone named Ali Reynolds. How do you know my name?"

"I talked to your mother just now—to one of your mothers," Ali corrected. "Cassie Davis is the one who gave me this phone number."

"I don't want to have anything to do with her. I'm hanging up now."

"Please don't," Ali said urgently. "I need to talk to you. It's about your brother."

"Look, lady," he said. "You're nuts. No matter what Cassie Davis may have told you, I don't have a brother."

"Actually, you do," Ali countered, "a half brother, but a brother nonetheless. His name is Evan Munsey, and it would appear that the two of you share the same sperm donor. Evan is hoping the two of you can meet."

There was a slight pause on the line before Rory spoke again. "You know about that, too—the sperm-donor thing?"

"I do," Ali breathed, grateful that he hadn't hung

up on her. "Cassie told me." Since that was how Rory referred to his birth mother, Ali did, too. "I did an interview with Evan and his mother last night. Your mother saw the program and came here this afternoon to talk to me about it."

"What makes you think this Evan guy and I have the same sperm donor?" he asked. "And what kind of interview? Is this supposed brother of mine some kind of criminal? Did he kill somebody?"

"Instead of my trying to explain all this over the phone, how about if I ship you a copy of the interview?" Ali asked. "Do you have a DVD player?"

"Of course."

"If you'll give me your physical address, I can FedEx it to you. You'll have it tomorrow. That way you and your . . . mother . . . can watch it together."

"My real mother, you mean."

"Yes."

"I'm not sure I should give you our address," he said. "What if this is some kind of scam?"

"It's not a scam," Ali assured him. "I just want to send you a copy of the interview. I'll include my contact information. That way, if you want to be in touch with me after you watch it, you can be. If you don't want me to tell Evan and his mother about you, you have my word that I won't mention any of this without your express permission."

Finally, reluctantly, he gave her a street address in Tempe, Arizona.

"I'm going to ship this FedEx," she said. "I'll specify an early-morning delivery. Will anyone be home to sign for it?" Requiring a delivery signature was the only way she could be sure he had actually received it.

"It's spring break right now, so I'm off school," he said. "I'll be here."

In case he didn't contact her again, in case this was the end of Ali's involvement, there was one more thing she needed to do—pass along Cassie Davis's final words.

"Cassie asked me to give you a message if I spoke to you," Ali said. "She said to tell you that she's sorry and she misses you."

The only reply was the sound of Rory Davis hanging up the phone.

Once the call ended, Ali hurried downstairs to production and got one of the guys there to burn a DVD with copies of both the Evan Munsey interviews. She slipped them into a FedEx envelope and dropped it off in the mail room just minutes before the driver was due to stop by for his pickup.

The clerk in the mailing office checked the shipping instructions. "Early delivery and signature required? What are you shipping here, the crown jewels?"

"Close," Ai answered. "What's in this envelope could very well mean the difference between life and death."

The next day Ali came to work early with the old spring in her step. The malaise that had been besetting her had evaporated. She was upbeat, focused, and on her game. She sat in her office watching the clock and waiting for the estimated delivery time to pass. It was spring but not yet daylight saving time, so Arizona was an hour ahead. Eventually time slowed to a crawl. No matter how badly she wanted her phone to ring, her device remained stubbornly silent. As the hours passed, Ali suppressed her disappointment and was grateful that she'd kept her word and not mentioned any of this to Alex Munsey. Knowing about Rory's existence would have gotten her hopes up only to have them dashed when he failed to respond.

Ali had given Rory her direct number, but when her phone finally did ring at two o'clock that afternoon, the call came through the switchboard. "I have Alexandra Munsey on the line," the operator said. "Are you available?"

"I'm here," Ali said. "Send it through."

"Oh, my God!" Alex exclaimed when Ali came on the line. "I can hardly believe it."

"Believe what?" Ali asked. "What's going on?"

"You did it!" Alex gushed breathlessly. "You found the needle in the haystack. I just got off the phone with Evan. This morning a stranger named Rory Davis called him from Tempe, Arizona. Rory told Evan that the two of them may be half brothers. They talked for the better part of an hour, and now they want to meet. Rory is flying in from Phoenix tonight. His flight is due to arrive at LAX at 7:20. Evan and I are going to the airport to pick him up. We're supposed to meet him at baggage claim. And Rory said to tell you that he's sorry he didn't call you back, but he wanted to cut out the middleman. He also mentioned that if you want to bring a film crew along to the airport, you're welcome to."

Ali felt a wave of goose bumps pass down her legs.

"And that's not all," Alex continued.

"What else?"

"Rory says that if he and Evan are related, and if Rory turns out to be a match, then Evan has found himself a donor. I can barely believe that he'd do this for someone who's a complete stranger, but he seems to be willing. I don't know how to thank you, Ali. This means everything to me. Everything!"

"You're most welcome," Ali replied. "And thank you for the scoop. What airline?"

"American. Flight 3690."

"Fair enough," Ali told her. "I'll be there with bells on, along with a film crew, but there's one more thing."

"What's that?"

"Do you happen to have a color photo of Evan when he was fifteen or so?"

"I think so," Alex replied. "I believe I have one that I took at a tennis tournament. Why?"

"Bring it along if you can," Ali said. "This is TV, after all, and comparing two photos side by side will make for a good visual."

"Will do," Alex said. "See you there."

For the next few minutes, Ali sat at her desk and stared out her window. The smog had lifted. The sun was out. The mountains were visible in the distance. For the first time in a very long time, Ali Reynolds felt as if she had done something useful—that she'd made a valuable contribution, that what she did for a living actually mattered.

It was a lesson her parents, Bob and Edie Larson, back home in Sedona had drilled into her head the whole time she was growing up. "There's nothing more worthwhile," her father always said, "than helping someone else."

"You were so right, Dad," she whispered under her breath. "It just doesn't get any better than this."

5

For Ali Reynolds that initial meeting between half siblings Evan Munsey and Rory Davis was also the beginning of the story of her lifetime. It was a heartwarming piece, one that had legs, enough so that eventually it was picked up on the network news outlets as well. She had to go to the airport in the same clothing she'd worn on the evening newscast, but that was okay. Her wardrobe wasn't the story, because Evan and Rory were the primary focus.

In order to get set up, she and her crew arrived at baggage claim a good forty-five minutes before the plane was due in. She expected they'd be the first to arrive, but Alex and her son were already there. Evan had been totally poised and at ease when he'd come to the station to do the interviews, but that night at the airport he was clearly a nervous wreck. He paced the floor, walking up and down the length of the baggage-claim area, waiting for an announcement to be posted that would tell them which baggage carousel would be in use once the plane touched down and the bags were unloaded.

As the cameraman laid out his equipment, Ali approached Alex, who appeared to be in a state that verged on jubilation. Alex introduced Ali to her husband, Jake, a man who seemed content to remain in the background and who held himself in careful reserve. His body language indicated he was there, all right, but he wasn't quite sure what any of this meant or even if he believed it. Ali's first impression was that Jake had distanced himself from his son's fight while his wife had been one hundred percent all in.

Evan paused his pacing long enough to express part of what was bothering him. "How will we recognize him?" Evan asked. "Other people are carrying signs with people's names on them. Maybe we should be, too."

"I wouldn't worry about that if I were you," Ali said, handing him the photo of Cassie Davis and Rory standing in front of the Disneyland entrance. "I think you'll recognize him on sight."

Frowning, Evan studied the photo before passing it along to his mother. "That's me, but who's the woman I'm with? I don't remember going to Disneyland with someone like her."

"That's because you didn't," Ali explained. "That's Rory Davis with his mother, Cassie Davis."

Evan took the photo back and stared at it again for a long moment. "Unbelievable," he muttered. He handed it back to Alex and resumed his pacing, leaving his mother staring at the photo.

"It's uncanny," Alex said, her eyes wide with amazement. "Is this why you wanted me to bring a photo?"

Ali nodded.

"Where did you get it?"

"From Rory's birth mother, who still lives here in L.A. Someone alerted her to the *L.A. Evening* piece. After she saw it, she came by the station yesterday and dropped off the photo."

"Why didn't you tell me about this?" Alex demanded accusingly.

"Because when I talked to Rory, he asked me not to mention it. I gave him my word that I wouldn't do so without his permission, and keeping my word is something I take seriously. But if you wouldn't mind giving me both photos, I'll go back to my cameraman and have him do a side-by-side shot so our viewers will be able to see the same thing you just saw."

Nodding, Alex dug a second photo out of her purse and handed both of them over to Ali. The two boys pictured there might have been carbon copies. After delivering the photos to the cameraman and waiting for him to film them, Ali did a brief introductory stand-up.

"Two nights ago a young man named Evan Munsey appeared on our newsmagazine, *L.A. Evening*. Evan is a twenty-one-year-old student at UCLA who suffers from kidney disease and has been on dialysis for the past three years. He's in desperate need of a kidney transplant. Evan's parents had difficulty conceiving, and he was born as the result of an artificial-insemination procedure. He and his mother came on *L.A. Evening* in hopes of locating other individuals who might be the biological offspring of his sperm donor and also in hopes that if they could find such a person, he or she might turn out to be a possible source for Evan's needed kidney. Two days later a miracle has occurred. I'm here at LAX with Evan and his parents, awaiting the arrival of Rory Davis, Evan's newly located half sibling. Even though the two brothers have never met, they've spoken on the phone. Rory, age twenty-four, has already indicated that if he turns out to be a suitable match and passes the medical requirements, he's willing to supply Evan with a healthy kidney."

By the time the stand-up was finished, the plane

was already on the ground. After the two photographs had been returned to the safety of Alex's purse, the welcoming committee moved to a spot near the bottom of the escalator to await Rory's arrival. The presence of a known news anchor and a cameraman on the scene was duly noted. Soon a small but excited crowd gathered in the background, hoping to catch a glimpse of whatever Hollywood notable was about to make an appearance. When a new set of folks started down the escalator, Evan stepped forward and stationed himself near the bottom.

"Is this the flight from Phoenix?" he asked a briefcase-carrying businessman who had hurried off the escalator and paused long enough to check the signage, looking for the appropriate carousel.

"Sure is," the man answered. "I was on a connecting flight. I hope like hell they didn't lose my luggage."

Evan stepped back again, leaving room for other people to pass. Ali was close enough to the action that she caught sight of Rory about the same time Evan did. The two young men looked so much alike that even though Ali was expecting it, she found the resemblance spooky. Rory was halfway down the escalator before the cameraman started filming.

Rory was smart enough to step off the escalator and move to one side before he stopped and stared. The two young men stood there like that, regarding each other with outright amazement. They were dressed differently, of course, but in terms of size, build, and features—from the bronze of their hair to the set of their hazel eyes—they might have been twins. After a long, uncertain pause, both of them moved forward at once, each greeting the other with hand extended. Grinning, they shook hands briefly. Then, as the camera rolled, that initial handshake morphed into a heartfelt embrace. They were brothers, all right. No one who saw them that night in the airport or on their television screens later on had the slightest doubt about that.

It was a heartwarming, wonderful story that remained on the news for days and wound back up to fever pitch when it was announced, several weeks later, that Rory was indeed a suitable organ-donor match and that he intended to return to L.A. at the end of May when school ended for the summer so he could gift his newly discovered sibling with a healthy kidney.

Yes, it was a feel-good story all the way around—at least at first. The problem is, those initial stories were only the tip of the iceberg. There was much more to come, and it wouldn't all turn out to be such good news.

6

Kaitlyn Martin Todd was addicted to TV. She had spent her early years living in a mountain-bound cabin outside a tiny community called Lyons, Oregon, twenty-five miles east of Salem. The house was remote enough that no television signals ever reached that far.

Kaitlyn's parents had divorced when she was in her early teens. She and her mother had left her logger father alone in his solitary cabin on the mountain and had moved to Salem, where she'd graduated from high school and attended Salem Community College, before eventually earning a nursing degree from Portland State. But once she moved to Salem and later, after settling in California, Kaitlyn had made up for lost time as far as TV viewing was concerned. Television was her passion.

Once out of school, Kaitlyn had reconnected with and married her high school sweetheart, Chuck Todd. The newlyweds had ended up in Santa Clarita when Chuck's uncle offered him steady work as a tow-truck driver, hauling stranded motorists off the treacherous Grapevine section of I-5. She had already landed a job at the Gilchrist Fertility Clinic in Santa Clarita when Todd ran off with another woman who happened to be a fellow tow-truck driver. Once Kaitlyn's husband had abandoned ship, her hooking up with her boss had started out as little more than revenge sex, but at the time what he had to offer seemed like a fair deal.

Edward Gilchrist was a good twenty years older than Kaitlyn. His sex drive seemed to be waning a bit, so he wasn't especially demanding on that score, and Kaitlyn's work in the clinic wasn't especially demanding either. The pay was good, and the boss had no problem with the tiny TV set she kept out of sight underneath the reception counter as long as she muted the sound when there were patients in the room. During quiet times she was able to keep abreast of her daytime soaps and afternoon talk shows, and she was usually home in time to never miss a single airing of her all-time favorite, *L.A. Evening*.

It was on a commercial break during one of the soaps when she saw the promo for that evening's program. There were no patients present, so she went straight into the office to tell Edward about it.

"Remember that woman who came in a few weeks ago looking for her records? I can't recall her name right now, but I recognized her face on the screen."

"What screen?" Edward asked.

"My TV screen. She and her son are going to be featured in a segment on *L.A. Evening* tonight, something called 'In Search of a Kidney.'"

"Alexandra Munsey," Edward said.

Kaitlyn was a little taken aback. She was surprised that he remembered the name right off the bat like that and had it on the tip of his tongue.

"That's the name they mentioned," she said. "But I thought you'd want to know."

That was the truth—Edward really did want to know. He left work at the stroke of five that day, something that was unusual for him. He went straight home without stopping off for a cocktail along the way. Kaitlyn had no idea that he was headed home to set his DVR to record that evening's edition of *L.A. Evening*. When the show finally came on, he watched the whole thing with a growing sense of fury. Once the segment ended, he replayed it several more times—listening to every word, searching for something that might rise to the level of outright slander.

In the course of the interview, Alexandra Munsey mentioned that she had conceived with the help of a fertility clinic in Santa Clarita. Since there was only one of those—his—anybody who knew the first thing about Santa Clarita would understand that she was referring to him and his practice. As Edward listened, his contempt for that unbearable woman knew no bounds. After all, hadn't he given the bitch exactly what she wanted—a baby? And now, here she was twenty-plus years later with that very same kid at her side, and was she grateful about that? Not on your life. Instead she seemed hell-bent on destroying him. How dare she go on the air and talk about him like that? How dare she?

As for the kid himself? Evan Munsey had kidney disease? So what? True, Edward's paternal grandfather had died of kidney disease sometime in his fifties, but surely that wasn't a genetic defect for which Edward could be held responsible at this late date. As for Evan— why couldn't he put himself on the kidney waiting list and take his place in line like everybody else? Why did he have to go on TV and kick open a hornet's nest? Because Edward Gilchrist knew that's exactly what it would be. Even on the television screen, he could see that Evan Munsey was the spitting image of his biological father—not the way Edward looked now, of course, but the way he'd looked when he was much younger, back when he was in high school and college.

After watching the segment three times in a row, Edward finally switched off the TV set and went over to the wet bar to pour himself another stiff drink. He'd already indulged in one earlier, before the program even aired. All he could hope was that this sympathy-seeking emotional appeal sent out over the airwaves would come up empty. And if it didn't? Thank God he and Dawn had already shredded those damning records back in the nineties when he'd first spotted that unstoppable freight train called DNA speeding in their direction.

And that brought up another sore subject—Dawn. A few weeks earlier, for no apparent reason Edward could understand, she'd gotten some kind of wild hair up her butt and had moved out. Not only had she moved out, she'd even gone so far as to contact an attorney and file for divorce. As far as Edward was concerned, Dawn and Alexandra Munsey were birds of a feather—ungrateful bitches from beginning to end. He knew where Dawn lived. He was tempted to drive over to her place right now and raise hell with her about it, but eventually he calmed down. With all the Alexandra Munsey crap circling the drain, what Edward needed to do at that moment was absolutely nothing. Instead he'd lie low and wait for things to blow over, as he hoped they would.

They always did.

The next morning at work, Kaitlyn showed up brimming with enthusiasm about the *L.A. Evening* piece. "It's too bad the Munsey kid is so sick, but the show was good PR for you, don't you think?" she asked. "After all, there he was, sitting next to his mother as big as life and testifying to the fact that when it comes to fertility issues, you know what you're doing."

"Alexandra Munsey can go to hell," Edward snarled back. "And if records have gone missing, you can bet that useless bitch Dawn was behind it."

With that he stalked into his office, slamming the door behind him, leaving Kaitlyn to wonder what she'd said that had sent him into such a spasm.

"Sounds like someone got up on the wrong side of the bed today," she muttered under her breath, and then she walked behind the counter and switched on her tiny television set. Regis and Kathie Lee were just coming on, and she didn't want to miss a minute of it.

7

The explosive story of the half brothers' first meeting was initially aired on the eleven o'clock news that very night, but it was rebroadcast the following day on every newscast there was—the morning show, the noon show, and the evening one as well. It was all a part of the gathering storm, and Ali Reynolds's participation continued to be front and center. Two days later, again just when it was almost time for her to go down to the green room for makeup, Diane called again.

"You have a visitor here in the lobby," she said.

"Is it someone I know?" Ali asked.

"Her name is Jolene Browder," Diane replied. "She says it's about Evan Munsey and Rory Davis."

"Did any of these people ever hear of calling ahead for an appointment?" Ali muttered.

"Do you want me to send her away and have her come back later?"

"Pardon my grumbling, but no, don't do that," Ali said. "I have a couple of minutes. I'll make it work."

She hurried downstairs. Once again the lobby area was filled with a crowd of people lined up to be part of the live audience for the show preceding the newscast. One slight woman, probably in her fifties, was clearly different from the others. She was seated on the same love seat where Ali had first caught sight of Alex Munsey. The audience members were all in casual Southern California attire. Jolene wore a timeless knit suit, sensible heels, and most astonishing of all—pantyhose. Her gray hair was pulled back in a carefully constructed upsweep that was held in place by some beaded combs and an armor-plating layer of hair spray. She sat bolt upright with her hands resting on a small purse that was perched on her lap, but what struck Ali most about her was the undeniable air of sadness that hovered around her like a visible cloud.

"Ms. Browder?" Ali inquired. "I'm Ali Reynolds. You wanted to see me?"

"Oh, thank you," Jolene said, startling out of some faraway reverie. "I meant to be here earlier, but there was a big traffic tie-up on the 101. It was one of those multi-car wrecks that had the freeway coned down from four lanes to one, and it took forever to get past it. You probably need to get ready to go on the air. If it's inconvenient, I can come back another time."

"No," Ali said quickly. "That's all right. I have a few minutes. Where were you coming from?"

"Westlake Village."

"So let's take care of this now if we can," Ali said with a reassuring smile. "What can I do for you? The receptionist said it had something to do with the Evan Munsey/Rory Davis story."

Jolene nodded in reply, but rather than answering aloud, she reached into her purse and pulled out a photograph and passed it to Ali. The somewhat faded color snapshot, most likely taken with a cheapie throwaway camera, featured a young woman—mid-teens, maybe—seated on a saddled black-and-white horse. The girl was grinning from ear to ear, and under the white Stetson she wore, Ali caught a glimpse of bright red curls.

"That's my daughter," Jolene said. "Her name was Cindy. Her horse was named War Paint."

"Was?" Ali asked tentatively.

The question was answered with another sad nod. "War Paint was already in his twenties when we got him. We had him put down shortly after we lost Cindy."

"I'm sorry," Ali said. That was all she could think of to say.

Jolene suddenly seemed to lose heart. "I'm sorry, too," she said. "This is a long story. I'm sure you need to go. I can come back later."

"No, continue, please," Ali insisted. "Tell me now."

"My late husband, Robert, lost his first wife and daughter in a car wreck when the child was little more than a baby. When we met, he'd been a widower for years, but he was only thirty and I was five years older. That five-year difference didn't seem insurmountable at the time, not like it would have been if we'd met when we were in high school, but still he made it clear from the start that he really wanted a child. We tried, and when it didn't work . . ."

"Let me guess," Ali interjected, "you went to see a fertility doctor in Santa Clarita."

"That's right," Jolene replied, "Dr. Edward Gilchrist. I was thirty-eight when we went to see him and forty-two when Cindy was born. Robert was absolutely over the moon. He spoiled her rotten, including getting her that blasted horse."

"You said you lost Cindy. What happened to her?"

Jolene sighed. "We were on a camping trip in Yellowstone. Cindy and Robert were into the outdoors. I wasn't especially wild about it, but I went along to get along. We were booked for a week in Yellowstone, camping here and there along the way. We had a dual-cab pickup with one of those fifth-wheel camp trailers hooked on behind it, so it's not like we were sleeping on the ground in a tent or something. But Cindy just wasn't herself the whole time—not feeling well, lethargic, not wanting to eat, losing weight. I thought maybe she was coming down with a form of the flu or maybe even mono. So one morning when we were supposed to go on a daylong trail ride, she didn't want to go. I would have been happy to stay with her, but she insisted that her father and I go, so we did."

Jolene's voice had faded to almost nothing as she spoke. She paused for a moment, and when she resumed, even with the audience members drained out of the lobby, Ali had to strain to hear her. "When Robert and I came back that evening, she was sleeping. When I woke her up for dinner, she was confused. She didn't seem to know who she was or where she was. She didn't even know who I was. She tried to get out of bed, and her legs . . ." Jolene paused again, struggling. "Her legs were swollen to almost twice the size they should have been. When she stood up, she almost fell. I grabbed her to keep her from falling, and her breath smelled awful—like ammonia."

Ali felt the hair rise on the back of her neck. She knew that smell. She had encountered it before—at the hospital when Dean was dying. "Kidney failure," Ali murmured. "Acute kidney failure."

Nodding, Jolene dabbed tears from her eyes. "Robert went to talk to the park ranger and was told the nearest ER was forty miles away in West Yellowstone. The ranger offered to call for a helicopter, but Robert figured if we left right then, we'd be able to get her to help faster than waiting around for them to send in an air ambulance. Even so, by the time we got her to the ER, it was too late. Cindy was gone."

"And your husband?" Ali asked, fearing the worst.

"Robert never got over it," Jolene answered. "He blamed himself for not calling for the helicopter. He committed suicide two years later. That's what his death certificate says, but as far as I'm concerned, he died of a broken heart."

Ali was stunned to silence. She couldn't think of a single thing to say. The word "sorry" simply didn't cover a heartbreak of this magnitude.

"I heard your talk at the luncheon," Jolene went on after a bit. "Thank you for doing that, by the way. As you can well imagine, I'm involved in the Kidney Foundation. I run the local chapter in the Village. I raise money. I donate. One of my friends mentioned the upcoming piece on *L.A. Evening,* and of course I watched. I also watched the follow-up two nights later. As soon as I saw those two red-haired young men standing together, I was almost sick to my stomach. Robert had red hair, and so when we were shopping through the donor book, we specifically looked for a red-haired donor. That's the one we picked, but do you know who else had red hair back then?"

"Who?" Ali asked.

"Dr. Edward Gilchrist."

Again the hair rose on the back of Ali's neck. "What are you saying?" she asked. "Do you think he was substituting his sperm for his donors' sperm?"

"Don't you?" Jolene replied.

Ali was appalled at the very idea. "Is he still in business?"

Jolene nodded. "That's what I wanted to know, so I checked first thing this morning, before I got ready to come here. I called the office and asked if Dr. Gilchrist was accepting new patients. The person who answered the phone said, 'Yes, he is.'"

Ali glanced at her watch. She had spent more time than she should have and was already late. "I've got to go get ready now," she said. "But if you wouldn't mind waiting until after I finish up with the evening news, there's someone I want you to meet."

"Alexandra Munsey?"

"Yes, I'll call her and see if she could meet us for a bite of dinner."

"I'd like that," Jolene said. "I'd like that very much."

8

lex was at the station by the time Ali's stint on the evening news was over. That night it was just the three of them—Ali, Alex, and Jolene. The next day, when they added Cassie Davis to the mix, the three moms made as unlikely a set of Three Musketeers as you can imagine. There was the prim and proper widow from Westlake Village, the concerned mother still fighting the good fight to see her son's organ transplant through to completion, and the tough-as-nails lesbian lady who looked as though she'd just stepped out of a dusty horse corral—which happened to be true. Cassie worked for a man who trained Thoroughbred racehorses on a swath of land in Orange County that had once been covered with citrus groves.

The three women soon became fast friends. When it came time for Evan's kidney transplant in early June, all three of them gathered at the hospital together. Since Ali was an integral part of the story, she was invited to come along, too. When the dual operations were over and both Evan and Rory were in the recovery room, Ali watched as Alex and Jake Munsey went in to see him. A few minutes later, a pale-faced Jake emerged from the recovery room, walking through the waiting room without exchanging a word with anyone. Not long after that, Alex came out as well. As soon as Ali saw the stricken expression on Alex's face, her heart fell.

"What's happened?" Ali asked, hurrying up to her.

"He's gone," Alex choked, bursting into tears. "Gone."

"But I thought the surgeon said Evan was okay," Ali objected, "that he'd come through the operation in good shape."

"Not Evan," Alex managed. "Jake. He's leaving me. He wants a divorce."

A few minutes later, while the other women were still trying to comfort Alex, Rory's mother, Emma, came out of the recovery room as well. During the course of the operation, Emma and her former partner, Cassie, had stayed on opposite sides of the room, like boxers stuck to their respective corners. This time, rather than avoiding Cassie, Emma walked straight to her. "Rory says he'd like to see you now. You can go in."

After leaving the hospital that night, Ali drove back to the station to give the viewers who'd been avidly following the Rory and Evan story an update on the successful transplant operations. Later that night, driving home to Robert Lane, she was struck by the stark contrasts the day had presented for that whole cast of participants.

According to the doctors involved, it looked as though the surgeries themselves had been entirely successful. Ali hoped that the few words of reconciliation exchanged between Cassie and Emma and between Cassie and her son were signs of better things to come for that set of fractured relationships. And yet, on a day that had finally seen the happy conclusion of Alex's long fight to save her son's life, she had also had to come face-to-face with the end of her marriage. *But isn't that the way life works?* Ali wondered. Good news and bad news always seemed to be rolled up into one complex, multicolored ball of yarn.

For the next several months after the transplants, Ali Reynolds had watched the activity from afar as Alex, Jolene, and Cassie embarked on their next battle—a concerted effort to bring down Dr. Edward Gilchrist.

That was about the time Ali's own life plunged off track.

The following January, one night after the eleven o'clock news, the station's new news director, a hotshot young guy named Cliff Baker—the guy considered to be the network's next golden boy—came looking for her. He caught up with her out in the hallway for a late-night ambush in which he let her know that she was yesterday's news and that her days as an anchor were over. Baker blamed Ali's dismissal on falling ratings, of course, and the fact that it was "time to take the station in a new direction." But Ali knew as well as Cliff did that the ratings—hers especially—hadn't changed all that much. She suspected that her dismissal had far more to do with the advent of high-def television broadcasting—a hypervisual venue in which the slightest blemish was there for all to see. In those kinds of circumstances, it was common for female newscasters to reach their pull-by dates far earlier than their male counterparts.

At the end of his late-night tirade, Baker had her summarily escorted from the building. With the rest of the newsroom staff looking on in stone-cold silence, Ali had been required to hand over her key to the building, her elevator pass, her name badge. Finally she'd loaded her personal effects from her office into a banker's box. The man designated to escort her out of the building was Eddie Duarte, the station's nighttime security guard. For years he had been the person who'd watched over her as she made her way out to her vehicle in the parking lot at the conclusion of her newscasts. That night he saw her out of the building and safely to her car in the parking lot, but this time she was going into exile rather than just going home from work, and Eddie was lugging her banker's box. He was also the only person at the station who ever expressed a word of regret over the way she was being treated.

Ali had gone home that night, expecting some show of sympathy from her husband, but none was forthcoming. Paul Grayson worked for the network. For all Ali knew, Cliff Baker was one of Paul's personal hires. In the course of their conversation that evening, it became painfully obvious that Paul had known well in advance that Ali was about to be handed her walking papers, and he hadn't had the simple decency or the courage to offer her a word of warning.

For Ali that was the last straw. Her marriage to Paul had been in a downward spiral for a long time. Her work on the Rory/Evan story had rekindled her love for her job, but it had done nothing for her relationship with her husband. She'd known it would come to a head eventually, but with Chris still in school, inertia had taken over and it had been easier to stay put and do nothing.

But that night when Paul had walked away from her, leaving her alone in her misery, his slamming the door behind him had been the final catalyst, one that prodded her into overcoming her reluctance to make some necessary changes. The very next day, she started emptying her closets of all the clothes she had accumulated over time, packing them into bags and delivering them to a charity she had done work with over the years, My Sister's Closets. Out of curiosity's sake, she tuned in to the noon news to see what, if anything, would be said about her sudden departure. Instead she saw a promo touting the arrival of the pert young thing who had clearly already been vetted and was due to be Ali's on-air replacement.

Weeks later, offended by the idea that someone in her late forties would be sacked from the station, Ali met with an attorney and launched the process of filing a wrongful-dismissal suit based on age and sexual discrimination. She had arrived at the house that evening in time to learn that her best friend from high school back home in Cottonwood, Arizona, Irene Holzer Bernard, who'd been reported missing several days earlier, had been found dead in the wreckage of her vehicle on a snowy mountain road north of Sedona. That very evening Ali and Chris had set off for Ali's hometown so she could be there to support Reenie's widower and their two kids.

Two critical pieces of the puzzle had fallen into place on that momentous drive home. Along the way Paul had called, demanding that she drop the lawsuit against the station for fear it might adversely affect his career. A few miles later, Chris had unleashed the real bombshell—the shocking news that Paul had been carrying on simultaneous affairs with both his personal assistant, April Gaddis, and Ali's PA as well.

Those illicit relationships might have been apparent to everyone else, but they had been invisible to Ali, and for her, learning about them was also the last straw. Driving east through the barren desert landscape, Ali understood firsthand exactly how Alex Munsey must have felt that night in Evan's recovery room when Jake had told Alex that their marriage was over and he wanted a divorce.

In this case Christopher had been the one who'd delivered the bad news—Paul had been too much of a gutless wonder. Ali had left L.A. thinking she was going home to deal with Reenie's funeral. Now, she decided, she was going there for good. A year or so before, she had inherited her Aunt Evie's double-wide mobile home on Sedona's Andante Drive. When the mobile had come her way, Ali's intention had been to go home long enough to help her mother sort through Aunt Evie's belongings in advance of selling the place. Fortunately, she had never quite gotten around to carrying through on that.

For the past seven years, she'd led what had seemed on the outside to be a charmed life of apparent luxury. Instead, she realized now, she'd been trapped in a reality that had been little more than a gilded cage. Some people might have considered the prospect of abandoning a literal mansion on Robert Lane in favor of a double-wide in a mobile-home development called Sky View Terrace as a huge step down, but Ali didn't see it that way. In fact, from where she was right then, living alone in humbler surroundings sounded more like heaven. Aunt Evie, bless her heart, had provided her niece with a priceless gift—a place to go—a haven where Ali could regroup, regain her strength, and figure out what the hell she was going to do with the rest of her life.

Yes, on that day in March Ali left both Paul Grayson and her life in California in her rearview mirror. She turned her back on them and slammed the door shut without giving either one of them so much as a second thought.

9

As Alex Munsey, Jolene Browder, and Cassie Davis went to war with their former fertility physician, the first battles were little more than minor skirmishes. They had approached Dr. Gilchrist's office en masse, with the three of them carpooling to Santa Clarita together, riding in Jolene's Buick. Jolene and Cassie gave the young blond receptionist their names and requested access to their records. She disappeared into a back room and was gone for what seemed like a very long time. When she finally returned, they were given the news that the files for the other two women were, like Alex's, also among the missing.

"It must be some kind of clerical error," she told them. "According to Dr. Gilchrist, when the office converted from paper records to electronic ones in the nineties, some of the files dating from the eighties inexplicably disappeared and couldn't be retrieved."

"You expect us to believe they just went missing?" Cassie demanded. "We'd like to hear that from Dr. Gilchrist himself."

"Sorry," was the answer. "He's currently out of the office and unable to meet with you. If you'd like to schedule an appointment . . ."

Had Edward Gilchrist bothered to speak to them—if he had acknowledged their concerns—things might have been different—but the three women left his office in a state of outrage.

"Clerical error my ass!" Cassie exclaimed once they were back in the car and headed south. "What a bunch of hogwash!"

"And delivered with a totally straight face," Jolene added. "The man downright lied to us back when we were his patients, and that woman in there is lying to us now. What Edward Gilchrist did wasn't just medical malpractice, it was out-and-out fraud, and yet here he is, still in business when he ought to be in jail."

"Right," Cassie said. "Remember that so-called catalog they showed us? I'll bet all those photos and profiles were phony as three-dollar bills."

"And I can already predict what's going to happen if we go after Gilchrist," Jolene continued. "He'll claim the only reason our kids are related is due to the fact he used the same sperm donor on each of us. Never in a million years will he admit that he was the clinic's primary sperm donor, and without access to our records and with no DNA evidence to back up our claim, he knows we've got no proof, so what do we do now?"

They were heading south on Interstate 5, inching along in rush-hour traffic toward Alex's apartment complex in Sherman Oaks. With the Munseys' divorce still pending, she had moved out of the house and into a nearby studio. She and Jake had agreed that Evan would stay on in the house, but for the time being a tiny apartment nearby was all she needed. And that was where they were heading now—back to the apartment where they'd met up earlier in the morning.

For several minutes after Jolene asked that question, no one spoke. "I'll bet we can find more DNA," Alex said quietly.

"What do you mean?"

"Do you think we're the only ones Gilchrist tricked?"

"Not on your life," Cassie muttered. "There are bound to be others. I'm betting we're just the tip of the iceberg."

"Think about our three kids," Alex continued. "Evan, Rory, and Cindy. They're all still relatively young, or they would be, and yet two out of three of them have already had serious issues—fatal in one case—with kidney disease, and we all know that a propensity for kidney disease can be passed from parent to child."

"If I remember correctly, all the catalog profiles included health overviews," Jolene said thoughtfully. "It seems to me that the donors were described as being in excellent health."

"But those were all the pretend donors," Alex said. "What about the real donor? We never saw a catalog listing for Edward Gilchrist. What if there's a history of kidney disease lurking on his family tree? And what if any other children he might have fathered are also unknowingly susceptible to the same thing?"

A moment of silence followed before Cassie murmured sadly, "And poor Rory's already down to one."

That quiet comment from the backseat crystallized the whole issue for all of them, framing it in another light entirely. This was no longer just about the three of them—about Edward Gilchrist lying to them and withholding their medical records. Suddenly the situation was much bigger and much more significant. Now other lives were involved, along with other families potentially facing the same kind of heartbreaks and hurdles that Jolene Browder's and Alex Munsey's families had endured.

"If people know they're prone to kidney disease," Jolene said, "there are preventive measures they can take, and if they're warned in advance, they can be on the lookout for the onset of symptoms before they become deadly. So what do we do?"

"We find those other people," Alex said simply, "Edward Gilchrist's other patients. We find them and their children and warn them."

"How?" Cassie asked.

Alex responded to the question by asking one of her own. "How did the three of us meet?"

"We met because of your interview with Ali Reynolds, of course," Jolene replied. "Without you and Evan showing up on *L.A. Evening*, none of us would have had a clue."

"Exactly," Alex agreed. "And that's what we need now—more publicity."

"Should we call Ali Reynolds?" Cassie asked. "I'll bet she'd help us in a heartbeat."

"We need to fight our own battles. We should hit the bricks on our own and find other media outlets so we can let people know," Alex told them. "We have to get out and see the people."

When they arrived at Alex's place in Sherman Oaks that evening, a fire had been lit under all three of them, and Cassie and Jolene weren't nearly ready to head home. Instead they all went inside and gathered around Alex's tiny kitchen table to brainstorm.

"What about the others?" Cassie asked once they were seated.

"Gilchrist's other kids?" Jolene asked with a puzzled frown.

"No," Cassie said, "what if there are other Gilchrists out there? He's probably not the only lying piece-of-crap fertility doctor in the universe. There may be a lot of other mass-produced progeny out there—people whose births came as a result of artificial-insemination procedures and who now have no access to half of their own medical history. There may be unpleasant and undisclosed illnesses lurking in their futures as well. Shouldn't they be warned, too?"

"They probably should," Jolene agreed, "but I'm guessing the rules in those other practices would be the same as Gilchrist's, where the identities of the donors are kept confidential."

"And weren't we all required to sign nondisclosure agreements?" Jolene asked.

"I'm pretty sure we did," Alex agreed.

"Those are NDAs," Cassie said, "but what about DNA?"

"What about it?"

"I know a guy who's creating a racehorse DNA database. Maybe he'd be willing to work with us on the side and create a human DNA database as well—DNA from people whose births were the result of artificial insemination. That might not lead folks back to their actual donors, but it could possibly give them access to half siblings who could help fill in the blanks on a few of their medical histories."

"Tracking down affected people won't be easy, and DNA testing doesn't come cheap," Jolene objected. "We'd have to raise a lot of money to make that happen."

"What the hell?" Alex Munsey asked. "I don't have

anything better to do at the moment, so I'm in. And if we're going to do it, what are we going to call this thing?"

Cassie Davis raised her hand. "I move we call it the Progeny Project. All in favor?"

In the end the vote was unanimous.

10

Once Ali went off to college, she'd spent very little time back home in Sedona. She'd come there occasionally for short visits, but until now she hadn't hung around as an adult for any extended period. It was something of a shock to her system and a come-down, if you will, to be demoted from being an easily identifiable celebrity in Southern California to being "Bob and Edie Larson's daughter."

Because Bob and Edie, owners and operators of the Sugarloaf Café, were a known quantity in town and had their own particular brand of celebrity. Edie's baking prowess—including her infamous Sugarloaf Café sweet rolls, which she made fresh every day—was literally the talk of the town, and Bob was considered to be the best short-order cook in the Verde Valley. Running a restaurant that was open from 6:00 A.M. to 2:00 P.M. seven days a week required a kind of industry, cheerfulness, and steady perseverance that Ali found both amazing and humbling.

In the beginning the restaurant had belonged to her grandmother, who had passed it along to her twin daughters, Edie and Evie. Ali's father, Bob, had been a latecomer to the partnership, but the three of them—the two sisters and Bob—had worked together for decades before Aunt Evie's death—and their hard work along with that scholarship was what had enabled Ali to go off to school, earn her degree, and live what had seemed to be a charmed life. Now that she was back, Ali couldn't help but feel ashamed that as a kid she'd looked down on her parents because they didn't have more money. Other families went on family trips. Bob and Edie worked seven days a week, day in and day out, with no time off for vacations. Other kids had fancy houses. The Larsons lived in a tiny place—a two-bedroom cottage—out behind the restaurant. Ali had a room of her own, but it was little more than a closet. And when it came to weekends and school vacations, other kids could hang out together listening to music or swimming in Oak Creek while Ali was drafted into helping out at the restaurant, busing tables or waiting on customers.

"I was such an arrogant twit when I was a teenager," Ali said. "What kept you from throwing me back?"

She and her mother were sitting in the restaurant drinking coffee. There were still a few customers, but it was near closing time. Having been up baking since 4:00 A.M., Edie was glad to be off her feet.

"You weren't arrogant," Edie said with a smile, "you were young and smart. Your father and I both knew that you were destined for better things than working in a restaurant. So did your Aunt Evie. We all wanted you to go off to school and make something of yourself, and you did."

It was Edie Larson's sister who had pointed Ali in the direction of that first Askins scholarship.

Ali peered into the depths of her almost empty coffee mug. "That much-vaunted degree isn't doing me a whole lot of good these days," she said. "When Cliff Baker gave me my walking papers, he told me I was 'yesterday's news,' and I guess he was right. I've put out feelers to stations in the area, but no one's hiring—at least they're not hiring women my age. What am I going to do with myself, Mom? What am I going to be when I grow up?"

"I'm sure you'll figure it out," Edie assured her. "Look what you did about Reenie."

When Ali had first come home from California, it was because her best friend from grade school, Irene Holzer Bernard, had died in a car wreck on Schnebly Hill Road, a treacherous back-road route that wound its way down the face of the Mogollon Rim, between Flag-staff and Sedona. Schnebly Hill was dangerous under the best of circumstances, and Reenie had chosen to tackle it in the midst of a fierce winter snowstorm. When word came out that Irene had recently been given an ALS diagnosis, it was easy for people to assume that she had chosen that route on that particular night as a way of committing suicide.

Ali knew her friend—and she knew Reenie's kids, Matt and Julie. Unwilling to accept the idea that Reenie would have left her children behind a moment before she had to, Ali had dug deeper into the case, eventually uncovering the sobering reality that her friend had been murdered.

"Yes, I did," Ali agreed, "and look what that got me—ownership of a one-eyed, one-eared, fifteen-pound cat named Samantha."

When Reenie's kids had gone to live with their grandparents, their grandfather's severe cat allergy had meant that Sam couldn't go along. Instead she'd taken up residence at Ali's double-wide on Andante Drive.

"When you say it that way, it makes me want to hum

that old song about the Flying Purple People Eater," Edie said with a laugh.

"It's not funny," Ali objected. "With nothing to do, I'll probably end up being one of those weird old ladies who live alone with nothing but a cat for company. Sounds pretty bleak to me."

"I doubt that," Edie said. "Based on Reenie's case, maybe you'd make a better cop than you do a reporter."

"That's not going to happen," Ali told her, "never in a million years."

Still, the seed was planted. Was that why, a few years later, Ali Reynolds found herself enrolled for six weeks of law-enforcement training at the Arizona Police Academy down in Peoria? Probably so, because whether Ali Reynolds meant to or not, she tended to take her mother's advice.

11

Over time the Progeny Project became an all-consuming passion for the three women involved. Cassie Davis, despite her rough-hewn looks, was a tiger when it came to strong-arming donations from hapless acquaintances, many of whom were big spenders at the racetracks. Jolene Browder, a retired CPA, set Progeny Project up as a 501(c)(3) charitable organization. She handled the IRS filings and did all the necessary accounting. Yes, she was supposed to be retired, but this was a labor of love, something she did in memory of both her cherished daughter, Cindy, and her late husband, Robert.

As for Alex? She took her show on the road, sometimes on her own and sometimes with Evan along, and went out to preach the gospel of the Progeny Project. She spoke to civic-minded groups, such as Kiwanis and Rotary clubs, and did countless radio and television interviews. Without mentioning Edward Gilchrist's clinic by name, she told the story of how she and other families had been bamboozled by an unethical doctor who was suspected of using his own sperm rather than that of his alleged donors to impregnate his patients. Yes, something good had come from her former doctor's fraudulent behavior, but it also meant that offspring conceived that way risked susceptibility to a potentially life-threatening health risk that had been concealed from the families directly involved. When it came to that part of the story, Alex always had before-and-after photos of Evan and Rory along for show-and-tell.

With practice, Alex morphed into an effective public speaker, bringing more and more people into the fold and uncovering a growing community of families who had been forced to resort to artificial insemination to conceive. Alex's concerns were their concerns, too. As word got around, more and more people swabbed their cheeks and submitted their DNA samples for testing. For some of the progeny involved, this was the first time they learned that the person they'd always believed to be their biological mother or father wasn't, so questions were raised about their origins that they might have wondered about but never dared ask.

In the beginning, Rick—Cassie Davis's racehorse-DNA guy—processed all their DNA samples on a contract basis. By the time Evan Munsey was a senior at UCLA, majoring in microbiology, the load had grown exponentially, and he was the one in charge of doing the profiling. While other databases focused on law-enforcement issues, Evan masterminded the creation of one of the country's first-ever civilian DNA databases of donor siblings. As Progeny Project's only paid employee, he managed their Web site as well as their Facebook page, creating a forum where both children and parents could discuss the pros, cons, and sometimes unintended consequences of creating babies and families by non-traditional means.

Over time Progeny Project's efforts paid off. Along the way, profiling brought to light three more twenty-somethings, two girls and another boy, whose DNA designated them as additional Gilchrist half siblings. From Evan's point of view, the last of those three turned out to be the best. Crystal Lucas happened to be a newly sworn officer with LAPD. She had red hair that matched Evan's and Rory's, but her facial features were entirely different. She was estranged from both of her parents for reasons she never quite specified, but she was willing to pitch in and help out with Progeny Project wherever her services were needed. Crystal had grown up loving video games and all things computer. Once she joined the group, she relieved Evan of his Web-site duties and greatly expanded Progeny Project's social-media presence, turning what had once been a California-centric organization into a national one.

As the library of DNA samples expanded, so did the stories that came to them in heartfelt Facebook comments, in e-mails, and occasionally in handwritten letters. Many of the resulting children had been told up front that the man who was their dad wasn't necessarily their father. For them none of this was an earth-shattering revelation. More than once, however, those stories about artificial insemination were themselves bogus and had been used to provide cover for long-standing extramarital affairs. In other cases the parents had never mentioned the truth of the matter, but the kids themselves, feeling a mysterious sense of not belonging, had discovered it for themselves from information gleaned from Progeny Project's growing database. For some, finding out that they had half siblings in the world was a blessing, for others a curse.

In what felt like a real triumph, longtime sperm and egg donors began coming on board as well. While still preserving their anonymity, they voluntarily offered to provide not only DNA samples but also pertinent health and medical information that could then be passed along to their biological offspring. It was as though the Progeny Project had finally come full circle.

By then Alex had grown tired of the constant traveling. With social media bringing in a steady supply of new Progeny participants, Alex Munsey was ready to unpack her suitcase and hang up her microphone. As a result of the divorce settlement, the Munsey family's summertime cabin on Kuffel Canyon Road near Lake Arrowhead came to her free and clear. She'd hired a contractor to winterize the place so she could live in it year-round. After she'd spent a long stretch out on the road, the cabin provided a welcome retreat. Now, though, it seemed to her that the time had finally come to settle in at home and turn her hand to writing the book she'd always meant to write, one with a telling working title—*A Mother's Tale: A Fertility-Clinic Nightmare.*

One at a time, she laid out what she regarded as Edward Gilchrist's misdeeds and his growing collection of fraudulently conceived offspring. Because Evan's and Rory's identities had previously been made public, she was free to use their real names. She shielded the other victims' privacy with pseudonyms, but she offered no such courtesy to Edward Gilchrist himself. With him she pulled no punches—she named names and laid out the whole story, chapter and verse.

Once the manuscript was in what she thought of as final form, she ran it by an attorney. After reviewing the manuscript, the attorney offered advice that was short and to the point:

"Put this away in a drawer, or else turn it into fiction," he told her. "If you publish it this way while the man's still practicing medicine, he's likely to sue you for slander and/or libel. You've written it and gotten it out of your system. Now let it go. There's no sense in poking a hornet's nest."

Having asked for the advice, Alex Munsey was smart enough to take it. She put the completed manuscript for *A Mother's Tale* away in a locked filing cabinet and left it sitting there gathering dust.

12

In early 2008 Alex Munsey was summoned out of her self-imposed retirement and called to assist in the handling of a newly discovered cluster of half siblings that had been located in and around Phoenix, Arizona. The doctor/sperm donor in that case turned out to be a guy named Kenneth Brennan, who had died unexpectedly in a car accident in 1986 and whose widow still lived in the area.

"What do you want me to do?" Alex asked when Evan phoned to apprise her of the situation.

"I'd like you to contact her," he said. "We don't have DNA on the doctor, so we don't have any real confirmation that the doctor himself was responsible for this cluster of sperm donations. Occasionally people have gone public with these kinds of unanticipated results. Since the doctor has been dead for decades, I think we have an obligation to reach out to his widow and let her know that she might be caught up in a storm of bad publicity."

"You're right," Alex agreed. "If I were in her place, I would appreciate having some advance warning. Do you have her contact information?"

"Sure thing," Evan said. "Her name is Marcella Brennan, and she lives in a place called Paradise Valley. I'll text you her address and phone number."

Minutes later, when Alex picked up the phone to

dial Marcella's number, she had no idea what to expect. The phone rang several times. Just when she was expecting a voice-mail announcement, someone picked up. "Hello," a woman said.

"Is this Marcella Brennan?" Alex asked.

"It is. Who's this?" Marcella asked.

"My name's Alexandra Munsey, Alex for short, and I'm with an organization called the Progeny Project."

"If you're looking for a donation, I'm not interested in making any of those at this time," Marcella replied. "Please put me on your do-not-call list."

"I'm not calling for a donation," Alex put in quickly. "The Progeny Project is a charitable organization devoted to using DNA profiling to enable people conceived via artificial insemination to access information about their biological parents for health and medical reasons."

Holding her breath, Alex fully expected to have the phone slammed down in her ear. That didn't happen.

"Oh," Marcella murmured after a pause. "What took you so long? I always knew someone would come around asking questions about that sooner or later. That's why I saved all Kenny's records. I thought they might be important later on."

Alex could barely believe her ears. "You kept his records?" she asked. "You still have them?"

"I sure do. When Kenny died, most people around town, including our friends and acquaintances, expected that I'd sell his practice and bring home a nice hunk of change, and I certainly could have used the money. Without my knowledge he had run up huge gambling debts, but by then I had some idea that things at the office might not be as they should be, and I was afraid that if I tried to sell the practice, the whole thing might blow up in my face. Instead I dispatched a crew of movers to clean out his office to the bare walls. Then I had them haul all the office furniture, file cabinets, and suchlike to Goodwill, but I had them box up all the records and bring them here. They're still down in the basement, untouched. But all of this happened a long time ago. Why are you calling me now?"

"As I said before, Progeny Project is an organization focused on providing pertinent medical information and occasionally emotional support for people whose lives have been impacted by artificial insemination. Sometimes offspring resulting from those kinds of procedures are the ones who come to us, sometimes it's the parents, and sometimes it's both together. By submitting and comparing DNA samples, we're able to match children with their biological donors, who can—"

"Then provide the necessary medical information," Marcella said impatiently, finishing Alex's sentence.

"Exactly," Alex agreed. "Occasionally our research has revealed unusual clusters of several half siblings located in close geographical proximity. This may indicate that the clinic involved was overusing the sperm from a single donor rather than relying on a variety of donors. My own son, Evan, was part of one of those single-donor clusters. When he was in his early twenties and needed a kidney transplant, we were able to locate a half brother who was willing to be a living organ donor. That's actually how the Progeny Project got started."

"The operation saved your son's life?"

"Yes, it did. He's still on antirejection drugs, but he's fine."

"What does any of this have to do with me?" Marcella asked.

Alex paused for a moment before continuing. What was coming next would be tough to hear, and she wasn't sure how Marcella would react. "We've recently discovered a collection of several half siblings located in and around the Phoenix metropolitan area. One of the mothers involved has indicated that your husband, the late Dr. Kenneth Brennan, was the physician who performed her IUI."

"I see," Marcella said. Then, a moment later, she asked, "How many half siblings are we talking about?"

Alex took a breath. "Six," she answered quietly, "six so far. It could be that your husband simply used the same donor for all of them, or—"

"Or," Marcella interrupted, "my late husband could be solely responsible for this 'cluster,' as you call it."

Alex, surprised by Marcella's matter-of-fact tone, was stunned to momentary silence. "That's a possibility," she admitted finally, "but without DNA evidence there's no way to ascertain that."

"My husband has been dead for many years," Marcella said. "Are you calling because one or more of the six individuals you mentioned are looking for some kind of financial restitution?"

"No," Alex murmured quickly, "not at all. We were concerned that one or more of them might decide to go public with this recently discovered information and mention your late husband's name. We thought you should have some advance warning."

"What happens to the donors?" Marcella asked. "Do you release their names?"

"Some of the donors have come forward and voluntarily identified themselves. Others prefer to remain anonymous, and we respect that. We collect their medical information and pass that along but leave their names out of it."

Again there was dead silence on the phone. Alex checked the screen to see if the call had failed. It hadn't.

"What a son of a bitch!" Marcella breathed at last.

"Excuse me?"

"I said that dead husband of mine was a son of a bitch, and I meant every word of it. And if you talk to some of the birth mothers involved, you might discover that the so-called scientific procedures he used were far more hands-on than scientific. As far as I'm concerned, if Kenneth Brennan turns out to be your repeat sperm donor, he lost his right to anonymity long ago. Give me a bullhorn and I'll shout his name from the highest rooftop."

The ferocity in Marcella's voice was nothing short of astonishing.

"One of his 'hands-on' patients blew the whistle on him to me years ago," Marcella continued. "I was beyond furious and was getting my ducks in a row to divorce the man when he had the good sense to die on me. As far as I was concerned, that car accident was a win-win. But knowing what he'd been up to, I figured it wouldn't be long before some of his former patients came calling, ready to file malpractice suits.

"That was the real reason I cleared out his office. I was afraid there might be some real damning information hidden in those files, and I didn't want anyone else having access to them. Years passed, and I knew there was no longer any danger of malpractice suits, but by then it was too much trouble and too expensive for me to hire someone to haul the records away. I'm on one of those reverse-mortgage things, you see. Once I'm gone and the house goes back to the bank, I figured I'd leave it up to them to foot the bill for moving the files out and getting rid of them. But for right now what do you want from me?"

Alex took a breath. "If you believe that your husband may be responsible for this cluster of half-sibling births, would there be any possibility of having a sample of his DNA? That would be helpful, as would having access to his family's medical history."

"If Kenny turns out to be their biological father, they'd be well advised to stay away from alcohol," Marcella suggested. "He was a drinker, you see—driving drunk when he died. Other than that, he was healthy as a horse. As for his DNA? He had a collection of Montblanc pens that he kept in a locked glass display case in his office. They're still there, and as far as I know, he's the only person who ever touched them. Those pens are all collector's items, and they've grown quite valuable over time. I've been saving them for a rainy day. So yes, if there's any of Kenny's DNA still around, it would be on one of those pens, or maybe on some of the paperwork down in the basement."

"Tell me about that paperwork," Alex said. "Does it include your husband's patient files?"

"It certainly does," Marcella answered, "and the donor profiles as well, insofar as the miserable jerk might have used other donors. It's all there, filed away in stacks of clearly labeled banker's boxes. I don't know if I should give them to you, though. Even after all these years, I'm pretty sure that handing them over to a third party would constitute a violation of patient privacy. However, if some of my husband's former patients came forward asking for their records, or if their offspring did, I'd have no problem turning the files over to them. In order to do that, I'd need to have proper identification, of course, but releasing those old patient files to the people directly involved seems like a no-brainer to me. You'd best tell those folks to get a move on, though," Marcella added after a moment. "After all, I'm getting on in years, and I won't be around forever."

13

By 2008 Ali Reynolds had been out of the news business and back in Sedona for years, but just because
she was no longer involved in the news, that didn't
mean the news was out of her blood. With the help of her
newly found ally, a man named Leland Brooks, Ali had
recently purchased and was in the process of rehabbing a
midcentury modern that, without her intervention, would
have been a prime candidate for the wrecking ball. She
had worked for the Yavapai County Sheriff's Office for a
while, but that gig had ended due to budgetary consider-
ations. Once more a lady of unintended leisure, Ali spent
more time than was good for her watching the news, both
local and national.

One morning during a telephone conversation with
her architect, she had muted the sound on the TV set.
When she looked back at the screen, she was amazed
to see a familiar face from her old news-anchor days
back in L.A. Ali remembered Alex Munsey, of course,
along with the whole drama surrounding her son's
urgently needed kidney transplant. The two of them
had been more casual acquaintances than close friends,
and after leaving California, Ali had lost track of the
woman entirely.

Ali turned the sound off mute just in time to catch
the last minute or so of a three-person interview. An older

woman named Marcella Brennan was involved somehow, but Ali had tuned in too late to hear what she'd had to say. Instead she heard Alex talking about something called the Progeny Project. When the show went to a commercial break, Ali reached for her cell phone. She'd replaced her phone twice since coming home, once because she had broken the screen and once because she'd been offered a free upgrade. Both times Christopher had obligingly transferred her contacts list.

Checking it now, she discovered that Alex's name was still there, along with two phone numbers—one listed as a home number and the other a cell. Since Alex and her husband were in the process of divorcing the last Ali had heard, she didn't bother with the home number. Instead she dialed the cell. Evidently Ali was still in Alex's contacts list as well, because when she answered the phone, she knew who was calling.

"Why, Ali," Alex said pleasantly, "how good to hear from you! What are you up to these days? I heard that your ex passed away under some pretty challenging circumstances. I should have been in touch back when that happened. I'm sorry I wasn't."

Paul Grayson had been found murdered the night before their divorce would have been finalized. The person responsible for his death was finally caught but not until after Ali herself had come under suspicion.

"Calling it challenging doesn't quite cover it, but it takes two to tango," Ali replied. "You'll notice I haven't reached out either. I left California with my tail tucked between my legs and didn't stay in touch with anyone, but I just now saw the final seconds of this morning's interview. How long are you in town for? Sedona's just a couple of hours north of Phoenix. It would be great if we could get together for a meal and bring one another up to date."

"Marcella and I are booked with interviews for most of today and early tomorrow, but I don't fly home until tomorrow evening, so lunch tomorrow would work."

"Where are you staying?" Ali asked.

"At a Travelodge near the airport," she was told. "There's an IHOP just up the street, but not much else."

Because Ali and Paul were still married at the time of his death, Ali's financial situation had taken a big upswing afterward. Ali suspected, however, that the same wasn't true for Alex and that she was most likely living in considerably reduced circumstances.

"If I remember correctly, you always loved Mexican food," Ali ventured. "How about the Macayo's on Central around eleven thirty?"

"Sounds good," Alex replied. "See you then."

"One more thing," Ali said. "What's the organization you mentioned in the interview?"

"The Progeny Project," Alex answered. "That's my baby now—mine and Evan's. It's a forum for people whose lives have been affected by artificial insemination."

"Speaking of which," Ali said, "how is Evan?"

"He's great. He has a new girlfriend. I think he's working up his courage to pop the question, and that's all thanks to you, Ali. If you hadn't helped us find Rory and that matching kidney, chances are Evan wouldn't have lived long enough to fall in love, let alone get married or maybe even have kids of his own. So thank you for that."

"You're welcome," Ali said quietly.

Once off the phone, Ali went online, searched out

the Progeny Project, and found more than she expected. In the early 2000s, law enforcement had embarked on the collection of DNA samples for crime-fighting purposes, but the DNA database dreamed up by Alexandra Munsey, Jolene Browder, and Cassie Davis back then was considered to be one of the first private-sector DNA databases ever established.

A quick search of Marcella Brennan's name revealed that she was the widow of a physician, a sole practitioner running a fertility clinic. Ali wondered if the guy was a carbon copy of the one who'd victimized Alex Munsey's and a number of other families years earlier and whose abuses had come to light only in the aftermath of Alex's determined search for a suitable donor for her son's much-needed kidney transplant. Try as she might, Ali couldn't remember the name of that offending doctor, and she wondered what had become of him.

Before long she needed to dress and head off on a series of interviews with contractors interested in tackling her construction project, but by the time Ali met up with Alex in downtown Phoenix late the next morning, she knew far more than she had previously.

The first thing Ali noticed about Alex when she entered the restaurant and walked up to the table, holding out her arms in greeting, was that the woman appeared to be years younger than she'd looked back when they first met. Alex was tanned and fit, as though she spent a good deal of time in the outdoors. The biggest change was in her face, and not because of some plastic surgeon's artistry either. The careworn expression that had etched her features when her son had been so gravely ill had seemingly been erased. There were laugh lines around her mouth now, and the worry lines in her forehead had disappeared.

"It's so good to see you again!" Ali exclaimed. "You look terrific!"

"Thank you," Alex responded. "You look pretty good yourself."

"And I'm sorry we lost touch."

"Don't be sorry," Alex said with a genuine smile. "That's what today is all about—we both get a do-over."

They spent a few minutes examining menus and deciding on what to order. "So where are you living these days?" Ali asked once their glasses of iced tea had been delivered.

"Up in the family cabin in the San Bernardino Mountains near Lake Arrowhead," Alex replied. "We used to go there mostly in the summers, but when Jake and I divorced, I ended up with the cabin, and now I live there year-round. I have an all-wheel-drive Subaru for getting in and out in bad weather, but I also keep plenty of food and firewood on hand. I have a generator, but if push comes to shove and the power is out too long, I also have backup kerosene lamps and battery-powered lanterns."

"I remember when you found out he wanted a divorce."

"I do, too," Alex said ruefully, "in the recovery room right after Evan's transplant. Talk about poor timing! I could hardly believe it. Now I know it's par for the course. When families end up spending years dealing with an ailing child, eventually the illness is the only glue holding some of those marriages together. Once the crisis passes—because the child either recovers or dies—the relationships aren't able to survive. That's exactly what happened to Jake and me. I had spent years focused on Evan and his needs. By the time I finally came up for air because it looked like Evan was going to be okay, Jake was ready to call it quits. He and I had grown apart. We'd become virtual strangers, and he didn't want to be married anymore."

"A girlfriend?" Ali asked.

Alex nodded. "Her name is Nancy, and they married eventually. She's not a bad person, by the way, and she's been good to Evan. I sometimes spend major holidays with them at our old house, because weather can make getting back and forth to my place for Thanksgiving and Christmas dicey at times. So we're fine now, all of us."

"Don't you get lonely living out in the wilderness all by yourself?"

Alex sipped her tea and shook her head. "I did at first," she answered thoughtfully. "For one thing, I was really angry with Jake and blamed him for kicking me out of the house and sending me off into exile. But I wasn't there all that much, because I was on the road with the Progeny Project."

"After I saw you on TV yesterday, I looked up Progeny Project," Ali offered. "It seems to have come a long way from some very humble beginnings."

Alex nodded. "To begin with it was just Cassie Davis, Jolene Browder, and I."

"How are they?"

"Jolene passed away a couple of years ago from congestive heart failure."

"I'm sorry. What about Cassie? Where's she these days?"

"She's living here now . . . well, in Mesa. She had a pretty serious horseback-riding accident and ended up having to get out of the horse-training business. She's retired now, and she and Emma are back together. I had hoped to see her this time around, but they're out of town this week."

"From what I saw online, it sounds like Evan and Rory are still involved with each other."

"They are," Alex said with a smile. "The two of them have become great friends. Now most of our outreach takes place over social media, so I've been able to take a step back from all that—the situation with Marcella here being an exception to that rule. Rory is living in L.A. again, so he helps out some of the time."

"And Evan?" Ali asked. "What's he doing?"

"He's doing great. He graduated from UCLA with a degree in microbiology. He had intended to go on and get an advanced degree, but PP, as we like to call the Progeny Project, sidelined him into the world of DNA profiling. After he caught that bug, he got even more sidelined when he ended up designing our DNA database. With Evan at the helm, PP was one of the first kids on the block to establish a private-sector DNA database. Things have changed over time. Now there's a lot more interest in establishing non-law-enforcement DNA databases. One of them—an outfit in Utah—is trying to woo him away from us by making him an offer he may not be able to refuse."

"And what about you?" Ali asked. "What have you been doing?"

"When we first launched the Progeny Project, I put myself in charge of PR. I did a lot of traveling and speaking, doing TV and radio interviews much like the ones Marcella and I were doing yesterday and this morning—just raising awareness of the long-term complications that can arise for people whose births resulted from artificial insemination."

"And that's what brought you to Phoenix," Ali concluded.

Alex nodded. "Marcella Brennan's late husband, Kenneth, ran a fertility clinic here. As far as I can tell, he was a carbon copy of Dr. Edward Gilchrist."

That was the name Ali had forgotten. "The guy up in Santa Clarita?"

Alex nodded. "That's the one. So far PP has turned up eighteen donor siblings in what we refer to as the Gilchrist cluster. Kenneth Brennan was evidently doing the same thing here in Phoenix. One of the mothers in this new cluster mentioned him by name. By the time I contacted Marcella, we had located six people in the Phoenix cluster. After yesterday's media blitz, several additional people have contacted us and will be sending in their cheek swabs. I wouldn't be surprised if more turn up once word gets around.

"And that's the only reason I came—to help get the word out. I've done countless interviews on the subject. Marcella hadn't done any, and I was glad to be able to help out. But I'll be equally glad to go back home. When I'm not on the road, I'm afraid I become something of a hermit."

"What do hermits do to keep busy?" Ali asked.

"This hermit sits in her favorite chair next to a wood-burning stove with a laptop on her lap, writing."

"You're a writer now?"

"Trying to be," Alex said with a laugh. "I'm one of those thousands of yet-to-be-published authors, but that's how I see myself—as a writer. My first manuscript, *A Mother's Tale*, is about my nightmare experience with

Dr. Gilchrist. It starts with Jake and me trying to get pregnant and ends with the kidney transplant."

"Unpublished? Why?"

"On the advice of counsel, it's stowed away in a file drawer, because if I put all that stuff out in print, Gilchrist is likely to sue my socks off."

"He's still around?"

"Not only is he still alive, he's still in business."

"You're kidding. I thought he'd be done for by now," Ali said.

"So did we," Alex replied. "The problem is, by the time all this came to light, it was too late to file malpractice suits. We tried reporting him to the medical board but didn't get to first base there either. One of the Gilchrist donor siblings, Crystal Lucas Manning, is a detective with LAPD. She's hooked us up with a trial lawyer who's hoping to file a class-action suit against him. We have thirteen separate families who've given depositions on what they were told about their respective sperm donors, all of which turned out to be lies."

"Thirteen?" Ali echoed. "You've found eleven more people who are half siblings with Rory, Evan, and Cindy?"

"We've found more than that," Alex replied. "Eighteen in all. Thirteen of those have given depositions."

"I can't believe Gilchrist is still in business," Ali added.

"I can't either," Alex agreed. "Believe me, it's not for lack of trying. So far we've been unable to obtain a sample of Gilchrist's DNA, but Crystal Manning, the detective I mentioned earlier, might have found a way around that."

"How so?"

"It's called discarded DNA. Last week, during her off hours, Crystal staked out Gilchrist's house and came away with a whole box of tossed-out tissues, paper cups, and beer bottles. There's a young woman living with him these days, but any male DNA found in trash at his address will most likely be from him. We're in the process of having those items analyzed now. If the resulting profile comes up as a match to the people in Progeny's database, then our lawyer says the gloves come off and we take the bastard to court."

"Be sure to let me know how it turns out."

"I will," Alex replied.

"And when you finally get around to publishing that book, will you send me a signed copy?"

"Absolutely," Alex answered with a grin, "but that's enough about me. What's been going on with you?"

Ali gave her a general overview in all its boring detail—a grown son and a relatively new daughter-in-law, housing, dealing with aging parents—in other words, the usual. "If you had come along a couple of months ago, I would have added that I had a totally nonexistent love life," Ali told her. "All that seems to have changed."

"You've got a boyfriend now?"

"I'm not sure I'd go so far as to call him a boyfriend," Ali allowed. "His name is B. Simpson—as in initial B. only. His given name was Bartholomew, but once *The Simpsons* came on the air, he endured a world of teasing on that score. As a result he ditched his first name altogether and kept the initial."

"What does he do?"

"He's into computers. He made a fortune in the computer gaming world, but now he's in the process of starting a cybersecurity company."

"So an entrepreneur, then?" Alex asked.

Ali nodded.

"Are you serious about him?"

"I'm not serious," Ali replied. "Turns out he's just a kid—fifteen years younger than I am. I believe that makes me what's commonly referred to as 'a cougar.'"

"Fifteen years is nothing," Alex told her. "As far as I'm concerned, you should grab on to happiness wherever you find it."

"I'll think about it."

When their luncheon ended and they were on their way out the door, they hugged and promised to stay in touch. Two weeks after their get-together, Alex sent an e-mail update saying that Kenneth Brennan's DNA was indeed a match to the people in the Phoenix cluster.

The next time Ali heard from Alex Munsey was again via e-mail:

> OMG! Our attorney had been trying to reach out to Gilchrist's former wife, Dawn, asking her to come testify against him at our trial. Last night someone attacked the poor woman in her garage and stabbed her to death. Edward Gilchrist killed her, I'm sure of it. He claims he was in Las Vegas at the time she died and that he had nothing to do with it, but he's a liar, and liars lie. I hope the cops can nail the bastard in a hell of a hurry. He deserves to rot in jail.

A month or so later, Ali received another e-mail from Alex:

Yesterday was supposed to be our big day
in court. Gilchrist showed up with a hotshot
attorney in tow who managed to have our
case thrown out. Completely. Even if we'd
lost in court eventually, at least we would
have been able to say out loud and in public
exactly the kind of lowlife the man is, but
now it's over. He'll never be held accountable
for his actions, and he'll probably end up
getting away with murder, too.

Ali wrote back, sympathizing with the disappointing
outcome, but Alex did not respond. For the next three
years, Ali went on with her life while Alex Munsey maintained radio silence. Ali tried sending e-mails from time
to time, but when there was no reply to those either, she
finally gave up. Evidently Alex had retreated to being a
full-time hermit and was determined to stay that way.

Besides, Ali had other interests to occupy her time
and attention. For one thing, she had grandkids now—
the twins, Colin and Colleen. She had finally overcome
the age-difference issue, and she and B. got married. She
went to work with him on his cybersecurity business,
High Noon Enterprises, which had suddenly morphed
from a humble start-up into a booming international
entity. In her spare time, Ali volunteered at a homeless
shelter in Flagstaff, where she was helping shepherd a
group of traumatized girls rescued from a polygamous
cult called the Encampment. The young women had
been brought up in what was essentially a nineteenth-
century existence, and the challenge now was to help
guide them into the twenty-first.

From time to time, Ali searched the Internet and

L.A.-area news sites to see if the cops were making any progress on the Dawn Gilchrist homicide investigation, but couldn't find any updates. The investigation had gone cold, and it seemed likely the case would never be solved. Yet then one day it happened. Early in 2011 there was an arrest in the case, followed shortly thereafter by a second one.

First a gangbanger named Leo Manuel Aurelio was taken into custody and charged with first-degree murder in the Dawn Gilchrist homicide. Three weeks later Edward Anthony Gilchrist, Dawn's former husband, was arrested as well. He was charged with first-degree murder and conspiracy to commit. At his preliminary hearing and despite his lawyer's pleas to the contrary, the judge looked at the seriousness of the crimes and refused to grant bail.

Ali read about it online and was surprised that she hadn't heard about it from Alex Munsey herself, but it was still very welcome news.

Amen, Ali thought. *It's about damned time.*

14

O n the day Edward Gilchrist was arrested, he was allowed a single phone call. Despite the fact that he hadn't spoken to his mother in months, Hannah was the person he called.

"Mummy," he said when she answered. "I'm under arrest. I need an attorney."

"All right, son," she said at once. "Don't worry. I've got this covered. And remember, don't say a word until your attorney, whoever he happens to be, is right there with you."

"Do you think I'm stupid?" Eddie demanded.

Hannah chose not to answer that question at the moment, because she suspected Eddie wouldn't be at all pleased with what she had to say. Not only did she think him stupid, she also regarded him as arrogant, self-centered, and any number of other things that were best left unsaid. Besides, she was far too busy circling the wagons to stand around making idle conversation.

It was three years now since Hannah's wretched former daughter-in-law, Dawn, had turned up stabbed to death on the floor of her two-car garage in Santa Clarita. Soon after the murder, the town's then police chief had announced at a press conference that they had a "person of interest" in the case. He didn't say it was Eddie, but he didn't have to. Everyone assumed that the culprit had to be Dawn's husband, because it's always the husband, right? From that moment on, Hannah had expected that sooner or later this day would come, and her son would be placed under arrest. Between then and now, she'd done her best to prepare for that ugly eventuality.

Hannah had spent weeks researching the best criminal defense attorneys available in the Greater Los Angeles Area and had kept a notebook listing the ones she considered to be the top five contenders. Now that push had come to shove, she wasted no time. She consulted the results in her notebook and picked up her phone. Money had never been a problem for Hannah Anderson Gilchrist, and it still wasn't, so she went all in and started with her number one choice.

The firm of Wilkins, Wilkins and Clancy had its offices in a high rise on Wilshire Boulevard. As part of her due diligence, she'd had her longtime chauffeur, Marco Gregory, drive her into the city for a little recon trip. After lunch at the Brentwood Country Club, she had Marco drive her past the high-rise building, dropping her off long enough for her to step inside to check things out. The offices of Wilkins, Wilkins and Clancy occupied the top two floors of the building. She had ridden up to the penthouse and stepped inside to be greeted by a receptionist.

"May I help you?"

"Oh, no," Hannah said quickly. "I believe I'm on the wrong floor."

She wasn't, of course. Everything about the snazzy office space and its interior décor told her that this was a high-powered outfit, one that would deliver plenty of bang for the buck. As far as she could tell from the swanky address and the building, things had appeared to be up to snuff. It would no doubt be expensive, but money wasn't the issue here. What Hannah was looking for was someone who would be effective.

To that end, after Eddie's pleading phone call, when it was time to feed a number into her landline phone, that was the one she dialed.

"Wilkins, Wilkins and Clancy," a voice answered. "How may I help you?"

It sounded like the same receptionist who'd greeted Hannah before. "I'd like to speak to Calvin Wilkins," she announced. "By that I mean Calvin Wilkins Sr. as opposed to Calvin Wilkins Jr."

"I'm not sure Mr. Wilkins is available. If I could have your name, I'll be glad to put you through to his secretary."

"My name is Hannah Anderson Gilchrist," she said. "I have absolutely no interest in speaking to a secretary or an underling. My son has been arrested on capital murder charges, and I'm in need of a top-notch criminal defense attorney. Edward's bail hearing is the day after tomorrow at the courthouse in Santa Clarita. Before that happens, I'd like to have Wilkins, Wilkins and Clancy on retainer."

That was evidently enough to get Hannah past the gatekeeper. "One moment, please," she was told before being put on hold.

It was several minutes rather than a single moment before a male voice finally came on the line. "Calvin Wilkins here," a man said cheerfully. "How may I be of service?"

"My son, Edward, has been arrested on homicide charges in the death of his former wife three years ago," Hannah told him. "I would like your firm in general and you personally to undertake his defense."

"I trust you're aware that this might turn out to be a very expensive endeavor," Wilkins cautioned.

"That's readily apparent," Hannah snapped back at him. "Penthouse office suites on Wilshire Boulevard don't come cheap. What I need to know at the moment is the amount you would require up front and whether you prefer payment to be made by way of a personal check, a cashier's check, or an electronic transfer."

"Twenty-five should cover the initial bail hearing," Wilkins replied. "And a personal check would be fine, but are you sure your son will consent to having you obtain counsel for him? You do realize that he'd need to sign off on that."

"Mr. Wilkins, Edward has very little leeway in this regard. Either he accepts the representation I obtain for him or he asks for a public defender. Which of those options do you think he'll choose? So when you say 'twenty-five,' I assume you're really saying twenty-five thousand, correct?"

"Yes."

"All right, then. I'll make arrangements to transfer that amount into my checking account. I want you on board as soon as possible, so I'd like to deliver the check today, if you don't mind. It's eleven right now. Traffic between Santa Clarita and L.A. probably isn't too bad at the moment. What about if we meet for a late lunch at Brentwood Country Club? I'm assuming you know where that's located."

"Of course, but wouldn't you rather come by the office?"

"No, thank you," Hannah sniffed. "I'm one of those old-fashioned, three-meals-a-day kind of girls, and by meal I don't mean one of those ungodly boxed lunches delivered from some nearby deli to a corporate conference room. Let's say one thirty. I'll call ahead. The reservation will be in my name. My grandfather, Augustus Anderson, was one of the club's founding members, you see. The waitstaff always makes sure I have a good table."

"I have no doubt they do," Calvin Wilkins said. "One thirty it is."

It was no accident that Hannah had dropped Augustus's name into the mix. Almost a century after his death, her pioneering grandfather's name still resonated in the city. Wilkins might have started to say something more, but Hannah hung up before he could do so. She had called him on her landline, the number of which was listed as private and would not have shown up on his caller ID. She hadn't given a phone number to the receptionist, so there was no way for him to call her back. Calvin Wilkins might be a big shot, but a check for twenty-five thousand dollars along with the expectation of a lot more where that came from would be too much of a temptation to resist. He would be there, with bells on.

As for Hannah? This was exactly how she liked to initiate business relationships—with herself firmly in charge.

As a young woman, Hannah had been considered "handsome" rather than "pretty" or "beautiful," and as a child she'd never been regarded as cute either. To overcome her shortcomings in the looks department, Hannah made certain that whenever she went out in public, she was carefully put together. Painfully thin for most of her life, she favored trim but stylish pantsuits and sensible heels, always with her grandmother's antique cameo pinned firmly to the throat of a spotless white blouse.

Growing up, Hannah had often wondered if she and

another baby had somehow been switched at birth. She and her mother, Isobel, had nothing in common. Her mother, a gorgeous creature and former debutante, was a socialite from beginning to end. Isobel had expected to give her daughter the benefit of the same kind of upbringing Isobel herself had enjoyed—an education provided first by at-home tutors and later tony private schools, topped off with a stint at finishing school and finally by a lavish coming-out party. All that activity was designed to achieve but a single end—to reel in a suitable husband for Hannah, who was in turn expected to give birth to a pair of children—preferably a boy and a girl. That was Isobel's game plan, and since going to college hadn't been part of her own life, she saw no need for a college degree in Hannah's future either.

Isobel was a natural beauty with a figure that could still turn heads when she was well into her fifties. Unfortunately, in the looks department her somewhat horse-faced daughter took after her father's side of the family rather than her mother's. To Isobel's immense disappointment, Hannah grew from being a clumsy, awkward child into a gawky plain-Jane adolescent, and finally into an even plainer adult. Hannah's enforced stay at that incredibly expensive Swiss-based finishing school ended up being a complete flop. Too homesick to finish out the course, she had returned to California much the same as when she left. When Hannah adamantly refused to have anything to do with a coming-out party, Isobel had despaired of ever finding her daughter a suitable match. Hannah was barely twenty at the time, but as far as Isobel was concerned, she was most likely headed for a life of spinsterhood.

Isobel made it her whole purpose in life to guarantee

that that didn't happen. During the forties, fifties, and sixties, Isobel Anderson had been a mover and shaker and a high-end fund-raiser in local and statewide Republican politics. One of her most treasured mementos was a color photograph featuring a smiling Isobel seated next to future first lady Mamie Eisenhower, both of them sipping tea. The photo was the first weapon Isobel had deployed in her newly launched effort to marry off her difficult daughter.

"See there," Isobel said, holding up the photo for Hannah's benefit. "Mamie was a lot like you. She was never a great beauty, and you won't be either. Obviously Mamie did the best she could with what she had, and I advise you to do the same."

Much to Isobel's surprise, Hannah had taken both her mother's words and her interest in politics to heart. Decades later on that drive into L.A., Hannah Gilchrist was still a card-carrying Republican, and to this day her hairdo of choice remained a carefully trimmed, gunmetal gray bob with a fringe of very short bangs. Hannah sometimes felt sorry for all the beautiful women out there, and L.A. was full of them. If the poor dears hadn't yet lost their looks, inevitably they would soon enough, and when that happened, they'd be screwed. If you'd never been beautiful to begin with, you had the distinct advantage of having nothing to lose. Yes, good looks counted for a time, but they definitely came in a distant second if you just happened to have a seemingly bottomless checkbook, because it was clearly money rather than looks that landed Gordon Gilchrist.

From day one, Hannah's marriage to Gordon was never a love match so much as it was an "arrangement," a marriage of convenience. For Gordon, marrying an heiress gave him standing in the community, a solid financial basis, and the necessary connections to advance what he hoped would be a long and successful political career. Marrying Hannah to Gordon checked off one of the mandatory boxes on Isobel's list of what her daughter needed to do with her life. For Hannah, marriage got her away from home and gave her an escape from being trapped under her mother's thumb.

Gordon might have been ambitious, but he was also self-involved, relatively weak, and not particularly kind. He had died of a heart attack at age thirty-eight, but all through their marriage he managed to sneer at his wife for not having the benefit of a college education. As far as Gordon was concerned, spending time in a finishing school was no substitute for a college degree, and Eddie, mirroring his father's attitude, had done the same thing.

But Hannah had learned that, degreed or not, whatever she might have lacked in diplomas, she made up for with a strong streak of pragmatism and common sense which, along with her unfortunate looks, had come down to her on her father's side of the family tree. She had used that pragmatism to advance Gordon's political prospects while ignoring his occasional dalliances and indiscretions. It was a time when divorces just weren't done, but she had retaliated by keeping a very tight hold on the family purse strings and by making sure Gordon understood that the money was hers rather than theirs.

Since common sense and pragmatism had seen her through any number of difficult situations, she fully expected the same would be true today.

With Marco carefully shepherding the Rolls through traffic, they made their way into the city. It might have been noon, but traffic was already a nightmare. The drive from

Santa Clarita to the country club, a distance of only a bit more than thirty miles, took an hour and twenty minutes, but the extra time gave Hannah a chance to settle into her comfy leather seat, close her eyes, and plan her strategy.

Try as she might, Hannah continued to regard her former daughter-in-law's death as no great loss. She had adored Jeanette, Eddie's first wife. When her son had thrown Jeanette over for a bottle-blond floozy named Dawn, who happened to be his then nurse/receptionist, Hannah had been beyond furious. The poisonous level of antipathy that sprang up between the two women had been instantaneous, mutual, and utterly unrelenting.

Hannah and Eddie had been estranged the whole time he and Dawn were married, and that had continued to be the case even after she'd helped him survive his second divorce. But when her son's carefully constructed world began to implode again, he'd been forced to come to his mother looking for help. Hannah had decided early on that if he ever showed any interest in reconciling, she would welcome him with open arms. Eddie might have been arrogant and obnoxious growing up, but she'd loved him all the same. If his being in crisis was the only way she could have her son back in her life, then Hannah would take whatever she could get.

When it came time for him to shuck off Dawn, Hannah had been more than happy to step in and foot the bill. She'd had her own attorney negotiate the divorce settlement, thinking that would give them the best deal. Things hadn't quite gone their way, and the settlement had been more generous than Hannah had anticipated. Still, from her point of view, if it meant getting rid of Dawn, it was money well spent.

The problem was, unloading Dawn wasn't nearly the

end of Eddie's troubles. About that same time, Eddie's formerly prosperous fertility clinic began running into difficulties. Some of his earlier patients—people he had assisted in their quests to conceive—had begun claiming that he'd misled them concerning the donors he'd used. Hannah was offended. What was wrong with those people? Without Eddie's help they never would have had kids in the first place, and now they were complaining about the very children Eddie had helped provide? Talk about ingratitude!

It wasn't until after Dawn's death that Eddie had finally told her that some of those same dissatisfied former patients, now part of a group called the Progeny Project, were initiating a class-action lawsuit against him. Hannah had immediately swung into action. She sent in an attorney who, for a pretty penny, had managed to have the case dismissed. But just because the lawsuit went away, that didn't mean the ugly rumors did.

As long as Eddie remained a person of interest in the murder of his ex-wife, it was hardly surprising that his practice continued to nosedive. His nurse, Kaitlyn, quit—or maybe Eddie simply let her go, Hannah never knew which. Patients dropped him left and right. New patients stopped showing up. He tried selling the practice, but in view of all the scandal surrounding it, no one was interested. For a long time, Eddie continued going into the office every day even though he no longer had patients to see. Eventually, though, he was forced to close his doors and put the building itself on the market. Disgraced, out of business, and now under arrest for murder, Eddie might have led a life of utter failure, and yet his mother was determined to do everything in her power to help him.

Marco Gregory dropped Hannah off at the clubhouse's

front door with barely ten minutes to spare before her one thirty luncheon appointment. Just as she'd requested, the hostess led her to one of the prized tables next to the windows. This one happened to overlook two of the course's more challenging sand traps. Hannah wasn't all that interested in golf, but her guests generally were, and she liked to make sure the immaculately kept course was front and center in their line of sight.

Shortly after she was seated, the hostess returned, leading a confident-looking man Hannah pegged to be somewhere in his mid-fifties. She'd expected someone older and more seasoned. He had a trim, athletic build and boasted a full head of silvery hair. He approached her with a self-assured smile, dressed in a designer suit topped by a neatly tied bright yellow bow tie. It was a look designed to intimidate and put people in their place. Hannah wasn't impressed.

"Ms. Gilchrist?" he asked, holding out his hand. "A pleasure to meet you."

"*Mrs.* Gilchrist rather than Ms.," she corrected primly. "Won't you have a seat?"

Calvin Wilkins sat, passing a business card across the table as he did so. She studied it, frowning in displeasure.

"This says Calvin Wilkins Jr. I believe I distinctly said that I wished to conduct my business with Calvin Wilkins Sr."

"Calvin Wilkins Sr. was my father," the man explained. "Unfortunately, he suffered a massive heart attack and passed away almost a year ago."

"I'm sorry to hear that," Hannah offered.

"My son, officially Calvin Wilkins III, finished law school third in his class and passed the bar exam on the first try three years ago. He works in the firm, but it's still a little early to bring him in as a managing partner. I've left the name on the wall as is for the time being, while we give him a chance to grow into the role. As the granddaughter of Augustus and Alberta Anderson, I'm sure you understand the value and importance of carrying on with a legacy name."

Hannah nodded her assent, pleased that in the time between her original phone call and now, her selected attorney had done some homework. He knew who she was without her having to tell him. Whether he was Junior or Senior meant little as long as their meeting was off to a good start. She had prepared a check for him before leaving home. Pulling it out of her purse, she slid it across the table. Calvin picked it up, looked at it briefly, and then slid it into the inside pocket of his jacket.

"Your son will need to sign off on your paying for his representation prior to the bail hearing. I have the form with me, so he can sign it this afternoon when I go to the jail to meet him. That won't be a problem, will it?"

"Not at all," Hannah answered. "Beggars can't be choosers."

Their waitress arrived at the table. "Can I get you two something to drink?"

"Since I need to head north to meet with my client right after lunch," Calvin said, "I believe I'll stick to coffee."

"And you?" the waitress asked, turning her attention on Hannah.

"I have a car and driver waiting outside," Hannah told her. "I believe I'll have a dry martini."

15

Eddie's preliminary hearing turned out to be a complete disaster. Hannah arrived at the courthouse fully prepared to post whatever bail the judge might deem necessary. In terms of strategy, it was probably a bad idea on Hannah's part to have Marco drive her to the courthouse in the Rolls. The judge involved wasn't someone Hannah knew personally, but the prosecutor was.

The assistant district attorney's wife and Hannah had served on the board for the local Friends of the Library for several years. At those gatherings Hannah had never made a big deal of who she was, but it was one of those things that went without saying, unless of course you counted the catered afternoon tea she hosted at her home each September—the home Ambrose and Isobel Anderson had built and gifted to the newlyweds shortly after their daughter's marriage to Gordon Gilchrist, a Santa Clarita native. Compared to Hollywood mansions, the place would be considered modest, but by Santa Clarita standards it was distinctly upper-crust.

Naturally, when asked how he pleaded, Eddie, with Calvin Wilkins at his side, announced clearly and distinctly, "Not guilty."

But then things went sideways. "The defendant is a long-term member of the community," the ADA allowed, "but his business has recently failed and his house is in danger of going into foreclosure."

Hannah sighed when she heard that telling detail. It was one more thing Eddie had neglected to mention.

"Nonetheless," the ADA continued, "with his mother's Rolls-Royce parked outside the courtroom, I believe it's fair to say that Dr. Gilchrist still has access to considerable financial resources, and that makes him a flight risk. Given that as well as the seriousness of the crime, the prosecution asks that the defendant not be allowed to post bail."

Calvin Wilkins objected, of course, but to no effect.

"The defendant will be returned to the county jail facility here in Santa Clarita, where he's to be held without bail pending trial," the judge announced with a quick rap of his gavel. "Next case."

No trial had been held—no guilty verdict rendered—but the rap of that gavel at midafternoon on a Wednesday sentenced Hannah Gilchrist to the next stage of her life as surely as if her son had already been convicted. And three days later, on a Saturday morning, it began in dead earnest.

That day and every Saturday afterward, from then until the end of the trial, Hannah got up early, ate her solitary breakfast, made herself presentable, and then headed off for the jail. Just because her son had hit a rough patch, that didn't mean she was going to abandon him, not at all.

With Marco behind the wheel and Hannah once again in the backseat of the Rolls, she was dismayed to notice, for the first time but not the last, that the Santa Clarita jail was located on Magic Mountain Parkway. There was nothing magic about it.

At the jail Hannah exited the car, leaving behind both her purse and her phone. She had done some checking in advance. Hannah knew she'd be required to pass through security in order to gain access to the visitors' room, and she had no intention of allowing some grubby jail guard to paw through her belongings. She'd also learned that in order to be given a pass, she'd be required to provide photo ID. Hannah had never learned to drive, so presenting a driver's license was out. Instead she brought along her passport.

"I expect I'll be about an hour," she told Marco. "You don't have to wait here. If you have something to do in the meantime, feel free."

She breezed through the metal detector and then went to a scarred Formica-topped counter where, after signing in and presenting her passport for examination, she was issued a name tag and a visitor's lanyard. Eventually she found herself in a grim, airless anteroom, waiting with a small crowd of people outside a locked metal door with the word VISITATION painted in heavy black letters on thick, wire-reinforced glass. Once the door was unlocked, Hannah was the first person in. A guard examined her lanyard, made a notation on a clipboard, and then motioned her inside.

The barren room was lined with narrow cubicles divided by tall panes of plexiglass that kept the prisoners on their side of the cubicle and visitors on the other. There were no chairs in the room. Each cubicle came complete with a pull-out metal seat permanently attached beneath a gray Formica countertop. No physical contact was allowed. There were no pass-throughs. The only means of communication between one side and the other was by way of a pair of old-fashioned telephone receivers mounted at shoulder height on the walls on either side of the glass partition.

"Wait here," another guard told Hannah, directing her to a cubicle. "I'll have someone bring Mr. Gilchrist right out."

The fact that Eddie's identity had already been divested of the word "doctor" made Hannah want to weep, but eventually she got a grip. She was here to support her son, not to fall apart. She sat up straight, folded her carefully manicured hands in her lap, and waited. At last a guard escorted Eddie into the room. It pained her to see her son dressed in an orange jumpsuit and shuffling along in prison-issue slippers. With his fading and thinning ginger hair, orange was definitely not a good color for him, most especially in a room lit by ugly fluorescent fixtures. There were dark circles under his eyes, so most likely he hadn't slept well. Neither had Hannah for that matter, but the makeup she'd carefully applied before coming here had helped.

She waited until he was seated before picking up the telephone receiver. "Good morning," she said.

Holding the phone to his ear with his shoulder, Eddie used his hands to send his mother a signed response. "It sucks," he said.

When Hannah's father, Ambrose, had come down with mumps at age five, his mother, Alberta, had been stricken with mumps as well. She had recovered eventually but was left profoundly deaf. As a result, her husband, Augustus, had decreed that everyone in the household, hired help and their son included, should learn sign language. For Ambrose sign language really became his second language, something he had passed along to his own daughter once Hannah arrived on the scene. The fact that Ambrose and Hannah could carry on private conversations in Isobel's presence without her being able to understand what they were saying was something that had driven Hannah's mother crazy, but not so crazy that she bothered learning the skill on her own. And remembering how she and her father had navigated around Isobel, from the time Eddie began learning to talk, Hannah had taught her son sign language.

Armed with the same steadiness that had once allowed Hannah to prop up a weak-willed husband, she had come to the jail fully prepared to prop up Gordon's weak-willed son. And in view of the fact that the signs outside clearly stated that all phone calls in the visitors' room were recorded, being able to resort to using sign language was a real boon. As they chatted back and forth, sometimes speaking and sometimes signing, Hannah Gilchrist couldn't help but think she was doing exactly what mothers are supposed to do—supporting her son. She did so with no idea that she had just taken the first step on a very dark road.

For the next thirteen months, while Eddie awaited trial, she was there at the county lockup every Saturday morning, come rain or come shine, dropped off early and picked up an hour later. Over time she and Eddie managed to sort out a shorthand version of sign language that required only one hand and was less likely to be spotted by the guards. Eddie never told her that she was his only visitor, but the lady at the check-in counter did. Other than occasional visits by someone from Calvin Wilkins's legal team, Hannah was it. She was the only one who cared.

Finally, after what seemed forever, the trial started, and Hannah was there for that, too, every single day.

It was only then, in the courtroom with Judge William Ratcliff presiding, that Hannah finally learned the truth about the charges lodged against her son and about the many betrayals that had destined him for that spot at the defense table in a murder trial.

The first time Hannah entered the courtroom, she took her place in a front-row seat directly behind Eddie's chair. Looking around, Hannah was reminded of the two separate churches that had been the sites of Eddie and Dawn's wedding and of Eddie and Jeanette's wedding before that. In both instances the pews had been divided by a central aisle into two separate sections—one side for the bride's guests and the other for the groom's.

The layout for the courtroom gallery in Santa Clarita was eerily similar. On one side, the prosecutorial side, were Dawn's family members and friends, along with people from what Hannah now recognized as the Progeny Project—the ultimate source of Eddie's downfall. In the months leading up to Eddie's trial, the ugly realities behind his once-profitable fertility practice had become common public knowledge.

Unfortunately, the results were there in the courtroom for all to see. Two women—the original founders of the Progeny Project, Alexandra Munsey and Cassie Davis—were there, as were their two sons, Evan and Rory. The two young men looked so much alike that they might have been twins, and together they both bore a striking resemblance to Eddie.

Hannah considered their visible presence to be prejudicial, as far as the jury was concerned. Calvin Wilkins went so far as to move that the two young men in question be barred from the courtroom—a request

Judge Ratcliff denied. They, along with their mothers, were there every single day for the duration of the three-week trial. And every time Hannah looked at the two young men, she felt nothing but loathing. These were not her grandchildren. If they along with their mothers and surrogate fathers were Eddie's sworn enemies, they were hers as well.

The courtroom was filled almost to capacity every day of the trial, but on Eddie's side of the room Hannah alone occupied the front row, with the seats on either side of her left conspicuously empty. The rows behind her contained even more of Eddie's former patients as well as a motley crew of media types. None of them were there on Eddie's behalf. Rather than offering Hannah or her son any moral support, they were there for no other reason than to witness his total humiliation and cheer his undoing. Eddie's former patients might have lost out on their ability to sue him for damages, but they were on hand to partake in his final defeat.

And Hannah Gilchrist hated them all, every last one of them.

16

Day after day the prosecution laid out its case. Zero forensic evidence was offered to link Eddie to the murder, but the circumstantial evidence was overwhelming. Hannah's first glimpse of the alleged hit man came when Leo Manuel Aurelio took the stand. Other than a facial image grabbed by a neighbor's security footage, he had left no physical evidence at the scene of Dawn's homicide. If he'd kept his mouth shut, he might have gotten away with it. Unfortunately for him and for Eddie, while in jail in San Diego on an unrelated charge, Leo had made the mistake of bragging to a cellmate that he'd gotten away with slicing a woman's throat two and a half years earlier in Santa Clarita.

The cellmate, looking to cut a deal with the DA on his own charges, had turned jailhouse snitch. Trying to verify if there was any truth to the story, prosecutors in San Diego had contacted authorities in Santa Clarita. The Dawn Gilchrist homicide investigation might have gone cold by then, yet it was anything but forgotten.

After comparing Leo's mugshot to the image from the security footage, detectives from Santa Clarita headed for San Diego. They read Leo his rights and then stayed on for the better part of a week, interviewing him on a daily basis. During that entire time, Leo spoke to them willingly enough, denying all knowledge of the crime without bothering to ask for an attorney. It wasn't until the cops played their winning hand by placing the two telling photos side by side on the table that Leo finally cracked and asked for an attorney. A young public defender, barely out of law school, had negotiated a deal—that Leo plead guilty to second-degree murder rather than first in exchange for testifying against Eddie, which is how Leo ended up with a sentence of twenty years to life rather than receiving the death penalty or life without parole.

Hannah and everyone else in the gallery listened with rapt attention while Leo told his story. He might have been a gangbanger thug when he committed the homicide, but the young man who came to court to testify against Eddie was a totally sanitized version of his former self. The smooth-shaven, cherub-faced young man—all decked out in a suit and tie and with his gang tats invisible under the sleeves of his jacket—looked more like an upstanding college kid than a convicted murderer. He told how Eddie had come looking for a contract killer and had paid him five thousand bucks in cash, half before the hit and half after. In well-rehearsed testimony, Leo reported how he had snuck into Dawn's garage as she was parking her car, dragged her out of the vehicle, and then slit her throat, standing over her and making sure she was dead before exiting the garage.

Hannah had watched the shock reflected in most of the jurors' faces when Leo related that chilling detail. She knew then that there was nothing Calvin Wilkins could do and that all was lost, but she didn't let on. With people watching her every move, she kept the expression on her face completely impassive. The spectators in the gallery probably thought she would fall apart, but she refused to give them the satisfaction.

Then the prosecution called Kaitlyn Todd to the stand. Hannah knew that the young woman had been Eddie's nurse/receptionist. It wasn't until she was on the stand that Hannah learned she'd also been first Eddie's girlfriend and later his lover, but that was hardly surprising. Like father like son.

Ms. Todd reported that one night, after Dawn's death and with the Progeny Project trial date approaching, she and Eddie both had a bit too much to drink. In the course of the evening, Kaitlyn had asked him about the missing records, the ones Alexandra Munsey had come asking for when she was in search of a matching kidney for her son.

"What did he tell you?" the prosecutor asked.

"'I had her shred them,'" Kaitlyn reported.

"Those were his exact words?"

"Yes," Kaitlyn said.

"And when he used the word 'her,' who do you think was the person to whom he was referring?" the prosecutor continued.

Calvin Wilkins objected. "Calls for a conclusion on the part of the witness."

"I'll allow it," Judge Ratcliff said. "Witness may answer."

Kaitlyn had seemed to shrink in her chair each time she glanced in Eddie's direction. This time, though, she straightened and stared directly at him. "Dawn," she said quietly but accusingly. "Ed's ex-wife. At the time the files disappeared, they were married, and she was his nurse. I came to work for him later on."

"How much later?" the prosecutor inquired. "Were the defendant and the deceased still married at the time you went to work for him?"

"Yes."

"No more questions of this witness," the prosecutor said.

When it was Calvin Wilkins's turn, he did his best to discredit her. "How would you characterize your relationship with the defendant?"

"He was my boss," Kaitlyn said, "but we were also lovers."

"While he was still married to Dawn?"

"Yes."

"Were you ever under suspicion with regard to her homicide?"

"I guess," Kaitlyn admitted with a shrug. "I was the one who made the travel arrangements for his trip to Vegas, the one that gave Ed an alibi at the time of Dawn's death."

"Were you ever charged in connection with this crime?"

"No."

"Were those charges dropped because you agreed to come testify against him—a quid pro quo arrangement, as it were?"

"As I already said, I was never charged, so how could the charges be dropped?"

"I understand that sometime after Dawn Gilchrist's homicide you went home to care for your father, who had been seriously injured," Calvin said. "How is he doing?"

"Some of his injuries are permanent."

"So he continues to need help?"

"Yes."

"And yet you flew down here—at the prosecution's expense, I assume—to testify against your former lover?"

"Yes."

"Why did you do that?"

"Because I believe he killed her," Kaitlyn declared defiantly. "And I want to see him get what he deserves."

"Or was it maybe to get revenge on the man who had dumped you?" Calvin asked accusingly, letting his words hang in the air.

When Kaitlyn replied, her voice was barely audible. "He didn't dump me," she said softly. "I left."

Hannah shook her head. Instead of undermining Kaitlyn's testimony, Calvin had instead made her more believable.

Next up was Curt Clavell, the attorney who had handled the Progeny Project's short-lived class-action suit, who spoke about his unsuccessful efforts to contact Dawn Gilchrist in hopes of persuading her to come to court and testify against her former husband.

"What kind of testimony did you expect her to offer?"

"We had heard from more than one source that she had personal knowledge about what had become of the missing records from Dr. Gilchrist's office."

"This is hearsay," Calvin objected.

"Disregard."

"Did you believe that she would have come to testify?"

"I do."

"Calls for a conclusion on the part of the witness."

"I'll allow it," Judge Ratcliff said.

"And why did you believe she would have done so?"

"Because we were given to understand that she continued to harbor ill will toward Mr. Gilchrist."

Calvin Wilkins objected to that, too, but again he was overruled, and once that testimony was allowed to stand, it was the capper on the jug. The prosecution rested, because Clavell's testimony had given them exactly what they needed, a final piece of the puzzle—motive.

When Calvin Wilkins took over, he offered a spirited defense, but there was little he and his team could do to overcome the damning testimony. On advice of counsel, Eddie declined to testify on his own behalf. The defense rested at one thirty on a Thursday afternoon. Hannah stayed where she was while the jury filed out and Eddie was led away. Only then did she make her way through the crowd. No one spoke to her. Since she was clearly there in support of her son, the people milling around outside the courtroom regarded her as their enemy, a feeling that was, as far as Hannah was concerned, entirely mutual.

The next evening when Calvin called at 7:00 P.M. to say that the jury had a verdict, Hannah returned to the courthouse, once again in the backseat of the Rolls and once again down that now all-too-familiar stretch of road along the Magic Mountain Parkway. During the trial she'd had Marco drop her off and return for her later. This night she asked him to wait.

When the jury filed into the room, Hannah was back in her accustomed place. She had watched enough crime TV to know that if jurors enter the courtroom without looking at the defendant, it usually spells bad news for the accused, and that was definitely the case here. Not one of the passing jurors glanced in Eddie's direction, and not in Hannah's either.

Leo Aurelio's judicial outcome was already a done deal. He had been transported to and from prison to offer his Judas-worthy testimony, but right that moment, as the jurors took their seats, the decision as to Eddie's guilt or innocence was still very much up in the air. He was charged with murder in the first degree along with conspiracy to commit.

A conviction for murder in the first degree called for either the death penalty or life without parole, no exceptions. The conspiracy charge could possibly result in a similar sentence. So either he was innocent or this Friday evening would end up being the worst day in Hannah Gilchrist's life. She sat ramrod straight in her usual chair, the one positioned directly behind Eddie's. When her son was led into the courtroom and seated at the defense table, she forced herself to maintain her composure, smiling and nodding at him as he took his seat. Then she sat there, staring at the back of his head.

For some reason the only thing that came to mind just then were the lyrics to one of Helen Reddy's long-ago songs—"You and Me Against the World." That's exactly how it was now—Hannah and Eddie against everyone else.

A moment later the bailiff called, "All rise for the Honorable Judge William Ratcliff."

The black-robed judge entered from his chambers, marched to his seat behind the bench, pulled down the pair of horn-rimmed glasses he wore on top of his head, and turned to address the jurors. "I understand you have reached a verdict?"

Nodding, the foreman rose to his feet. "We have, Your Honor." With that he walked over to the judge and passed him a single sheet of paper before returning to his place in the jurors' box.

"And how do you find?" Judge Ratcliff asked.

"With regard to the first charge of murder in the first degree," the foreman replied, "we find the defendant guilty."

Gasps and at least one muted cheer were heard inside the room. The judge immediately rapped his gavel. "Silence," he ordered.

"With regard to the second charge," Judge Ratcliff asked, "conspiracy to commit, how do you find?"

"We find the defendant guilty," the foreman responded.

"Thank you, jurors," the judge said. "You are free to go." Then, after delivering another sharp-eyed glare to the gallery, one designed to stifle any additional emotional outbursts, he added, "The defendant will be remanded into custody and returned to the county jail to be held there until his sentencing hearing, one week from today."

With that the judge departed the room. Ignoring the hubbub around her, Hannah sat unmoving and watched as a pair of uniformed deputies stepped up to the defense table. Each took hold of one of Eddie's arms to lead him away. Before they fastened the cuffs around his wrists, he signed her a quick message: "Thank you."

"You're welcome," she signed back. "I love you."

She understood that the sentencing hearing was a mere formality. The mandatory sentence for first-degree murder would most likely be life without parole. All the hearing would do was give Dawn's relatives a chance to vent their feelings in public. Like it or not, Hannah supposed she'd be there to hear them do so. She had been her son's only ally throughout the ordeal of his trial, and she would serve in the same capacity when it came time for his sentencing.

Hannah stayed where she was until the room finally emptied. "Ma'am," the bailiff said at last. "If you wouldn't mind going, I need to lock up."

"Of course," she said, getting to her feet.

Hannah stumbled out into the marble-tiled corridor in time to see two uniformed deputies escorting a jumpsuit-wearing prisoner down the hall. At first Hannah didn't recognize Leo Aurelio, the formerly suit-clad man who had served as her son's primary accuser. She wasn't sure why he'd been allowed to remain in the gallery for the duration of the trial. Maybe that was another gift from the prosecutor, just like his conviction for second-degree murder.

The three men boarded an elevator. Just as the doors were closing behind them, a woman Hannah recognized as one of the local TV reporters managed to squeeze in behind them. Hannah was happy to stay behind in the corridor and let the elevator descend without her. She had no intention of breathing the same air as Dawn's knife-wielding killer, who had just ensured Eddie's conviction.

Hannah knew that Leo had been sentenced to twenty years to life, but she also knew that with good behavior he could be out in far less than that. Unless Calvin Wilkins could make a successful appeal of this conviction, Eddie wouldn't be out ever, and that wasn't fair—not at all.

Hannah went home that night and turned on the TV. All through the trial, she'd been conflicted—torn between wanting to know how the local media were reporting the story while at the same time not wanting to know. She turned on the news right at eleven o'clock, where the conclusion of Eddie's trial was the top story. A news anchor with very white teeth and long blond hair introduced the segment.

"Earlier this evening a jury found longtime Santa Clarita physician, Edward Anthony Gilchrist, guilty of first-degree murder and conspiracy to commit murder in the death of his former wife, Dawn Lorraine Gilchrist, who was stabbed in the garage of her town home more than three years ago. Shortly after the verdict was read, our crime reporter, Magda Herman, who has been covering the trial for the past three weeks, caught up with one of the case's star witnesses as he was leaving the courthouse. What's the story here, Magda?"

The moment Hannah saw the reporter's face, she recognized her as the woman who'd hopped into that descending elevator at the last moment.

The reporter smiled to acknowledge the introduction and then took up the story. "Because I was separated from my camera crew at the time, I'm sorry to report that I don't have any film of this incident, but after leaving the courtroom I rode down in the elevator with the prosecutor's primary witness against Dr. Gilchrist, the hit man who at Gilchrist's behest actually committed the crime. Leo Aurelio pleaded guilty to second-degree murder four months ago and is currently serving a twenty-year-to-life sentence for his participation in the homicide. He was transported from the Protective Housing Unit at Corcoran State Prison to the Santa Clarita Courthouse in Santa Clarita in order to testify. I asked him if he had any comment on Dr. Gilchrist's conviction and was able to record his reply on my iPhone." She held the device up to her microphone and pressed play. "Yeah, I got a comment all right," a man's voice replied. "He ruined my life. He's going down, too, and that's just what he deserves."

"Sounds like there's a little bad blood there," the smiling anchor commented.

"Yes, it does," Magda agreed. "No love lost at all."

And again completely unfair, Hannah thought as she shut off the TV set and went into the bedroom to get ready for bed. Leo was the one with the knife. He was the one who spilled the blood and did the actual killing. Why should he get off with such a light sentence when poor Eddie was losing everything?

In the bathroom Hannah removed her wig before she removed her makeup. Years earlier, after she'd undergone chemo for a bout with breast cancer, her hair had fallen out. That was a given, but when it grew back in, it was so spotty and thin that ever since she had resorted to having her head shaved and wearing a wig whenever she left the house. That had been five years ago, and her oncologist assured her she was in remission, but Hannah couldn't help feeling as if she were living on borrowed time. And what would become of Eddie once she was gone? Who would look after him then?

She lay awake for a long time thinking about that. She might not be able to do anything for Eddie after she died, but maybe there were things she could do for him on her way out.

17

Ali Reynolds was surprised and a little disappointed that Alex Munsey didn't break her silence and contact her about Gilchrist's upcoming trial. She'd had to learn about it on her own. Far from the courthouse in Santa Clarita, California, Ali kept track of the progress of the trial by checking with L.A.-based news sites, sometimes even live-streaming the evening news onto her computer screen. On Thursday afternoon the jury had retired to deliberate. When she tuned in to the evening news on Friday and there was still no verdict, she figured the coverage for the week was over. It seemed unlikely that the jury would return a verdict earlier than Monday.

Ali shut down the computer, feeling more than a little blue. The reporter who had delivered the "live report" from the courthouse steps in Santa Clarita, Magda something-or-other, was clearly a new hire, a sweet young thing who looked like she was barely out of high school. Liz Cassidy, the news anchor now seated behind the desk where Ali had once held sway, was a known entity. Liz had been a pushy beginning reporter back then, and Ali remembered their having had several run-ins along the way. Liz had probably done her best to wipe Ali's name out of her random-access memory. Magda, on the other hand, had most likely never heard the name Ali Reynolds. Yes, it seemed as though she had left her news-anchor days without leaving behind so much as a trace of her presence.

She had embarked on a self-imposed journey of reading the classics that she was supposed to have read much earlier but never did. When B. was off traveling—as he often was—that was how she occupied her long evenings, reading in front of the gas-log fireplace in the library, with Bella asleep in the chair beside her.

Shaking off the mood, Ali tried to return to the book. When her phone rang a few hours later, she had dozed off with the book still open in her lap. Seeing Alex Munsey's name in the caller-ID window, she could barely believe her eyes.

"Guilty!" Alex Munsey squealed in her ear. "They found the son of a bitch guilty as charged! When deliberations passed the twenty-four-hour mark, I started to get worried. We were called back to the courthouse a little more than an hour ago. It's over, Ali. It's done."

"Thank God," Ali said. "I've been keeping track of the coverage from here, but I didn't expect a verdict before Monday. It's taken a long time."

"Almost ten years," Alex agreed. "We didn't nail him with the class-action suit, but we got him all the same. They convicted him on both counts—first-degree murder and conspiracy to commit. Those both call for mandatory sentences of life without parole. The sentencing hearing is a week from today. I've been asked to be a part of the victim-impact statement, and that's why I'm calling. Would you come to that? Please?"

"Why?" Ali asked.

"Because you were there at the beginning, Ali, and it would mean so much to me if you could be here for the ending," Alex answered. "Cassie was here for part of the trial, but she can't stay for the sentencing, and with Jolene gone . . ."

"I'm the only one left."

"Pretty much."

Ali could feel her earlier mood brightening. Her time on the news desk in L.A. hadn't been for naught after all.

"I guess I'm up for a road trip," she said. "Do we know what time on Friday? And should I come to your place or go directly to Santa Clarita?"

"The courtroom doesn't open until ten, but the trial has attracted a lot of attention, and we should probably be in line early to get a seat. As for coming to my place? The cabin's a good two and a half hours from here. I've been staying at the Holiday Inn Express in Santa Clarita during the trial. Why don't I book us two rooms for two nights, arriving on Thursday? Friday night we'll go out on the town and celebrate."

"Sounds good," Ali said. "See you then."

18

The morning after the verdict, just as she had every Saturday morning for the past thirteen months, Hannah Gilchrist got up, ate her breakfast, and prepared to go to the jail. Before she left the house, she called one of her good friends—someone who specialized in high-end real-estate transactions—asking her to stop by later on in the afternoon to talk about listing her house.

Hannah loved the old place. She had come to it as a bride more than six decades earlier. The house was located in one of Santa Clarita's most prestigious neighborhoods. She knew she'd have no difficulty finding a willing buyer, and at this point Hannah was ready to let it go. Once the sentencing hearing was over and she knew where Eddie would be incarcerated, her intention was to rent or lease something much less ostentatious near wherever her son ended up going. He might be heading off to prison, but he was still her son and her number one priority. She had visited him once a week for as long as he'd been in jail awaiting trial, and she planned to continue visiting him on a regular basis in the future.

What Hannah needed to do now was simplify her life, starting with unloading the house and most of its contents. That also meant pensioning off her longtime staff, Marco and Bettina Gregory, her driver and housekeeper. Bettina was several years older than Marco—old enough to start collecting Social Security and receiving income from her IRA. In envisioning her new life, Hannah also realized that she'd need to be responsible for her own transportation—that meant buying a smaller, more modest vehicle and getting a driver's license for the first time in her life. As for her beloved Rolls? Marco had often spoken longingly about wanting to start his own limo service. As her parting gift to him, and in honor of his years of faithful service, she'd hand over the keys to the aging Rolls-Royce and help set him up in business. After all, there was no one on earth who knew more than he did about keeping that decades-old engine tuned up and running.

The guards at the jail were used to Hannah by now, and Eddie was already seated in their usual cubicle when she arrived in the visitors' room.

"I'm so sorry about the verdict," she told him now. "Do you have any idea where they'll send you?"

Eddie shrugged. "Rumor has it that it'll be Folsom, but there's no way to know that for sure until the sentencing hearing next week." That's what he said aloud. His signed message said something else. "I hope that little weasel Leo is there, too, so I can take him out."

Hannah smiled and nodded. Eddie was all she had left. If he set his course on vengeance, that's what she would do, too. Why not?

"Leo's not in Folsom," she signed back without specifying how she'd come to be in possession of that knowledge. "He's in Corcoran." Aloud she said, "On my way in, I added some money to your commissary account. Not very much, since I doubt you can transfer the funds from one place to another."

"Probably not," Eddie agreed.

"Leo's in the Protective Housing Unit," she signed.

"Good to know," he added. Hannah knew that Eddie wasn't referring to the extra money in the commissary account.

"We'll set up a new account when you get wherever you're going."

"Thanks, Mom," he said. "You're the best."

"I'm glad to do whatever I can to help."

Eddie resorted to signing once again. "I need to know more about where Leo is—his inmate number, if possible."

"How would I go about finding that?"

"Maybe you could reach out to him—write to him. Act like you're willing to be his friend. You should be able to locate prisoners by contacting the prison system. You may even be able to do it over the Internet."

During the past three years while Eddie's situation had continued to deteriorate, she had, out of necessity, spent plenty of time at her local library branch, becoming quite adept at using their computers.

"I haven't been on the computer much lately," she said aloud. "There were just too many ugly e-mails coming in. I ended up deleting most of them without even reading them, but I've heard computers are good for doing genealogical research. With you away I'll need something to occupy my time, and I may buy my own computer and try my hand at that."

"Genealogy?" Eddie asked.

Hannah nodded.

"As for computers," Eddie continued, "you're a fast learner when it comes to things like that. I'm sure you'll do very well."

Hannah appreciated her son's unexpected compliment. Those were few and far between.

"Yes," she said aloud. "I intend to get started right away. Now, is there anything else I can help you with? Anything else you need?"

"Yes," he signed. "I want to take them down—every single one of them."

He didn't have to mention anyone by name. She knew exactly who he meant. "That makes two of us," Hannah signed back.

Eddie's verbal answer to her earlier question, the one that was recorded on the phone, was completely harmless. "Not really," he said aloud. "For someone who's about to spend the rest of his life in prison, I guess I'm good."

"Stay strong, son," she said. "I love you."

With that, Hannah broke off the connection. She stood up and left the desolation of the visitors' room with her shoulders pulled back and walking with a purposeful step. If her son was bent on a war of vengeance, it was her war, too, and she'd just been given her first mission. She had something to do now, and she would do it.

On the way home, she had Marco stop by her neighborhood branch library, where she sought the help of her favorite reference librarian, Susan Attwood.

"I heard about the verdict," Susan said in a hushed voice when Hannah appeared at her counter. "I'm sorry."

"I'm sorry, too," Hannah said. "But that's why I need your help. Once Eddie is sent off to wherever they're sending him, I'll need to know how to contact him. Do you know if there's a phone number where people on the outside can locate prisoners and get their mailing addresses?"

"Let me see what I can do," Susan said.

It took the librarian less than ten minutes to come up with a toll-free number where Hannah could find the needed information. Back home Hannah called the number and had to wait on hold for forty-five minutes before an agent gave her Leo Aurelio's mailing address. "We expect to have an inmate e-mail system up and running soon," the woman told her over the phone, "but for now snail mail is your only option."

Snail mail was fine with Hannah, and if befriending Eddie's betrayer was the best way to help her son, she couldn't wait to get started. Once she had the address in hand, she took a seat at the dainty writing desk in her morning room and set out to compose a letter on her elegantly monogrammed stationery. The words spooling out of her Montblanc fountain pen and written in royal-blue ink were penned in time-honored Spencerian Method cursive, the only style recognized as acceptable by Hannah's first-ever penmanship instructor.

Dear Mr. Aurelio,

> *My name is Hannah Gilchrist. Edward is my son. As I sit here tonight grieving that his life as a free man is over, I felt constrained to write to you. As I'm sure you will understand, I am deeply saddened by Edward's current situation. I certainly didn't raise him expecting him to grow up and become a convicted killer.*
>
> *Although you contributed in large measure to that conviction, I wanted to reach out to you today, as a good Christian and in an attitude of friendship and forgiveness. Although you*

*provided much of the testimony offered against
him, I'm well aware that Edward's actions in
this matter destroyed your life every bit as much
as they destroyed his own.*

*That being said, I trust you have good people
in your life—caring loved ones—who are able
to sustain you and offer encouragement in your
present and very difficult circumstances. I just
want you to know that I am wishing you the
best, and if I can do anything to help, feel free
to contact me.*

*Sincerely,
Hannah Anderson Gilchrist*

Once she finished writing the missive, Hannah read it through twice. It was so much balderdash, of course. She didn't wish Leo Aurelio well at all. In fact, she wished him nothing but ill. Still, this was a good start. She addressed and stamped an envelope, and then, carefully folding the letter, she put it inside and licked the flap to glue it shut.

"Make no mistake about it, Leo," she said aloud as she walked outside to place the letter in the mailbox at the end of her driveway. "Eddie Gilchrist is coming for you, and I'm going to help him."

19

On Thursday morning the following week, Ali was up and out early, hoping to make it through L.A. prior to rush hour. Somehow she'd managed to forget that rush hour in L.A. was a never-ending nightmare and one she'd lost the knack of negotiating. She arrived at the hotel in Santa Clarita late in the afternoon, worn to a nub, only to find the lobby teeming with throngs of seemingly unsupervised preadolescents. She checked in, made her way to her room, and then called Alex.

"This place is a madhouse," she complained.

"Right," Alex returned. "I forgot. It's coming up on the weekend, and Magic Mountain is just up the street. Don't worry, there's a wine bar a few blocks away that's quieter and a whole lot more welcoming. Why don't we go there?"

The wine bar was exactly as advertised. Once they were settled into comfortable leather chairs with glasses containing generous pours of Merlot on the table in front of them, Ali gave Alex a pointed look. "You went dark on me again," Ali said accusingly. "I sent e-mails and got nothing back. What happened?"

Alex nodded. "Sorry about that," she acknowledged. "Once the judge dismissed our lawsuit, I fell into a deep, dark hole."

"And became even more of a hermit?"

"Pretty much," Alex replied. "A despairing, clinically depressed hermit. For the better part of three years, I could barely get out of bed. I was in such a bad place that I couldn't even write. Gilchrist seemed to be getting away with everything, even murder. The cloud didn't start to lift until after he was arrested. I should have called you then, but I didn't, because by then I was too embarrassed."

"Not to worry," Ali replied. "Now that you've finally gotten around to calling me, all is forgiven."

Alex resumed her story. "Once I got myself sort of pulled together, I started working on *A Mother's Tale* again, bringing the story forward from the transplant on and talking about the Progeny Project. Now that the verdict is in, I'm finishing the last few chapters."

"Do you have a publisher?" Ali asked.

"Yup, I do," Alex said. "I had planned to self-publish the book as a fund-raiser for Progeny, but it's been disbanded."

"The Progeny Project is disbanded?" Ali asked in disbelief. "How did that happen?"

"That's another story," Alex told her. "What I have now is a deal with a regional press. They have national distribution, but they expect that the biggest demand for the book will be here in Southern California. Most of the editing is done. The book can be ready to go in a matter of weeks. They're planning on putting it out in conjunction with another book, *Tell No Tales*, an almost completed true-crime treatment of Dawn Gilchrist's homicide."

"Are both books coming out simultaneously?"

Alex nodded. "As companion pieces. The guys in marketing think sales of the one will drive sales of the other—that's why the titles are so similar. Once *Mother's* is finally put to bed, I'm planning on going back to my next book. It's a novel—a murder mystery. Spoiler alert, when you read it, don't be surprised to learn that a doctor is the very first victim."

They both laughed about that. "It's one way of getting even," Ali observed. "If you can't knock them off in real life, kill them in fiction. Now tell me about Evan. Will he be here tomorrow?"

Alex shook her head. "He was here for the trial, but he needed to get back to work. He lives in Salt Lake now, with his wife, Kathleen. Their son, Rory, is about to turn two."

"So Evan did get married," Ali concluded. "What's he doing now?"

"A company out of Utah called Family Ties is starting a commercial DNA operation, and Evan's experience in creating Progeny's database was just what they needed. They're rolling all of Progeny's data into theirs and planning a big launch for next year. Since Evan is in on the ground floor, if it takes off like they expect it to, he'll be set for life."

"Here's to Evan," Ali said, raising her glass.

"And here's to you, Ali," Alex returned. "Without you I wouldn't have a son or a grandson."

Ali and Alex ordered salads, a cheese plate, and second glasses of wine. Although the evening ended early, there wasn't much sleep to be had, because the still-unsupervised kids spent most of the night marauding up and down the hallway. The next morning Ali and Alex were first in line to go through security at the Santa Clarita Courthouse, and they were first inside the courtroom as well. They were already seated when a grim-faced older lady marched past them with all the dignity of a dowager empress. Without nodding or speaking to anyone else in the room, she took a place in the front row of seats directly behind the defense table.

"That's Gilchrist's mother, Hannah," Alex whispered to Ali. "She's from old money here in Southern California, and I'm guessing she's the one paying for her son's high-priced defense team."

Ali expected that as the room filled up, other people—friends and supporters of the defendant—would join Hannah in the front row, but they did not. That whole set of seats—three on either side of her—remained empty throughout the proceedings, so presumably Edward Gilchrist had no friends, and neither did his mother. Without meaning to, Ali couldn't help but feel sorry for the old woman, sitting there alone in a kind of regal isolation. All the other spectators in the room had come there to celebrate the prosecution's victory. Hannah was the only one there to mourn the very real loss of her son.

As a convicted killer, Edward Gilchrist came to the sentencing hearing dressed in an orange jail jumpsuit and wearing handcuffs and shackles. Ali watched him throughout the proceedings. During the victim-impact statements he listened impassively, with no sign that they affected him in the least. If he felt any remorse, it certainly wasn't visible.

Although not directly affected by Dawn Gilchrist's murder, Alex was allowed to speak during that portion of the hearing.

She stared at an unblinking Edward Gilchrist as she spoke. "You, sir, are a liar and a cheat. I and many other people in this room came to you looking for help with our reproductive issues. Instead of using your purported stable of donors, you lied to us, and we suspect that you fathered many of our children yourself. Five of those are here in this courtroom today. They may share your despicable DNA and bear some physical resemblance to you and to one another, but they are nothing like you. They have been raised by loving parents in loving families and have grown up to be responsible, hard-working, loyal people.

"You are a disgrace to the practice of medicine, Edward Gilchrist. I regret that an ill-fated class-action lawsuit started by some of us might have been the underlying cause of Dawn Gilchrist's death. For that I'm truly sorry. She might have been responsible for the shredding of all those files, but you probably lied to her the same way you lied to everyone else, most especially when you swore that oath to do no harm.

"I'm glad the jury found you guilty. I'm glad you'll be spending the rest of your life in prison. You're a contemptible human being, and you're getting exactly what you deserve."

Alex's statement ended, and the room erupted in a round of enthusiastic applause which the judge stifled with a loud bang of his gavel. When Judge Ratcliff's sentence was delivered, it was almost as an afterthought. And then it was over.

As the deputies led the prisoner out of the court-room, Ali noticed something odd. He didn't so much as glance or nod in his mother's direction. How could he show such disdain for someone who had most likely been at the trial the whole time, sitting front and center and supporting him throughout the entire ordeal?

Outside the courtroom a full-fledged celebration

was in progress. Alex Munsey made her way through the crowd accepting high fives, hugs, kisses, and handshakes as she went. For several minutes Alex and Ali stood side by side on the courthouse steps, posing for photographs.

They went to dinner as a group—Alex and Ali, along with a whole troop of people from the Progeny Project. The organization itself might have been disbanded, but the connections made during its existence remained in place and as strong as ever. The evening was a night meant for celebrating, and a good time was had by all.

The next day, Saturday morning early, Ali Reynolds and Alexandra Munsey stood outside the Holiday Inn Express and made their good-byes, ending with a long, heartfelt hug and another round of mutual promises that from now on they really would stay in touch. As Ali drove out of the parking lot, waving as she went, she had no way of knowing it was the very last time she would see Alex Munsey alive.

20

A full month after Edward's arrival at Folsom, he was summoned to the visitation room, where he was surprised to find his mother, seated in yet another cubicle, awaiting his arrival.

"Mom," he said, picking up the phone. "What are you doing here?"

"I came to visit you."

"Did Marco drive you over?"

"No," she said with a bright smile. "I live here now, right here in Folsom. I decided it was time to simplify my life—to downsize, as they say. I sold the house, unloaded most of my goods in an estate sale, and moved into a gated retirement community here in town called Arbor Crest. I have a two-bedroom town house unit that comes with a two-car garage."

"A garage big enough for the Rolls?" Eddie asked.

"Oh, no," she told him. "I unloaded that, too. I gave it to Marco and Bettina Gregory as a going-away present."

Hannah didn't bother telling her son that before she'd left Santa Clarita, she'd gone to the trouble of drafting a new will, one that removed Eddie as her sole heir and left her entire estate to the Gregorys. With Eddie in prison until his dying day, he had no use for her money. She might just as well give it to people for whom it would make a difference.

In terms of relatives, Hannah still had a few extant cousins left on her mother's side of the family, but during the hard times—during the years of disgrace and the awfulness of the trial—the cousins had kept to themselves. They'd never so much as picked up the phone to see how she was doing, so the cousins' ship had sailed. The Gregorys, on the other hand? Marco and Bettina had stuck with Hannah through it all—through thick and thin. Since they weren't blood relatives, there would be hell to pay as far as estate taxes were concerned, but nonetheless they'd be thrilled with whatever was left.

As for parceling out her wealth in charitable contributions? The new Hannah Gilchrist was done with those.

"If you dumped the Rolls," Eddie asked, drawing her back to the present, "how are you getting around?"

"Oh, that," she said dismissively. "I bought myself a new car—the first one ever. It's just a little Lexus LS, but the insurance premiums are through the roof because they consider me to be an inexperienced driver."

Eddie was astonished. "You got a driver's license at your age?" he demanded. "How did you do that?"

"I took lessons and passed the driving test my first try," she told him. "I told my driving instructor that I was a widow and needed to learn to drive on my own. The instructor was very kind and very understanding. I'm glad he didn't ask me how long ago my husband died."

"I am, too," Eddie echoed.

"But all that aside, I just learned that Alexandra Munsey is publishing a book," Hannah continued. "It's going to be called *A Mother's Tale*."

"About me?" Eddie asked.

"Presumably. It's being published concurrently with another book by a local true-crime writer."

"Also about me?" Eddie asked.

"I believe so."

"Can I sue them for libel?"

Hannah shook her head. "I already checked with an attorney on that. You're a convicted killer now as opposed to an alleged one. I'm pretty sure people can say whatever they like about you."

"Alexandra Munsey is a bitch," Eddie said, switching over to signing. "I wouldn't be here if it weren't for her. This is all her fault."

That was when Hannah caught sight of the tattoo on his arm for the very first time. "What's that?" she demanded.

"It's a list of people," he said. "They're the people who owe me, or maybe I owe them."

"What do you mean?"

He pointed toward the first letter in the row where the image of a capital *D* was almost entirely obscured by a black *X*. "That *D* is for Dawn," he signed. "The other letters are for Leo Aurelio, Kaitlyn Todd, Alexandra Munsey, and Ali Reynolds, that busybody news anchor who started it all."

"What are you planning on doing about them?" Hannah asked.

"I've already gotten even with Dawn," he said. "Now I need to figure out how to get even with the rest of them."

"Will you need my help?" Hannah asked.

Eddie looked at her in stunned surprise. He had planned on talking her into helping him, but he was astonished that she'd come right out and offered. "Are you serious?"

"Of course I'm serious," Hannah said. "You've never been one to walk away from a fight. Why would you

start now? And if you need help, I'm here, just as I was
in court with you every day of the trial—because you're
my son, Eddie."

Eddie appeared to be profoundly touched by that
declaration. He dabbed a tear from the corner of his
eye. "Thank you," he murmured aloud. "Thank you for
being in my corner."

"You're welcome," she replied. "You're all I've got,
and I'm all you've got, so whatever you need me to do,
just let me know."

In that short signed conversation, their mutual intent came through loud and clear. If Eddie was out for
revenge, Hannah would have his back every step of the
way. End of story.

"I can't quite see you living in a two-bedroom apartment," Eddie said aloud, going for a bit of harmless conversation to make up for the extended period of silence.

No one in the jail in Santa Clarita had ever commented on the long silences between them, but here
someone might be paying closer attention.

"Tell me about it," she countered. "I can't see you
living the rest of your life in a cell either, so we're even
there, but I believe we're both fully capable of making
the necessary adjustments. Besides, Arbor Crest seems
to be quite nice. No upkeep to do—no yard to look after
or pool to maintain. If there's a plumbing problem, all
I have to do is tell the front desk.

"The community center includes a dining room, and
residents can purchase a meal plan or make do on their
own cooking. A lot of people come and go from there on
golf carts. Since I've never learned to cook, I came here
intending to follow the meal plan route, but it turns out
the food there is pretty iffy, so I've started going to a nearby

restaurant. It's in a shopping center just down the street, where there's also a grocery store, a bar, and a beauty shop. I've tried the beauty shop, but so far the results are disappointing. The manicurists and hairdressers here don't hold a candle to the ones back home in Santa Clarita."

"But you're settling in?"

"Yes, very much so," Hannah assured him. Then, glancing at her watch, she added, "Our time's almost up. On my way out, I'll make a deposit in your commissary account. It won't be much, but it should be enough to tide you over."

"Thank you," he said.

Hannah could tell that his gratitude was sincere, but she was pretty sure he was thanking her for a lot more than the promised deposit.

"Will you be needing cash?" That was her next signed question. "I've set some aside—quite a bit, as a matter of fact, in case you need it."

"Having money would probably be a good idea, but I'll need to figure out how best to handle it. From what I'm hearing, getting contraband in and out of here used to be a lot easier than it is now. I'll have to let you know." Then, switching back to the spoken word, he added, "How's your genealogy research coming along?"

"I bought a computer and spent some time at the Expert Bar learning to use it. As for the genealogy research? It's slow but steady," she replied.

A nearby guard caught Hannah's eye and motioned toward the clock on the wall. Nodding to the guard, Hannah got to her feet. "I'd better be going now," she told Eddie. "But don't you worry. I'll be back."

"Thanks again," Edward added as his mother rose to go. "Thanks more than you know."

That evening at dinner, Edward strolled over to Luis Ochoa's table and was gratified when he was invited to have a seat.

"I hear you had a visitor today."

Edward wasn't surprised. Luis had his sources. There was very little that went on inside the walls of Folsom Prison that he didn't know about.

"And?" Luis inquired.

"As far as the A List is concerned, she's all in."

"Glad to hear it," Luis said. "So who's up first?"

"That would be Leo Aurelio my turncoat hit man."

"The one who's in protective housing?"

Again Edward Gilchrist was startled at how much Luis Ochoa knew about him and his business, but he nodded. "Yup," he said, "that's the one."

"I've handled protective housing hits before," Luis said, "but they can be a lot of trouble. They're also very expensive. I recommend we wait until Aurelio gets moved into the general population."

"Whatever you say," Edward told him. "You're the boss."

21

Rather than being allowed to visit Eddie once a week as Hannah had done in Santa Clarita, at Folsom she was limited to one visit per month. On the day *A Mother's Tale* and *Tell No Tales* were both available for advance purchase, Hannah logged on to her Amazon account and ordered two copies of each volume, one set to be shipped to her and the other to be sent directly to Eddie. The idea that they would both be reading the same book at the same time made Hannah feel closer to him somehow.

She set the true-crime book aside and went straight to the other one. It began with the saga of the Munseys' long, unsuccessful struggle to conceive. Alex Munsey told how they'd been referred to Eddie by a "friend of a friend." The story covered the part about how they'd carefully shopped through the profiles in the clinic's catalog of donors, looking for their "perfect match." Hannah was surprised to find herself dismissively put off by Alexandra's unmitigated joy at the birth of her son, Evan.

So what? Hannah wondered. *Isn't that how mothers are supposed to feel? Isn't that how I felt when Eddie was born?*

As the story moved along, Hannah was struck by how that one little event—Alexandra Munsey's search for information on her son's biological father—had set off this whole series of cascading catastrophes. It reminded her of what she'd learned about avalanches all those decades ago at the finishing school in Switzerland. It took only a tiny chunk of ice and snow knocked loose from a ledge to set off a deadly avalanche, engulfing unsuspecting skiers and hikers on the slopes below. And that's exactly what had happened here with one small exception. Instead of taking out hapless skiers and hikers, this deadly stream of events had led directly to her son's ruin.

Looking up from the pages, Hannah was forced to acknowledge that Eddie was anything but blameless in the situation. What in all that was holy had made him think he could use his own sperm and get away with it? Whatever had made him think no one would ever notice and call him on it?

Arrogance, she decided at last. *Arrogance and stupidity at the same time.* In that regard Eddie was spookily like his father. Gordon had lorded it over Hannah and lied to her face, most likely thinking she was too dim to see through him. She had chosen to put up with his shenanigans—even pretending that she believed his tall tales—because it was the path of least resistance. She'd stayed married to someone with numerous "outside interests" because it had suited her and because, as long as he was screwing around with one of his several mistresses, he wasn't bothering her. Besides, divorcing Gordon would have been frightfully expensive and emotionally complicated. Her mother, Isobel, was still alive back then, and she would have pitched a fit.

Shortly before Gordon's death, his doctor had raised an alarm about his "numbers," hinting that there were indications he might be leaning toward the specter of kidney disease, but then a fatal heart attack had intervened and taken him out. Despite the incredible relief Hannah had felt once Gordon was gone, she had played the role of grieving widow in a decorous and properly restrained manner. When the prescribed period of mourning ended and prospective suitors began lining up on her doorstep, she sent them all packing. She had no intention of marrying a second time, because she was perfectly fine on her own and happy to be left to her own devices. Decades later she still was.

When she went back to reading and got as far as Alexandra Munsey's account of the trial, she raced through it from beginning to end, and that was a real eye-opener. Hannah had lived through every word of that trial—every nuance—but it was surprising and somewhat disorienting to read about the same events from someone else's point of view.

As she'd expected, *A Mother's Tale* ended with Eddie's sentencing hearing. When it came to the victim-impact statements, Dawn's parents had both spoken up, tearfully saying how much they missed their wonderful daughter. Hannah had a hard time accepting the idea that anyone could have a high opinion of Dawn Lorraine Gilchrist, but then again these people were her parents, after all, and you had to consider the source.

One of Dawn's friends, someone from a divorce support group, told about how Dawn had died the very night of one of their regular dinner gatherings. She claimed that Dawn's brutal murder, ultimately at the hands of her former husband, had left the entire group feeling shaken and vulnerable.

Only when the others had finished did Alexandra Munsey step forward to speak on behalf of what she referred to as the defrauded families. When she finished, the Munsey woman had sat down to a burst of spontaneous applause. A printed version of the words she'd spoken in the courtroom was included in the book. Hannah remembered exactly what had been said. She didn't need to read through it a second time.

There were black-and-white photos scattered throughout the book. The last one, apparently taken on the front steps of the courthouse after the sentencing hearing, showed Alexandra Munsey standing shoulder to shoulder with another woman. The caption underneath identified Alexandra's companion as Ali Reynolds, the long-retired news anchor whose coverage of Evan's search for a new kidney had turned the whole story into a media event.

All these years later, here she was again, come back to gloat along with everyone else. No wonder Ali's initial was one of the five displayed on the A List on Eddie's arm. Without the free publicity Ali's generous news coverage had provided, none of this would have happened. None of it.

Hannah finished the book and moved on to the epilogue. She expected it to be a schmaltzy piece in which the author went out of her way to thank everyone who'd made writing the book possible. That wasn't it—not at all.

Despite numerous requests from the Progeny Project, Dr. Edward Gilchrist refused to provide a sample of his DNA to be used for comparison purposes with the cluster of eighteen half siblings resulting from insemination procedures conducted at his fertility clinic. However, thanks to discarded

DNA retrieved from material found in a trash bin on the street outside his home, we were able to obtain his complete profile, thus verifying that he was the sole donor for those eighteen individuals, one of whom is now deceased.

In addition, we also discovered a separate cluster of seven half siblings, also originating from Dr. Gilchrist's medical practice. With the assistance of a detective from LAPD, we were able to secure a DNA sample from material collected at the time of Dawn Lorraine Gilchrist's autopsy, which gave us her DNA profile as well. Genetic comparisons have confirmed that the seven additional individuals were conceived from eggs provided by Dr. Gilchrist's murdered wife.

Hannah was shocked. The idea that Dawn had provided some of the eggs Eddie had used was news to her. Hannah had never come straight out and asked her son why he and Dawn had divorced or why he'd been so quick to knuckle under to all her demands when it came to the divorce settlement. Now Hannah understood. Dawn's exit strategy had been a form of legal blackmail. Since she'd been an active participant in Eddie's scheme and had known too much, he'd forked over cash in order to guarantee her silence. Later on, worried that she might renege and break that silence, he'd taken her out.

If only we'd been closer, Hannah thought now. *If only he'd confided in me about what was really going on, I could have brought my lawyers to bear on the class-action case soon enough to have prevented all this from happening.*

But Eddie had chosen to leave her in the dark. By

the time Hannah got wind of the situation, it was already too late, yet now she knew why Kaitlyn Todd's *K* was tattooed on Eddie's arm. She had obviously known too much as well, and that generous severance package he'd given her had probably been a somewhat less expensive way of getting Kaitlyn to keep her mouth shut, too, but that hadn't worked either. Once the prosecutor had come around asking, Kaitlyn Todd had boarded the first available plane and flown into town to testify against him.

From Hannah's point of view, Kaitlyn was almost as bad as Dawn had been, and it was a crying shame Eddie hadn't already gotten rid of her, too.

22

The Professor read his copy of *A Mother's Tale* with a rising sense of outrage. Despite what he did for a living, he had always thought that the downside of having kids of his own had far outweighed the upside. That had been a bone of contention between him and his first wife. Jeanette had wanted kids; he hadn't. She'd gotten them, too, with her second husband. As for Edward's second wife? On that score he and Dawn had been on the same page. She hadn't wanted kids any more than he did.

But the people depicted in Alexandra Munsey's book—that miserable collection of Edward's former patients—had all been hell-bent on having kids. For whatever reason, they hadn't wanted to go the adoption route. They'd wanted kids of their own. Those desperate childless couples had come to Dr. Edward Gilchrist with their sad faces and their tales of woe, begging him for help which he had gladly supplied. But then, after he'd helped them conceive the little brats they wanted so badly, were any of them grateful? No, not in the least! Alexandra Munsey was a prime example. The woman had devoted the past ten years to trying to destroy both

Edward's life and his livelihood. What kind of thanks was that?

Alexandra and her husband, Jake, had come to Edward's office in search of viable sperm, and he had provided same. What did it matter if the sperm involved was his or someone else's? Why complain about that? Maybe his father had died at a young age of a heart ailment, but Edward himself was healthy enough, wasn't he? And if it hadn't been for the fact that he'd used his own sperm more than once, chances are that harridan of an Alexandra never would have located that half sibling with his matching kidney who'd saved her son's life. So not only had Edward Gilchrist's actions given the Munsey kid a chance to be born in the first place, he'd also kept him from dying. And what did he get in return? An evil woman out there spreading garbage about him far and wide.

The whole time he'd been in business, there had never been a single malpractice suit filed against him. In the book Alexandra kept referring to herself and the other parental units involved as "defrauded families." But he'd never had a fraud charge filed against him either, and when those same supposedly "defrauded" families had tried to sue him for damages in a class-action suit, the judge had tossed the case, saying more or less that they didn't have a leg to stand on. Now, though, with him in prison, Alexandra Munsey could go public with this kind of crap, and there wasn't a single damned thing Edward could do about it. It was infuriating!

And what about that nosy, interfering bitch from the TV station? Ali Reynolds—what was the deal with her? What gave her the right to come around stirring the pot? As soon as he'd seen them together on that

TV show when Alexandra was asking for help in locating a matching kidney, Edward had suspected that the two women spelled trouble for him. He'd assumed it would blow over eventually, but of course it never had, all because of Ali Reynolds who had conspired against him from beginning to end.

As the deputies had led him into the courtroom for the sentencing hearing, he noticed that the vaguely familiar woman seated next to Alexandra Munsey was someone who hadn't been in the gallery during the trial itself. Now, though, after reading the book and seeing the photos, he knew exactly who she was and why she was there. After trashing his life, the two women had teamed up again, standing in celebratory triumph on the courthouse steps while he was cuffed and marched back to his cell. Insult to injury.

Edward was somewhat surprised by the piece at the end of the book that focused on children born as a result of his having used Dawn's eggs. How had Alexandra made that connection, and how had she talked the ME into providing tissue from Dawn's autopsy to obtain a DNA sample? Then he remembered from reading the book that one of his so-called offspring was now an LAPD detective. That probably explained the ME connection.

Statistically speaking, fertility procedures where donor sperm was used outnumbered those utilizing donor eggs. So far Alexandra and her pals had located eighteen kids attributable to him as opposed to only six for Dawn, but Edward was pretty sure there were more of both types out there. He also knew that each and every time another one surfaced, it was likely to unleash yet another media storm.

Finished with Alexandra's book, he turned immediately to the second one, Lacey Dutton's *Tell No Tales*, which wasn't much better. Who the hell was Lacey Dutton anyway, and what had made her decide to write a book about Dawn's murder? Edward studied the cover photo. Lacey wasn't someone he knew personally, but he recognized her as someone who'd been a regular attendee during the course of his trial—another interested bystander who had come to savor seeing him go down in flames.

Reading *Tell No Tales* cover to cover reinforced Edward's fury with both Leo Aurelio and Kaitlyn Todd, while *A Mother's Tale* had done the same as far as Alexandra Munsey and Ali Reynolds were concerned. They had all turned on him, and his determination to make them pay burned as brightly as the flame on a welding torch.

And who was Edward's only ally in all this? His mother, someone he would have thought to be the last person on earth to back him to the hilt. When he had shown her the tattooed letters on his arm and explained what he intended to do, she barely batted an eyelash. In fact, she told him that she would help no matter what, that she loved him no matter what. She had uprooted her life in Santa Clarita and moved to Folsom for no other reason than to be close to him. For the first time in Edward Gilchrist's life, he was actually humbled. His mother loved him far more than he loved her and far more than he deserved. He might not have respected her back when he was growing up, but he sure as hell respected her now.

And if she did follow through on what she'd said—if she did help him go after the people who'd wronged him—what would happen if someone figured it out and the two of them ended up being caught? At this point Eddie was already doing life without. He himself had nothing to lose, nothing at all.

Hannah had indicated much the same thing on her part. She was old. Her health might go south on her at any moment. She'd given up her home—the home she'd lived in for most of her life—to come here to Folsom to be close to him. She'd told Edward that he was all she had and that from where she was now, she didn't much care what happened to her one way or the other.

That declaration certainly leveled the playing field. As Edward saw it, the coming battle would be fought between two very different sets of people—four with everything to lose and two with nothing to lose. The have-nots would be all in, and the haves wouldn't be. They wouldn't even know they were under attack until something hit them in the face, and by then it would be too late.

What could be better?

23

Gradually Hannah Gilchrist settled into her new life in Folsom. Among her fellow residents at Arbor Crest, she made no secret of the fact that her son was a convicted murderer serving his time in the state prison just down the road. That became something of a status symbol for her, and she wore it like a red badge of courage. It was the main reason that once she finished reading the two *Tales* books, she donated both copies to the community library.

Over time Hannah's clear devotion to her disgraced son made her a bit of a legend. Some of the ladies with whom she played bridge began inquiring after Eddie's health once she returned from one of her regular monthly visits.

"He's fine, thank you," Hannah would tell them. "He's bearing up."

At the Arbor Crest Community Center, bridge was considered a late-morning or early-afternoon activity. Late afternoons and early evenings were devoted to working five-thousand-piece jigsaw puzzles. Donna, one of the "puzzlers," as they liked to be called, was openly envious of Hannah's close relationship to her son.

"My Darryl shut me out forty years ago, right after he graduated from college," Donna complained. "I never knew what it was I did or didn't do that drove him away.

When Darryl married, my ex-husband, his father, was invited to the wedding. I wasn't. He has a daughter, and she has kids now, too, but I've never met any of them."

On hearing those words, Hannah's first thought was that Donna's Darryl was most likely a jackass, but she was diplomatic enough to keep that notion to herself.

"Children are like that," she said stoically. "Sometimes all they're good for is to break their mothers' hearts."

The truth was, Hannah actually enjoyed the simple pleasures of playing bridge and working puzzles. They were a far cry from the complex duties her social standing in Santa Clarita had demanded of her. And to her surprise she actually relished living on her own. Marco and Bettina had lived in their own quarters, of course, a casita out back, but they'd been in and out of Hannah's space throughout the day. Here she was blessedly alone. Yes, she was doing without a live-in cook for the first time in her life, but she had figured out a way to cope with that, too.

As she'd told Eddie, Arbor Crest's meal plan had proved to be woefully inadequate, and she'd taken her business elsewhere—to the restaurant just up the street. There, with a judicious use of generous tips to both the waitstaff as well as the kitchen help, Hannah soon had them eating out of her hand—the other way around, really. Items that weren't necessarily on the regular menu would show up as "specials" whenever she requested them.

Something that really surprised her about life in Arbor Crest was that living in a two-bedroom unit was honestly no hardship. Yes, she'd lived in a spacious mansion, but in reality she'd used precious little of all that space, and she'd held on to only a few pieces of furniture that were more than adequate in Hannah's current downsized digs.

Grandmother Alberta's four-poster bed and matching dresser took up most of the space in one bedroom. That was where Hannah slept. The chintz easy chair and matching sofa from the sitting room along with a wall-mounted TV set filled up the minimal space that was designated as a living room, while her trimmed-down dining-room needs were handled by the maple kitchen table where she and Bettina Gregory had occasionally shared a cup of afternoon coffee. In the second bedroom, now Hannah's office, her treasured antique writing table and chair held sway. That was where she sat to work on her laptop. It was also where she penned her weekly missives to Leo Aurelio, the only dark spot on Hannah's horizon.

For some strange reason Eddie had decreed that Leo would be the first item of A List business. Determined to be her son's partner in this enterprise, Hannah kept her mouth shut and went along with the program, but two years in, not only was Leo still alive, he was also still in the Protective Housing Unit. Eddie didn't seem concerned about the passage of time, but Hannah was. Eddie had all the time in the world. Hannah did not.

Because her main function was to supply whatever funds Eddie required, her initial worry had been how she'd go about doing just that. She kept a surprisingly large stash of cash in her garage refrigerator, but as Eddie had pointed out early on, getting it inside the walls of the prison was a problem. But then Eddie's pal and fellow inmate Luis Ochoa had stepped up to the plate.

Luis was in the business of getting things done,

and he was the one who had solved Hannah's money-transfer problem. Early on, he'd looked into the source of Edward Gilchrist's plentiful cash. After some research Luis had learned that Hannah Gilchrist was indeed loaded. She lived in a gated retirement community in Folsom called Arbor Crest, drove a brand-new Lexus LS, and had a standing appointment at Arbor Crest's nail spa for weekly manicures. Realizing that Edward had the potential of becoming one of his top clients, Luis had invited Eddie to join him at his private table in the mess hall and laid out his plan.

If Eddie wondered how Luis knew where Hannah lived or that she liked having regular manicures, it seemed best not to ask. The very fact that he'd been invited to share Luis's table had let everyone know his change of status, and the next time Eddie's mother came to visit, he had dutifully passed along the new game plan.

"Weren't you complaining about not liking the way the nail place here does your nails?" he asked aloud through the phone.

"I was. I've gone through three nail techs so far, and they're all hopeless."

"One of my friends in here has a niece who runs a traveling nail-spa operation called Nails to Go. Why don't you give her a try?"

Out of sight from both the cameras and the guard, he signed the rest of the message. "She's Luis's runner. You give her cash, and she'll handle the transfers. If she comes to see you on a regular basis, no one will pay any attention to her."

Hannah had received that news with a flood of relief. By bribing one of the visitation-room clerks, she'd been able to smuggle small sums of money into the prison, but if it ever came time to pay for a hit, she didn't relish having to go out on her own and meet up with a potential killer in some dark alley or deserted parking lot.

Hannah had immediately looked up Nails to Go on the Internet, and Gloria Reece came into her life doing biweekly gel manicures. With the slow passage of time, Hannah may have been losing heart, but in that interval she had also given Gloria thousands of dollars as bankable deposits toward Eddie's current and future needs. No paperwork was involved, no receipts were signed, but Hannah kept a formal ledger, which was also safely tucked away inside her piggy-bank fridge. By her reckoning, Eddie should already have accumulated more than enough to pay in full for the destruction of the people on his A List—every last one of them.

24

And then at last, just when Hannah thought it would never happen, it did happen. She received a letter from Leo.

Dear Hannah,

    Good news. I finally got moved to general population. It's like a whole new life—more yard time, more opportunities to take classes. I can't believe I'm going to college now—well, at least taking college-level courses. And that never would have happened if you hadn't encouraged me to get my GED. So thank you for that.

    And surprise, surprise. I even got an A in English 101. Thank you for that, too. And for being my friend all this time.

                       Leo

Leo had been moved to general population? That was such good news that Hannah could hardly contain herself. She could have called Gloria right then and relayed the message through her, but she wanted to deliver it herself. She sat on it for almost a week and a half until her next scheduled visit to the prison.

"Leo's out," she signed gleefully. "They've moved him to general population."

"Way to go!" Eddie signed, grinning back at her. "I'll let Luis know that we're on."

Hannah was still giddy on the drive back to Arbor Crest, but then—disappointingly—nothing happened for several long weeks. While she waited, she turned her attention to tracking down Kaitlyn Todd, although Kaitlyn Martin was the name the woman had used when she testified against Eddie in court. These days she was married and living in Mill City, Oregon, under the name Kaitlyn Holmes. It took time to ferret out all those details—her husband's name, what she did for a living, where she lived, and where she worked.

While Hannah tracked down all those details, she kept a close eye on news feeds coming out of Corcoran. Almost a month after letting Eddie know about Leo, Hannah found what she was looking for in an online news feed from the *Corcoran Statesman*:

CORCORAN INMATE COMMITS SUICIDE

Leo Manuel Aurelio, an inmate at the Corcoran State Prison, was found dead in his cell early this morning. He was discovered hanging by the neck, and his death is being treated as a presumed suicide.

A guard from the Protective Housing Unit, speaking anonymously, questioned the ME's decision. "Leo didn't cause us no trouble. He was a young guy who would have been up for parole in another couple of years. Why would someone like that kill himself?"

Aurelio was five years into a twenty-years-to-life sentence for second-degree murder in the 2009 stabbing death of Dawn Lorraine Gilchrist, the former wife of disgraced Santa Clarita physician Edward Anthony Gilchrist.

Although Aurelio was the one who actually delivered the fatal blows in the Gilchrist homicide, he was offered a reduced sentence in exchange for testifying against the victim's former husband in what was deemed to be a murder-for-hire scheme.

Convicted of both first-degree murder and conspiracy to commit murder, Edward Gilchrist is currently incarcerated at Folsom Prison, where he is serving life without parole.

That time Hannah couldn't wait around for her regular visit. Pleading a health emergency, she managed to make an unexpected visit to Eddie that very day to give him the good news. There was a triumphant smile on her face as she signed, "Time to add another X. Leo is history."

"Time to haul out the needles and ink," he agreed, signing back.

Early the following week, a pair of investigators from the California Bureau of Investigation showed up at the reception desk at Arbor Crest looking for Hannah Gilchrist. When the receptionist called to announce that some detectives wished to speak to her, Hannah decided against meeting with them in private.

"Since this may have something to do with my son, it's probably better that we conduct whatever business they have in mind in public," she said into the phone. "Have them wait for me in the lobby. I'll be right down."

Hannah had been taking a wig-free nap when the

call came in. With her wig back in place and her makeup reapplied, she drove the three blocks to the community center, which also functioned as the reception area, and marched inside with the confident air of a woman fully in charge.

The receptionist caught Hannah's eye and pointed her toward two men in suits, one younger and one older, who were seated on a sofa in front of the room's immense and entirely decorative gas-log fireplace. Even without the receptionist's help, Hannah would have had no trouble spotting them. The two plainclothes cops stuck out like a pair of sore thumbs—to her as well as to everyone else in the room. The curious eyes of people supposedly reading books, playing cards, or working jigsaw puzzles were actually discreetly focused on the visitors.

Hannah approached the two investigators, stopping directly in front of them. "I'm Hannah Gilchrist," she announced perfunctorily. "How may I help you?"

"Thank you for seeing us," said the older of the two, hurriedly rising to his feet and holding out his ID wallet. "I'm Agent Bill Mansfield with the California Bureau of Investigation, and this is my partner, Agent Bob Owens. We'd like a word if you don't mind."

Hannah remained standing while taking her time to examine the ID.

"All right, Agent Mansfield," she said at last, handing the wallet back to him. "What can I do for you?"

"Won't you have a seat?" he asked.

Clearly he wanted to put her at ease, and Hannah wasn't buying it.

"No, thank you," she said, crossing her arms and speaking clearly enough that her words carried throughout the room. "I prefer to stand, and if this concerns my son, I should probably consult with my attorney before I say another word."

"Your attorney's presence won't be necessary," Agent Mansfield assured her quickly. "This isn't about your son. It's about Leo Manuel Aurelio. Do you happen to know him?"

"Of course I know him," Hannah snapped. "He's the man who testified against my son during Edward's murder trial. I also happen to know he's dead."

Agent Mansfield looked surprised. That was precisely the news he'd come to deliver, and he obviously hadn't expected Hannah to be aware of Leo's death in advance of his announcement. "You do? How do you know about that?" he asked.

"Leo and I have been corresponding for some time," an unblinking Hannah replied, "for years, in fact. The last letter I sent to him was returned marked 'Deceased.'"

"Would you care to go somewhere else so we can discuss this in private?"

"That's not necessary. I don't mind having my neighbors hear what's being said. Most of the people here at Arbor Crest are fully aware of my son's situation."

"Very well, then," Agent Mansfield replied. "Your correspondence with Mr. Aurelio is actually the reason we're here. A packet of your letters was found among his personal effects."

"He kept my letters?" Hannah asked.

Agent Mansfield nodded. "Yes, he did. Did you happen to keep any of the ones he sent to you?"

Hannah shook her head. "No, I did not. Our exchanges were private conversations. I saw no need to preserve them. They were no one else's business."

"Since Mr. Aurelio's testimony was largely responsible

for your son's conviction, I'm a little puzzled as to why you would write to him."

"Are you a Christian?" Hannah shot back at him.

Again Mansfield seemed taken aback by the question. "Yes, I am," he began, "but—"

"So am I," Hannah interrupted with a superior smile that easily laid claim to the moral high ground. "If you are, too, I suppose you've heard all those things about turning the other cheek and forgiving those who trespass against us."

"Yes," Agent Mansfield agreed. "Of course I'm aware of those teachings."

"They're not just teachings," Hannah corrected, moving in for the kill. "They are words to live by. At least they're the words I choose to live by. I wrote to Leo for the first time shortly after my son was transported to the prison here in Folsom. I wrote to my son's accuser offering my forgiveness and my friendship, and I'm happy to tell you that he accepted both. I don't believe he had anyone else in his life. He was an orphan, you know."

The younger agent, the one named Owens who had yet to say a word, nodded discreetly in Agent Mansfield's direction as though verifying what Hannah had just said.

"Are you aware of the circumstances surrounding his death?" Mansfield continued.

Hannah indicated that she was. "After my letter was returned from the prison, I went online and did some checking. I learned that Leo committed suicide. That he was found hanging in his cell."

"Although you may no longer have your set of letters, do you remember him ever mentioning to you anything about his being depressed?"

"Not at all," Hannah replied. "According to what Leo told me, he was doing well. He had earned his GED, had started working toward getting an associate's degree, and was looking forward to his first parole hearing. I believe he was going to be eligible for parole sometime relatively soon—in a couple of years or so."

Mansfield asked, "Did he mention feeling as though he might be in any danger or that he might have gotten crosswise either with one of the other inmates in the facility or with one of the gangs?"

"He said nothing of the kind to me," Hannah replied. "The Leo I knew was intent on serving his time, being released, and being able to live a productive life after paying his debt to society."

"All right, then, Ms. Gilchrist," Agent Mansfield said, holding out his hand. "I guess that's all. We'll be going. Thank you. You've been very helpful."

Hannah allowed the two agents to get as far as the door before she said anything more. She hadn't been inside a church in years, not since Dawn and Eddie's disaster of a wedding. On this occasion, however, she was determined to out-Christian the Christians.

"Agent Mansfield," she called after him, "one more thing. As I said, I'm aware Leo was an orphan. I'm sure that's why he fell in with such a bad crowd long before he ever came to this country. Have you located any other relatives?"

"Not so far."

"What will happen to his remains if you don't find someone to claim them?"

"When bodies of prisoners go unclaimed, they are generally buried on the prison grounds."

"If you're unable to locate any other relatives, I'll be

glad to handle Leo's final arrangements and any expenses those might incur," Hannah said.

"Really?" Agent Mansfield asked in astonishment. "Are you sure? That's incredibly generous of you."

"As I told you before," she said, "Leo and I became friends. It's the least I can do."

Agent Mansfield took out a notebook. "I'll be sure to pass along your contact information. Someone from the morgue will be in touch."

A month later a box marked "Human Remains" and addressed to Hannah Gilchrist arrived at the reception desk at Arbor Crest. From the surreptitious glances sent in her direction as she went to retrieve the package, Hannah realized that everyone in the room most likely knew exactly what the shipment contained. Back in her unit, after removing the sealed urn from its shipping box, Hannah put the urn on front-and-center display in the middle of the side table in her small living room—an action that set Arbor Crest tongues wagging for months to come.

The people who saw the costly bronze piece had only the nicest things to say about it and about the caring thing Hannah had done for "that poor man." When those words came back to her, as they inevitably did, they always made her smile. As far as Hannah herself was concerned, the contents of that urn said nothing at all about the milk of human kindness and everything there was to say about Edward's campaign of getting even.

In gaining possession of Leo Aurelio's remains, Hannah Anderson Gilchrist had successfully claimed her very first trophy.

One down on her watch, and now there were three to go!

25

On December 22, 2016, feathery snowflakes were already falling as Kaitlyn Martin Todd Holmes maneuvered her father's wheelchair onto the lift on the passenger side of his minivan and locked the chair in place before pressing the lift-gate button. With snow falling on her glasses and blinding her, it seemed to take for-damned-ever, but thanks to her husband, Jack, she no longer had to load her father in and out of a vehicle by hand. That had been a killer.

The van was old, bought secondhand from a poor woman whose husband had recently died. The best thing about it was the automatic wheelchair lift. The old rust bucket definitely wasn't a thing of beauty, but it ran. The lift worked. As far as Kaitlyn was concerned, it got them from Point A to Point B, and wasn't that all that mattered?

"There's gonna be an ice storm later today," Rex Martin announced to his daughter when she climbed in behind the steering wheel, slammed her door shut, and paused long enough to clean her glasses. "Arctic winds from Canada will be blowing in from eastern Oregon. Heard it on the radio just before you got here."

Kaitlyn shivered when she heard the news. Storms like that were notorious in this part of the world, and they had the power to bring traffic in western Oregon to a complete standstill for days at a time. As for the radio her father had mentioned? It wasn't anything like what most people thought of when they heard that particular word.

Rex's home, the one Kaitlyn had grown up in, was a small, shingled frame dwelling—little more than a cabin, really—situated deep in a canyon in steep, mountainous terrain high above the town of Lyons, Oregon, which could easily have been called a village. The nearest city of any size was Salem, some twenty-five miles to the west.

The thing that set Rex Martin's place on McCully Mountain Road apart from other houses in the near neighborhood was a towering ham-radio antenna that reached skyward from the end of his moss-covered shake roof. No ordinary radio or TV signals of any kind penetrated this far into the canyon. Cell-phone service was spotty at best, even if you walked as far as the end of the driveway, but navigating the driveway in his wheelchair wasn't exactly an option, so Rex relied on an old-fashioned Princess phone from decades earlier, and the dial-up Internet access for his computer was slow as molasses.

As a consequence, Rex's primary source of news from the outside world was through the ham-radio equipment that occupied a surprising amount of space in his tiny living room. From his remote outpost in the mountains of western Oregon, Rex had made friends with people all over the world. It was also where he got his morning weather reports, delivered each day compliments of an amateur meteorologist named Mort who lived in Mountain View, California, and whose greatest joy in life was providing individualized commercial-free weather reports for anybody who wanted one.

"Great," Kaitlyn muttered, "an ice storm blowing in is exactly what I don't need today. Buckle up, now," she added. "Getting down the mountain won't be a problem. The snow's not sticking enough yet, but we'll probably need chains for getting back up. Maybe we should leave the van here and take my RAV4 instead. It has four-wheel drive."

"Naw," her father said. "You learned to drive on these roads, girl, and it's just like riding a damned bicycle—you don't forget. If we have to use chains to get me back home, we'll use 'em. But it'll be too much trouble getting me out of the van and loaded into your little SUV. By the time we're done, we'll be late for that danged doctor's appointment, and you know how that'll go over."

Kaitlyn did know how that would go over—it wouldn't. In the seven years she'd been back home managing her injured father's complex medical care, she'd dealt with more than enough doctors' offices. This appointment happened to be a first visit with a brand-new physician—not a good time to turn up late. She shifted into gear and then, with a look of regret, drove out past the parked Toyota to get back on the road.

"It'll be dark when we're coming home," she objected.

Rex dismissed her concern with an impatient wave of his hand. "Not to worry," he said. "We'll be fine."

Six weeks earlier, when Kaitlyn had called for an appointment and been told that the doctor's first availability was on December 22 at three thirty in the afternoon, darkness had been her primary concern. One day past the winter solstice, it would be dark by four thirty or so, just as they'd be heading back up into the mountains. If the doctor happened to be running late—as doctors often did in the afternoons—they would be that much later. At the time Kaitlyn hadn't taken the possibility of bad weather into account. Today not only would it be full-on dark, there was no telling how rough the weather would be.

They drove most of the way into town in silence. Glancing in her father's direction halfway there, Kaitlyn wasn't surprised to see he had dozed off. Rex had probably been too concerned about his upcoming appointment to get much sleep. Ditto for his daughter—she hadn't slept either.

Eight years earlier Rex Martin had been horribly injured in a logging accident out in the woods. He and his crew had been felling a tree—something he'd done hundreds of times over the years, but this time something went haywire. The tree zigged when it should have zagged, and Rex was caught in the wrong place at the wrong time. The accident left him with two smashed legs and a permanently damaged spine. The doctors had managed to jury-rig his legs back together with titanium plates, screws, and full-length casts, but there was nothing they could do for his permanently injured back.

Long divorced, Rex was accustomed to living alone. Once he was released from the hospital and rehab some two months later, he was confined to a wheelchair and his world had changed. The day of the accident, the youngest guy on the crew had been an inexperienced kid named Jack Holmes. The other guys on the scene were of the opinion that it had been a greenhorn's error in judgment on Jack's part that had caused the nearly fatal accident. None of them ever said that aloud, though, including Rex Martin.

"Not your fault, kid," he had told Jack. "It coulda happened to anybody."

The only one laying blame was Jack Holmes himself, and he dished it out in spades. Jack tried his best to convince Rex to sell out and move into town. When that didn't work, Jack stepped up to the plate. He organized an army of volunteers—friends, neighbors, guys from the crew—who showed up, toolboxes in hand, ready to make Rex's longtime family home wheelchair-accessible—installing ramps, lowering countertops, widening doorways, and putting in grab bars.

It had been in the middle of that remodeling effort when Kaitlyn's life in California blew up and she came home to stay, ostensibly to look after her dad. Neither Jack nor Kaitlyn had expected what followed. Jack was busy trying to assuage his guilt over what had happened to Rex. As for Kaitlyn? Betrayed twice over, she was done with men. Just to make that point perfectly clear, she'd gone to court and spent some of her severance pay to take back her maiden name.

Given all that, it came as something of a surprise to both of them when the two fell hopelessly in love. They had married the following year, in Jack's home church, St. Augustus Lutheran in Mill City. No longer willing to work in the woods, Jack hired on at the Home Depot in Salem, commuting the sixty-plus miles every day, rain or shine. Kaitlyn was able to find part-time work at a clinic in Mill City that was open three days a week. With their combined incomes, they were able to buy a small bungalow that wasn't much bigger than Rex's place up in the mountains. Between them they continued to function as Rex Martin's primary caregivers. Jack generally stopped by on his drive home from work in the afternoons, bringing along the mail and picking up groceries as needed along the way. Kaitlyn's more time-consuming part of the equation was to keep Rex's house clean, look after his finances, and manage his health issues, including doctor's appointments and medications. A visiting nurse stopped by once a day to help with meal preparation and personal-hygiene issues.

Kaitlyn didn't say much to Jack about her time in California, either before or even after they married, and Jack didn't press her. He had some things in his own past—juvenile drinking, car theft, and a joyriding car wreck when he was fourteen—that he didn't like discussing either. But in the spring of 2012, when an assistant district attorney from L.A. showed up telling Kaitlyn about Edward Gilchrist's arrest and asking questions about his first wife's death, she decided it was time to come clean and tell her husband about what had happened.

"Gilchrist told you straight out that he did it?" Jack asked when she told him about Ed's drunken confession.

Kaitlyn nodded. "He was pretty much out of it at the time. He may not even remember that he told me, but I always suspected that was why he gave me that severance package. He didn't have to. I ended up spending it, but it always felt like blood money."

"You think he gave it to you just to shut you up?"

"Yes."

"Then you have to tell the cops what you know," Jack concluded.

"What if they ask me to testify against him?"

"Then you testify," Jack told her. "It's as simple as that, because it's the right thing to do."

That was one of the things she loved about Jack—he was a straight arrow, and she did as he suggested. She flew down to L.A. to testify against Edward Gilchrist, looking him right in the eye as she did so. The Kaitlyn who showed up at the courtroom at Santa Clarita had been Kaitlyn Martin. Having spent good money to return to her maiden name, she hadn't changed her name again when she and Jack married. After the trial was over and Ed was put away for good, she came straight home and changed her name once more, this time from Martin to Holmes.

The trial and all it had entailed was years in the past now. She seldom thought about it anymore, and she didn't think about it that day either. To begin with she worried about the weather, and then she worried about traffic. Much later in the afternoon, though, when it was time to head home after the doctor's appointment, she barely noticed the amount of accumulated snow on the ground or on the minivan's windshield, nor did she worry that the world had been plunged into darkness. No, right then Kaitlyn's only preoccupation was with her father's health. She understood that they were in for the fight of their lives, and it would probably not end well for Rex Martin.

26

The onset of a persistent cough and episodes of short-ness of breath had prompted Rex's regular GP to refer him to the internist they'd seen today. The doctor had listened to Rex's chest, studied the X-rays, and then ordered another round of tests. Scheduling an MRI would be next up on Kaitlyn's agenda. The doctor hadn't come right out and said so directly, but she was pretty sure he suspected lung cancer. So did she.

Kaitlyn turned the key in the ignition and then used the wipers to clear away the accumulated snow. If there was this much snow in the lowlands, it was bound to be worse up in the mountains.

"I wish you kids would hurry up and have kids," her father muttered as she pulled out of the parking lot and into traffic. "The doctor made it sound like this could be serious, and I'd like to see a grandkid or two before I cork off."

Talk about their getting pregnant was a sore subject. Jack and Kaitlyn both wanted kids, and they'd been trying. So far it just wasn't happening. Considering her experience with Dr. Edward Gilchrist's fertility clinic, she sure as hell wasn't going to try going to one of those.

"We're working on it, Dad," she said, and let it go at that.

The rush-hour storm made for stop-and-go traffic all

the way through town. Jack went into work early and got off at three. That meant that most likely he was already home. At least they both wouldn't be caught up in this seemingly endless traffic jam.

"If this weather is gonna stick around for a couple of days, we should probably stock up on groceries," her father suggested.

Getting the hint, Kaitlyn sighed. Buying groceries in the Pacific Northwest with a snowstorm bearing down was always a free-for-all, and it would make the trip home that much later.

"Why don't you just come stay with us in Mill City for a day or two?" she asked.

"No way," he told her, "absolutely not. I'd rather be home in my own place."

With a reluctant sigh, she turned in to the Fred Meyer parking lot. "What all do you need?"

"Just the usual—bread, milk, a couple of frozen dinners, and maybe a few paperbacks if they have any."

Available grocery carts were hard to find. She finally followed a shopper out into the parking lot and grabbed her cart as soon as she finished loading groceries into the car. Inside the store the shelves in the bread aisle were already picked clean. Ditto for the fridge where the milk should have been. Kaitlyn made do with a selection of the frozen dinners and containers of microwavable soups. For bread she bought several packages of refrigerated rolls that he could heat up in the oven. In the book section, she managed to score a single western and two murder mysteries. The shopping excursion, which should have taken ten minutes under normal circumstances, took forty-five instead, and while she waited in line at the check stand, she called Jack to bring him up to speed.

"Why won't your dad come here?"

"Because he's old and he's stubborn," Kaitlyn answered.

"Isn't that the truth!"

Rex was still awake when she returned to the minivan and loaded in the groceries. Once she turned on the engine and the vehicle started warming up, he immediately dozed off again. His sleeping in the car like that was another cause for worry, but it was also a huge favor to her. Given the road conditions that night, his propensity for backseat driving wouldn't have been welcome.

There was still stop-and-go traffic the rest of the way through town, and out on Highway 22 it was white-knuckle driving every inch of the way. A snowplow with flashing orange lights rumbled past her heading east. If the Department of Transportation was dispatching snowplows to clear the highway, that most likely meant the road through Lyons was already toast, and the narrow track up the canyon to her dad's place would be even worse. Still, home was where her father wanted to be, and given the way the doctor's appointment had gone, she was determined to get him there.

Having grown up in the mountains, Kaitlyn was accustomed to the hazards of wintertime driving. She knew how to put on chains, but she wasn't looking forward to doing it. Fortunately, when she turned off Highway 22 and crossed the newly sanded bridge over the North Santiam River, she found that a group of guys from the local Grange were out in force, installing chains in exchange for small donations.

When Tommy Robins, the guy in charge, approached the minivan, Kaitlyn rolled down her window. "How bad is it?" she asked.

"Pretty bad and getting worse," he said. "Beyond this point, you'll need either chains or four-wheel drive."

"Chain me up, then," she said, clicking open the luggage compartment. "The chains are in back under the floor mat."

Just then a dark-colored Toyota 4Runner swung off the highway and flashed by, almost clipping Tommy in the process.

"Asshole," Tommy muttered. "Somebody will be digging him out of a ditch before the night is over."

On the passenger side of the car, Rex stirred. "What's going on?" he asked.

"Putting on chains," she explained.

Tommy was running the show, which meant he wasn't doing the actual work. "Hey, Tommy," Rex said, "how's it going?"

"It's okay now," Tommy allowed, leaning against her window frame, "but that ice storm is supposed to hit any minute. You're lucky you got here when you did. Once there's a coating of ice on all this snow, there'll be hell to pay. When it starts to get real bad, we're shutting down. You gonna stay up on the mountain with your old man?"

"No," Kaitlyn answered ruefully.

Tommy looked across her at Rex. "You sure you'll be all right out there all by yourself? It might be a day or two before anyone can get to you."

"I'll be fine," Rex told him. "I've got food, books, plenty of wood, and a generator. I'll be snug as a bug in a rug."

Once the chains were on, Kaitlyn paid what was owed and drove on. With a good six inches of snow on the ground and more falling, the chains made all the difference. Kaitlyn turned off 226 and headed up the

McCully Mountain Road. Due to a lack of guardrails, locals sometimes referred to that stretch of roadway as "Killer Mountain Road." Once they got to the house, it took time to operate the chair lift, wheel her father inside, and unload and put away the groceries.

To facilitate Rex's care and give him a measure of dignity, Jack and his pals had redesigned his bedroom space to allow the use of a remote-controlled lift that made it possible for Rex to get himself in and out of his chair, on and off the pot, and into and out of bed. By nine o'clock, when he was tucked in for the night and Kaitlyn was ready to go, she was able to leave him there with a totally clear conscience.

On her way to the RAV4, she noticed that the snow had changed to freezing rain. Heading back down the narrow canyon road, she saw that the minivan tracks she'd left behind in the snow on the way up had completely disappeared. Four-wheel drive or not, she didn't risk speeding. She was far too aware of the steep inclines that fell away from the roadway and down the mountainside to the right.

Shortly after driving past the turnoff to the next-door neighbor's place, she noticed a vehicle shooting out onto the slender roadway behind her. Driving far too fast and with the headlights on high beam, the speeding vehicle pulled in directly behind her, following almost on her bumper—close enough that the headlamps themselves disappeared, leaving a blinding glow that made it difficult for her to see what was in front of her. She couldn't tell what kind of vehicle it was, but it had a high profile.

"Asshole," she muttered into her rearview mirror. "What the hell's your big hurry?"

It was probably another mile or so to the next driveway where she could pull in and let him pass. In the meantime he'd just have to be patient.

Just then the vehicle nosed even closer and bumped into her from behind. It wasn't a hard hit—just a gentle nudge, not enough to do any damage but enough to scare the hell out of her. Gripping the steering wheel and trying to avoid going into a skid, she tapped on the brakes, but nothing happened. Instead of slowing, the RAV4 seemed to pick up speed. Not only was the guy literally on her bumper, he was shoving her toward the cliff.

Moments later Kaitlyn's SUV plunged off the side of the road and tumbled down the mountainside. It flew through the air for some distance before landing nose down, and then it continued moving, turning end over end three times before finally coming to rest at the base of a towering second-growth tree. The plunge down the mountain might have been accompanied by screeching metal and the sound of shattering glass, but pelting sleet muffled any noise. And if Kaitlyn screamed as she went over the edge, there was no one out in the forest on that frigid night to hear her.

Far above her the black Toyota 4Runner that had shoved her off the roadway paused long enough for the driver to survey the carnage. He rolled down his window briefly and listened to hear if there was any sound coming from the wreckage. In the falling sleet, the night had gone dead quiet. The driver up above didn't bother getting out to go check for survivors. That wasn't necessary. His target might have survived the first impact, but not the subsequent ones.

After a minute or so, he took his foot off the brake and eased on down the road on snow that was already topped by a thin layer of ice. Vague humps showed where distinctive tire tracks might have been left earlier, but there were none there now. And between now and the time someone came looking for the victim, these tracks would be completely obliterated as well, and that was just how the killer wanted it—as though he'd never even been here.

27

Mill City, Oregon, December 2016

Back home in Mill City, Jack Holmes watched the clock and the weather reports and worried. By nine the temperatures were falling and the snow had turned to freezing rain. Soon every road in the county would be covered by a layer of treacherous ice.

Kaitlyn had called him from the grocery store in Salem around seven. He estimated it would take at least an hour for her to get from there back to her dad's place above Lyons, depending on traffic and on whether or not she'd had to stop and put on chains. Then it would take time to arrive at Rex's place and get him offloaded and settled in. By Jack's estimate Kaitlyn should have been on her way home from there by around eight thirty, and certainly no later than nine. On a good day, the seven-and-a-half-mile drive took around fifteen minutes. On a night like this, it would be longer, but still, by nine thirty he was pacing the floor.

Jack could have tried calling, but he didn't. The roads were too iffy tonight for Kaitlyn to be talking on the phone and driving at the same time. "And if she's stuck somewhere and needs help, she'll call."

That's what Jack told himself, but by ten o'clock he was having a hard time believing it. Where the hell was she? By ten fifteen he lifted his temporary call ban and tried dialing her number. Naturally the call went straight to voice mail. There were spots along McCully Mountain Road where you could get a cell signal, but Rex's place didn't happen to be one of them. At ten thirty and frantic with worry, Jack dialed Rex's landline. His father-in-law's muffled answer said he'd been awakened out of a sound sleep.

"Did Kaitlyn decide to stay over with you?" Jack asked.

"Stay over?" Rex responded, instantly awake. "No, not at all. Isn't she home yet?"

"She's not, and I'm worried sick. What time did she leave?"

"A little after nine," Rex replied. "What time is it now?"

"Ten thirty."

"You've tried her phone?"

"She doesn't answer. It goes straight to voice mail."

"Have you called the cops?" Rex asked.

"Not yet," Jack said, "but I will now."

Wanting to calm himself before dialing 911, Jack sank into Kaitlyn's chair and was astonished to discover that she'd left her iPad at home, on the charger and almost out of sight, tucked between the seat cushion and the arm of the chair. By the time he finished dialing, he had the device in hand with Kaitlyn's Find My Phone app up and running.

"911," a woman responded. "What are you reporting?"

"It's my wife," he said. "Her name is Kaitlyn Holmes. I think she might have been in a wreck. She left her father's house on McCully Mountain Road outside Lyons an hour and a half ago. It's not quite eight miles from his house to ours in Mill City. I've used her iPad to locate her phone. It appears to be a little over a mile or so from her dad's place. It seems to be close to the road but not on the road. The problem is, she isn't answering. My calls go straight to voice mail."

The operator took Jack's name and phone number. "We'll send someone out as soon as a unit becomes available," she told him, "but the roads are such a mess tonight, we're completely backed up."

The words "as soon as" weren't nearly soon enough for Jack Holmes. Once off the phone, he got dressed, bundled up against the freezing rain, and headed out. The weather was appalling. Other than his Jeep Cherokee and an occasional snowplow, there was no one else out driving—not on Highway 22, or on Highway 226, or even on McCully Mountain Road. If there had been tracks on the road earlier, they weren't there now. Jack inched his way up the steep incline in low gear, stopping every now and then to compare his position with the blinking green dot on Kaitlyn's iPad that supposedly indicated the location of her phone.

When he finally drew even with the indicator on the iPad, there was no sign of any kind of police presence. Jack was the first to arrive. Parking in the middle of the road, he turned on his hazard lights, climbed out of the Jeep, and gingerly crept close enough to the edge to be able to see over the side. By then, the freezing rain had tapered off and finally stopped. Overhead, the cloud cover was breaking up, showing distant stars here and there while the temperature dropped even more. Far below, Jack's eyes were drawn to a tiny red dot. Instantly he knew exactly what he was seeing—the fading glow of a dying taillight.

Hoping beyond hope that Kaitlyn was still alive,

he didn't hesitate. Slipping and sliding on his butt, he made his way down the steep slope, yelling her name as he went. "Kaitlyn, Kaitlyn, can you hear me?" But in that snow-covered, icy landscape, his voice seemed to go nowhere, and there was no reply.

When he reached the driver's door, the glass was completely blown out. The dashboard lights, like that one remaining taillight, provided a dim and ghostly illumination as he peered inside. Kaitlyn was still strapped into the driver's seat. Her eyes were open. Her head hung loosely at an awkward angle. Jack reached inside to take her pulse, but as soon as he touched her icy skin, he knew it was too late. She was gone.

He fell to his knees in the icy snow and covered his face with his hands. "No!" he howled skyward. "Nooooo!" His anguished cry was answered by the wail of an arriving police cruiser, nosing its way up the mountain.

Later on, people would note that the arriving cops made no effort to preserve the crime scene, not that anyone realized at the time that it *was* a crime scene. Even had they attempted to do so, it would have been hopeless, because Mother Nature herself had already obliterated most of the evidence. According to the broken clock in the dashboard, the RAV4 had crashed to earth at 9:20 P.M. During the subsequent investigation, a snowplow driver heading out to clear Highway 226 reported almost colliding with a dark-colored SUV ten minutes or so later. The vehicle, speeding onto the highway without hesitating at the stop sign, had careened off McCully Mountain Road and onto 226, almost T-boning the larger vehicle.

"It would've been a lot worse for him than it was for me," the driver said.

Since there was no way to tell if the unidentified vehicle had anything to do with Kaitlyn's accident, that part of the investigation went nowhere.

The first cop on the scene, Deputy Les Kinsey, happened to be someone who knew both Jack Holmes and Rex Martin personally. Needing to clear the area to make room for arriving emergency vehicles, Kinsey advised Jack to drive to his father-in-law's place up the road. While a team from the local volunteer fire department extricated Kaitlyn's body from the wreckage, Kinsey conducted his initial interviews with both Rex and Jack Holmes in the living room of Rex's home.

Neither man had much to say. Kinsey had Rex recount the details of their day. Kaitlyn had driven him into Salem to see a doctor, and they'd stopped on the way home to pick up some groceries. No, she'd had nothing to drink, other than a cup of coffee she'd purchased in Fred Meyer. As for Jack's day? He'd been at work at 5:00 A.M. and left for home at 3:00 in the afternoon. He'd made dinner—macaroni and cheese—and had kept it in a warming oven so it would be ready for Kaitlyn to eat when she arrived. He had been at home in Mill City at the time of the accident and had called Rex from there sometime around ten thirty.

And that was that. A few days later, the Linn County ME delivered his autopsy findings to the sheriff's department. His report revealed that although Kaitlyn Holmes had suffered blunt-force trauma, the actual cause of death was a broken neck. Her manner of death was termed "accidental."

With that the Linn County Sheriff's Office labeled the case closed.

28

Folsom, California, March 2017

Once she finally had the right name, Hannah's search for Kaitlyn had been relatively easy. Lyons, Oregon, was tiny, and Mill City wasn't much bigger. The real difficulty had been inserting someone into the area who could carry on discreet surveillance long enough to sort out the target's movements. Luis's preference was to keep as much business as possible inside the family—the hits and the money both. Eventually Gloria tapped the Bakersfield cousins to do the job, and they pulled it off without a hitch.

Once again Hannah scoured local news sources, looking to see if there had been any problems with the operation. The first notice she found was a tiny piece in the *Oregonian*:

MILL CITY WOMAN DIES IN ICY CRASH

Longtime Mill City resident Kaitlyn Martin Holmes, age 34, perished in a one-car rollover accident on McCully Mountain Road outside Lyons on Friday night. The accident occurred during a fierce storm that left both ice and snow on the roadway, making for extremely hazardous driving.

The vehicle, which may have been going too fast

for conditions, plunged off the highway and crashed into a tree, killing the sole occupant instantly.

Ms. Holmes is survived by her husband, Jack Holmes, of Mill City, and her father, Rex Martin, of Lyons. She was preceded in death by her late mother, Leona Martin.

Services are pending.

The other accounts Hannah found didn't vary much from the first one. No suspects were mentioned, nor were any persons of interest. She went to see Eddie two days later and was disappointed to see that the tattooed *K* on his arm had already been obliterated by an *X*.

"Who told you?" she signed.

"Luis," he answered. "Gloria gave him the news."

Hannah found herself surprisingly let down that she hadn't been the first to tell him. It was as though the others were quietly edging her out of the game. Later on, though, sitting in her living room and seeing Leo Aurelio's urn, she knew what was needed to make her feel better—another trophy.

The next time Gloria stopped by to do a manicure, Hannah didn't hassle her about spilling the beans to Eddie. Instead she had cash on hand and a request of her own.

"What's that for?" Gloria asked when Hannah placed a stack containing several hundred-dollar bills on the table and pushed it in her direction. "We've already been paid in full. So what's this?"

"I'd like to obtain a copy of Kaitlyn Holmes's death certificate," Hannah told her.

"What's the matter?" Gloria demanded. "Are you

saying our guy is a liar—that he says he took care of her and you don't believe he did?"

"No, no," Hannah said soothingly. "It's not that, not at all. I saw an article about the incident online, and I know everything is in order. I just need a copy of Kaitlyn's death certificate."

"Why?"

"For my personal records."

"All right," Gloria agreed at last, silently counting the bills before slipping them into her pocket.

"Is that enough to cover it?"

"It's fine," Gloria said. "I'll get back to you with it as soon as possible."

Gloria dropped off the document two weeks later when she came by for the next manicure appointment. After she left, Hannah took some time to examine it. Kaitlyn's death certificate was almost like a report card—an official acknowledgment of a job well done. When it came time to put it away, she folded it carefully. Then she pried the lid off the urn containing Leo Aurelio's remains and placed the death certificate inside that.

Hannah Gilchrist had claimed her second trophy. She'd taken two names down from Eddie's A List. Two down. Two to go. Next up was Alexandra Munsey.

29

When Alex Munsey's second novel, *The Changeling*, showed up on Ali Reynolds's "recommended for you" list on Amazon, she picked up her phone and dialed. In the years since the Gilchrist murder conviction, she and Alex had rekindled their friendship, staying in touch through phone calls and e-mails. Alex had been on the sidelines during Ali's romance, courtship, and marriage with B., while Ali had cheered Alex on through the tough times as she ventured into writing fiction rather than nonfiction.

"Hey," Ali said when Alex answered. "I see your new novel is about to hit the shelves."

Alex laughed. "Yes, it is, and that means I'm about to hit the road. Publicity has booked a killer schedule that's going to have me on tour for almost a month. And the book editor for the *L.A. Times* is due here at the house any minute to do a profile interview."

"I know all of that sounds great and fun to someone on the outside," Ali said, "but on the inside I'm guessing it probably isn't."

"You're so right about that," Alex agreed with a laugh. "Having to be charming 24/7 isn't nearly what it's cracked up to be. I used to do it all the time when I was on the road with Progeny, but now I'm out of practice."

"Being a hermit will do that to you. Are you coming to Phoenix?"

"They gave me a choice between Phoenix and Salt Lake City. With the kids there, I chose the latter. Hope you understand."

"Of course I understand," Ali replied. "Visiting with grandkids trumps visiting with grown-up friends six ways to Sunday. How old is Rory these days?"

"Five going on six," Alex replied. "Evan just signed him up for T-ball. According to him, he's going to be either a baseball player or a fireman when he grows up."

It was interesting that although there was more than a decade and a half between Ali and Alex, their kids and grandkids were almost the same age. And she clearly remembered when her son, Christopher, had said the same thing about wanting to be either a baseball player or a fireman. Now he was a high school teacher who sculpted life-size metal animals on the side.

"If you're not coming to Phoenix," Ali said, going back to the topic of the upcoming book, "where will I be able to get a signed copy?"

"One of the first events is at Vroman's in Pasadena. If you order it to be shipped from them, I could sign yours when I stop by before the official signing."

"Good enough," Ali said. "Will do."

"So how's it going with you? Did that weird guy who works for you have any luck in rehabilitating that stray AI he took in?"

The "guy" in question was Stuart Ramey, and the stray AI's name was Frigg. Stu had always been B.'s second-in-command at High Noon Enterprises. Months earlier he had been instrumental in helping the authorities bring down a serial killer named Owen Hansen.

Hansen might have been a mediocre serial killer, but as far as computer science was concerned, he was brilliant, and in terms of AI engineering, he was head and shoulders above everybody else. He had created an artificial intelligence which he named Frigg to be his partner in crime.

Unfortunately for Hansen, in the process of turning Frigg into a successful accomplice, the deep-learning techniques he'd employed had inadvertently also taught Frigg the fundamentals of self-preservation. When the authorities, with Stu's help, were closing in on Hansen, he began ignoring Frigg's threat assessments and strategic suggestions. Understanding that Hansen's endgame would be hers as well, Frigg had gone looking for a new human partner. Operating on the assumption that if Stuart was smart enough to take down Owen, Frigg determined that he might also be smart enough to function as Owen's successor.

Stuart had been both enthralled and appalled by the man's AI creation. Frigg's voice-recognition skills alone were nothing short of astonishing. Having been created for the sole purpose of being a crook's accomplice, the AI had no algorithms that would help her differentiate between good and bad, right and wrong. What worked was right no matter how wrong it might be. Yes, she was extremely adept at assembling and assessing information, but most of the tools she used, including her superb hacking skills, were also unlawful. In the process of bringing down Hansen, Stuart had inevitably become aware of Frigg's illegal proclivities and had immediately taken steps to permanently disable her.

That hadn't worked. Not only had the AI outmaneuvered Owen Hansen, she had rightly concluded that

Stuart would try to undermine her. Before Stu could scrub her files, Frigg had installed some financially astute countermeasures that had effectively coerced Stuart Ramey into rebooting her several months down the line. Once she and her eight-hundred-blade mainframe were again operational—this time under Stu's supervision—he began the challenging process of attempting to turn a crooked AI into a law-abiding one.

"From what Stu tells me," Ali said with a laugh, "it's a lot like housebreaking a puppy. You teach it not to pee in one place and it immediately turns around and pulls the same stunt somewhere else. There are evidently enough redundancies in the AI's system so that removing all those programs is far more complicated than he expected it to be."

The sound of a ringing doorbell on Alex's end of the phone call brought the conversation to an end. "That's probably my interview," she said. "Gotta go. Talk to you later."

30

Once it came time for Hannah to target Alex Munsey, her social-media presence might have been all over the Internet, but her physical location was much more difficult to pin down. The author bio posted on her Facebook page, her Web site, and book covers usually referred to her as a "California-based author living near Los Angeles." Unfortunately for Hannah, the words "near Los Angeles" included a whole lot of territory.

Hannah's maiden name had been Hannah Marie Anderson. After a lifetime of ignoring her middle name, she used it to create an online handle—HMAnderson. That was the name she used to sign up as a follower for both Alex Munsey's Facebook page and her Twitter feed, always posing as a devoted fan.

Alexandra Munsey, going by the gender-fluid pen name of Alex Munsey, was now a bestselling author, turning her modest success with *A Mother's Tale* into national acclaim as a novelist. Hannah had ordered and read her first book, *The Silver Lining*, when it was released, without bothering to send a copy along to Eddie. Why rub his nose in the fact that while he rotted in prison, Alexandra Munsey was free to go on with her life—a shiny, new, successful one—that had grown out of having destroyed his? Nope, he was better off not seeing it.

Based on Hannah's previous purchases, when the next book was about to be released, Amazon sent out a reminder to see if she was interested in buying the new one as well, a book called *The Changeling*. A cover blurb announced Alex Munsey to be the "new Maeve Binchy." Hannah read the book and didn't care for it much. It was long on relationships, with all the loose ends neatly tied up by the end of the story. These days her reading tastes tended to land on the darker side of the literary spectrum, focusing on true crime, preferring the rare ones where the bad guys got away with murder.

The release of Alexandra's book resulted in a flurry of author interviews, and links to those articles were often posted online. That was how, a week after *The Changeling* was published, Hannah clicked on a link leading to the author profile in the *L.A. Times*:

Three years ago, when Alex Munsey's first novel, *The Silver Lining*, unexpectedly landed on the NY Times Best Seller list, no one was more surprised than the author herself, who happened to be sixty-eight at the time it was published. Now she's seventy-one, and with her second novel, *The Changeling*, due to hit the shelves next week, everyone is wondering if literary lightning can strike twice in the same place. If that happens, Alex Munsey may be surprised again, but her myriad fans won't be—not in the least.

In order to speak to her, I drove to an isolated cabin on a rural road, high in the San Bernardino Mountains near Lake Arrowhead, where she lives alone as a self-described hermit and plies her new-found trade on an ever-present laptop.

One might assume that a bestselling author would be ensconced in more palatial digs, but Alex Munsey's rustic three-room cabin—combination kitchen and living room, bedroom, and bath—is anything but palatial. Her cozy book-lined living room has only two chairs—a rocker and a leather easy chair—and looks more like a study than anything else. On a chill mid-March morning, a woodstove in the corner kept us warm and toasty.

"How did you come to be a writer?" I ask as we settle down to talk, with her in the rocker and me in the easy chair. "Was it your life's ambition?"

Alex Munsey is a plainspoken woman with a ready smile and a lighthearted laugh. Considering the challenges she's endured, both the smile and the laughter are surprising.

"I'm a walking, talking example of how good can come from bad," she tells me. "I'm a writer now, but I never expected that to happen. When I was growing up, the only thing I ever wanted to be was a mother. That almost didn't happen, and that's why I'm here."

It's no accident that her customary writing chair is the one she's sitting in right now. "Originally this chair belonged to my grandmother," she explains. "It was in my son's nursery on the day I brought him home from the hospital. When my marriage ended years later and I moved out of the house to come here, this was the only piece of furniture I brought along with me."

Alex Munsey's story is a complicated one, filled with unexpected triumphs and heartbreaks. After years of being unable to conceive a child on their own, Alex and her former husband sought help from Dr. Edward Gilchrist, a physician who at the time was operating a well-respected fertility clinic in Santa Clarita. They selected what they thought to be their preferred sperm donor from a catalog of donor profiles, and their son, Evan, was born as a result of artificial insemination.

Years later, when Evan was diagnosed with kidney disease and needed a transplant, Alex went searching for a possible organ donor. A request for assistance from Dr. Gilchrist's office for more health information and medical history on the sperm donor was rebuffed, but Alex didn't give up. She continued her ultimately successful search, but doing so led to the unwelcome discovery that Dr. Gilchrist had fathered any number of children—Evan included—by using his own sperm in his procedures rather than that of his alleged donors—the ones whose profiles he had shown to prospective parents.

After relating that part of the story, Alex gestures toward a photo, one hanging in a place of honor over the rough-hewn log mantelpiece. In a room where the walls are covered with framed photographs, this is by far the largest. It shows two young men standing side by side and leaning against the hood of a pickup truck. The young men could be twins. They look so much alike as to be indistinguishable.

"Evan is on the right, Rory Davis is on the left," Alex explains. "Rory was the first of Evan's many half siblings to surface. He also donated the kidney that saved Evan's life. This photo was taken about six months after the transplant. By the way, that's why my five-year-old grandson is named Rory Davis Munsey.

"If I were to show you a photo of Edward Gilchrist, you'd see there's a distinct family resemblance. But all those years ago, finding first Rory and then a third half sibling after that told us there was a problem involving the operation of the fertility clinic, and that's when we started looking for additional half siblings."

"Which you found?"

"Yes, we did."

"How many?"

"So far we have more than twenty-eight individuals whose DNA links them directly either to Dr. Gilchrist or to his co-conspirator, nursing assistant, and wife Dawn Gilchrist. As more and more half siblings surfaced, I was shocked to discover how many families had been bamboozled by Dr. Gilchrist. Eventually we attempted to file suit against him. Worried that his ex-wife might come forward to testify against him, he murdered her. Eventually our lawsuit was dismissed, but Edward Gilchrist is now in prison serving life without parole for the murder of Dawn Gilchrist. So although we lost one battle, we won the war."

"And that's where the silver lining thing comes from?" I ask.

"Exactly," Alex answers with a smile. "And it's also how I became a writer. My first book, *A Mother's Tale*, was a nonfiction treatment of the Dr. Gilchrist scandal and all it entailed. In the process of writing it, however, I discovered that writing is something I love to do, and it turns out I'm good at it.

"My agent suggested that I try turning that true story into a novel. That's how my next book, *Silver Lining*, came about. As they say in literary circles, it was 'informed' by my own experience, but it's fiction—similar to the real story though not the same. Writing that gave me an opportunity to use my literary license, or at least my literary learner's permit."

"And what about *The Changeling*?"

"*The Changeling* is a novel that reflects the lessons I've learned through living life."

"Like what?"

"You have a baby and think your life is going to be perfect, but it turns out being a parent is a crapshoot. That baby you love so much might grow up to be a concert pianist or he could turn into a serial killer—you never can tell. And life's the same way—also a crapshoot. You choose someone you think is the perfect partner and swear to stay together 'until death do us part,' but then one day—surprise, surprise—your husband shows up and tells you that it's all over."

"Is that what happened to you?" I ask.

"Yes," she says. "When Jake and I were married, we used to come to this cabin on weekends and for vacations. Back then it was a happy place. When the divorce came along, I ended up with the cabin as part of the property settlement. When I first came to live here, I felt as if having to live here was a kind of exile—a punishment for having been forced to choose between the health of my child and the health of my marriage.

"What I didn't see coming was that eventually this cabin would become my refuge and a place to find my own voice. It was while living here that I launched my journey of becoming a writer. And this summer I expect that Evan will come here to visit with his wife and son. This place may be my refuge, but I'm hoping it will become my grandson's happy place."

No, it won't, Hannah Gilchrist vowed silently to herself, *not if I have anything to say about it.*

That very day she launched a search of San Bernardino County property records, hoping to pinpoint the exact location of Alexandra Munsey's supposed "refuge." When she finally found what she was looking for, an address on Kuffel Canyon Road, Hannah felt as though she'd just won the jackpot. The next time Gloria showed up to do her nails, Hannah would be ready to place her next order.

31

After a hectic month of being on tour, Alexandra Munsey was thrilled to finally be heading home to the quiet simplicity of her mountain retreat. For weeks she'd been in and out of bookstores, airports, airplanes, hotels, and car-service limos. She'd stayed up late and gotten up early. She'd eaten fancy food in equally fancy restaurants at oddball times and had found that none of it really agreed with her—the food, the surroundings, the timing.

At home she seldom wore makeup, sticking to sunscreen and lip gloss most of the time and letting her hair air-dry once she got out of the shower. On the road she'd had to use a blow dryer, a hairbrush, and gallons of hair spray day in and day out in order to keep her hair under control. And the daily applications and reapplications of a full array of makeup had been a pain as well.

But was it worth it? Evidently. *The Changeling* had hit the list. Her editor was happy. Her publisher was happy. Her agent was happy. As for Alex? What she was happy about was going home.

On the tour she'd traveled from the West Coast to the East Coast with stop-offs and appearances here and there along the way, coming and going. Her last two appearances had been in Salt Lake City. Spending two nights in the same hotel had been almost like a vacation. With two daytime Salt Lake events, she'd been able to have dinner with Evan and his family, where they'd celebrated Rory's sixth birthday a couple of days early, and she'd given him the collection of colorful books she'd gathered for him from bookstores en route. In the course of dinner, she'd learned that he had a scheduled T-ball game the next day. Wanting to see Rory play, Alex had rebooked her afternoon flight to LAX to later in the evening, and she had flown home to L.A. having seen her grandson hit his first-ever home run. It had made for a wonderful but tiring day and by the time she met up with the car-service driver in baggage claim for the drive home to Lake Arrowhead, she was beyond weary.

"How long is this going to take?" she asked.

"A little over two hours," he said, "but you never know. That could change."

With the driving left to someone else, Alex spent some time on her phone. The marketing department was totally sold on the importance of maintaining a social-media presence. They had created a Web site for her and a Facebook page where they posted her daily schedule along with photos of previous signings and events. They had also established a Twitter account for her, which she used dutifully if reluctantly:

> On my way home. I can hardly wait to sleep in my own bed. By staying late in Salt Lake, I got to see my grandson's first T-ball homer.

After sending the tweet, she sent Evan a text, letting
him know she was on the ground and headed home.
After that she replied to a couple of e-mails that had
come in over the course of the afternoon and evening.
By ten o'clock, with the Escalade bogged down in a
traffic jam that would turn that projected two-hour trip
into a three-hour trip, Alex ran out of energy. It wasn't
that late, but with her body on no known time zone,
she gave herself permission to put the phone away, lean
back in the seat, close her eyes, and sleep.

32

Hannah Gilchrist had spent most of the night binge-watching multiple episodes of *I (Almost) Got Away with It* on Investigation Discovery, but she had been asleep in her chair for some time when her ringing phone awakened her at eleven thirty. If you live in a retirement community, late-night phone calls hardly ever come with good news. Donna, the jigsaw-puzzle lady, had been going downhill for weeks now, and Hannah expected that one of the neighbors was calling to say that Donna was gone. She did not expect to receive a late-night call from Gloria Reece.

"Where the hell is she?" Gloria Reece growled into Hannah's ear. "According to the schedule you gave me, she was supposed to be home by four o'clock this afternoon. My people are in place and waiting, but they're wary about hanging around in the area for fear of being spotted. I don't blame them in the least."

Hannah felt more than a little put out by Gloria's tone and attitude. She seemed to be getting more and more uppity lately, as though she had somehow forgotten who was paying the piper here, as though she were the one in charge. Once Hannah had handed off the Munsey project to Gloria, her job had been to keep Gloria apprised of Alex's travel plans, but other than that she had no idea about when the hit would be scheduled. Scheduling was up to Gloria and she didn't like answering to anybody.

With a sigh Hannah used the remote to put the program on pause and then rose to go sit at her computer, parked as it usually was on the writing desk in her office.

"Since this was one of her travel days, maybe you should have waited a day or two," Hannah suggested mildly.

"And maybe you should keep your opinions to yourself."

Hannah was bristling by the time she settled in front of the computer and checked the Twitter feed. "Okay," she said, "there's a tweet from ten fifteen that says she stayed to see her grandson's T-ball game and caught a later flight. It also says she's in the car and on her way home. There's no way to tell where she was when she sent it or how close she was to Lake Arrowhead."

"She isn't there yet," Gloria said. "She's supposedly coming from LAX?"

That word "supposedly" rankled. It was as though Gloria were holding Hannah personally responsible for Alex Munsey's last-minute change in schedule.

"If you have to call it off for tonight and take care of it some other time, that's entirely up to you," Hannah replied. "Now, if you don't mind, I have better things to do than to sit here jawing about things I can't fix. Please let me know how it turns out."

With that, Hannah hung up the phone. She returned to the TV set long enough to shut it off, then went to bed. Tossing and turning, she didn't sleep, and not because someone was somewhere out there in the night stalking Alex Munsey. Being a part of Eddie's quest for vengeance had given Hannah a chance to be close to her son—to be there for him. But did that closeness have to come at the cost of being reprimanded by her manicurist? Maybe that was a steeper price than Hannah Gilchrist was prepared to pay.

33

I t was almost eleven thirty when Alex's driver awakened her. "We're here," he announced, pulling up to the walkway that led to her front door.

Alex had left the inside lights on a timer so it would look as though someone were home. She stepped out of the SUV and breathed in the cool nighttime mountain air. It was late May. The weather at LAX had been hot and muggy. Hurrying ahead, she unlocked the front door while the driver followed behind, bringing the luggage. When she stepped inside, the house had that slightly musty, airless smell of having been shut up and abandoned for some time, but nothing was out of place. It was her home sweet home.

"Where do you want these?" the driver asked. He had somehow managed to haul everything into the house at once—the two large suitcases along with her carry-on.

"Just drop the bags by the front door is fine," she told him. "I'll drag them into the bedroom later."

Alex reached for her purse and wallet. No doubt the driver's tip was included in her publisher's billing, but it had been a long, late drive, and he'd helped with the luggage. A little something extra was definitely in order.

"Am I your last job for the night?" she asked, handing him her tip.

He nodded.

"How far do you have to go to get home?"

"Just to Whittier is all," he said. "It's not that bad, and it's late enough now that traffic should be better."

"Right," she said. "Famous last words."

He grinned back at her. "Isn't that the truth!"

She walked out onto the porch and watched him drive off, then stood there for a time, savoring the clear night air and the scent of the forest. When the night-time chill caught up with her, she went inside, shivering slightly, closing and locking the door behind her. She looked at the pile of luggage, but she wasn't ready to tackle it just yet. There would be plenty of time to un-pack in the morning. For right now, if she ever had to wear most of that clothing again, it would be too soon.

She went into the bedroom, undressed, and slipped into her favorite flannel nightie. After that two-hour nap in the car, she knew there was no point in trying to go to bed just yet. She was tired, yes, but she wasn't at all sleepy. Back in the kitchen, she glanced at her phone and discovered that it was almost out of juice. She put it on the charger, poured herself a glass of chardonnay from the boxed wine in her fridge, then settled into her rocker and clicked on the TV. Having traveled all over the country, she was eager to find out what was hap-pening on the local news, but by the time she was ready to watch, the news was long over. She went channel-surfing, settling at last on an episode of *Forensic Files*.

The show was almost finished, with the bad guy in custody, when sometime after midnight Alex caught sight of flashing lights piercing the dark sky outside. Checking through the living-room window, she saw that a cop car with a pulsing light bar was parked in front of her house. As a uniformed deputy exited

the vehicle and walked toward the front door, Alex's
heart dropped. When cops were sent out at this time
of night, it probably meant some kind of bad news.
She hurried across the room, unlocked the dead bolt,
and switched on the porch light. She wrenched open
the door just as a female deputy stepped up onto the
porch. She was young and pretty, with her dark hair
pulled back into a bun. Alex could see the bulge of a
holster on the belt at her waist. The badge on her shirt
glittered in the light.

"What's wrong?" Alex demanded. "Has there been
an accident? Is someone hurt?"

"No, ma'am," the deputy replied. "Several nearby
residents have reported seeing an especially aggressive
bobcat roaming the neighborhood. We're coming around
advising people that if they have pets or young children,
they should keep them inside. It's possible that the animal is rabid. Game and Fish has been notified, but they
probably won't be out here until sometime tomorrow."

Weak with relief, Alex covered her face with her
hands and took a step backward into the house. When
she dropped her hands, she was surprised to see that
the deputy had followed her inside and was kicking the
door shut behind her.

"Wait," Alex said, catching sight of the handgun
in the deputy's hand. "What's going on? What do you
think you're doing?"

Alex tried to back away, but by then it was too late—
too late to run or even scream. Face-to-face with the
weapon the deputy had pulled from her holster, Alex
instinctively held her hands in front of her as if to ward
off the attack. The nine-millimeter slug passed through
the palm of her left hand, but that didn't slow it down.

It slammed into her heart, killing her instantly. She was dead before she hit the floor.

The assassins Gloria Reece had contracted to do the job were pros. Once the front door closed, the light bar turned off and disappeared. The getaway driver listened for and heard the muffled gunshot, but there was no audible or visible reaction from the surrounding neighborhood. No dogs barked. No lights came on. Before exiting the house, the shooter picked up her shell casing, then she left the same way she had entered—through the front door, closing it firmly behind her. Since the shooter had worn gloves, she left behind no fingerprints or DNA. The fatal slug was embedded in her victim's chest, and blood spatter would provide the only forensic evidence.

Outside, the getaway driver waited beside the darkened car, holding open a black plastic trash bag. Quickly the shooter slipped off her outer garments—gloves, uniform, and shoes—lifted from the costume shop of a television soundstage. By morning all of it would be reduced to cinders in a burning barrel on a farm outside Bakersfield. If someone came looking for gunshot residue, there wouldn't be any of that either.

The killers had entered the neighborhood late in the afternoon. Other than Alexandra Munsey, no one on Kuffel Canyon Road had noticed their presence, and there were no witnesses to their unhurried departure. They left the scene and drove back home without speeding or doing anything that might attract undue attention.

"Good job," she told her driver as he steered their long-retired Crown Victoria, a former cop car, away from the crime scene. "Uncle Luis would be proud."

34

It was the middle of the night, and the Professor was sound asleep when someone rattled the bars on his cell. An unexpected presence outside a cell at night often spelled trouble or danger. Fully awake and alert, Eddie stiffened slightly under his blanket, but other than that, he didn't move.

"Hey, wake up, dude," someone said. "I've got news."

Recognizing the voice of the cell block's usual night-time guard, Eddie sat up on his cot.

"What kind of news?" Eddie asked.

"From your friend Luis. He says to tell you it's a done deal."

"Thanks," Eddie muttered. "Good to know."

Not wanting to show too much emotion, he lay back down. Then unable to quell his sense of triumph, he sat back up. The guard was someone he knew fairly well—a guy who could be counted upon to look away if the need arose and the price was right.

"I'm gonna need a little quiet time here," Eddie said.

"The usual price?"

"Maybe a little more than the usual," Eddie told him.

"Fair enough," the guard said. "Have a ball."

These days Eddie kept his cubbyhole fully stocked with tattooing supplies just in case, up to and including the candle and matches. Minutes later, grinning to himself in the flickering candlelight, he pricked his skin with a needle and sent the first drop of india ink into the tattoo on his forearm. High on adrenaline, he barely felt a thing. He was a far more experienced tattoo artist now, and it took only forty-five minutes of working in near darkness for him to create an *X* that completely blotted out the first letter *A* on his arm, the one that stood for Alexandra Munsey. She was out of the way now, and that meant there was only one letter remaining—the *A* that designated Ali Reynolds.

She was next on his list, and Eddie could hardly wait.

35

When Gloria called Hannah the next morning to tell her that Alexandra Munsey had been handled, Hannah was so ecstatic that she almost forgave Gloria for her previous transgressions—almost but not quite.

One more target had been removed from the list, and Hannah could hardly wait to give Eddie the news. That very afternoon she fired up her Lexus and drove straight to the prison. She was in her eighties now, and age was catching up with her. She'd had to have cataract surgery, and although her vision was much improved, when venturing out she seldom strayed far from her beaten path, the one that led directly from Arbor Crest to the prison. It wasn't her regularly scheduled visiting day, but by now she was enough of a known quantity that the people at the visitation counter could be counted on to give her some slack.

When the guard led Eddie into the visitation room, Hannah was shocked by how unwell he looked. There were dark circles under his eyes which meant he hadn't slept well.

"Are you all right?" she asked.

"I'm okay," he said, "just a little under the weather."

"Maybe you should see the doctor."

Even as she said the words, Hannah knew she could have saved her breath. As a former doctor, Eddie hated having to see the prison physician. That meant he'd have to be dreadfully ill before he'd stoop to making an appointment. On the health front, Hannah had some news of her own, but now wasn't the time to share it.

"Why are you here today?" he asked. "This isn't your usual day."

"Chalk it up to mother's intuition," she said aloud. "I had a feeling something might be amiss."

With that she switched over to their customary sign language. "Alex is gone."

"I know," he said, pointing to his already updated tattoo. "Luis told me."

Hannah was instantly furious. It had happened again. With Gloria's help, Luis had stolen Hannah's thunder. Instead of treating her as a full partner in their joint endeavor, the others seemed to be shutting her out. Together they had demoted her to the point that she was little more than an afterthought to that operation. Realizing that, Hannah squared her shoulders and said the rest of what she'd come to say.

"I'm going to the funeral," she announced.

"To the funeral," Eddie echoed. "Why on earth would you want to do that?"

"I have my reasons," she snapped at him, although in reality she had only one. Hannah wanted her trophy, and she had decided overnight that a printed program from Alex Munsey's funeral was exactly what was needed, a conclusion she didn't bother sharing with her son.

A horrified look appeared on Eddie's face. "No!" he

signed. "Absolutely not! That makes no sense. What if someone recognizes you?"

"They won't," she assured him. "People don't look at women my age. We're invisible."

"You may think you're invisible," Eddie signed, "but you're also incredibly stupid. Don't do this."

In all the years he'd been locked up—all the years when she'd gladly done his bidding and carried out his vendetta—this was the first time Eddie had crossed that line. In that moment Hannah was transported back to those years when both her husband and her son had looked down their collective nose at her lack of formal education. Invisible or not, she had no intention of just sitting there and taking it.

"I may be stupid," she said, "but I'm not the one in prison." That was what she signed. What she said aloud was a little different. "Eddie, I'm so sorry. Suddenly I'm feeling a bit ill myself. I'll have to be going."

With that she got up. Her three-pronged cane clicked on the tiled floor as she marched out of the room. She was still angry when she got home. No mother could have done more for a son than she'd done for Eddie, and yet he dared treat her that way? Dared talk to her that way? It was unacceptable! Intolerable!

Still wounded by their quarrel, Hannah spent the next several days scanning local news sites and broadcasts, searching for some hint that Alexandra Munsey's body had been found. The first arrived several days later on Memorial Day afternoon, when a headline on the *San Bernardino Examiner*'s Web site reported that the body of an unidentified female had been found shot to death in a cabin near Lake Arrowhead earlier that morning. No other details were available at that time.

On Tuesday, though, once the body had been identified and the name released to the media, the story shifted into a higher gear.

LOCAL AUTHOR FOUND MURDERED

Alexandra Munsey, a local bestselling author, was found shot to death in her Lake Arrowhead home late last week while her most recent novel, *The Changeling*, remains at number five on the New York Times Best Seller list.

The San Bernardino Sheriff's Office reports that the body was found on Monday morning by the victim's former husband, Jake Munsey, who had gone to the home to check on her after multiple phone calls made to her residence the day before went unanswered.

"I knew she was dead the moment I opened the door," Mr. Munsey reported. "I never even went inside."

At a press conference earlier today, Sheriff's Department spokeswoman Amanda Roberts reported that Ms. Munsey evidently died shortly after returning from a monthlong national tour promoting her latest book.

"Her luggage was found near the body, just inside the front door, and her purse was located on the kitchen counter," Ms. Roberts said. "Nothing seemed to be missing from the home. Her jewelry and watch were still there, and more than several hundred dollars in cash was found inside her wallet, leading us to believe that this was a targeted hit rather than a robbery gone bad. There was no sign of forced entry or sexual assault."

So far no suspects have been identified in the homicide, but according to Ms. Roberts investigators are currently interviewing a person of interest.

The Changeling is Ms. Munsey's third book and her second novel. Her first published work, *A Mother's Tale*, tells the story of her long-running feud with her onetime fertility doctor. That physician, Dr. Edward Gilchrist, was later convicted of homicide in the death of his former wife and is currently serving life in prison due to that crime.

Ms. Munsey was instrumental in forming an organization called the Progeny Project, which became a resource of information and a community gathering place for families impacted by the unintended consequences of having children born by means of artificial insemination.

Her literary agent, Moira Van Dorn, expressed her shock by saying, "This is a terrible loss for her family, for me personally, and for the literary world in general. In terms of her writing, Alex was truly coming into her own, and I can't imagine why anyone would attack her in such a horrific way."

Ms. Munsey was born on February 14, 1946, to Mason and Ellen Olson of Van Nuys, California. A graduate of UCLA, she is survived by her son, Evan, of Salt Lake City. Funeral services are pending.

It was the last few words of the article that caught Hannah's attention. Funeral services pending. Eddie had forbidden her attendance, but would she still go? Enough time had elapsed between the incident with Eddie and now for Hannah to realize that he wasn't completely wrong. Some of the people from the funeral were likely to have been present at Eddie's trial five years earlier, but she doubted that any of them would recognize her. People saw what they expected to see—a frail old woman, a harmless little old lady leaning on her cane, not a stone-cold killer.

Hannah could have asked Gloria, of course, and had her delegate someone to drop by the funeral home and pick up a program the same way someone had been sent to retrieve Kaitlyn Holmes's death certificate. But that's not what Hannah did. Instead she sent Gloria a message saying she'd have to cancel that week's manicure appointment. And that week on her regular visitation day, Hannah didn't bother going to the prison to see her son.

Eddie had created a terrible breach when he had called her stupid, and if he thought Hannah was over it, he was dead wrong.

36

Late that Friday afternoon, Ali Reynolds, seated at her desk in High Noon's corporate offices, was more than ready for her workweek to be over. A long-delayed order of computer blades and racks had finally arrived on Tuesday afternoon. The frenzy of unpacking and installing had meant having all hands on deck. When her phone rang, she expected the call to be from B. Simpson, her husband, telling her that his flight home from Japan had been canceled or delayed. Instead a strange number showing a Salt Lake City location turned up in the caller-ID window.

"Hello," she said.

"Ali?" a male voice responded. "Ali Reynolds?"

"Yes," she said. "Who's this?"

"It's Evan, Evan Munsey."

Ali could tell from the tone of his voice that something was wrong. "Why, Evan," she said, "how good to hear from you again. Is everything okay?"

"No, everything is not okay," he said. "It's about my mom. She's dead."

The shocking news took Ali's breath away. Her signed copy of Alex's new book, *The Changeling*, was right there on the corner of her desk. She had finished reading it the previous afternoon while everyone else in the office had been up to their ears in computer installation. She had planned on calling tonight to let Alex know how much she'd enjoyed it.

"Oh, my goodness," she said. "I'm so sorry. I talked to your mom several weeks ago when she was about to go on tour. What happened?"

Ali heard the catch in Evan's voice before he answered. "She was murdered," he said in an anguished whisper. "Someone went to her cabin up by Lake Arrowhead and shot her to death."

Ali was appalled. "When was this?"

"We're not sure of the exact timing. The cops may know more now, but they haven't released that information to us. The last I heard from Mom was a text she sent a week ago yesterday. She had just gotten off a flight from Salt Lake. She said she'd met up with the car service and was on her way home. We had seen her that same day. The tour had taken a lot out of her. She said she was tired and that she was going to spend the weekend in her robe, taking it easy. After being on the go for a month, she just wanted to veg, so I didn't think too much about it when I didn't hear from her on Friday or Saturday.

"But Sunday was my son's birthday. Rory turned six that day. He also lost his first tooth. We sent Mom a video of him with his front tooth missing, and I was surprised that we didn't hear right back from her. When I tried phoning her later that night, the call went straight to voice mail. That's when I started to worry. On Monday, when she still didn't answer, I called Dad and asked if he could go up and check on her. He's the one who found her. The front door was unlocked, and she was lying right there next to the pile of luggage she'd had with her on tour."

"A home invasion, then?" Ali asked.

"The cops don't think so. She evidently opened the door to her attacker. There was no sign of breaking and entering."

"So it must have been someone she knew," Ali suggested, "someone she invited into her home. Any sign of a physical confrontation?"

"None," Evan replied. "Other than the gunshot wound, there was no sign of a struggle. The television set was on. There was half a glass of wine on the side table next to her chair. So I think she was just sitting there by herself when the killer showed up on her doorstep. The cops say it wasn't a robbery gone bad. Her purse was found nearby with a good deal of cash still inside it. And valuable jewelry was left behind as well. She was still wearing both her Omega watch and the diamond pendant she gave herself when *Silver Lining* hit the *New York Times* list."

"Did your mother have any enemies?" Ali asked.

"The cops asked me the same question. I told them I didn't know of any current ones, but there's always that old one—the one from way back then—that Gilchrist guy who's still in prison doing life without parole. From what I'm hearing, the detectives seem to be fixated on my dad as a person of interest. That's probably because he's the one who found the body, but he only did that because I asked him to. The problem is, however, he's the ex-husband."

"And husbands or ex-husbands are always the ones who do it," Ali offered.

"Exactly," Evan breathed. "I tried to tell them that was nuts, because he and Mom had buried the hatchet years ago. Nancy, my stepmother, tried to tell them the same thing—that Mom often spent the holidays at their house—but it sounds like their minds are made up, and they're not buying it no matter what we say."

He fell silent after that. While Ali struggled with what to say next, someone tapped on the frame of her office door. She looked up to see Stuart Ramey, High Noon's second-in-command, standing in the doorway. She motioned him to come inside and have a seat while she turned back to her phone call.

"Is there anything I can do to help?" she asked.

"That's why I'm calling now," Evan said, "and I'm sorry I didn't call sooner, but things have been so nuts. . . ."

"Evan, please don't worry about not calling me. Just tell me what you need me to do."

"This morning the ME's office finally released the body to our mortuary, Longmont Funeral Home in Sherman Oaks. The story has been all over the local news for days so several of the people from the Progeny Project have called or e-mailed, expressing interest in coming to the services. Everyone had been standing around with one foot in the air waiting to hear when we could schedule it. When we finally did, it seemed likely more people would be able to attend on a weekend than during the week. With that in mind, we've scheduled the memorial for Sunday afternoon at two P.M. so people wouldn't have to miss work."

"This Sunday afternoon?" Ali asked.

"Yes, and it was when we started talking about planning the service that I thought of you." Evan paused for a moment before continuing. "I know this is a big ask, but would it be possible for you to speak at the memorial? You were there with Mom at the very beginning, when the whole thing with Rory and me got started. Since it was such a defining issue in her life, I thought it was important that we acknowledge it. Cassie Davis would have been the other natural choice, but Rory tells me that Emma is having serious health issues right now and Cassie can't get away."

"Of course I will," Ali answered at once. "I'm honored to be asked, and I owe it to you and to your mom to be there. As soon as we get off the phone, I'll see about booking a flight. I'll probably fly in tomorrow and then fly out on Monday morning."

"Thank you, Ali," Evan said softly. "I really appreciate this. I'll be picking up Kathleen, my wife, and Rory—our little Rory—from LAX tomorrow. Kathleen's a teacher, and she and Rory both had to finish out the last week of school before they could come. Depending on your schedule, I can pick you up at the airport or else I can send someone to get you."

"Don't worry about me," Ali said. "You have enough on your plate. I'll rent a car and get wherever I need to be on my own."

"Do you know where you'll stay?"

"Since the memorial service and reception will both be in Sherman Oaks, I'll probably book somewhere in Hollywood. The W, most likely. My husband, B., travels so much that we have a never-ending supply of points with them. Where are you staying?"

"With my dad and Nancy," Evan said. "And they'll probably be hosting a small private reception at the house after the public one at the funeral home."

"Send along their address," Ali said. "You can text it to this number."

"Will your husband be coming as well?"

"I doubt it. He's somewhere over the Pacific right now, and he's due home later tonight. Since he's been traveling all week, I suspect he'll want to stay home."

The call ended, and Ali looked over at Stuart Ramey, who'd been sitting there during much of the conversation. "Did someone die?" he asked.

Ali nodded. "A friend of mine from back when I was living in California. She was murdered late last week, shot to death in her home up near Lake Arrowhead."

Stuart's face registered genuine alarm. "Are you all right?" he asked.

Ali was stunned to momentary silence. "I think so," she said at last.

"I lost my friend, too," he added quietly. "I know how much it hurts. I'm sorry."

Ali knew the story of Stu and his lost friend. Stuart had grown up suffering from an undiagnosed case of Asperger's syndrome. Hopelessly bullied at school, he'd been on his own until another equally smart outsider named Roger McGeary had turned up in his life, and the two of them had become fast friends. They'd lost track of each other after high school. Years later, in the course of unraveling the cause of Roger's inexplicable suicide, Stu had unmasked Owen Hansen as a serial killer. Solving that case and facing down a diabolical bad guy had awakened something in Stuart Ramey and given him a degree of self-confidence he'd never had before. Still, the idea of Stu being able to step away from himself long enough to ask after someone else's emotional well-being was remarkable.

"It does hurt," Ali agreed. "It hurts terribly."

"Who was it?"

"Her name was Alex—Alexandra Munsey. She's . . .

she was . . . a writer. In fact, I just finished reading her book last night." Ali picked up her copy of *The Changeling* and handed it to Stu. "That was her son, Evan, on the phone asking if I'd come to L.A. and speak at her memorial service on Sunday afternoon. I agreed to go, on the assumption that you guys can keep the doors open and the lights on in my absence."

Still holding the book, Stu nodded. "Cami and I should be able to manage," he assured her.

Cami was short for Camille Lee, a young computer-science graduate who was, Ali supposed, third-in-command at High Noon. She'd been hired originally to serve as Stu's assistant, stepping in when he needed help relating to human beings as opposed to interacting with machines. Now that he was requiring less of that, Cami had been able walk away from being Stu's emotional Sherpa and focus on work that was more in keeping with her own computer-engineering skills.

"Do you think he'll want to stay here, or will he want to go to the funeral with you?" Stu wanted to know.

"I'll ask, but I doubt he'll want to go," Ali replied. "For one thing, with that flight delay, who knows how late it'll be by the time he gets home? Besides, he doesn't know any of the people involved. Between interacting with a bunch of strangers and being able to keep an eye on his new computers, I'm pretty sure I already know what he'll choose."

Stu nodded. "Right," he said, "there's always the chance of a glitch of some kind in that initial upload, and someone will need to be here to fix it. I told Cami I'll hold the fort tonight, and she can come in tomorrow morning to relieve me, but I know we'd both prefer to have B. on hand in case anything goes wrong."

"Wait," Ali said, "you're staying over tonight? I thought today was supposed to be your official move-in day."

"It was," Stu conceded, "but it's not that big a deal. If I move out today or tomorrow or next week, what difference does it make?"

For years Stu had lived in a studio apartment on the far side of the computer labs. Living on-site had made it easier for him to keep up with B. Simpson's travel schedule, making him readily available for consultation no matter where his boss was in terms of time zones or the international date line. The arrangement had also been convenient for all concerned, since Stu hadn't possessed either a driver's license or a vehicle. That had recently changed, and days earlier he'd closed on the purchase of the home in Sedona that had been B. Simpson's bachelor pad before he and Ali married.

Cami showed up just then, popping her head in the door. "Hey, Stu," she said, "I got the last rack of GPUs up and running, so I'm off." Then, looking back and forth between Ali and Stuart, she added, "What's going on? Did I miss the memo about a staff meeting?"

"It's not a staff meeting," Ali explained. "One of my friends was murdered in California a little over a week ago, and I've been asked to speak at her memorial service on Sunday."

"I'm so sorry," Cami interjected.

Ali nodded. "I agreed to go, but I'm concerned that Stu is having to readjust his moving plans."

"His moving plans were already readjusted," Cami said with a grin. "Besides, he won't suffer. I told him I'd pick up his preferred staff of life—pepperoni pizza—and drop it off here on my way back from Krav Maga. The only reason he was wanting to rush home is because his sweetie, Frigg, is already there."

"Leave Frigg out of this. She is not my sweetie," Stu grumbled. "And when you pick up that pizza, don't forget my root beer."

"Yes, sir," Cami said, snapping to attention and giving him a mock salute.

The easy banter and constant bickering between the two young colleagues often made Ali feel like a dormitory house mother, or maybe a referee. They were opposites in every way. Cami was tiny, while Stu was a bear of a man. Cami was almost twenty years Stu's junior, but in many ways she was more mature and far more experienced. She was outgoing and friendly. He was painfully shy—a nerd's nerd—who preferred his own company to almost anyone else's. She was a health-food nut—organic and non-GMO foods all the way—while he was your basic junk-food addict. When doughnuts showed up in the break room, Stu dove right in, while Cami lectured everyone within earshot on the evils of white flour and sugar. Stu's childhood history of being bullied had made him someone who would rather dodge a fight than go to war. Cami, despite her diminutive size, was a devotee of self-defense. She spent her off hours developing her Krav Maga skills and doing target practice at the shooting range.

For all their differences, though, when the two of them were seated side by side in the computer lab with their keyboards at hand and monitors in front of them, they were the ultimate dream team, working in unspoken harmony and anticipating what the other needed without a word having to be exchanged.

Ali laughed. "All right, then," she said. "Get going, both of you. I need to check with B. so I can figure out my own travel arrangements."

Because he was still in the air, she didn't bother to call, resorting to texting instead:

I've been invited to
speak at a funeral in
Sherman Oaks on
Sunday afternoon. Do
you want to come along
for the ride, or do you
want to stay home?

                Who died?

A friend of mine, Alex
Munsey.

        The woman whose book
           you were reading the
               other day?

That's the one.

             What happened?

She was murdered—
shot to death
inside her own home.

        That's awful. So sorry to
               hear it.

The ME just released the
body, and her son asked
if I would do the eulogy. If
you want to be there, you
can just stay over in L.A.
tonight. That way we can
meet up tomorrow, go
to the memorial service
on Sunday, and fly home
together on Monday.

>   Do you need to have
>   me there?
>   If you do, of course
>   I'll be there.

But you'd much rather
be home watching over
your brand-new GPUs.

>   You know me too well.

Okay. I'm perfectly
capable of flying
back and forth to
California on my own.
When will you be home
tonight?

>   Who knows? By
>   the time the plane
>   took off, I knew I'd
>   already missed my
>   L.A.-to-Phoenix

connection. And
once I clear customs
and catch the next
flight, I'll probably
land there too late
to catch the shuttle
back to Sedona.

Rent a car, silly. If you
drive it home tonight,
I can take it back to the
airport tomorrow.

Good idea. Smart girl.

Isn't that why you keep
me around?

Ali smiled as she shut down the text app on her phone. Like Stu, B. Simpson was brilliant when it came to sorting out complex cybersecurity issues, but sometimes the simplest problems baffled him. Ali was B.'s real-world Sherpa in the same way Cami was Stu's.

Then Ali turned back to her computer, dialed into her travel folder, and went looking for flight reservations. She booked an early-afternoon flight so she wouldn't have to leave the house at the crack of dawn. Before heading out, she went to the computer lab and found Stu at his workstation.

"I'm on my way," she said. "I talked to B. He'd rather be here than attending a funeral, and I don't blame him. I fly out tomorrow at one, back on Monday afternoon."

"Okay," Stu said. "Travel safe, but what was your friend's name again—the one who was murdered?"

"Alexandra Munsey," Ali said. "Everybody called her Alex."

Back in her office to retrieve her purse, she paused long enough to pick up her signed copy of *The Changeling* and opened it to the inscription, written in blue ink with Alex's trademark flourish:

> Sometimes it pays to be a late bloomer. Thank you for always being there for me.
>
>   Alex Munsey

You're welcome, Ali thought. *I always have been, and I guess I still am.*

37

It was a thoughtful Stuart Ramey who sat at his workstation late that afternoon, once everyone else had left and he finally had the place to himself. As someone who'd had very few friends in his life, he had only recently come to the realization that Ali Reynolds his boss was also Ali Reynolds his friend. And knowing how deeply he'd been affected by losing Roger McGeary, Stu couldn't stop thinking about Ali's loss and wondering if there was something he could or should do to help her.

Who was this Alex Munsey? Hers was a name Stu had never heard before, even though she and Ali had evidently been longtime friends. Who had murdered her and why? And why had Ali been summoned to speak at the funeral? For all those unknowable questions, Stu Ramey had the perfect answer: his new pal and the reason he now had his own place—his AI, Frigg, thirty miles away, in the rack-lined man cave in his not yet fully occupied home in Sedona. Firing up his Bluetooth, he summoned her.

"Good afternoon, Stuart," Frigg said, "happy Friday. I hope you've had a pleasant day."

When Frigg had first come into his possession, he'd had to work hard on toning down the formality with which she addressed him. Having swung too far toward casual for a while, they now seemed to have arrived at a happy medium.

"I need you to look up someone for me," he told Frigg. "I'd like to see what you can find out about someone named Alexandra Munsey. She's a friend of Ali's from California who was murdered recently. I'm just curious, is all. I'd like to know what happened to her."

"Of course, Stuart," Frigg said. "I'll get right on it. Do you want me to send my findings to your Bluetooth?"

"No," he replied. "I'm going to be here most of the night. Send whatever you find to CC2."

CC was short for Command Central, the venerable Apple desktop that Owen Hansen had designated to be the AI's original user interface. Stu had created CC2, a much newer laptop that served as a system image of everything on the desktop and something Stu kept with him at all times these days. As for telling Frigg where "here" was? That wasn't necessary. Frigg's device-location capabilities kept the AI apprised of the locations for both CC2 and the Bluetooth at any given moment.

"Do you require anything else at this time?" Frigg asked.

It was still weird to find himself conversing with what he knew full well was a computer program. "No," he said. "That's all I need. Thanks."

"You're welcome."

For a while Stu sat there keeping an eye on the slow progress of the upload, but soon notifications began showing up on the laptop. He hadn't asked for a deep dive into Alexandra Munsey's background. He had wanted information on the homicide itself, and that's what Frigg provided—recent bits and pieces of information culled from public sites on the Internet. News briefs described the initial discovery of the body, the subsequent identification of the victim, and overviews of the progress of the investigation—including the names of the detectives involved. There was an early mention of there being a person of interest in the case, which probably indicated that investigators suspected that either a husband or boyfriend, current or former, might be responsible for the crime.

The details seemed sketchy. It appeared that someone had paid a visit to the victim's house and then simply gunned her down just inside the front door without any evidence of a physical confrontation before taking her life. One paragraph in particular caught Stuart's attention:

> An anonymous source close to the investiga-
> tion, speaking without authorization, said that
> Ms. Munsey's death has the appearance of a
> hit of some kind rather than a crime of passion
> or a robbery gone bad. When asked about this,
> however, the detectives involved would neither
> confirm or deny.

"So what do you think about that?" Stu asked Frigg, knowing she would be aware of which file was currently pulled up on his screen. "Is this a hit or not?"

It was a testimony to Owen Hansen's computer genius that Stuart could speak to Frigg in a conversational fashion and elicit an equally conversational response. And since Frigg had been extensively schooled in all aspects of criminal behavior, who better to ask?

"A hit," Frigg replied at once.

"So who put out the hit?" Stuart asked. "The ex-husband?"

"Unlikely," Frigg answered. "Ms. Munsey's former

husband is Jake Munsey. Since he is listed as cohosting both the memorial service and the subsequent reception, that would suggest an absence of conflict between him and the victim. Most of the time, individuals directly involved in homicides choose to absent themselves from participating in public funeral activities, although occasionally they hover in the background gloating while at the same time appearing to be sympathetic."

Stuart scrolled forward until he located the file containing the text of a paid funeral announcement indicating that a public reception at the funeral home would immediately follow the service. An invitation-only private gathering would be held later at a separate address. Frigg supplied a notation that the second address led back to Jake and Nancy Munsey, Alex's former husband and someone who was most likely his current wife.

"Right," Stu muttered, more to himself than to Frigg. "In order to pull off a reception like that, you'd have to be a really good actor."

"Mr. Munsey is a CPA operating his own PLLC," Frigg said. "Nothing in either his educational background or his work history indicates an interest in the theater arts."

"Wait," Stu said. "That makes it sound as though you're already analyzing potential suspects?" He was joking. Frigg was not.

"Examining the possibility of Mr. Munsey's participation was a logical course of action to take," she replied primly.

Considering Frigg's extensive background and understanding of criminal behavior, it was hardly surprising that she would be curious about solving the case. That's what AIs were intended to do—to solve problems, and an open case of homicide was a problem in need of a solution. And since said homicide victim was a friend of Ali's, wouldn't helping solve the crime be a help for her as well?

Stu thought about that for a moment. Since reactivating Frigg, Stu had been at work identifying and removing what he thought to be the bulk of the AI's sketchier capabilities. Still, even if she used a few of her officially unsanctioned functions, it might be interesting to see what she could bring to bear in this instance.

"Okay, Frigg," he said at last. "Let's see what you can do about all this."

"You're authorizing a deep dive into Alexandra Munsey's background?"

"I guess I am," Stu confirmed with a laugh, "but do me a favor. Try to keep from landing me in jail in the process."

A notice showed up on one of Stu's screens indicating that the front security shutters had been opened by Cami using her key card. Moments later the aroma of hot pizza preceded her down the hallway. Cami was walking into the lab, pizza in hand, when an alarm sounded, and they both knew at once what that meant. The download had crashed. For the next several hours, the pizza sat forgotten and growing cold on the desk while they searched through the new GPUs trying to figure out which one had failed.

At 5:00 A.M. they finally located the faulty GPU, removed it from the network, and reinitiated the upload. At that point Cami packed it in and went home, while Stu staggered into his soon-to-be-former studio to grab some sleep.

As for Frigg? Since no one had bothered to tell her to stop working, the AI kept at it, all through the night.

38

It wasn't until late Friday night that Hannah finally found the funeral notice giving her the details on Alexandra Munsey's funeral. The fact that it was going to be held on Sunday didn't give her much time to prepare, especially since it was being held in Sherman Oaks—at least an eight-hour drive from Folsom. It wasn't a trip Hannah could undertake on her own.

A few months earlier, when she'd renewed her driver's license for the first time, she'd passed the tests—written, driving, and vision—with no difficulty at all. Even so, the high-handed bitch at the DMV had said that, due to her advanced age, she was restricting Hannah's license to daytime driving only with no freeway driving allowed. What Hannah needed more than anything right then was a car and a dependable driver, and when it came to drivers, there was no one she trusted more than Marco Gregory.

She still stayed in touch with Marco and Bettina, always exchanging Christmas cards and faithfully remembering their birthdays. They were nice to her because that's the kind of people they were. She had added a codicil to her will with a relatively small bequest to Gloria, with the verbal understanding that in Hannah's absence those funds were to be held on account and managed by Gloria's uncle for Eddie's benefit. Other than that the Gregorys remained her only heirs. By seven the next morning, she was on the phone with Marco.

"I need to come to a funeral in L.A.," she said when he came on the line. "If I flew in from Sacramento this afternoon, would you be able to pick me up at the airport and get me to my hotel and then drive me to the funeral tomorrow?"

"Absolutely, Mrs. Gilchrist," he told her. "I'll have to make some adjustments in my schedule, but I'm happy to do that. Do you prefer the Rolls? I usually trot it out only for special events, but if that's what you'd like . . ."

"No, no," Hannah said hurriedly. "For this I think something a little less ostentatious might be in order."

"All right, then," he said. "I have a nice Lincoln MKT that should do the trick. Let me know what airline and what time."

"I'll get back to you on that once I know."

She had just hung up when her phone rang again, and she was surprised to see Gloria Reece's phone number in caller ID.

"You canceled your appointment for today," Gloria said accusingly when Hannah picked up.

"Yes, I did," Hannah replied. "I have other plans."

"What other plans?" Gloria demanded. "You're not still expecting to attend Alex Munsey's memorial service, are you? We don't think that's a good idea."

Obviously Eddie had gone crying to Luis about Hannah's plans for the funeral, and Luis had dispatched Gloria with orders to get Hannah back in line. Good luck with that!

"Really," Hannah bristled. "Who exactly is 'we'?"

"Your son, my uncle, and me—all three of us," Gloria answered. "Right now the investigation into the 'event' seems to be focused in another direction, and we'd like to keep it that way. Your sticking your nose in at tomorrow's funeral might raise suspicions and cause someone to come looking at us. You could end up jeopardizing everything."

Hannah didn't know the full extent of the criminal enterprise Luis Ochoa operated from his locked cell inside the razor-wire-topped walls of Folsom Prison, but she suspected that she and Eddie weren't Luis's only cash customers. As for his niece? Gloria counted as little more than a glorified courier—and probably one of many. Hannah Gilchrist wasn't accustomed to taking orders from people she regarded as hired help, and she was in no mood to let Gloria's latest reprimand go unchallenged.

"You're all entitled to your opinions," Hannah replied, "and I'm entitled to mine. I have no intention of taking orders from you or anyone else, my son included. I'm entirely capable of making up my own mind about what I will and will not do. I've devoted the last five years of my life to doing Eddie's bidding, and I've done so in a way that has no doubt contributed to the well-being of you and your entire family. Going to that memorial service is something I'm doing for my own well-being, and I have no intention of depriving myself of that simply on your say-so."

With that she ended the call. After making her flight and hotel reservations, Hannah called Marco back to give him her ETA. All of that handled, she turned off her phone. She'd made up her mind to go to the funeral. She wasn't about to change her plans, and she had no desire to listen to any further comments from the peanut gallery.

39

Inmates inside Folsom Prison were not allowed access to cell phones—at least most of them weren't. They weren't supposed to have designated tables in the mess hall either, but Luis Ochoa was an exception to both those rules. Gloria purchased burner phones. Whenever a replacement was required, she handed the item off to one of Luis's pet guards, who was happy to make the delivery. The phones gave Luis access to the Internet and unfiltered news from the outside world. He surfed the Net usually under cover of darkness, and when he needed to consult with Gloria, texting worked better than talking. In the wee hours of Saturday morning, as soon as he saw the funeral notice for Alex Munsey, Luis sent out an SOS to Gloria.

Party is Sunday in L.A.
E. thinks H. is going. Do
you know?

Don't know, but I'll
check. What should I do
if she is?

Since she's no longer
taking instructions from

E. I'm worried she's
about to go off the rails.
Could be real bad for
business. See if you can
talk some sense into her.
Otherwise you'll have to
fix it.

Will do.

Gloria knew that when Uncle Luis wanted her to fix
something, he didn't mean patching it together with duct
tape or Gorilla Glue. By seven thirty the next morning,
having just finished that very testy phone conversation
with Hannah, Gloria sent Luis another text.

H. is not just going off
the rails. She IS off the
rails.

You talked to her?

Tried to, but she wasn't
listening. She's going,
come hell or high water.
She went all up in my
face. Told me where to
go. If she decides to
get too chatty, we're in
trouble, because she
knows way too much.

Like I said before, fix it,
the sooner the better.

While she's down in
L.A.?

Nothing noisy in
Sherman Oaks. Give
my old buddy Tank a call.
He's better at
staging believable
scenarios than
anybody I know.

Whatever we do will
probably have to happen
at the funeral home,
either before or after the
service.

You're a big girl.
Figure it out
and do what you
have to do.

H. is E.'s meal ticket.
What if he ends up
turning on us, too?

It may be time to cut
him out of the herd.
You take care of H. I'll
handle E.

When the text session ended, Gloria erased the thread, and no doubt Luis did the same. Luis had tried to be vague, but he probably was not vague enough. They'd both said more than they should have. Gloria knew that erasing their conversation meant nothing, since it probably still lingered somewhere out there in the cloud. If law enforcement really went digging, they'd be able to retrieve every word. That's why Luis was absolutely right about taking care of Hannah Gilchrist sooner rather than later.

Gloria paused for a moment, trying to get her head around the task at hand. This was a rush job, and the problem with rush jobs was that you couldn't phone them in. Someone had to be on the scene to take charge—calling the shots and making the tough decisions if things went sideways. In this case the person in charge had to be none other than Gloria herself. Flying down would have made for a quick trip, but Gloria didn't want to risk running into Hannah at the airport. Instead she would have to drive eight-plus hours to get there.

Gloria took a fast shower. Then, playing to her audience, she dressed in a pair of too-tight jeans topped by a low-cut tank top and a denim jacket. Once she had her clothing packed, she went downstairs to the converted wine cellar that served as Uncle Luis's armory and safe-deposit box. The guy Luis had suggested she use for the job—Johnny "Tank" Rowland—might have been known to her, but he also qualified as outside talent—expensive outside talent. With that in mind, she picked up more than enough cash to cover the job. After stuffing that into a duffel along with her clothing, she went over to the gun shelves and picked out a pistol, a Ruger LCP, along with a small-of-back holster. Tank was more or less trustworthy, but one of his underlings might try to play cute with her. With all that cash along, Gloria wanted to be prepared.

By eight fifteen she was in the car and headed west toward Sacramento, thinking and mulling the problem as she went. When it came to wet work, Tank had a reputation, and he was also Luis's first choice. Personally Gloria would have preferred to use the cousins from Bakersfield. They had carried out both the Kaitlyn Holmes hit and Alex Munsey's without leaving behind a single trace of incriminating evidence at either scene. The problem was, the cousins weren't right for this job. They routinely did extensive planning before carrying out a hit, and this one, of necessity, had to be done not only on the fly but also with very limited intelligence.

When it came to knowledge about what Hannah planned to do in L.A., Gloria had squat. Hannah intended to make an appearance at Alex Munsey's funeral—that was it. Gloria knew the location for that, as well as the service's start time and approximate end time. As for the old woman's plans for before or after the service? Gloria had no idea. Where she was staying was a complete mystery, as were her transportation arrangements. Would Hannah show up at the funeral driving herself in a rental car? Maybe she'd opt for a limo service or perhaps even an Uber. Taking all those unknowns into consideration, Gloria's participation was essential in carrying out the mission. She was the only one who would be able to identify the target and point the assailants in the right direction.

At nine Gloria phoned her answering service. Saying she'd been called out of town by a family emergency, she had them cancel her next three days' worth of appointments. Only then did she place the call to Tank Rowland.

Tank and Uncle Luis had met and become friends years earlier, when they'd both been in juvie. When they were in their twenties, their paths had diverged. Uncle Luis had earned his "life without" sentence for murdering both his ex and her new boyfriend, while Tank, on the other hand, had reinvented himself and taken up what was ostensibly a respectable line of work, first in car sales and later as a car dealer of sorts.

He supposedly made his fortune dealing in high-end secondhand vehicles, using cash on the barrel to help financially strapped owners get out from under their overpriced sales contracts and leases. In fact, it was through just such a deal with Tank that Gloria Reece had ended up with the Range Rover she was currently driving. But Tank's other line of work—his real moneymaker—was a full-service chop shop operating out of a scuzzy warehouse near the docks in San Pedro, where stolen vehicles could be stripped of their GPS locating devices and reduced to a collection of valuable spare parts within a matter of minutes.

"Why, Gloria, sweetheart," Tank gushed when he heard who was on the phone. "How's that new ride working out for you?"

"It's fine," she said. "I'm driving it and heading your way right now."

"You in the market for another one?"

"Nope, but I need your help, though. I'm looking for a couple of day laborers to do some work for me tomorrow."

"What kind of work?"

"Serious work—for Uncle Luis."

"Speaking of him, how's my good friend Louie doing these days?"

"About the same," Gloria said. "Things don't change much for him, but he keeps himself busy, and that's what this is all about."

"I see," Tank said, "so maybe we should discuss this in person instead of by phone. Why don't you stop by the house when you get to town? We can have a drink and a bite to eat, hash out the details, maybe have a little fun afterward."

Gloria knew exactly what kind of fun he had in mind, and she was fine with that and was in fact dressed for that very contingency. When she'd gone to bed with him before, he'd given her a surprisingly large discount on her car purchase. In addition, staying with Tank in his upscale Malibu digs would be better for her than checking in to a hotel, where she'd end up leaving a paper trail and have to deal with avoiding countless security cameras. Tank's uppity neighbors—people who would have been appalled had they known the details of his real background—would have security cameras, too, but they wouldn't be capturing her face. Hers would be just another Range Rover in an area where Range Rovers were thick on the ground.

"Sounds like a deal," she told him.

"What time will you get here?"

"I'll pull off at the next rest area and put your address into the GPS," she said. "Once I have an ETA, I'll let you know."

40

When Stuart Ramey awakened, it was three o'clock in the afternoon. He could hear voices outside in the computer lab and was able to ascertain from listening that both Cami and B. were in the other room. His packed clothing was still there, loaded into boxes and ready for his stalled move, so after starting a pot of coffee he showered and changed into clean clothes. Fortunately, there was one remaining piece of leftover pizza in the box. He gobbled that down. Then, with coffee in hand, he ventured into the lab.

"How's it going?" he asked.

"Good afternoon, sleepyhead." Cami grinned at him. "It's about time you climbed out of bed."

"How are our newbies working out?"

B. answered without taking his fingers off his keyboard or his eyes off his monitor. "They're great," he said. "You guys did a terrific job with both the install and upload. Once you got rid of that one faulty blade, everything seems to be working well. As far as I'm concerned, the two of you are welcome to take off. With Ali out of town, I can stay here as long as necessary to finish fine-tuning the connections."

"I can stay, too, if you'd like," Stu offered.

"Not necessary," B. replied. "I know for a fact that both you and Cami have put in way more hours this week than you should have. And what about your move? I thought you would be out of here and into the house in Sedona by now."

"That was the plan," Stu said, "but a few other things came up in the meantime."

"Which you two took care of quite admirably," B. told him. "But right now I want you to look out for you and get that move handled once and for all."

"Okay, then," Stu said, turning back the way he had come. "I guess I'll go get started."

"How much do you have left to do, and would you like some help?" Cami offered. "As you've already learned, I'm pretty good when it comes to hauling boxes around."

"Not a whole lot," Stu said. "Clothes and shaving kit. That's about it, except for my computer collection, that is."

Stu's extensive computer collection was hardly a small matter. He had been collecting computers of all sizes, shapes, and pedigrees for years. Their boxes filled most of the studio's generous closet space and were stacked floor to ceiling along the back wall of the main room.

"What about food? Have you done any grocery shopping yet?"

"No," Stu admitted. "Haven't quite gotten around to buying groceries."

"That's about what I thought," Cami said. "So we'll do one load only of whatever will fit into your truck and my Prius. After that we'll go grocery shopping so I can give you your first cooking lesson."

"Appreciate the help," Stu said grudgingly, "but I'm not so sure about that cooking lesson."

After Stu decided to buy the house, Cami had done most of the strategic planning. Never having owned a house before, he'd been at a loss as to what he would need, what it would look like, or where it would go. Cami, with an instinctive eye for interior design, had sat him down in front of a free-shipping furniture Web site and walked him through the entire process, helping him select everything—indoor furniture, outdoor furniture, rugs, linens, pots and pans, silverware, and dishes. Because the house was being sold by B., they'd been able to have most everything delivered and put in place well before closing. When it came to sorting out Stu's new kitchen, Cami had gone looking for equipment that would wean him away from his total dependence on carry-out dining. She was eager to help him start cooking for himself, and in order to do that he needed groceries.

While Cami went to retrieve a dolly, Stu returned to the apartment. As he did so, he realized he hadn't heard anything from Frigg. That was unusual. Most mornings she provided him with a cheery wake-up call. Walking by his bedside table, he understood why. Both of his iPhones as well as his Bluetooth were lying right there. None of the pieces of equipment was on its respective charger, and they were all out of juice. No wonder Frigg was maintaining radio silence.

As soon as he put his Frigg iPhone on a charger, it started pinging with incoming messages. When he opened the CC2 laptop, he was greeted by a flashing red message, one of Frigg's "howlers," that filled the whole screen.

WHERE HAVE YOU BEEN?

Frigg had been carefully taught that human interaction needed to be conducted with a certain degree of civility. She usually began with a polite inquiry about his health or about how he'd slept. That was definitely missing here. Stu had gone AWOL on her, and obviously his AI was pissed.

> Sorry about that. We had a network crash. By the time Cami and I finished up, I was so tired that I fell into bed without charging my devices. Why? What's up?

Where is Ms. Reynolds right now?

> Ali? She's either in California or on her way there. She's supposed to speak at a funeral tomorrow afternoon. Why?

Alex Munsey's funeral, correct?

> Yes, why? What's going on?

In that case I believe we need to move

Ms. Reynolds's threat
level from green to
orange.

One of Frigg's major responsibilities for her cre-
ator had been making and delivering threat assessments for Owen Hansen. These days, when people
from High Noon were out on the road, and especially
when B. was gallivanting around the globe, Stu fed
all travel arrangements into Frigg. That way, in case
of a crisis, whether a natural disaster or some kind of
terrorist activity, Frigg could spot the problem early on
and provide assistance in terms of making alternative
arrangements. Stu didn't remember giving Frigg the
information about Ali's heading for California, but he
must have done so.

Cami swooped into the room just then, pushing the
same dolly they'd been using all week long while moving crates of computers. "What's going on?" she asked.

Stu shook his head and motioned for her to be quiet.

What are you getting
at? Tell me. Switch the
display over from CC2 to
the wall monitor here in
Cottonwood. Cami just
showed up. Whatever
you have, she'll want to
see it, too.

Good afternoon,
Ms. Lee. I hope you're
having a pleasant day.

Cami rolled her eyes, but Frigg's pointed polite-
ness demanded the same in return. "Tell her thank
you."

> She says thank you.
> Now, tell us!

You asked me to look
into the Alex Munsey
homicide. In doing so
I located information
about the memorial
service, but I've found
several things that are
very concerning.

> Like what? Walk us
> through it.

I found some question-
able video footage.

> Video footage from
> the homicide? My
> understanding is that
> it happened in the
> middle of nowhere, in
> an area with no video
> surveillance available.

Not footage of the
homicide itself, but
possibly related to the

homicide. The footage
has both audio and
video components,
although the sound
quality is defective. We
are in the process of
remastering the sound.
In the meantime I can
send you what we have.

Okay, I'm turning on the
CC2 speakers. Show us
what you've got.

When the monitor came on, the video was some
sort of interior shot with two people—a man and a
woman—displayed on a split screen. Each of them
held what appeared to be a black landline telephone receiver. The man in the left-hand screen was gray-haired
and probably in his sixties. Since he was dressed in an
orange jail-type jumpsuit, this was obviously a lockup
facility of some kind. On the right was a reserved and
properly attired woman wearing a dark blazer and a
high-necked white blouse. At the base of her throat
was an old-fashioned cameo brooch.

"What are we seeing here, and where are we?" Stu
asked.

"Looks like a prison visitation room," Cami supplied.

"That is correct, Ms. Lee," Frigg said, "specifically
the visitation room in Folsom State Prison. The individual on the left is Edward Gilchrist. The person on
the right is his mother, Hannah Anderson Gilchrist."

"Wait just a minute here," Stu blurted out. "Don't

tell me that you've hacked into a prison's interior surveillance system!"

"It was quite simple, really," Frigg replied. "The state has dumbed down the password to make it easy for everyone to remember. Fido was able to unscramble it with very little difficulty. One moment while I fast-forward."

As the images sped by, allowing glimpses of the same two people, Stu shook his head in frustration. When Frigg had come into his possession, he'd begun the process of isolating and removing some of her more questionable programs, her "pet programs," as he had called them. Now, not only had she found a work-around for at least one of those forbidden programs, she had given it a petworthy name. Eventually Stu would need to dispose of Fido, too, but at this point, for good or ill, the damage was done. When Frigg hit the pause button and it was time for Stu to speak again, he made no effort to disguise his growing irritation.

"Look, Frigg," he grumbled, "the murder I asked you to investigate happened sometime within the last two weeks, so why are you showing me surveillance footage—illicit surveillance footage, by the way—of someone who's already in prison for some other crime and has been there for years? The time stamp here says we're looking at images recorded in 2013."

"When I researched material on the Alexandra Munsey homicide," Frigg explained, "I found any number of references to an earlier homicide case, one that went to trial in 2012 and resulted in this individual, Edward Anthony Gilchrist, being sentenced to life in prison without the possibility of parole. At your suggestion I have been making a systematic study of English language aphorisms. I believe the one that's most applicable here is something about avian creatures with similar markings preferring to remain in close proximity to one another."

"Yes, yes," Stu said impatiently. "You mean, birds of a feather flock together?"

"Exactly," Frigg said, "birds of a feather. I wanted to see if something similar might be occurring here—if one murder or murderer might be connected to another."

"And what did you discover?"

"Please watch and listen," Frigg replied as the video resumed. As she had said, the audio portion was difficult to make out, and watching the video portion was a frustrating process, not unlike trying to watch an online movie with the action being constantly interrupted by long periods of buffering. A few words would be spoken followed by extended periods of silence. At first Stu thought that the recorder wasn't functioning properly, but then he realized that there were some changes in facial expressions during the silences. Occasionally a stray hand gesture or two would appear at the bottom of the frame.

"What's the point of all this?" Stu asked. "From the little I can hear, they seem to be discussing pretty ordinary day-to-day stuff. I'm surprised the prison system would bother keeping it."

"They keep all of it," Frigg said. "It's stored in a library, with each prisoner's file footage saved separately. But if you look closely, you'll see that what they're saying aloud isn't all they're saying."

"What do you mean?"

"They're using sign language in those long silences when they're not speaking aloud," Cami interjected. "One of my classmates at UCLA was deaf, and they brought in a sign-language interpreter for all her classes."

"That is correct, Ms. Lee," Frigg replied. "I believe they're communicating by way of a nonstandard form of sign language. I can read both BSL and ASL. What they're using appears to be a shorthand version that requires the use of one hand rather than two, thus allowing each of them to hold the telephone receiver with one hand while continuing to sign with the other."

"What about those odd facial expressions?" Stu asked.

"Those appear to be part of the conversation as well. I have fed all the footage into the system, and my assets are currently attempting to locate the most common words."

"In other words, Code Breaking 101," Stu said. "Has anyone at the prison figured this out or noticed that something fishy was going on?"

"I don't believe so," Frigg replied. "I've checked through other files in addition to this one. When questionable footage is discovered, in either audio or video form, it is always flagged for future reference. So far there are no flags showing on any of the material I've found on Mr. Gilchrist."

"Anything else interesting about this?" Stu asked.

"Mr. Gilchrist has been incarcerated in Folsom State Prison since January of 2013. Prior to that, and between his arrest in 2011 and his conviction in 2012, he was held in the Santa Clarita jail. While in jail he had numerous visits from a Mr. Calvin Wilkins from the law firm of Wilkins, Wilkins and Clancy. There were some visits from the law firm early on in his stay at Folsom. Other than his attorneys, Mr. Gilchrist's only visitor has been the woman you see here—his mother, Hannah Gilchrist."

Stuart sighed as his fading patience took another direct hit. Obviously Frigg's pal Fido had penetrated the Santa Clarita visitor logs and their prisoner recording system as well. Clearly Fido had to go.

"Okay," he said, "so whatever's going on involves Gilchrist and his mother. This is all very interesting, but it's also ancient history. How about if we come back to the present homicide? What have you learned about that?"

"Wait," Cami interjected. "If Gilchrist and his mother are carrying on secret conversations designed to evade surveillance, don't we need to take a closer look at this? Shouldn't we find out what they're discussing?"

"Exactly, Ms. Lee, but first allow me to address Stuart's concerns. Here's what I've assembled so far on the Munsey homicide."

When the monitor lit up with a new chain of files, Stuart began clicking through them, starting with an obituary that had been posted just that morning. That was followed by numerous news articles and clips done by local media, reporting on the homicide. But on the far side of that, Stu discovered something that brought him up short again. This time Frigg had managed to obtain copies of actual police reports as well as investigative notes from the detectives working the case.

Stuart was thunderstruck. None of that confidential information should have been accessible to the public. It could only mean that Frigg had penetrated the San Bernardino Sheriff's Office as well. How the hell was she doing it?

"Frigg," he said in exasperation, "what the hell are you thinking?"

"Excuse me, Stuart," Frigg said. "I noticed audible stress indicators in your speech pattern just now. Have I somehow offended you?"

"Yes, I'm offended. We don't have permission to access internal sheriff's-department documents. In addition, you have no business analyzing my speech patterns."

"I find it helpful in gauging how I should frame my response."

"Here's an idea," Stuart growled, "gauge this. Hacking into confidential police records is illegal, yet you've been wandering through them with wild abandon and forwarding that improperly obtained material to my computer. Having said material in my possession means I'm breaking the law, too. I thought I told you up front that I didn't want to end up in jail."

"You can always exercise Command D and delete the material permanently. When you do that, it's gone."

"Done!" Stu said, punching Command D. "The problem is, I can delete it until the cows come home, but I sure as hell can't unsee it. Now, what in God's name does any of this have to do with changing Ali's threat assessment?"

"You asked me to do a deep dive into Alexandra Munsey's death, but I ended up diving into her life as well. Every time I encountered a new name, I initiated the creation of a separate dossier on each of those individuals."

"And you found what?" Stu asked.

"Three people involved in Edward Gilchrist's homicide trial are deceased—two prosecution witnesses, Leo Aurelio and Kaitlyn Holmes, along with Ms. Munsey, whose participation was limited to delivering a victim-impact statement during his sentencing hearing."

"Okay," Stu said. "I can see that three people involved with the trial are dead, but what does that have to do with Ali?"

"Edward Gilchrist went to prison for murdering his ex-wife, who was expected to testify against him in a lawsuit brought by several of his former patients. That lawsuit had been spearheaded by three individuals— Cassie Davis, Jolene Browder, and Alex Munsey. Jolene and Alex are both dead, one an apparent murder victim and the other one possibly of natural causes."

"And the third?"

"Cassie Davis is retired and living in Mesa."

"What about Ali?"

"She was the catalyst that brought that initial group into being in the first place."

Cami was the next to speak. "If Gilchrist and his mother are clearing the decks of people involved in his going to prison, what's to stop them from coming after Ali and after Cassie Davis, too?"

"Exactly," Frigg said.

Stu was already on his feet and headed for the other room. "Thank you, Frigg," he said over his shoulder. "Please line up whatever material you've collected. I'm going to go get B. He needs to hear this."

41

B. is here now, Frigg," Stu announced a few moments later. "Show us what you've got."

"Good afternoon, Mr. Simpson," Frigg said. "I hope you're having a pleasant day."

"I *was* having a pleasant day, but that's no longer the case," B. replied. "If Ali and this other woman are really in danger, we need to let them know, so let's get on with it."

"Stuart," Frigg said, "before we proceed, would you like me to begin by recalling the material on Ms. Munsey that was previously deleted?"

"No," Stuart said. "Let's see the story in chronological order."

A copy of Jolene Browder's death certificate appeared on the monitor. "There appears to be little out of the ordinary here," Frigg supplied. "Her death in 2005 is much earlier than the others, and as you can see, her manner of death is listed as natural causes. She died of congestive heart failure while in a hospital and under the care of a physician. No autopsy was performed. Ms. Browder was connected to Ms. Munsey through an organization called the Progeny Project. Her death may not be related to the others', but I've included it here for completion's sake."

"Who's next?" B. asked.

"One moment," Frigg said.

Seconds later the monitor displayed video footage of a visitation room. "This is the visitation room at Folsom State Prison," Frigg stated. "Edward Gilchrist is on the left side of the screen. His mother, Hannah Gilchrist, is on the right," she explained for B.'s benefit. "This is the first time she came to visit her son after his incarceration there. I'll need to fast-forward."

When the image slowed, Edward Gilchrist's hand was moving.

"Leo," Cami said aloud. "He just signed the name Leo."

"Yes," Frigg agreed. "This is early in the process—2013. They had not yet fully developed the one-handed signing method. I interpreted that sign just as you did—Leo—and since there was already someone named Leo in the Munsey database system, I created a timeline. Mr. Aurelio and Mr. Gilchrist were both involved in the death of Mr. Gilchrist's former wife Dawn. Once convicted, they were held in separate facilities—the former in Corcoran State Prison and the latter in Folsom. Most of the time Mr. Aurelio was held in what is referred to as protective housing. He was Mr. Gilchrist's hired hit man. In return for a reduced sentence, Mr. Aurelio agreed to testify for the prosecution during Mr. Gilchrist's trial."

"Which explains why Aurelio was held in protective housing," B. surmised. "He was a snitch."

A series of images appeared on the screen, handwritten notes, but the images were too blurry for the people in the room to make out the words. "What are these?"

"Letters from Hannah Gilchrist written to Mr.

Aurelio. She started corresponding with him shortly after her son's trial ended and continued to do so the whole time Mr. Aurelio was locked up. The prison makes photocopies of all incoming mail just as they maintain recordings of all telephone conversations and in-person visits. I'll be able to send you enhanced copies of these shortly, but Hannah seems to be encouraging him to take classes and work on completing his education. Due to overcrowding, prison officials removed him from protective housing early in 2016. Within a matter of weeks, he was dead."

The next image that appeared on the screen was Leo Aurelio's death certificate. "Please go to the lines dealing with manner of death and cause of death. He was found hanging in his cell. Initially his manner of death was listed as suicide. Two months later, when the toxicology report came in, the finding of suicide was amended to read undetermined."

"Why?" Stu asked.

Frigg brought up the next screen.

"Fentanyl," Stu whispered aloud when he saw the word.

Suicide by fentanyl poisoning was something people at High Noon had encountered before. The report indicated that the quantity found in Leo Aurelio's body amounted to a fatal dose. "Wait," Cami said. "Go back to the death certificate." Frigg switched back to the previous screen. "If he had taken all that fentanyl, why is the cause of death still listed as asphyxiation?"

"Because he was alive when the noose went around his neck, but he might well have been unconscious," B. suggested. "That's why the manner of death is now listed as undetermined."

The next image was a showstopper—a copy of a billing statement from a funeral home covering the final expenses for one Leo Manuel Aurelio. The bill, sent from a funeral home in Corcoran, California, was addressed to Hannah Gilchrist at 45 Arbor Crest Court in Folsom, California, with a copy of it sent to the California Department of Corrections. Listed items included transport of remains, cremation, funeral urn, and cost for shipping. The ship-to address was the same as the billing address. The bill was stamped paid in full, and the method of payment was an Amex card.

"Presumably that credit card belongs to Hannah Gilchrist?" Stuart asked.

"That is correct," Frigg replied.

Stu shook his head. He didn't ask how she knew that, because he didn't want to know.

"If this was the guy who testified against Hannah's son and got him sent up for life, why would his mother pay those final expenses? Why have his cremains sent to her?"

"Maybe because she was stalking him," B. said. "Remember, 'Revenge is a dish best served cold,' and she and her son might have been playing a long game. Hannah could have befriended Leo and offered to become his pen pal as a means of keeping track of him. For all we know, Leo himself might have been the one who supplied them with the information that he was being moved out of protective housing. And what do you know! A few weeks later, the guy turns up dead in his new cell."

"So is Gilchrist on the inside directing the action while Hannah is on the outside making it happen?" Cami asked.

"That's how it looks," Stu said. "Frigg, what can you tell us about Hannah?"

"We are currently assembling our dossier on Ms. Gilchrist and will post it as soon as it is complete," Frigg replied. "In the meantime here is the information on the death of Kaitlyn Martin Todd Holmes. At one time she was Edward Gilchrist's nurse and his lover. Like Leo Aurelio, she testified for the prosecution during his homicide trial."

The collection of material that showed up next included the usual items—news clips and articles gleaned from local media outlets, Kaitlyn's death certificate, and—unsurprisingly this time—numerous police reports, including audio-only interviews with both the victim's father and her husband done the night of the accident. After a brief investigation, law enforcement determined that Kaitlyn's car had been traveling "at a high rate of speed and too fast for conditions" when it plunged off an icy roadway. She had died two nights before Christmas in what Oregonians would later refer to as the "Christmas Eve Eve Storm," a period of ferocious winter weather that had ultimately shut down Oregon's stretch of I-5 for close to twenty-four hours. Five weather-related traffic deaths were attributed to the storm, including that of Kaitlyn Holmes. By the middle of January, the investigation into her case was officially closed.

That probably would have been the end of it, but there were several additional items. In early March, Rex Martin, Kaitlyn's wheelchair-bound father, and Jack Holmes, her widower, had taken to the airways with a campaign to have the case reopened. The most telling item was a taped television interview with both men together.

"Law enforcement claims that my daughter, Kaitlyn, died in a motor-vehicle accident for which she was partially at fault. I don't believe it. I think she was murdered," Rex Martin asserted during his part of the interview. "We have reason to believe there was another vehicle traveling on McCully Mountain Road at that time, an SUV that might have forced her off the road."

"You also believe that to be the case?" the newscaster asked, turning to Jack Holmes.

"I do," he replied. "The local Grange had a volunteer chain-up gang out working that night. One of those guys, Tommy Robins, told me that a black SUV—a Toyota 4Runner—turned off Highway 26 and almost took him out while they were putting chains on Kaitlyn's minivan. At the funeral, Howie Barth, a snowplow operator, told us that an SUV with a similar description almost creamed him when it came speeding off McCully Mountain Road around nine thirty that same night. He told us about it and reported it to the sheriff's department, but nobody ever bothered to interview him."

"So why are you here?" the interviewer asked.

"I want justice for my daughter," Rex said. "If somebody knows something, please come forward and tell us."

"I understand you're offering a reward?"

Jack Holmes nodded. "That's correct. So far it's only five thousand dollars, but we're hoping to raise more."

"Good luck to you, then," the interviewer said. "Thank you for stopping by this morning."

"And that makes three," Stu said. "Leo Aurelio, Kaitlyn Holmes, and Alex Munsey. Four if you include Jolene Browder. So what do we do about Cassie Davis and Ali? Do we call them and warn them?"

"Based on how we've gathered all this information, we can't exactly call the cops," B. replied. "The thing is, we sure as hell need to let them know they might be targets, too, and Alexandra Munsey's memorial service would be a perfect place for the next hit." With that B. reached for his phone. "I'll call Ali and have her get in touch with Cassie."

Just then another image appeared on the monitor—a copy of Hannah Gilchrist's recently renewed California driver's license, one that restricted her to daytime and non–freeway driving only. Looking at the screen, B. returned the phone to his pocket without pushing the send button.

"Anything else, Frigg?" he asked.

"Ms. Gilchrist is something of a reclusive figure," Frigg replied. "She seems to maintain no social-media presence. I've been able to use facial recognition to locate her in television footage from the time of her son's trial, but I'm unable to locate any public statements or interviews. She was once active in the Friends of the Santa Clarita Public Library, but her participation in that came to an abrupt end when she sold her home there and moved to Folsom."

"How much did she sell the home for?" B. asked.

"According to Zillow the house sold in 2013 for $4.6 million," Frigg replied. "I can find no other properties listed in her name, so presumably she didn't reinvest. Units similar to hers in Arbor Crest rent for approximately $5,600 a month, so that means she's probably still sitting on a large chunk of that cash and likely far more as well."

"Are there any other children involved?" B. asked. "Any other heirs?"

"No, Edward Gilchrist is an only child."

"And he just happens to be in prison for life," Cami breathed.

"I'm not sure what the going rate on murder-for-hire is right now, but I'm guessing she may have decided to spend some of her cash to carry out a vendetta against the people she believes wronged her son," Stu said. "I get that, but where's she finding her help? She may have money to burn, but she'd need to have some serious criminal contacts to make stuff like this happen."

"Right," Cami agreed. "You can't just dial up a friendly neighborhood handyman service or look in the want ads to find someone willing to knock off a guy in prison, shove a woman's vehicle off a narrow road in the middle of a blizzard, or gun down an unsuspecting author in her own home."

"All right, Frigg," Stu said. "We need to know Ms. Gilchrist's friends and associates, and we need to know her son's friends and associates as well."

"Of course, Stuart," Frigg replied. "I'll get right on it."

"And in the meantime," B. said, "we're definitely dialing Ali's threat level up to full-on red."

42

As the sun sank in the west, Ali was sitting under an umbrella by the pool at the W Hollywood, having a contemplative glass of wine. She was supposed to be working on her eulogy, but she wasn't. She had booked into the W because it was familiar to her and she could pay with points. She knew how to get there like she knew her own name. Back in the day, the hotel had been Paul Grayson's favorite go-to place. Once upon a time, she'd been thrilled to function as his bit of arm candy while he wined and dined various celebrities and visiting dignitaries. The thrill of that had dissipated before long, and there were plenty of memories of being in the bar or one of the conference rooms when things got ugly.

That was why she'd chosen to go outside and sit by the pool rather than stay inside. She had no actual memories of the pool area, but bad vibes from the past seemed to lurk there, too, and thinking about poor Alex Munsey wasn't helping.

When her phone rang with B.'s name showing in caller ID, she was only too happy to pick up. "Hey," she said. "How's it going?"

"Are you carrying?" he asked.

Fortunately, Ali had already swallowed her last sip of wine; otherwise she might have spewed it back into the glass. It had taken a long time for B. to adjust to the fact that she was generally armed with a Taser and/or her Glock. The fact that he was even asking about it came as something of a surprise.

"As a matter of fact, I'm not," she said. "It's a three-day trip. I flew commercial and decided to do carry-on only. As you know, getting weapons of any kind through TSA these days is a nonstarter."

"Crap!" B. muttered.

His response was even more unexpected. "Why?" Ali asked. "What's going on?"

"Frigg just raised your threat level, and I'm afraid she may be right."

Ali listened in stunned silence while B. recounted the details from Frigg's earlier briefing. "So Frigg thinks that both Cassie Davis and I might be targets?"

"Yes," B. replied. "Unfortunately, we can't take any of this to the cops—"

"Because it all came from Frigg," Ali finished.

"Yes."

"And you're thinking someone might come to the funeral expecting either one or both of us to be there?"

"That, too."

"You don't need to worry about Cassie," Ali said. "I already know she's not coming."

"The one I'm really worried about is you," B. said. "I know I've not always approved of your being armed and dangerous, but this doesn't happen to be one of those times."

Ali looked around the hotel patio. There was a young family—a couple with three little kids splashing in the shallow end of the pool—while an older man, a single-minded exerciser, swam lap after lap on the far side. There was nothing out of line. Everything seemed perfectly normal. Still, Ali couldn't help feeling exposed and vulnerable. Despite the warmth of the early-evening air, she felt a flash of gooseflesh run up her legs.

"You think an assassin of some kind might show up at the funeral?" she asked.

"I do."

"So what do you suggest?"

"That we attempt to turn a soft target into a hard one," B. said.

"How?"

"I have a friend, retired Secret Service, who runs WWS, a personal-security company in L.A."

"Wait, you're proposing I go to the funeral with an armed bodyguard?"

"I am indeed!"

Ali hesitated. On the one hand, this might be an overreaction on B.'s part. On the other hand, with four people already dead maybe he wasn't wrong, but did she want to show up at her friend's funeral accompanied by a bunch of tough guys in suits?

"I can tell you're not thrilled by the idea," B. said, "but please humor me on this one, Ali. I'll text you her number."

"*Her* number?" Ali echoed.

"Sonja's number. Sonja Bjornson is the woman who owns WWS. I'll bet when I said retired Secret Service, you assumed I meant a he."

"Guilty as charged," Ali admitted.

"I've run into Sonja and some of her operatives at various conferences," B. continued. "It turns out high-profile women prefer having female security details as opposed to the other kind."

"That would be my preference, too," Ali said. "I'll give her a call. But isn't today Saturday? Would calling on a Saturday be a problem?"

"I think WWS is pretty much a 24/7 operation. Someone will be on hand to field incoming calls."

"Even though Cassie's not coming to the funeral, I'll give her a call as well," Ali added, "just to give her a heads-up. If these people were willing to travel as far as Oregon to take out Kaitlyn Holmes, there wouldn't be anything keeping them from going to Arizona as well."

"When you talk to her, be sure to mention that there was no sign of forced entry at Alex Munsey's place in Lake Arrowhead. She obviously opened the door for her attacker, so it was either someone she knew or someone she considered trustworthy."

"It sounds as though you might have gotten a look at some of those police reports."

"Yes, we did," B. admitted.

"Frigg again?"

"Frigg again," he confirmed.

"I thought Stu had gotten rid of all Frigg's dubious hacking programs."

"I think he thought so, too," B. allowed, "but for right now I'm happy as hell to have Frigg up and running and working and on our side."

By the time the call ended, the lap swimmer had left the pool and gone inside. As the family with the little kids began gathering up floaties, towels, and gear, Ali decided it was time for her to go inside, too.

If she was walking around with a target painted on her back, sitting alone on a hotel pool deck seemed like a bad idea. Up in her room, she tried dialing Sonja Bjornson's number, but the call went to voice mail after four rings. It was Saturday evening, after all, so Ali left a message:

"My name is Ali Reynolds. I believe you know my husband, B. Simpson. I'm in town to attend a funeral service tomorrow for Alex Munsey, a friend who was murdered a week or so ago. B.'s worried that whoever went after Alex might also be coming for me. I know it's late to schedule this kind of thing, but if you have any operative availability tomorrow, I'd like to hire someone."

She closed by leaving both her e-mail address and her phone number. Next up was Cassie Davis.

"Good to hear your voice again after all this time," Cassie said, "just not under these particular circumstances. I can't believe Alex is dead."

"I can't believe it either."

"Are you going to the funeral?"

"Yes, I am," Ali answered. "I'm delivering a eulogy."

"Emma's doing chemo right now," Cassie said. "It's just not possible for me to leave her alone."

Ali felt a tiny lump in her throat. She remembered the scene in the waiting room when, shortly after Rory's and Evan's transplant surgeries, Rory's parents, a long-estranged lesbian couple, had somehow found enough common ground to start making their way back to each other. She was glad to hear that a tiny moment of recovery-room détente had turned into something lasting.

"I'm sorry to hear that," Ali said. "Evan had told me Emma was ill, so I knew you weren't coming, but that's not why I'm calling. We have some concerns."

"We? Who's we?"

"I have a team up in Sedona doing some private investigating into Alex's murder. We've developed information that leads us to suspect that whoever targeted Alex might have killed at least two other people."

"Which people?"

"Two prosecution witnesses from Edward Gilchrist's homicide trial—Leo Aurelio and Kaitlyn Todd Holmes."

"And now Alex, too?"

"And maybe even Jolene Browder. That gives rise to concern that you or I might be targeted as well."

"Anybody who comes looking for me will have a fight on their hands," Cassie declared with a laugh. "Arizona is an open-carry state. I have a weapon and, believe me, I don't leave home without it. As for those supposedly 'gun-free zones,' like the ones posted in the hospital? Screw 'em. If the crooks don't pay any attention to those signs, why the hell should I be a sitting duck?"

Why indeed?

When the call to Cassie ended, Ali went back to working on the eulogy. An hour later Sonja called back. "Sorry it took me so long to return your call," she said. "There are some big doings in town this weekend, and my team of ladies is stretched pretty thin. Your message made it sound as though you wanted me to field a complete security detail. The problem is, for tomorrow I have only one asset available. Her name is Shaelyn Green. She's ex-military—young but effective. So bring me up to speed on the nature of your threat, and let's see if she fits the bill."

It took another half hour of niggling details, but by the time they hung up, Shay was scheduled to arrive at Ali's hotel at eleven the next morning to meet up and strategize. Off the phone at last, Ali ordered a room-service dinner and sent B. a text:

Sonja Bjornson lined me
up with someone named
Shaelyn Green.
I'm meeting her at
eleven in the
morning. Now I'm going
to have something to eat
and finish writing that
eulogy.

> Good. I'm relieved. I'm
> glad you called her. I
> was afraid you'd play
> stubborn and drag your
> feet.

Nope, when you're right,
you're right.

> I may be right, but I'm
> also time-zone-
> challenged. Going to
> bed now. Talk to you in
> the AM. Night.

Good night and sweet
dreams.

43

When Gloria Reece hit the city late in the afternoon, she didn't head straight to Tank Rowland's digs in Malibu. Instead she took a detour through Sherman Oaks and scoped out Noble Avenue just off Ventura. There was a coffee shop with outdoor seating directly across the street from the Longmont Funeral Home's parking lot. That would be a convenient spot from which she could function as a lookout, observing the situation and alerting members of her hit team when the time came for them to spring into action.

She had hoped for a relatively lively neighborhood. Unfortunately, this one was the exact opposite. Getting her team in and out without their being spotted would be a challenge, something she immediately addressed with Tank once she finally arrived at his house. Seated on his patio and drinking vodka tonics, she told him about the difficulties of having hit men escape the crime scene after the fact. Tank, it turned out, wasn't the least bit worried.

"My guys don't 'escape the area,'" he told her with a grin. "They simply disappear—poof, like a puff of smoke. For a hit-and-run operation like this, I've got an experienced three-man tag team. One guy drives a stolen vehicle, of which I happen to have an unending supply. The next one drives a stolen motorbike, and the third one drives a box truck with stolen license plates.

"Once the crash occurs and before the dust settles, the driver exits the stolen car, hops on the back of a motorbike, and away they go. Within a few blocks and once out of sight, they drive the bike up the loading ramp and into the truck. While everybody's still focused on the car wreck and frantically dialing 911, the third guy calmly packs up the loading ramp, closes the back gate, and drives away—easy peasy. The truck with only one person apparently on board leaves the scene and melts into traffic. It heads straight back to San Pedro, observing every posted speed limit along the way. Once inside the warehouse, both the truck and the bike get carved up into parts."

"Sounds as though you've done things like this before," Gloria observed.

Tank grinned and nodded. "I think it's safe to say that there are any number of unsolved vehicular-homicide cases in and around the Greater Los Angeles Area that might have my name on 'em."

"For a deal like this, how much are we talking about?" Gloria asked.

"Naturally, since you're working for Luis, you'll get the friends-and-family discount," he said. "You do want this target dead, right?"

"Absolutely."

"Man or woman?"

"Woman."

"Armed, do you think? It's always a good idea to know if you're messing with someone who might fight back."

"I doubt it," Gloria said. "She's in her eighties."

"And you've got no idea what kind of vehicle she'll be using?"

"None at all," Gloria said with a shrug.

"Okay," Tank said. "The best maneuver here is to T-bone the target vehicle. Side air bags can do a lot to keep people safe, so you have to make sure enough metal penetrates the body of the other car to get the job done. For that I prefer something big. We just got in a Chevrolet Suburban that should fill the bill."

"But wouldn't a car like that come equipped with On-Star or some kind of interior GPS locating technology?"

"Honey lamb," Tank said with a satisfied smile, "when my guys go car shopping these days, they always carry a GPS jammer. Once the car gets to the warehouse, I've got a guy who's a wizard at disabling the damn things. For chop-shop jobs, the GPS is the first thing to go. But my little jammer technology—privately developed, by the way—can be very useful for other kinds of work as well—like when you need to be in one place and make the cops think you're somewhere else."

"Sounds handy," she said.

Tank reached into his back pocket and pulled out a device about the size of a cell phone. "Help yourself," he said, passing it to her. "It's on the house. Takes a standard iPad charger, and all you need to do to operate it is switch it on or off."

"What about the GPS on my Range Rover? Did you mess with that, too?"

"Nope, you don't need to worry your pretty little head about that," Tank said. "I bought that one fair and square—maybe not so fair, come to think of it. The guy was in a jam and needed money real bad."

After a few more drinks, they settled on a price and Gloria counted out the money, paying the whole amount up front and in cash. That wasn't Gloria's preferred way of doing business, or Luis's either, but with someone like Tank exceptions needed to be made. Over the next hour or so, Tank made several calls, verified all necessary details, and sorted out the communications issues. Gloria was impressed by that. When it came to murder-for-hire, Tank Rowland really was a one-stop shop. His housekeeping skills, on the other hand, were far less satisfactory.

From the outside, Tank's place looked downright palatial—genuine high-end real estate, but the interior was seriously low on upkeep. There was plenty of booze but not much food. While Tank heated up a Papa Murphy's pizza, Gloria mixed the next set of drinks, generously doubling Tank's dose and lightening her own. When it was time to go to bed, the sheets weren't exactly pristine. Despite being more than slightly drunk, he must have noticed her sniff of disapproval.

"Maid quit," he explained. "I haven't had time to find a new one."

Gloria had come to Tank's house fully expecting to take a hit for the team, but that didn't include having to sleep on dirty sheets. Leaving him there, she went down the hall. Two doors away she found a bedroom where the now-departed maid had left behind a neatly made bed with freshly laundered sheets. By the time she went back to Tank's room, she found him passed out cold on the bed.

"Sometimes," Gloria Reece told herself aloud, "you really do get lucky."

44

Since B. was adamant about their taking some time off, once the phone call with Ali was over, Stu and Cami began hauling dolly after dolly of computer boxes out of the building and loading them first into Stu's dual-cab F-150 truck and then into Cami's Prius. By the time both vehicles were loaded to the max, they'd barely made a dent in the wall of boxes.

"It's a start," Cami said, turning away from the ones that were left. "We'll get the rest of them later."

On their last trip through the building, they stopped off long enough to pick up CC2. "Okay, Frigg," Stu said. "Cami and I are about to leave here and head for Sedona. I'm shutting down the living-room monitor."

"Would you like me to send updates to the Bluetooth while you're in transit?"

"Nope," Stu said. "I'm leaving that off, too. It's too distracting to listen to updates and drive at the same time."

"Very well, Stuart," Frigg said. "Drive safely."

Unsure if he wanted to hear the answer, Stu asked the next question anyway. "Are you making any progress?"

With Ali under threat, they had left Frigg alone to do her thing without any stipulations or caveats about which programs the AI could or could not use. If she came up with something actionable, the folks from High Noon would simply have to find a way to explain to law enforcement how they'd managed to obtain so much information they shouldn't have had.

"Yes, I am," Frigg announced confidently. "I believe I have identified the man who is most likely Edward Gilchrist's closest associate inside Folsom State Prison. His name is Luis Ochoa, and, like Mr. Gilchrist, Mr. Ochoa is also doing life without parole. He was sent to prison thirty-three years ago for the first-degree murder of his wife and her male companion. I've obtained details on that trial and am placing those in the dossier I'm assembling on Mr. Ochoa."

"How did you land on Mr. Ochoa?" Stu asked.

"Inmates are allowed out of their cells on a limited basis, and there are only a few places where they are permitted to mingle freely. One of those is in the mess hall, so I've studied the surveillance footage from there. Most of the tables seat five or six people at a time. Naturally, people tend to seat themselves in groups. Depending on the space available in the mess hall, those groups move from location to location. There is, however, one notable exception. One table in the far corner of the room and well away from the serving lines often has only two occupants—Mr. Gilchrist and Mr. Ochoa. Occasionally other inmates join them, but generally speaking it is as though the two of them have a private dining arrangement."

Stuart sighed. Frigg had penetrated yet another surveillance network, but this time he didn't complain about it. "How did you identify Mr. Ochoa?"

"The California Department of Corrections maintains a statewide database of incarcerated individuals, which includes mug shots that are updated on an annual basis."

This was another unapproved-of activity on Frigg's part, but Stuart didn't quibble about that, either. In order to protect Ali from a credible threat, this was information they needed, regardless of how Frigg had ferreted it out.

"The fact that those two individuals dine together in relative privacy suggests that they must wield a good deal of influence inside the prison," Frigg continued. "I'm currently researching Mr. Ochoa's background. By the time you reach Sedona, I hope to have added far more detail to his profile. Are you sure you don't want me to send updates while you're in transit?"

"Yes, I'm sure," he said. "Again, just collect the material into a file. It'll be easier for me to read it off a monitor later than to listen to it as I drive."

"Very well, Stuart, have a good trip."

Because Cami was determined to do the grocery shopping and deliver her first cooking lesson that night, they offloaded the computers into the unused part of the garage and immediately headed back out for their shopping trip. A bewildered Stuart trailed Cami through the grocery store, pushing a cart while she collected an assortment of staples, fresh vegetables, and meats, along with an amazing assortment of spices.

Partway through the store, he tried to lure her over to the deli. "Shouldn't we pick up something for dinner? The deli's mac and cheese is pretty good."

"We're not buying dinner at the deli because you're *making* dinner," Cami told him, "with some assistance, of course. In fact, you're making two separate dinners. Pork chops for tonight, cooked in your NuWave, and a Crock-Pot beef stew to have for tomorrow and the day after that."

Stuart Ramey had never cooked a meal from scratch in his whole life. He'd never cut up or browned stew meat, never peeled a potato, never chopped a vegetable, never owned a Crock-Pot or a NuWave. By late Saturday evening, under Cami's capable tutelage, all that had changed. Cami had spent enough time at her maternal grandparents' restaurant in San Francisco's Chinatown to know her way around a cutting board, and they had come home from that one trip to the store with enough ingredients to create a one-pot masterpiece. They were making good progress when they were rudely interrupted by the blaring screech of a smoke alarm.

"Is something on fire?" Cami asked.

"It's not a real smoke alarm," Stu told her. "It's Frigg pretending to be the smoke alarm. I forgot to turn my Bluetooth back on."

"Okay, Frigg," he said once he had the Bluetooth working, "now that you've got my attention, what do you want?"

Trying to keep from giggling, Cami followed Stu into the man cave.

"I have two folders that require your immediate attention," Frigg said, "one on Luis Ochoa and the other concerning Luis's niece, Gloria Ochoa Reece, the only daughter of Mr. Ochoa's late brother, Antonio."

"What does his niece have to do with anything?"

"She runs a traveling nail salon called Nails to Go," Frigg replied. "Through analyzing Hannah Gilchrist's credit-card expenditures, I've learned that for the past several years Ms. Reece has been Hannah Gilchrist's nail technician."

"Does Gloria have any kind of criminal record?"

"None," Frigg replied, "not even a traffic violation."

"So she's squeaky clean."

"She also visits her uncle at least once a month, sometimes more often."

"Okay," Stuart said. "We've got Luis Ochoa and Edward Gilchrist hanging out together on the inside, with Luis's niece and Hannah Gilchrist getting together on the outside under circumstances that appear to be totally above suspicion."

"I suggest you study Ms. Reece's folder before you turn to Mr. Ochoa's. Hers is far more interesting. According to my research, nail technicians working in Folsom, California, earn an average of twenty-three thousand dollars a year, and that is the amount reported in her IRS filings. Ms. Reece is a divorced single woman. She owns her own home—a distressed bank-owned property on Rugosa Drive, which she purchased in 2009 for one hundred fifty-nine thousand. It is now valued at three hundred fifty-four thousand and is currently mortgage-free. She is also the owner of a 2016 Range Rover."

"All of that on twenty-three thousand a year?" Cami asked. "That doesn't add up."

"No, it doesn't," Stu agreed. "She must be getting extra money from somewhere else, lots of it—money that she doesn't report to the IRS."

"Wait a minute," Cami said excitedly. "Frigg, how long has Luis Ochoa been in prison?"

"Thirty-three years, ten months, and two days," Frigg replied at once. "He received his sentence on September fourteenth, 1983."

Cami's voice was alive with excitement. "Okay," she

said. "We have four people here—Luis, Edward, Hannah, and Gloria—who are all tied in together. Luis is the hard-core criminal who's been incarcerated long enough to have private-dining-room status inside the prison and probably plenty of criminal contacts outside prison. He hooks up with Gilchrist, who's a relative newbie in the prison but who wants to get even with everyone who put him there. Hannah, Edward's mother, is the one with money to fund whatever kind of vendetta her son has in mind, and Gloria—the innocent-looking manicurist living way beyond her means—is the person who links all the others together."

"You're absolutely right, Cami," Stu marveled. "Luis is the brains of the outfit, Hannah is the banker, and Gloria's the gofer."

"Excuse me," Frigg interjected. "Why would a burrowing rodent of the family Geomyidae be involved in all this?"

"Not a G-O-P-H-E-R," Stu corrected, spelling the words aloud. "A G-O-F-E-R. That's an employee who runs errands. Gloria Reece is someone with no criminal history. As such, she can come and go as she pleases, doing pickups and deliveries without arousing any suspicion. I'm guessing she collects the money from Hannah and then makes sure it ends up in the proper hands."

"What if the Gilchrists aren't Luis Ochoa's only customers?" Cami asked. "Just a glance at Gloria's financial records tells us that there's lots of money coming and going here. I think we may have stumbled into a major criminal enterprise operating from inside Folsom Prison."

"Agreed," Stu said.

"So what should we do about it, then?" Cami asked. "Wake B. and let him know?"

"No," Stu said. "The last time I talked to him, he was running on empty and was going to grab a nap. Let's call Ali and bring her up to date. We'll let her decide on whether or not we should awaken B. In the meantime, Frigg, I want you to keep on digging."

"Of course, Stuart," Frigg told him. "Is digging considered an errand?"

"I suppose," Stu answered. "Why?"

"Does that make me a gofer, too?"

"Yes," Stuart said, "under the circumstances, I believe it does."

45

Stu and Cami called Ali a few minutes later and laid out what they had learned. "In other words, it sounds like there could be a whole team of assassins out there gunning for me—and for Cassie, too."

"Possibly," Stu agreed. "Frigg would most likely exchange that 'possibly' for a 'probably.'"

"And does B. know about this?"

"Not yet. He hit the wall and went to grab a few z's. We decided to let you make the call about whether or not to wake him up."

"Why, so he can be worried sick, too? No, leave him be and let him sleep. Now, tell me, do we have photos of any of these bad actors?"

"We have photos of the ones we know about," Stu allowed. "The problem is that in terms of sending them to you, most of the current ones are off-limits."

"Why?"

"Because they're all state-issued photo IDs—driver's licenses, Gloria Reece's beautician's license, in-prison ID photos of Luis Ochoa and Edward Gilchrist. If I send them out over the regular Internet and someone finds out, the sender is in trouble, and so is the recipient."

"In other words, once again it's all stuff Frigg has managed to access that we're not supposed to have?"

"Correct," Stu agreed. "I'm sending the exceptions

to that along to you as pdfs. Those are all older photos that Frigg culled from ordinary news-site sources. The one of Hannah Gilchrist is from 2008. The ones of Luis Ochoa and Edward Gilchrist were taken in the course of their homicide trials. Luis was twenty-two at the time; Edward was in his early fifties."

When the first text came in, Ali tapped on the pdf to open it. Once it came into view, the reproduction was grainy but she was able to make out enough of the features to recognize Hannah. "That's her, all right," Ali said. "That's how she was wearing her hair when I saw her at Edward Gilchrist's sentencing hearing—cut short with those Mamie Eisenhower bangs. My mom used to wear her hair like that. I hated it."

"What kind of bangs?" Cami asked.

"Short ones," Ali said. "Very short."

"And who's Mamie Eisenhower?"

"She was the first lady once," Ali explained, "married to President Dwight D. Eisenhower. That was long before your time. Both my mother and my Aunt Evie adored the woman."

"Frigg," Cami said. "Can you bring up Hannah Gilchrist's driver's license? And could you show us a photo of Mamie Eisenhower, please?"

"Of course, Ms. Lee, one moment."

A short time later, Cami added, "I see what you mean about the resemblance, Ali, and it looks like Hannah's hairdo hasn't changed at all over the years. She still has short bangs, and her driver's license was renewed just a couple of months ago, so that photo for sure is reasonably up to date."

"What can you tell me about Gloria?" Ali asked.

"According to her driver's license, she has brown hair

and brown eyes. She's five-six, and weighs a hundred forty pounds."

"There are a lot of people around here who would match that description, so it's not much help, but I'll manage. Thanks for the update, guys."

After the call ended, Ali sat with the phone in her hand for some time, considering whether or not to make another call. If Sonja's Shaelyn Green was supposed to provide for Ali's security, they both needed to have access to this latest information.

"Sorry to bother you again," Ali said when Sonja came on the phone. "Remember those two people I mentioned earlier who might be the source of the threat?"

"Yes," Sonja answered. "Edward Gilchrist and his mother, Hannah."

"I just found out there are two more names that should be added to that list—a guy named Luis Ochoa and his niece, Gloria Ochoa Reece. He's a lifer in Folsom Prison, right along with Edward. Those two guys, Edward and Luis, appear to be best buds, and Gloria stays in close contact with her uncle. Gloria has been Hannah's manicurist for a number of years, and according to my sources, she seems to be living far beyond her means."

"You think the four of them are in on this together?" Sonja asked.

"That's what my people back home in Sedona are telling me, and I tend to believe them." The fact that one of those "people" turned out to be an AI didn't seem especially relevant.

"You wouldn't happen to have photos of any of these folks, would you?" Sonja asked.

"I wish. I believe you can find old photos of Hannah

and Edward on the Internet, and probably Luis as well. My understanding is that Gloria is five-six and one hundred forty pounds, with brown hair and brown eyes," Ali said. "Sorry I can't be more specific."

"Not to worry, then," Sonja said reassuringly. "We'll take it from here. You get a good night's sleep."

Except a good night's rest wasn't in the cards. Ali went to bed, all right, but she couldn't sleep. Instead she tossed and turned, wondering about this seemingly deadly group of people who were supposedly coming after her. Facing down an eighty-something-year-old woman was one thing, but what about the others? Luis Ochoa, a convicted killer, was clearly a hardened criminal. Gloria Reece didn't have a record, but maybe she simply hadn't been caught. So just how dangerous was she, and how were Shaelyn and Ali supposed to fend her off, especially if they had nothing more to go on than a vague description?

It was almost five the last time Ali glanced at the clock before she finally dozed off. She was sleeping peacefully four hours later when a phone call from B. awakened her.

"Why the hell did you tell Cami and Stu not to wake me once Frigg made those connections?" he growled into the phone when she answered. "For that matter, why didn't *you* call me? If I hadn't called Stu just now to see how things were going, I'd still be in the dark."

"I made an executive decision that you needed sleep more than you needed to spend the night worrying about something completely out of your control. Besides, that way at least one of us got a decent night's sleep."

"You didn't?"

"Barely," she admitted, "and when I finally did

doze off, I had terrible nightmares about being chased through the streets by a bunch of people I didn't know who were all trying to kill me."

"Sounds about right to me," B. observed.

"But what if it's not?" Ali asked. "What if we're wrong about this situation and have worried ourselves sick about something that may never happen? What if Frigg's wrong and we've overreacted and gone to so much trouble and expense for nothing?"

"Believe me," B. said, "I'm all for this being a false alarm, and spending money to overprepare for something that comes to nothing is still money well spent. In the meantime Frigg's been busy doing some forensic accounting. It turns out Gloria Reece isn't the only member of Luis Ochoa's extended family who seems to have come into financial windfalls of dubious origin. Her mother, a widow with no visible means of support, did the same thing her daughter did. She bought a distressed condo in Vegas on the cheap and had the property completely renovated to the point that it's now appraised at three times what she paid for it. Like Gloria's property, this one is also mortgage-free. Several other cousins on the father's side of Gloria's family have also benefited substantially."

"Is this some kind of money-laundering scheme?" Ali asked.

"That's Frigg's assessment," B. said. "Luis sits in prison making illegal money hand over fist. Since he can't spend any of it himself, he doles it out in cash among his various relatives in amounts small enough that they so far have avoided attracting any attention from law enforcement."

"How much money are we talking about?"

"According to Frigg it adds up to several hundred thousand dollars," B. replied. "I think we've stumbled onto a major prison-based criminal enterprise, and although it may include murder-for-hire, there might be other components to it as well, including possible connections to drug cartels."

"So if Edward and Hannah Gilchrist are two of Luis's customers, surely they're not his only customers."

"Probably not," B. agreed.

"Now that we know about this, what can we *do* about it?" Ali asked. "If we try to bring in law enforcement, the blowback is likely to take us out right along with Luis."

"Or put us in some kind of squeeze play between the good guys and the bad guys," B. added. "We'll have to do something, but not until after you're safely home, right?"

"Right," Ali agreed. She glanced at the clock. "I'm planning to be dressed for the funeral when I meet up with Shaelyn at eleven, so I should go hit the shower."

"Take care," B. told her with an audible catch in his throat.

"I'll do my best."

46

By 11:00 A.M. Gloria had scored on-street parking and was settled in at a prime spot outside the coffee shop located directly across the street from the Longmont Funeral Home. She had dressed in jogging attire and had spent an hour walking the neighborhood—scoping out the presence of security cameras and verifying the game plan she and Tank had tentatively worked out the night before.

The funeral home was located on Noble Avenue, halfway between Ventura and Dickens Street. Ventura was lined with businesses, traffic, and multiple surveillance cameras. Dickens Street, a block away, was lined with apartments and, presumably, with far fewer cameras.

Without knowing what kind of vehicle Hannah would use and whether it would be turning right or left on Noble when exiting the funeral home's parking lot, Tank had suggested that the Suburban be parked facing north on Noble, giving the driver a straight shot toward the target and enough time and distance to achieve sufficient speed leading up to the crash. The motorbike was to be tucked into the far corner of a bank parking lot, directly adjacent to the one belonging to the funeral home. As for the box truck? Decorated with magnetic signage for a nonexistent carpet-cleaning service, that would be parked on the far side of Dickens facing east. When it was time for all hell to break loose, the wreckage, the motorbike, and the getaway car would all be located within a single block of one another.

Being on-site, Gloria had to give Tank credit. His assessments had been pretty much on the money. Now she was the one charged with making them work.

47

Sonja had asked Ali for a photo and had forwarded one of Shaelyn Green to Ali so they would each have an idea of what the other looked like. When a raven-haired beauty walked into Delphine's at exactly 11:00 A.M., Ali recognized her on sight. She was dressed in a flashy turquoise pantsuit with equally flashy silver sandals. Carrying an immense Michael Kors purse as well as an oversize Nordstrom shopping bag, the new arrival sashayed into the room like she owned the place and went directly to Ali's table.

"I'm Shaelyn, but most people call me Shay," she said, holding out her hand. "From the look on your face, I'm assuming I'm not exactly what you expected."

Ali was embarrassed to have been caught so flat-footed. "Sorry," she said. "I would have thought you'd show up looking like someone who wanted to blend in."

"Shorts and T-shirts are what I wear when I want to blend in," Shay said with a smile. "This is what I wear when I don't want to blend in. Bad guys tend to underestimate women who look like this. They're usually of the mistaken opinion that I'm perfectly harmless, and on that score they're perfectly wrong."

"So you've been out shopping?"

"Not exactly," Shay said, shoving the bag in Ali's

direction. "I keep the bag on hand to use as needed, and I brought along a little something for you."

Ali opened the bag far enough to peer inside. "Body armor?" she asked.

Shay nodded. "You'll need to try it on up in your room, but if someone gets past me and comes after you, that body armor is your second line of defense."

Wondering about the sizing, Ali examined the tag and noted that medium was probably about right. "It should fit," she said. "How did you know what size?"

"We got your height and weight off your driver's license," Shay said.

Somehow it warmed Ali's heart to know that Frigg wasn't the only entity in this fight with unauthorized access to governmental databases.

Their waiter showed up just then. At his recommendation they both ordered eggs Benedict and coffee. When he suggested champagne or mimosas, they both declined.

Shay nodded approvingly as he walked away. "Under the circumstances it's best to keep a clear head," she said. A moment later she reached into her purse and withdrew several pieces of paper. "Take a look at these," she urged.

Accepting the papers Ali found herself staring at photocopied photographs of four different people, two of whom she recognized at once—Edward Gilchrist and his mother, Hannah. Clearly prison didn't agree with him. He looked gaunt and unwell in his orange jumpsuit. At the sentencing hearing, he'd had a head of thinning reddish hair just starting to go gray. Now he was nearly bald, and what little hair he had left had turned white. Hannah, however, looked exactly the same.

"The other two are Luis Ochoa and Gloria Reece?"

Shay nodded. "These are the known members of the opposing team. I doubt any of them will show up on the ground in person, but I thought we should have a clear idea about how they all look."

Ali studied Gloria's face the longest. She didn't look particularly threatening, but Ali knew instinctively that she was in all likelihood the most dangerous. Suppressing a shiver, Ali handed the photocopies back to Shay, who returned them to her purse.

"So what's the plan?" Ali asked.

"I spent the morning reconnoitering the neighborhood around the funeral home in my blend-in clothes, just so I'd know the lay of the land. The funeral home is a block off Ventura on Noble Avenue. There are theaters and lots of restaurants in the neighborhood, so even though it's Sunday, there'll be plenty of traffic. I propose that we go in my car and time our arrival so we get there at the last minute. I'll drop you off at the front door just before the service starts and go park. Once the service is over, I'll go fetch the car and come back to pick you up."

"Drop off and pick up?" Ali asked. "Why do that?"

"Because a client's greatest risk of exposure comes when entering or exiting venues. The less time you spend hanging around outside the building, the better off we'll be. There's a lobby area just inside the front door. During the service I'll stay out there to make sure no bad actor tries to slip in or out. The manager told me that another room has been set aside for after the service itself for a reception, where light refreshments will be served. Do you want to stay for that or bug out immediately after the service?"

"I should make an appearance at the reception and stay for a while at least," Ali said. "It'll be the only chance I'll have to talk one-on-one with some of those people."

"All right," Shay said at length. "I don't like it, but we'll do it your way."

Their food came then. As they tucked in, Ali attempted to turn the conversation from the day's stressful issues. "How'd you end up in this line of work?" she asked.

"I absolutely hated school," Shay answered. "Once I was through with high school, I had no interest in going to college. My dad was US Marine Corps all the way. So was my grandfather. I signed up thinking I was going to save the world and did two tours of duty in a part of the world that didn't seem very interested in being saved. When I came home in one piece, I was looking around for work and thinking about going into law enforcement. Then someone referred me to Sonja, and I've been with her ever since. The pay's way better, and so are the uniforms."

48

Shortly after noon on Sunday, Hannah, dressed in full funeral regalia, waited for Marco Gregory in the lobby of the Sherman Oaks Hilton Garden Inn. The hotel wasn't quite the five-star accommodation she would have used in the old days, but it had served her purpose, and it was less than two miles away from the Longmont Funeral Home on Noble Avenue.

Before wearing hats had gone out of fashion, Hannah had worn them often and had maintained an extensive collection. During her downsizing move from Santa Clarita to Folsom, she had limited herself to a few of her favorites, only as many as would fit in a single hatbox. For the funeral she'd brought out a stylish black felt cloche with a brim that came down almost to her eyebrows. Peering at herself in the mirror in the lobby, she decided that the hat suited her very well. It wasn't a disguise exactly, but it gave her quite a different look.

She had left her room wearing her grandmother's cameo, but while waiting for the elevator to come, she thought better of it. Fearing it might be a telling detail someone might remember seeing earlier, she had unpinned the brooch and slipped it into her pocket.

Marco pulled up to the front entrance, parked in the driveway, and then came inside to escort her to the car.

"Madame is looking very well today," he said, smiling and offering his arm.

"Thank you," she said. "You're very kind."

He opened the back door of an idling black limo and helped her inside. She didn't know what kind of vehicle it was, and she would have preferred the Rolls, just for old times' sake, but, like the Hilton, this vehicle served the purpose and wasn't nearly as flashy. He waited until she was settled and then handed her the cane.

"I've missed you so much," she said gratefully as they drove away from the hotel.

"Thank you, ma'am," he replied. "We've missed you, too."

They pulled in under the green awning at the funeral home at twelve forty-five, an hour and fifteen minutes before the memorial service was scheduled to start.

"Are you sure you don't want me to wait for you here?" Marco asked.

"I believe waiting somewhere nearby would be better," she told him. "I'll call when I'm ready to be picked up."

"Yes, ma'am," Marco agreed. "That will be fine."

Exiting the air-conditioned vehicle into a blast of early-summer heat, Hannah made her way to the funeral home's front doors only to discover they were still locked. Even in the shade of the driveway's canopy, it was surprisingly hot. After a few imperious knocks with the handle of her cane, an employee inside—someone dressed impeccably in a suit and tie—finally took pity on her and opened the door.

"May I help you?" he asked.

"I'm here for the Munsey memorial service," she told him. "I know I'm early, but it's dreadfully hot out here. If I could just have a place to sit . . ."

"Of course," the man said, speaking in the somber tone suitable to someone in his line of work. "Right this way, please."

He led her into a chapel-like room set up with a hundred or so folding chairs. On the way inside, she collected a program from a stack on a small table next to the door and immediately slipped the precious item into her purse. The usher tried to direct Hannah to a chair nearer the front of the room, but she chose a seat in the far corner of the last row, a vantage point that would allow her to observe the other guests as they entered. At the front of the room on a dais stood a table banked with a profusion of flower arrangements. The middle of the table held a decorative bronze urn and an enlarged framed copy of Alexandra Munsey's cover photo from *The Changeling*.

Hannah watched with interest as people began filing into the room. Among the first to arrive was a couple accompanied by a small boy. She recognized the man to be Evan Munsey. She had seen him coming and going from the courtroom every day during the course of the trial. Presumably the woman was Evan's wife. But the ginger-haired child walking with them was the one who took Hannah's breath away. The family resemblance was astonishing. When he looked up to say something to his mother, Hannah saw the gap where he was missing a front tooth. That meant he was probably six or seven years old, and it was like seeing Eddie again, back when he was a sweet little kid, back before arrogance had overtaken him, back when he still loved Hannah for who she was rather than for what she could do for him.

And that's when a light went off in Hannah's head. That little boy, whoever he was, was Eddie's grandson, which meant he was also Hannah's great-grandson. By now there might be others, but this was the only one Hannah had ever seen in person—the only one! To her tremendous surprise she felt something that she hadn't felt in a long time—the first fitful tinges of regret. As the room continued to fill, Hannah's focus remained glued to that nameless boy.

She had come to the funeral intent on relishing her victory and retrieving a trophy to remember it by. Digging the program out of her purse, she read through that sought-after prize. "Survivors include son, Evan Munsey, and wife, Kathleen, of Salt Lake City, and grandson Rory Davis Munsey." For Hannah, knowing the little boy's name made everything that much worse. Having him sitting there quietly next to his parents cast everything she had done over the course of the past five years in a different light.

She had forked over the money to pay for the hit on Alexandra Munsey without so much as a second thought and strictly on Eddie's say-so. But what about the little boy sitting in the front row? The room was filling up, and now too many people separated them for Hannah to have a clear view of Rory. She knew that his mother had handed him something—a coloring book, maybe—to keep him occupied. Did he know his grandmother well enough to have any memories of her to carry forward with him for the rest of his life? That thought gave Hannah another jarring attack of conscience.

No longer able to see Rory, Hannah studied the other people gathered there. Several of the men looked spookily like Edward. Given Alex Munsey's history, that in itself wasn't so startling. Hannah supposed she had seen several of these same men before, during the course of Eddie's trial. But then a woman wearing an LAPD dress uniform slipped into the row of seats directly in front of Hannah. A glimpse of the new arrival's face caused Hannah's heart to pound in her chest. It was as though her mother, Isobel, had been reincarnated. A small gasp of surprise escaped Hannah's lips, enough so that the woman glanced curiously in her direction, but then she looked away and sat down. For several tense moments after that, Hannah worried that she'd been recognized, but nothing was said, and she was finally able to breathe a sigh of relief.

Her prediction about going unnoticed was entirely accurate. In a roomful of strangers, many of whom were directly related to her, no one paid the least bit of attention to the old woman dressed all in black, sitting next to the wall in the last row of chairs. When the memorial service started, Hannah Gilchrist began to weep, dabbing away her tears with a dainty lace-edged handkerchief. No one noticed that either, because people shedding tears at funerals was hardly out of the ordinary.

Soon other people joined in, but the tears they shed were for Alexandra Munsey and her grieving family. Hannah's tears, laden with guilt and remorse, were strictly for Hannah.

Alex Munsey was dead—Rory Davis Munsey's grandmother was dead—and it was all Hannah's fault.

49

As they drove to the Longmont Funeral Home in Shay's Acura, Ali felt cranky, and Shay picked up on her sudden change of mood. "What's wrong?" she asked.

"Let's see," Ali said. "The extra padding from the body armor makes me look fat—as though I've gained twenty pounds and outgrown my clothing."

"You look fine," Shay said.

"And I hate having to wear an earbud," Ali added. "I've never liked having anything in my ears."

"You'll get used to it, because in this case it's necessary. If something goes wrong, communication is the name of the game. I need to hear everything you say and hear, and vice versa."

"And I hate being driven around," Ali grumbled. "I'd be better off driving myself."

"You do realize that none of those things are what's really bothering you, don't you?" Shay asked.

"What do you mean?"

"You're in limbo right now," Shay explained. "Is the threat real or not? If an attack comes, what's the best move, fight or flight? If the attack doesn't come, how do you move beyond it? And because you can't control any of it, you're stressed about all of it."

"Sounds about right," Ali conceded.

"By the way," Shay added, "welcome to my world. That's what bodyguards do day in and day out. Every morning we get up and prepare for the worst, and whenever nothing bad happens, that's a good day."

"What if nothing bad happens today?" Ali asked. "What if all of this turns out to be a false alarm and totally unnecessary?"

Shay grinned at her. "Then I get paid, and you get to go home safe and sound—win/win."

Eventually the pep talk worked its magic, and by the time they pulled up under the green awning of the Longmont Funeral Home, Ali was feeling marginally better.

"Okay," Shay said, stopping mere steps from the front door. "You go on in. I spotted a couple of parking places in the back corner of the lot. I'll grab one of those and then stand guard in the lobby during both the service and the reception."

"Got it," Ali said.

When she opened the car door, it was a surprisingly short distance from there to the entrance. Only after she'd entered the building and the door closed behind her did Ali realize that she'd been holding her breath from the moment she stepped out of the car.

A moment later a man in a dark suit approached her. "You wouldn't happen to be Ms. Reynolds, would you?"

Ali froze. Here was a stranger asking for her by name. Was this it? Was the attack going to happen now, while Shay was still outside parking the car? When fight or flight kicked in, Ali landed on the former.

"Yes, I am," she said firmly, squaring her shoulders and looking the man in the eye. "What can I do for you?"

"I'm on usher duty today. Mr. Munsey asked me

to be on the lookout for you. If you don't mind, he'd like you to be seated in the front row with members of the family. If you'd care to come this way, I'll be happy to escort you there," he added, offering his arm.

"Thank you," a relieved Ali said, accepting the proffered arm.

When they entered the chapel, the room was almost full and somber organ music was playing in the background. The usher dutifully led Ali down the right-hand outside aisle to the front of the room, then directed her to a spot at the end of the first row of folding chairs. She was seated next to a red-haired boy armed with colored pencils who was busily working away on a Spider-Man coloring book. Nodding to Evan Munsey and the woman who was presumably his wife, Ali took her own seat.

"You must be Rory," Ali said, speaking quietly in his ear. "I'm Ali Reynolds."

"Did you know my Grandma Alex?" Rory asked without looking up.

"I did," Ali said. "She and I were friends."

"She gave me this coloring book for my birthday," he said. "Mommy said I could bring it today and show it to people."

"You're doing a great job of coloring," Ali said. "And it sounds like you have a smart mommy."

At that moment the man who'd be officiating—the Reverend Justin Nugent, according to the program— stepped up to the lectern, and the service got under way. After a few words of welcome and an invocation, he introduced two young women—high school girls from a nearby charter school—who had been asked to perform a duet of what Reverend Nugent said was Alex's favorite hymn, "Whispering Hope."

It was a song Ali knew and loved, too. The words scrolled through her head as she listened:

> If, in the dusk of the twilight,
> Dim be the region afar,
> Will not the deepening darkness
> Brighten the glittering star?
> Then when the night is upon us,
> Why should the heart sink
>   away?
> When the dark midnight is over,
> Watch for the breaking of day.

That's what this is all about, Ali thought. *Without the darkness, there would be no light. You have to live through the night in order to see the morning.*

When the song finished, Reverend Nugent invited Evan Munsey to step forward. As Evan stood, so did Rory Davis. Although the two nearly identical men came forward together, Rory was the first to speak.

"Most of the people in this room know that I'm the guy with two mothers, but that's not quite true, because Alexandra Munsey was, is, and always will be mother number three. She was the moving force that brought Evan and me together years ago, and she brought many of the rest of you together as well. With her help many of us have been able to unravel the mysteries of our mutual births. Alex's determined search for a donated kidney to save her own son's life is what started the ball rolling. When I donated a kidney to someone who was essentially a stranger to me back then, I hoped I was saving his life, but I had no idea that I was also gaining a best friend. And now, because that replacement kidney is still working, I'd like to introduce my friend and brother, Evan Munsey, to say a few words about his mom and mine."

As the two men hugged, a round of applause erupted throughout the room. It took a moment after that for Evan to regain his composure.

"My mom," he said at last. "As Rory said, Alexandra Munsey was a force to be reckoned with. She was a woman who never took no for an answer. She was someone who went to the mat for whatever she believed in. If she thought something was wrong, she would go the extra mile to put it right. Now that I'm a parent, I have a better understanding of how hard she fought to keep me alive when the odds and the people around her were all telling her that I was a lost cause.

"That's my dad, Jake Munsey, on the end of the aisle, and my stepmom, Nancy, is seated next to him. Although my parents raised me together, some of you may never have met my dad before today. When I was so ill, it was Mom who took up the cudgels and fought for me tooth and nail while Dad worked, paid the bills, and kept food on the table. That kind of family dynamic—one where there is an extremely ill or dying child—is a recipe for tearing people apart. My parents divorced shortly after the transplant surgery, but all of them—Dad, Mom, and Nancy—were and are decent, loving people who made peace with themselves and with one another. For years we've all celebrated holidays together, either at Dad and Nancy's house or at Mom's.

"Why am I telling you about this today? As I'm sure all of you know, my mother was brutally slain a week and a half ago, gunned down by an unknown intruder at her home in Lake Arrowhead. The murder investigation is being headed by Detective Sam Douthit of the San Bernardino Sheriff's Office. Early on there was some indication that my father, Jake, was being treated as a person of interest in the case. I spoke to Detective Douthit earlier today and was told that is no longer true, something for which I'm eternally grateful, and so is the rest of my family.

"But here's the thing: We all need justice for my mom—Dad and Nancy, Kathleen and me, Rory Davis here, as well as Rory's namesake, my son, Rory Davis Munsey. I want us to be every bit as relentless about tracking down my mom's killer as she was about tracking down that kidney. The day she died, she was coming home from a book tour that had taken her all over the country. One of you may have been in touch with her somewhere along the way, and you may have learned something that might be helpful to this case.

"If you've seen or heard something, no matter how small or seemingly insignificant, please be in touch with Detective Douthit. We don't want Mom's murder to go unsolved. We don't want her case to be one of those that goes cold. Let's bring my mom's killer to justice the same way she brought us together—by piecing all those little details together, the same way she helped us all piece together our DNA.

"Thank you."

And then it was Ali's turn. Throwing out her prepared eulogy, she decided to try to lighten the mood. "Unlike most of the people in this room, I am not related to any of you." The quip was greeted by nods of approval and a sprinkling of laughter.

"What I am is a friend of the family," she continued,

"and, more important, Alex and I were friends—not kindergarten friends or high school friends or even college friends. I guess you could say we were kidney-donation friends, because, as with so many of the other people in this room, Alex's and my friendship dates from her ultimately successful search for Evan's new kidney in 2003, and it's a friendship that has endured through thick and thin ever since.

"And even though that kidney was found and Evan's life was saved, that wasn't the end of the story. Alex soon realized that advances in reproductive medicine gave otherwise barren parents the miracle of having children of their own, while at the same time ignoring or trampling on the rights of those very children. She came to realize that, like her own son, many other artificially inseminated children needed to have access to accurate health information concerning the donors who had provided the eggs and sperm that had given them life.

"They needed to know if there were genetically transmitted diseases lurking in the family trees of their biological parents that might threaten their own well-being or that of their offspring. They needed to know how many other half siblings might be out there in the world or in their neighborhood. And so Alex, along with two other courageous women—Cassie Davis and Jolene Browder—founded the Progeny Project, an organization devoted to using DNA as a tool to help individuals born via artificial insemination to have access to their own biological information.

"How many people in this room are here today because Alex Munsey's Progeny Project impacted your lives? Would it be possible to have a show of hands?"

Ali paused her presentation long enough as hand

after hand rose in the air. She counted at least thirty before giving up. While studying the room, however, she caught sight of an older woman, who, although she didn't raise her hand, was openly weeping. Not only was she sobbing into a hankie, she was also the only woman in the room who was wearing a hat.

Who is she? Ali wondered. *Is she a friend of Alex's, maybe, or a fan, or a distant relative?*

"So here you all are," Ali resumed. "Many of you share common strands of DNA, which means that you're related while not being actual family, not in the traditional sense. What you have instead is a sense of connection and community. That's a gift Alex Munsey gave all of you, and it's why so many of you are here today on this Sunday afternoon to honor and celebrate Alex's memory.

"Eventually Alex stepped away from motherhood and the Progeny Project in what some would call 'late middle age' in favor of pursuing her own life and dreams— including her determination to become a writer. Her first book, *A Mother's Tale*—an autobiography of sorts—was also the story of the Progeny Project and its aftermath. Her first novel, *The Silver Lining*, was published at a time when most people her age were already collecting Social Security checks. That book went on to become a surprise bestseller. When Alex signed my copy of her new book, *The Changeling*, she wrote these words: 'Sometimes it pays to be a late bloomer.' As I stand here, today's issue of the Sunday *L.A. Times* tells me that Alex's *The Changeling* remains at number five on the New York Times Best Seller list. Late bloomer indeed!

"I have no idea why such a remarkable woman would be taken from us in what can only be regarded as a horrific act of random violence. Along with Evan I trust that at some time in the future law enforcement will succeed in bringing the culprit or culprits to justice, but that's a concern for another time and place. Today is a day of remembrance.

"In closing I'd like to thank the two young women who graced us with their presence earlier and sang that wonderful song. We all came here today with heavy hearts. This is the darkness of midnight. When the service is over, coffee, tea, and light refreshments will be served in a room just off the lobby. You're all invited. Let's go there together not to shed tears but to celebrate the life of the wonderful woman we've lost—a woman who was a blessing in my life and in many of your lives as well. Perhaps sharing our memories together will be part of the breaking of day."

With that, Ali returned to her seat. Reverend Nugent asked if anyone else wished to speak. When no one raised a hand or stepped forward, he ended the service with a benediction. While the organist played "Amazing Grace" in the background, the usher who had escorted Ali into the room reappeared and began directing folks back out. The people in the front two rows filed down the center aisle first, with everyone else following along behind, exiting row by row. Ali left the chapel with the family and then found herself directed to join them as part of the receiving line once they entered the room reserved for the reception.

Ali supposed that made sense. In a room where so many people were related by blood and DNA, it stood to reason that a near stranger would be treated like a member of the family.

50

Hannah hadn't intended to stay for the reception. Her idea had been to leave the moment the service was over, but that was before she'd seen Rory Davis Munsey. She wanted to be close enough to him to hear his voice and maybe even touch his hair. She supposed that might be dangerous. There was always a chance someone might recognize her, although that hadn't happened so far. Besides, it wouldn't take long. She'd be in and out again in no time.

Before she ever left her chair in the chapel, Hannah sent Marco a text asking him to bring the car around and telling him that she'd be outside shortly. When she stepped into the reception room and saw that a receiving line had been organized just inside the door, she almost backed out. Unfortunately, there was a couple directly behind her who made a graceful exit impossible, so Hannah forged onward. It was easy enough to get past the Munseys—the grown-up ones, at least. All she had to do was murmur a few words of condolence and move on. A sprinkling of the words "I'm so sorry for your loss" went a long way, but she wasn't so sure it would work with Ali Reynolds, who was stationed at the end of the line.

During the service Hannah had been stunned when Evan had announced that the following speaker would be Ali Reynolds, Eddie's next target. Hannah's next target. It hadn't really occurred to her that Ali would be there. It might have crossed Eddie's mind or even Gloria's, but it didn't seem likely that either one of them would attempt another hit this close to Alex Munsey's. And so, as Hannah finished shaking Kathleen Munsey's hand, she decided to brazen it out and keep on going.

"Thank you for that very moving eulogy," she murmured to Ali, holding out her hand and peering up at Ali from under the brim of her hat, all the while thanking her lucky stars that Grandmother Alberta's cameo brooch was safely stowed in her pocket rather than pinned at her throat. "You're a remarkable public speaker."

"Thank you," Ali said. "That's kind of you to say, but you look somewhat familiar. Do I know you? Are you a relative or a friend of the family?"

"Neither, I'm afraid," Hannah said quickly, making it up as she went along. "I was a huge fan of Alex Munsey's work, starting with *A Mother's Tale* and right on through to *The Changeling*. I've already read that one, by the way, and I think it was by far her best work. When I saw the notice in the paper, I decided to come. I live only a few blocks from here. I hope no one's offended."

"I'm certain no one is," Ali assured her. "The service was open to the public, after all. Please help yourself to the refreshments."

Hannah made her way into the room. Stopping by the refreshment table, she declined all offers of tea, coffee, or punch. She had developed a severe essential tremor over the past year or so, and any cup of liquid that was more than half full was liable to end up spilled all over her. Instead she stood there and looked around the room, searching for little Rory, spotting him at last seated alone at a table with his coloring book spread out in front of him.

Seeing him like that jarred loose a shard of memory. Eddie had been like that when he was little, able to wall himself off from a roomful of people to concentrate on the project at hand—building a model airplane, doing his homework, or reading a book. So if that part of Eddie's DNA was part of Rory Munsey's makeup, what about the rest? He might be a cute kid now—polite and well behaved—but would he grow up to be a narcissistic asshole?

The fact that those last two words had even crossed Hannah's mind was shocking enough to make her stagger over to a nearby table and sink onto a chair. Maybe the idea of those words had been lurking around the edges of her consciousness at times, but this was the first time she'd come close to allowing them to surface in her brain, let alone consider giving voice to them. But she said them aloud now, whispering them under her breath.

"That's what he is—Eddie's a narcissistic asshole." And then, in order to stifle an inappropriate hoot of laughter, she pulled out her hankie and covered her face, hoping people would mistakenly think she was still emotionally traumatized by the memorial service.

When Hannah finally regained control, she got up and made her way over to the table where Rory was sitting. As she approached him, she couldn't help thinking how irresponsible it was of his parents to leave the boy alone and unsupervised in a room filled with relative strangers.

"Hello, Rory," she said, helping herself to a seat at the table.

"Hello," he replied. "Did you know Grandma Alex?"

"No."

"Then how do you know my name?"

"It was in the program."

"What's your name?"

And somehow, looking at Rory's deep blue eyes and charmed by that missing front tooth, it was important for Hannah to answer truthfully. "My name is Hannah." When he said nothing in return, she added, "Do you like coloring?"

"It's okay, I guess," he answered with a shrug. "Mommy said I should color and not bother any of the grown-ups."

For some inexplicable reason his simple response caused a new set of tears to spill from Hannah Gilchrist's eyes. Unable to restrain herself, she reached out and patted the top of Rory's head, marveling at the fine texture of his hair and all the while remembering Eddie's.

"You're a good boy," she said, rising to her feet, "and it sounds like you have a very good mommy."

A text came in on her phone from Marco Gregory:

I'm out front.

Good. I'll be right there.

Hustling through the crowded reception room as fast as flowing tears and her cumbersome cane would allow, Hannah made for the door, muttering under her breath. "Damn you, Eddie. If you'd just had brains enough to keep your nose clean and your pants zipped, I could have had a grandson, too—a real grandson just like Rory Munsey."

51

Ali circulated around the room with a glass of punch in hand, chatting up a storm. Some of the people she remembered from the sentencing hearing and some she did not. Finally, noticing a somewhat familiar woman in an LAPD uniform, Ali approached her. The name on her badge identified her as Lieutenant Crystal Manning. She had a tall, rangy build like Evan Munsey and Rory Davis. At this point their once-red hair was flecked with gray. Crystal's hair was a similar shade, but with no gray showing, most likely thanks to some help from a colorist at her local beauty salon. But similarities in hair color and build were where the resemblance to Evan and Rory ended. Crystal's facial features were entirely different.

"I believe I remember you from the sentencing hearing," Ali began, "or rather maybe from the party after the sentencing hearing, but I don't recall the name."

"I was Crystal Lucas back then, and it was quite the celebration," the woman agreed. "We were all staying over that night, so we gave ourselves permission to let down our hair. By the way, I liked what you said in there about Alex giving us a community. My parents claimed they'd always wanted to have kids, but once I showed up, I must not have been what they'd been expecting, because they never seemed to like me much. They always made me feel like an outsider. It wasn't until I hooked up with Progeny Project and the rest of these guys that I finally found a place where I felt I actually belonged."

"How long have you been with LAPD?"

"I signed on with LAPD in 2009," Crystal said. "My plan is to make captain by the time I'm fifty and then bail."

On the far side of the room, Ali caught sight of the old woman who had seemingly spent most of the service in tears crossing the room in a purposeful manner. While Ali watched, the woman limped over to the table where Rory Munsey was seated with his Spider-Man coloring book and his box of colored pencils spread out in front of him. The woman paused beside the boy and then, a moment later, sat down across from him. Ali felt a sudden sense of unease. If the woman was nothing more than a fan of Alex's writing who happened to live in the neighborhood, why had she gone looking for the boy? Because that's exactly what she'd done—she had sought him out deliberately and was speaking to him with no other adults present.

As their conversation continued, the boy showed no signs of distress—nonetheless alarm bells were ringing in Ali's head. She was a grandmother, after all. Rory's age wasn't so different from Colin and Colleen's, and she knew that Athena and Chris had already delivered more than one "stranger danger" lecture to the twins. If the woman were nothing more than one of Alex's fans, why was she engaging with Rory on his own? Why was she patting him on the head? What was going on?

At that point Ali quickly excused herself and started across the room. Before she made it, however, the old woman rose from the table and stepped away, leaving

Rory exactly as he was. Relieved, Ali allowed herself to be sidetracked by Rory Davis, who wanted to introduce her to his fiancée, Amber. After a short but polite exchange, Ali continued over to the corner.

"Hey, Rory," she said, approaching his table. "How's it going?"

"Okay, I guess," he said with an indifferent shrug.

"Can I get you something? Cookies? Punch?"

"My mommy will bring me something," he said. "I'm not allowed to take food from strangers."

"Good call," Ali said. "What about the woman who was here talking with you a little while ago?"

"The one with the cane and the black hat?"

"Yes, that's the one. Is she someone you know?"

"Nope," Rory said, putting down his pencil and holding up the book to examine his handiwork.

"What did she want?"

"Just to talk to me, I guess. She seemed pretty old, but she has the same name as a girl in my class."

"What name is that?" Ali asked.

"Hannah," Rory answered. "She said her name was Hannah."

Ali felt a sudden chill. "Holy crap!" Ali exclaimed under her breath, turning away from the child. "Shay, did you hear that?"

"I sure as hell did, and I'm on it. A lady wearing a black hat and walking with a cane is just now coming out of the building. A limo seems to be waiting for her."

"Can you stop her?" Ali asked.

"I've got no reason to stop her, but I'll go get the car," Shay said. "Maybe we can follow them and see where they're going."

By then Ali had fought her way through the reception

crowd, exited the room, and dashed across the lobby. Just outside the front doors, she came to a halt. Looking to the right, she saw a black Lincoln MKT stopped in the exit lane of the parking lot, signaling to turn left. That's when Crystal Manning caught up with her.

"I saw you race out of the room," she said. "You looked upset. Is something wrong?"

"You see that limo over there?" Ali asked, pointing. "The woman inside—the one with the cane—is Hannah Gilchrist."

"You're kidding! Edward Gilchrist's mother came to Alex's funeral? What the hell is she doing here?"

"That's what I'd like to know."

As Shay came to a stop beside Ali and Crystal, there was enough of a break in the traffic for the limo to pull out into the street. Ali had opened the Acura's door but had not yet gotten inside when she heard the distant revving of a car engine. There was no sign of a speeding vehicle, but from the sound she could tell that it was coming from somewhere off to her right, from somewhere just out of sight behind the building.

The limo was turning into the left-hand traffic lane when, with a squeal of burning rubber, a hulking black Suburban shot into view. It slammed into the passenger side of the Lincoln with so much force that for a moment the two vehicles seemed welded together. With a screech of rending sheet metal, they spun as one, then bounced up onto the far sidewalk, where they finally split apart. The Suburban came to rest against a fire hydrant, breaking it off and sending a geyser of water into the air, while the limo lurched farther into the opposing parking lot before finally coming to a stop with its nose plastered against the base of a light standard.

For a moment everyone looking on was too shocked to move. As water from the hydrant blew skyward, a black-clad figure wearing a motorcycle helmet emerged from the wreckage of the Suburban. He slithered backward out through the driver's-side window opening. Reaching up and grabbing the roof of the vehicle, he pulled himself the rest of the way out before dropping easily to the ground. He walked away from the mess without so much as a backward glance. As he stepped off the sidewalk, a south-bound motorbike pulled up beside him. He hopped onto the back of it, and off they went, speeding away, instantly disappearing from view behind the intervening building.

"That was no accident," Crystal declared, grabbing her phone and dialing 911. "That was a hit plain and simple. It'll be a miracle if anyone inside that limo survives."

As Ali and Crystal sprinted toward the wreckage, Shay rolled down her window. "I'll see if I can catch up with that bike."

"Don't," Crystal said. "Let them go." But Shay went anyway, speeding out of the parking lot and onto Noble.

As Ali and Crystal raced past the spewing hydrant, Crystal was still speaking into her phone. "Yes, I see movement. The driver might be alive. Hang on. I'll let you know."

As they reached the wreckage, Crystal went straight to the front door. Ali, dreading what was coming, approached the back. Much to her surprise, there was movement there as well. A thin edging of shattered safety glass lined the space where the window should have been. Peering inside, Ali caught sight of a bald and bloodied Hannah Gilchrist, wedged against the crumpled door on the driver's side of the vehicle and struggling to emerge from under a blanket of deployed air bags.

"Help me," she pleaded. "Someone please help."

The left side of her head was covered with blood from a jagged cut that ran from the top of her skull to the top of her ear.

"I'm right here," Ali said. Reaching into her purse, she dragged out the fistful of tissues she'd brought along to the funeral. "Hold still," she added, reaching in through the window. "I need to apply pressure to that cut."

"The cut's not the problem," Hannah groaned. "It's my hip. I think it's broken. I was having trouble fastening my seat belt. I got thrown all the way across the car and slammed into the door."

Ali knew that it was a miracle the woman hadn't been ejected through the missing window. "We've called 911," she said as reassuringly as she could manage. "Help should be here soon."

Reaching inside, she used a thick layer of tissues in the palm of her hand in an attempt to stanch the flow of blood. Ali knew from first-responder training that head wounds tend to bleed profusely, and that was the case here. Not only was it bleeding, the cut was so long that it took the whole length of Ali's hand to apply pressure. Even then blood soon oozed through the layer of tissue, running down her arm, soaking into the sleeve of her blazer, and pooling at the elbow.

"It hurts," Hannah managed through gritted teeth. "It hurts worse than anything."

Hannah Gilchrist had to be a tough old bat. With all the blood loss, Ali was astonished that the woman could still speak in a normal tone of voice when most people would have been screaming in agony. "I'm sure it does," Ali said.

"I saw her," Hannah added. "Just before we got hit, I saw her."

"Saw who?" Ali asked.

"Gloria, she was sitting right there watching, like she was waiting for it to happen—like she was expecting it to happen."

Gloria would have to be Gloria Reece, Ali realized, but had she really been there or had Hannah suffered a concussion and was simply hallucinating? Or maybe she was lapsing into shock, but as long as Hannah was talking, Ali wanted to keep her that way.

"Gloria who?" Ali asked, playing along.

"The three of them did this on purpose," Hannah declared.

"Who did this on purpose?" Ali asked. "Are you saying you know the two guys, the one in the Suburban and the one on the motorbike?"

"What motorbike? I never saw any motorbike."

"But you said three people were involved," Ali said. "Who do you mean?"

"My son," Hannah answered, beginning to sob for the first time, as if that admission hurt worse than the agonizing pain in her hip. "It's Eddie, Gloria, and Gloria's uncle, Luis Ochoa. I disobeyed Eddie's direct order, and they all three turned on me."

If true, this was a stunning revelation. Ali had heard it, but was she the only one? Crystal, tending to the injured driver, was totally preoccupied with him. Ali's only hope was that her earbud connection was still working.

"Are you getting any of this, Shay?" Ali asked.

"Every word," came the response. "I couldn't spot

the bike, so I'll try circling back to see if I can locate Gloria. Ask Hannah what Gloria was wearing."

Ali repeated Shay's question to Hannah.

"Something blue," Hannah answered. "A blue top of some kind."

"Okay," Shay said. "I'm on it."

From the street Ali heard the racket of multiple emergency vehicles arriving on the scene. Moments later an EMT came up behind her. "Okay, lady," he said to Ali. "Thanks for the assist, but you need to move away from the vehicle now." As Ali stepped aside, the EMT spotted the blood on her hand and arm and quickly focused his attention on her. "Are you hurt, too?" he demanded.

"No," Ali answered, dropping the wad of blood-soaked tissues. "It's Hannah's blood, not mine. She's got a cut on her head and maybe a broken hip."

"That's her name, Hannah?"

Ali nodded.

He turned toward the car. "Hello, Hannah," he said calmly. "Let's see what we can do to get you out of there."

As the adrenaline drained from her body, Ali staggered over to a nearby parked car and leaned against the fender for support, but what she was feeling inside was an immense rush of relief. All the suspects' names were out in the open now, and in a way that led back to Hannah Gilchrist herself rather than to Frigg. In that regard High Noon Enterprises had just dodged a bullet.

She looked down at her hands. Both of them were covered with blood. She tried rubbing them off on her already wrecked blazer, but it was no use. The blood was drying now and mostly caked as well, so it didn't wipe off. Just then her cell phone buzzed in her jacket pocket.

Ali had turned the phone on silent during the service and had never gotten around to turning the ringer back on. The whole time she'd been talking to Hannah, it had been buzzing like crazy with incoming messages and calls. This time she was finally able to answer.

"Are you okay?" Stuart demanded the moment she came on the line.

"Yes, I'm okay," Ali said. "Why?"

"Because I saw the whole thing."

"What whole thing?"

"The car accident," he answered. "We saw someone we assume was Hannah Gilchrist come out of the lobby and get into a limo. You came outside, too, but as soon as the wreck occurred, you ran across the street and disappeared from view. We were afraid something bad had happened to you, too. What the hell is going on?"

"Wait," Ali said. "You saw the car crash? How's that possible?"

"Frigg tapped into the surveillance systems for both the funeral home and the coffee shop across the street."

"She didn't," Ali said.

"Yes, she did."

Suddenly Ali was overcome with an uncontrollable urge to giggle.

"Why are you laughing?" Stu asked, sounding offended. "This isn't funny. I was scared to death."

"But it *is* funny," Ali insisted. "Whoever thought I'd end up being stuck with an AI for a guardian angel?"

52

Gloria stayed at the table throughout the service, waiting for the main event. When the Lincoln pulled up under the awning, she picked up her phone and dialed first the guy on the motorbike and warned him to be on the lookout. Then she dialed the guy in the Suburban and kept him on the line, holding off for just the right moment. She watched as Hannah came hobbling out to the car and as the driver handed her inside.

"Get ready," she said.

The driver walked back around the vehicle and got in himself. He drove up to the exit and sat signaling to turn left. "On your mark," Gloria said into the phone.

As the limo moved toward the northbound lanes of Noble Avenue, Gloria issued her final order. "Go!" she whispered urgently into the phone. "Go, go, go!"

The limo was almost finished with its turn when Gloria caught sight of Hannah staring directly at her through the back passenger window. Time seemed to slip into slow motion as their eyes locked. In that moment and even before the crash happened, Gloria felt a sudden sense of impending doom. Not only had she been seen, she'd been recognized.

Gloria remained where she was long enough for the speeding motorbike to appear and disappear. Then, while other people from the coffee shop rushed to see what had happened, Gloria abandoned the table she'd occupied for the better part of three hours. Her heart might have been pounding in her chest, but she forced herself to walk sedately away from the action. She had left the Range Rover parked around the corner on Dickens. Once inside, she took a few deep, calming breaths before grasping the steering wheel with hands that were still surprisingly shaky. Hannah had seen her, and if the old battle-ax wasn't dead, this was going to turn into a complete disaster.

Once Gloria felt capable of driving, she headed eastbound on Dickens, circled around to Ventura, and then pulled in to the theater parking lot from the opposite direction. She arrived in time to see a collection of emergency vehicles—at least two ambulances and a flock of police cruisers—converging on the scene. She parked in a remote spot, far enough away that her Range Rover wouldn't be caught up in any of the subsequent investigation.

Even while the crash was happening, Gloria had worried that the timing was slightly off. She had wanted the Suburban to make a direct T-bone hit on the other vehicle. Instead it had plowed into the limo at an angle that made the impact more of a glancing blow. Would that be hard enough to do the job? She certainly hoped so. The last thing Gloria wanted to do was go back home to Folsom and have to tell Uncle Luis that she had failed.

People flocked out of the theater entrances while others rushed across the street from the funeral home, all of them intent on seeing what was going on. Gloria waited long enough for a crowd to form before she got out of her car. As she neared the growing mob, a single ambulance threaded its way through the throng of onlookers before speeding out of the parking lot with its siren blaring, clearly heading for the nearest hospital.

Craning her neck, Gloria tried to see what was taking place, but she was too far away to catch any of the action. The man standing next to her was a full head taller than she was. "What's going on?" she asked.

"Car accident," he answered. "Hit-and-run. They got the driver out. Looks like they're using the Jaws of Life to rescue a passenger trapped in the backseat."

That wasn't the news Gloria Reece wanted to hear, not at all! She didn't want Hannah Gilchrist trapped— she wanted the woman dead. She'd been hoping for the arrival of a medical examiner's van rather than a pair of ambulances, but if Hannah was still alive, Gloria had to figure out where they were taking her, and she had to do it fast. If Hannah managed to live long enough to spill the beans, Gloria's whole existence was in jeopardy. If the cops didn't come after her, one of Uncle Luis's henchmen sure as hell would.

Without another word Gloria slipped away from the crowd and climbed back into the Range Rover. Long minutes later, when the second ambulance departed the scene, first turning right onto Noble, right on Ventura, and finally left onto Van Nuys, Gloria Reece managed to tuck in behind them, far enough away so she wouldn't be spotted but close enough to keep the flashing lights in view. That speeding ambulance was headed for the nearest ER, and so was she.

53

During the encounter with Hannah, Ali had been sustained by a burst of adrenaline. Once it dissipated, she felt woozy. She was leaning against the fender of a nearby parked car as the first ambulance left the scene. That's about the time Rory Davis showed up.

"Are you all right?" he asked, his face full of concern.

"I'm fine."

"Are you sure? You don't look fine. You've got blood all over you."

"One of the people was hurt," Ali explained. "I was doing first aid."

"Someone said a person leaving the funeral was involved in the crash," Rory continued. "Do you have any idea who it was?"

Ali nodded. "Hannah Gilchrist."

"Hannah Gilchrist?" he echoed. "Are you kidding me? She was at the funeral? I never saw her. What the hell was she doing there? Where was she?"

"In the back row. I noticed her sitting there crying when I was up front speaking, but at the time I had no idea who she was."

"And she was crying?"

Ali nodded again. "Like she'd lost her best friend. Later, when she came through the receiving line, she claimed she came to the funeral because she was one of Alex's devoted fans, but then when I saw her talking to Rory . . ."

Evan turned up then and joined the knot of people who'd gathered around Ali. "Who was talking to Rory?" he demanded.

"Hannah Gilchrist."

Evan's eyes widened in alarm. "She was at the funeral?"

"And at the reception," Ali replied.

"How did she even know we were holding the service?"

"There were announcements in the paper," Rory said. "She probably saw something either there or online."

"But why would she come here?" Evan asked. "What made her think she'd be welcome? She had no business showing up, and if I'd known she had, I would have asked her to leave. But she was talking to Rory? What did she say to him?"

"I don't know exactly what was said," Ali replied. "When I saw someone I knew to be a complete stranger talking to him, it worried me. It just didn't look right. I was on my way to find out what was going on when she got up and walked away. By the time I reached Rory, I could tell he wasn't the least bit bothered by what had happened. I asked him about her, and he said she told him her name was Hannah. I put two and two together and realized it had to be Hannah Gilchrist. I tried to catch up with her to find out what the hell was going on, but I got outside just in time to see the crash."

"How did it happen?"

"The driver of her limo was turning left into north-bound traffic on Noble when a speeding Suburban came charging up out of nowhere and rammed into it from behind."

"An accident, then?" Evan asked.

Crystal Manning, walking up to the group, answered Evan's question before Ali had a chance.

"Not an accident," she declared. "This was not a hit-and-run. It was actually a hit—attempted murder. The guy driving that Suburban just tried to kill Hannah Gilchrist."

Ali caught Crystal's eye. "That's what Hannah thinks, too."

"She told you that?"

Ali nodded. "While I was trying to stop the blood from her head wound."

"Did she have any idea who might be responsible?"

Ali nodded again.

"Then you'd better come with me," Crystal said. "We need to have a chat with the investigating officers." As they walked away from the others, she added, "Did Hannah happen to name names?"

"She did," Ali answered. "She said three people were involved—Edward Gilchrist, Gloria Reece, and Luis Ochoa. She said that because she'd disobeyed one of her son's direct orders, he and the others had turned on her."

"Orders about what?"

"I'm not sure," Ali hedged. "She didn't go into that, but I believe it may have something to do with Hannah's son trying to wreak vengeance on people who were involved in his homicide trial."

Crystal stopped short in midstride. "Wait, are you saying these same people might be involved in Alex Munsey's death?"

"It's possible," Ali answered. "And if they want Hannah dead, too, who's to say they won't try again?"

With a shake of her head, Crystal plucked her phone out of her pocket and dialed a number. "I've got a badly injured individual—a female—in an ambulance headed from Sherman Oaks to Van Nuys Central Trauma," she said into the phone. "Her name is Hannah Gilchrist. We believe her to be the victim of an attempted vehicular homicide. I'm worried that the people responsible may want to finish the job. Let the EMTs know that she needs to be admitted to the hospital under an assumed name. Properly identified law-enforcement officers may be allowed to see her, but she's to have no other visitors. Is that clear? Good. Give the hospital my name and let them know I'm on my way."

"Wait," Ali said as the call ended. "Do you want me to go along to the hospital?"

"No," Crystal answered. "Since you're an eyewitness, you need to go talk to the uniforms who are investigating the scene."

With that, Crystal galloped off in the direction of the funeral home's parking lot, intent on retrieving her car.

"Did you hear all that?" Ali asked. With no idea that she was speaking into her earbud, Rory and Evan both gave her puzzled looks, as though she'd suddenly lost her marbles.

"I heard, all right," Shay Green said in Ali's ear.

Ali turned away from the others before she spoke again. "Come get me," she said.

"Where are we going?"

"Van Nuys Central Trauma."

"But I thought she said you should go talk to the cops."

"Later," Ali replied. "Right now I want to be at the hospital. Lieutenant Manning may have a badge, but what she really needs is us. We're the only people who actually know what Gloria Reece looks like. Crystal has no idea."

"Shouldn't we at least discuss this?" Shay asked. "I'm supposed to be protecting you. From that point of view, it seems like a bad idea for you to be heading smack into the middle of a potential firefight."

"If you won't give me a ride, I'll call a cab," Ali told her. "If you won't help, I'll go it alone. I want to stop these people, and catching up with Gloria Reece is step number one."

"Got it," Shay replied after a pause. "I'll be right there."

By the time Ali crossed the parking lot, Shay's Acura was idling next to the curb. Ali hopped in, pulled the door shut, and fastened her belt. "Do you know how to get to Van Nuys Central Trauma?" she asked as the car shot forward.

"I do," Shay replied, then added, "We'll be using backstreets, but we'll get there in a hurry. The person I heard you talking to earlier, the one who said she was going to the hospital—is she a police officer?"

"Yes, she is," Ali answered. "Crystal Manning is a lieutenant with LAPD homicide. She's also one of the Gilchrist half siblings."

Shay remained quiet for a moment as the car shot across Ventura and continued northward, speeding through intersections with barely a pause to check for oncoming traffic. "All right, then," she said finally, "what's the plan?"

Ali looked down at her bloodied clothing. "You ever spend much time in ER waiting rooms?"

"Some," Shay conceded.

"Here's what we're going to do. We're going to walk into that ER just as big as life. You're going to claim to be my neighbor, and you're going to tell the admitting people that my husband beat me up. Since I won't be actively bleeding or puking, they'll have us take a number and wait. We'll sit off to the side and see if Gloria shows up. This was a hit, Shay. When the dust settled, Hannah was supposed to be dead, and the fact that she isn't is probably setting off alarm bells up and down Gloria's chain of command. If she comes to the hospital intent on finishing the job, the only way she'll be able to get to Hannah is to get by us first."

"But what happens then?" Shay wanted to know. "Are you planning on making a citizen's arrest, or do you expect to stage some kind of shoot-out in the middle of an ER waiting room?"

"Nothing of the kind," Ali said. "If Gloria shows up in the ER, we ID her first and then run up the flag to Crystal. I'm sure she can take it from there."

54

Stu Ramey had spent most of the day glued to his wall monitors in the man cave, studying the financial information Frigg had amassed on Luis Ochoa's numerous and relatively well-heeled family members. Most of them appeared to be living far above their means, which indicated they all had substantial amounts of undocumented monies flowing into their household accounts. Needing to give his head a rest, Stu had gone into the kitchen to collect another bowl of surprisingly delicious beef stew when Frigg sent him a howler that brought him back to the man cave on the run.

"What's going on now?" he demanded.

"There's something you should see."

Two neighboring wall monitors lit up, both showing CCTV of two separate street scenes. "Where is this?" he wanted to know.

"The coffee shop is located across the street from the Longmont Funeral Home in Sherman Oaks, California. The other one shows side-by-side views of the funeral home's parking lot, one from the entrance looking out across the parking lot and another view from the parking lot toward the entrance."

"You hacked into their surveillance systems?" Stuart asked. "Who told you to do that?"

"It's part of my standard security protocol," Frigg

replied. "If I know that one of my subjects will be in a certain location, I try to establish surveillance coverage if at all possible. I did the same thing at Ms. Reynolds's hotel last night—just the public areas and the hallways, not her room."

"Of course not," Stu replied sarcastically. "You'd never do anything that underhanded."

"Unfortunately, I had some challenges in establishing the connection here," Frigg continued. "I didn't manage to get either feed going until after the funeral was already in progress. I should be able to go back and capture earlier portions, but I thought you'd want to see this first."

Stu stared at the screen. A black limo was waiting underneath the shade of an awning. A woman walking with the aid of a cane emerged from the building. The limo driver leaped out and came around to the far side of the car to help her inside.

"According to my facial-recognition software, the woman in the limo is Hannah Gilchrist."

Stu felt his heart drop to his toes. "What the hell is she doing there?"

The limo moved out from under the portico and then stopped at a curb-cut driveway, signaling for a left-hand turn. Two more people emerged from inside the building and stood staring after the limo. "The individual on the right is Ms. Reynolds," Frigg reported.

And then, with no advance warning, as the limo moved into traffic a speeding vehicle appeared out of nowhere, smashing into the limo's rear passenger panel from behind and sending both vehicles spinning across two lanes of oncoming traffic. Moving as one, the two vehicles hurtled up and over a sidewalk before the wreckage disappeared from view. Ali and her companion were still stationary outside the funeral home when another vehicle pulled up beside them. A moment later that vehicle, too, shot off into the street, turning right rather than left. At the same time, Ali and the other woman sprang into action, sprinting off across the street before they, too, vanished from the camera's stationary view.

"What the hell just happened?" Stu demanded.

"It was a car wreck," Frigg explained unnecessarily.

The next person to appear in the frame was a man wearing a motorcycle helmet. He stepped onto the sidewalk and then looked off to his right—as though he were expecting someone or something. Moments later a motorbike pulled up beside him. Without exchanging a word, the guy with the helmet stepped off the sidewalk, hopped onto the back of the motorbike, and then it shot out of range. Because there was no sound, this all happened in a silent pantomime.

"Where's Ali?" Stuart demanded. "Did something happen to her, too?"

He immediately started dialing her number, but there was no answer, not for the better part of five agonizing minutes. And when she finally did answer, she actually laughed at him. Offended, Stuart Ramey did something he'd never done before in his whole life. He hung up on her—hung up on his boss. Then he sat there staring at the screen in real time while people poured out of the funeral home. Some of them got into their cars and drove away. Others dashed across the street, hurrying in the same direction the damaged vehicles had traveled after the crash. Stu was still watching when Ali suddenly reappeared in view and stepped into what seemed to be a passing vehicle, which immediately drove out of frame.

"What just happened?" he asked.

"A number of things," Frigg told him, "but you may want to take a closer look at the coffee-shop footage."

Preoccupied with the action surrounding the car wreck, Stuart had barely glanced at the other monitor. When he turned his attention in that direction, he saw a sidewalk-café arrangement with five or six outdoor tables set along the front of a building. The tables were all occupied, mostly with two or more people.

"Okay," he said. "I see outdoor tables. I see people sitting there. Why is this important?"

Frigg enlarged the image, bringing one woman's face into a close-up view. "According to my facial-recognition software, this woman, the one sitting alone at the far end table, is Gloria Reece. If I synchronize all three sets of film, you'll see that moments before the crash happens, she is speaking animatedly on her cell phone. The other people all turn in the direction of the crash. Not Gloria. Instead, she gets up, walks away, and disappears."

"No way to tell which way she went?"

"Not so far."

Stuart was sitting there trying to figure out what the hell he should do next when a text message from Ali came in on his cell phone. He read the message aloud:

"'Hannah badly injured in a car wreck. She's on her way to the ER at Van Nuys Central Trauma via ambulance. I'm going there, too. I hope you'll keep your eyes on the prize.'

"Eyes on the prize," Stuart repeated. "What the hell is that supposed to mean?"

"Ms. Reynolds has just identified her next destination," Frigg informed him. "I'll see what I can do to penetrate the hospital's video-surveillance system."

55

t took close to fifteen minutes to get from the parking lot to the hospital in Van Nuys. Since Shay knew the way, Ali was free to work her phone. After sending that one text to Stuart and hoping he got the underlying message, her next call was to Evan.

"Where the hell did you go?" he asked. "One minute you and Crystal were here, and the next you were both gone."

"Crystal was called away," Ali told him. "I was on my way to talk to the cops on the scene when something came up. Now I need your help."

"What?"

"Crystal Manning's cell-phone number. If you could text it to me, I'll have it handy in case I need it."

"I'll send it," Evan agreed, "but is there anything else I can do? Would you like me to call her and give her a message?"

A call to Crystal was the last thing Ali wanted. If she was going to be on hand to identify their suspect at the hospital, Ali couldn't afford to have a lieutenant from the LAPD telling her to sit down and shut up.

"No message," Ali said aloud. "This way I'll be able to contact her myself as needed."

56

It was disconcerting for Hannah to be wheeled into the emergency room lying flat on her back, faceup, and staring at the ceiling and the glowing light fixtures overhead. The first EMT had dosed the cut on her scalp with some kind of powder—a clotting agent, he told her. She couldn't see it, of course, but there seemed to be less blood dribbling into her ear and running down the back of her neck.

The pain from the cut was negligible compared to her hip. That was so intense that she wanted to scream in agony, but she'd been taught from an early age that Anderson women didn't scream. Her father had drilled that lesson into her head from the time she was little and came into the house sobbing because of a badly scraped knee.

"You need to be strong," he'd told her. "Don't go around screaming and crying and begging for sympathy. You're better than that."

But not right then in Van Nuys Central Trauma, because when the nurses and attendants picked Hannah up and transferred her from the gurney onto a bed, she screamed like crazy. She couldn't help it. A doctor showed up seconds later. The badge on his chest identified him as Dr. Pennington.

"Where does it hurt?" he asked once she quieted back down.

"It's my hip," Hannah gasped when she could speak again, "my left hip."

A woman's face—her mother's face, Isobel's face—appeared in Hannah's line of vision, standing behind the doctor. For a moment Hannah thought that she was hallucinating, or maybe she was already dead. Isobel couldn't be here. That wasn't possible. When the doctor turned to speak to the new arrival, Hannah caught sight of the uniform. That's when she remembered where she had seen the woman before—earlier, at the funeral.

"Unless you're a relative, you'll have to leave," Dr. Pennington was saying to the cop. "This patient isn't allowed to have any visitors."

"I'm not a relative. My name's Lieutenant Crystal Manning," the woman said, flashing a badge. "I'm with LAPD. Your patient is the victim of an attempted homicide, and she needs to be moved to a secure location."

"ER is a secure location," Dr. Pennington replied.

"Really?" Lieutenant Manning countered. "I got in, didn't I? I walked right in through those swinging doors without anyone making the slightest effort to stop me."

"Your uniform may have helped you get inside, but it doesn't give you a right to make demands," Dr. Pennington told her. "This woman is my patient, and she has HIPAA protections that guarantee her privacy, even from people in law enforcement. I'm going to have to ask you to leave."

"Hannah Gilchrist needs protection far more than she needs privacy," Lieutenant Manning insisted. "That's why I'm here."

Frowning, Dr. Pennington glanced down at the chart he was holding. "Look," he said, "we've admitted her as Jane Doe. What more do you want?"

"I want her safe."

Hannah listened to the exchange. She was a little foggy. In addition to the clotting powder, the EMT had given her something that was finally starting to dull the pain. But even with her faculties somewhat clouded, she knew that the cop was right. Gloria had tried to kill her. So far she hadn't succeeded, but she would try again. She was bound to try again.

"It's all right," Hannah murmured aloud to the doctor. "Let her stay."

"Very well," the physician conceded, but Hannah could see he wasn't at all happy about it. He lifted the sheet long enough to glance at Hannah's injured hip and shook his head at what he saw there.

"Somebody needs to find out if we have an orthopedic surgeon on call. We won't know for sure until after the X-rays, but I'm pretty sure she's going to need a new hip ASAP." He checked her pupils, looking for signs of a concussion and was surprised to find none.

"Once we get that head wound stitched back together, we'll get you to X-ray," Dr. Pennington told her. "You'll also need an MRI, but from what I'm seeing here, you are one hardheaded lady."

"That's what my mother always said."

Hannah glanced around the room, searching the faces of the scrum of nurses until she could focus on the detective. "You're one of Edward's children, aren't you," Hannah said. It was a statement not a question.

"How did you know that?" Lieutenant Manning asked. "Because I was at the funeral?"

"No," Hannah murmured, "because you have my mother's face. I'd recognize you anywhere."

"Wait," Dr. Pennington said, sending a puzzled look

back and forth between the two women. "Didn't you just tell me that you weren't related?" he said finally, addressing the detective.

"It seems I was wrong about that," she replied.

"All right, then," the doctor ordered. "Let's get those stitches in place. Fortunately, we won't need to shave her head."

57

Stu paced the floor while Frigg worked at accessing the surveillance system for Van Nuys Central Trauma. He wanted the hacking attempt to work while at the same time being afraid it would work. He hadn't mentioned that to anyone else—not even B.—because he didn't want anyone else to know what Frigg and Fido were up to.

And if Ali was right and Gloria Reece was there at the hospital, what was Stu supposed to do in that case? He sure as hell couldn't send her a text. Unable to decide, he kept right on pacing.

When Frigg said, "I'm in," Stu raced for the bank of wall monitors with his heart in his throat.

"Show me," he said.

"On the far left is an interior shot of the ER waiting room. Facial recognition identifies the woman at the counter as being Ms. Reece. The shot on the right is the portico outside the entrance to the ER. I believe that is Ms. Reynolds exiting a vehicle."

"Happening right now?" Stu asked, reaching for his phone.

"Live streaming," Frigg replied.

Stu watched as Ali paused outside the vehicle long enough to exchange a few words with the driver. By the time she closed the door, her phone must have been ringing. She reached for that before starting toward the hospital entrance.

"Hello."

"Stop right there," Stuart ordered as the automatic door slid open in front of her. "Do not go inside."

Ali complied, halting in her tracks. "Why?" she asked. "Is Gloria here? Is she already inside?"

"She's at the counter talking to a clerk. Where's your bodyguard?"

"She went to park the car."

"Damn!" Stu muttered. "Whatever you do, don't go in there on your own. If anything happens to you, B. will kill me."

"I'm hanging up now, Stu," Ali told him, cutting him off. "There's someone I need to call."

58

A li quickly located Crystal's phone number in Evan's text and dialed it. "It's Ali," she said. "Gloria Reece is here at the hospital. It looks like she's arguing with the ER admitting clerk."

"You're here at the hospital?" Crystal demanded. "I thought I told you to stay at the scene."

"And I thought you could use some assistance. Where are you?"

"I'm with Hannah. They've stitched up her head wound and are wheeling her down to X-ray. I'll come right down. Where are you?"

"Right outside the entrance to the ER," Ali answered. "What are you going to do?"

"I can talk to Gloria," Crystal answered, "but I can't detain her. I've got no probable cause, no warrant."

"But Hannah told me she was sure Gloria was responsible," Ali said. "She saw her at the crime scene, and now she's here at the hospital."

"An accusation like that, especially one made to a third party, isn't sufficient grounds for me to take Gloria into custody."

Ali looked around. Several yards away a uniformed security guard was smoking a cigarette and messing with his cell phone. Shay was nowhere in sight. She'd probably had a problem locating a parking place. And if she were here, she'd say the same thing Crystal just had: "Stay outside. Stand down." But Ali didn't feel like standing down. And she didn't feel like taking orders either.

"Ask Hannah," Ali urged. "See what she has to say. In the meantime I'll see what, if anything, I can do to get Gloria to hang around awhile."

With that thought in mind, Ali charged into the lobby just as a couple with a little boy tried to exit. The kid, looking miserable and chagrined, wore a newly applied cast on one arm. The parents looked stressed. All three of them shied away in horror when they caught a glimpse of Ali's bloodied clothing.

"As I said, we currently have no patients by the name of Gilchrist," the clerk was saying to Gloria as Ali came to a halt at the counter, "none at all. You must be mistaken."

"I am not mistaken," Gloria insisted. "I followed the ambulance that brought her here. My grandmother is somewhere inside this hospital, and I demand that you let me see her."

The frazzled clerk glanced in Ali's direction. "Excuse me, ma'am," she said, "you'll need to step away from the counter and wait your turn."

Backing away, Ali studied Gloria Reece, doing what Frigg would have described as a quick threat assessment. The woman was dressed in a loose-fitting light blue T-shirt, a pair of white shorts, and strappy sandals. There was a telltale bulge in the middle of her back that suggested the presence of a firearm, most likely carried in a small-of-back holster. The shorts precluded any kind of ankle-holstered backup weapon, but the purse anchored on Gloria's right shoulder might well hold one of those. If there was any kind of confrontation, both the purse and the holstered weapon had to be taken out of play at once.

Gloria and the clerk were still arguing back and forth when Shay entered the lobby and got in line with Ali, who immediately sent the new arrival a text:

> Gloria is at the counter.
> She's armed. Small-
> of-back holster. Maybe
> gun in purse.

> What should we do?

> Delay her long enough
> to give Lieutenant
> Manning a chance to
> talk to Hannah.

> Don't worry. She'll be
> delayed, all right. With
> help from the DMV,
> I located her vehicle
> down in the parking
> garage. Thanks to my
> box cutter, it currently
> has two flat tires. When
> it's time for her to leave,
> she'll need a tow truck.

> Good show. Keep an
> eye on her.

Where are you going?

**Outside for a minute. I'll
be right back.**

Ali remembered spotting that uniformed security guard standing outside, and that's precisely where she headed. He was still in the same spot, lighting up another cigarette well within the boundaries of the designated smoking zone. As she got closer, Ali saw that he wasn't armed, but there was something about his bearing that hinted at his being ex-military, maybe someone who'd done a couple tours of duty in the Middle East. His name tag said he was Brad Copley. Noting the hardness of his features, Ali realized that, armed or not, Brad was someone not to be taken lightly.

The only remaining question was how to engage him. What was the best way to enlist his help on Ali's side of the conflict? Should she come across as someone with some law-enforcement background and experience, or should she go all damsel-in-distressy? Seeing him stuff a pack of Marlboros back into his shirt pocket gave her the answer she needed. He was young, he was male, and he smoked Marlboros. If Brad was one macho dude, playing the DID card was Ali's best option.

"Excuse me," she said breathlessly, dashing up to him. "The sign over there on the door says this is a gun-free zone, right?"

Looking at her with concern, he stubbed out his newly lit cigarette in the sand of a waist-high ashtray. "Yes, ma'am," he replied.

"And that means no guns at all, right?" she asked.

"That's correct—no guns at all. Why, what seems to be the problem?"

"There's a woman inside the lobby arguing with the clerk behind the counter," Ali replied, feigning uncertainty. "I don't want to cause any trouble, but I'm pretty sure she's wearing a gun under her shirt. I was standing behind her in line and saw what looked like a gun right there in the small of her back."

Brad pressed a button on a shoulder-mounted radio. "Possible gun in ER lobby," he said. "Request assistance." With that he strode off toward the door while Ali followed close on his heels. Once inside the waiting room, he immediately took charge.

"Excuse me, ladies," he said, holding his hands in the air in an attempt to calm the raised voices emanating from the counter. "Is there a problem here? Anything I can do to help?"

"Yes, there's a problem," Gloria replied.

Seeing the uniform must have made her realize that she had overplayed her hand. With every eye in the room now on her, she made a concerted effort to lower her voice. "They brought my grandmother here by ambulance a little while ago, but now they won't tell me where she is or what they've done with her."

"I can see why you'd be concerned," Brad said, taking out a small notebook and a stubby pencil. "What's your grandmother's name?"

"Hannah," Gloria answered impatiently, "Hannah Gilchrist. She was involved in a serious car crash in Sherman Oaks."

"And your name?"

"Gloria," she replied, "Gloria Reece."

"Would you happen to have your ID on you, Ms. Reece?"

Brad was unfailingly polite, and he waited patiently while an exasperated Gloria fished her driver's license out of her purse.

"Thank you so much," he said. "Now, if you wouldn't mind stepping aside for a moment and giving me some details, I'll see if I can help you out." He walked away from the counter toward the far side of the lobby. With every eye in the room focused on her, Gloria had no choice but to follow.

Ali was impressed. Brad's professional de-escalation of the situation was something drilled into every wannabe cop during police-academy training—keep it calm, keep it light, keep it conversational. And once Brad and Gloria crossed the room, Ali noticed that Brad positioned himself so he would be facing the front entrance while Gloria would have her back to the door. A moment or two later, an arriving black-and-white slid silently to a stop under the portico, and two uniformed officers—a man and a woman, both carrying weapons—emerged. Their understated arrival went completely unnoticed by Gloria Reece.

"What time did you say the accident occurred?" Brad was asking.

"Probably close to an hour ago now," Gloria answered.

The two uniforms walked up behind Gloria. At that point, without changing his tone of voice, Brad Copley delivered his zinger. "Van Nuys Central Trauma is a gun-free zone, Ms. Reece. Is it possible that you're carrying a weapon in that small-of-back holster?"

As soon as he said the words, the female officer stepped forward. Before Gloria could react, the officer plucked the weapon from its holster and grabbed the purse before stepping away far enough to be safely out of reach. While Gloria spun around angrily to face the new arrivals, Brad maintained his professional composure.

"Do you happen to have your concealed-carry permit on you today, Ms. Reece?" he asked.

As confusion and outrage registered on Gloria's face, Ali found herself smiling. Gloria's weapon wasn't the only firearm in that gun-free zone that day, but it was most likely the only illegal one. In gun-control central Southern California, that would probably be enough for her to be taken into custody, and at that moment that was precisely what was required.

"I don't have it with me right now," Gloria muttered.

"So maybe we should all step outside to discuss this," Brad suggested. As the four of them exited through the sliding door, the woman behind the counter looked as though she was about to pass out.

"You mean she had a gun?" the clerk asked faintly. "The whole time she was standing here yelling at me, she was carrying a weapon?"

"She was," Shay said, stepping out of line and clearing the way for the next person to approach the counter. "And just for the record, she wasn't Hannah Gilchrist's granddaughter either."

While the conversation outside grew more and more animated, Ali picked up her phone and sent a text to Crystal:

I believe Gloria is about
to be taken into custody.

Taken into custody? I
told you we don't have
enough for an arrest
warrant.

Weapons charge. Hand-
gun in her possession
with no concealed-carry
permit.

How did that happen?

Sometimes you just get
lucky. Where's Hannah?

Still in X-ray.

If Gloria came looking
for Hannah, armed and
dangerous, maybe you
can get her to tell you
about what's really
going on.

The presence of an unli-
censed weapon should
give me enough prob-
able cause to obtain a
search warrant.

Good luck with that. And
when you go for
warrants, be sure to

get one for her vehicle
as well.

What kind of vehicle?

Range Rover.

Where is it?

It's down in the parking
garage, disabled.

Disabled? How did that
happen?

Anybody's guess.
Apparently it has a
couple of flat tires. And
there goes Gloria. The
cops just cuffed her and
are loading her into the
back of a squad car.

They'll probably take her
to Valley Station. I'll give
them a call and let them
know that we're looking at
way more than a simple
weapons charge. I'll ask
them to hold her in an
interview room until I can
get there.

What's happening with
Hannah?

> They took her
> directly from
> X-ray to have an MRI.
> I'm pretty sure they'll be
> admitting her after that.
> Where will you be?

We'll hang out down in
the lobby in case any
more bad actors show
up on the scene.

> Who's we?

Shay Green.
She's working
security for me today.

> Sounds like having
> security would have
> been a good idea
> for any number
> of people.
> Okay, I'll be in touch.

"What now?" Shay asked when Ali pocketed her
phone.

"Now we wait," Ali said. "Hannah talked to me. It
remains to be seen if she'll talk to LAPD."

59

Hannah Gilchrist lay perfectly still in the MRI tube and concentrated on not surrendering to a powerful urge to scream. The pain medication they had given her earlier was wearing off by the time the X-ray session ended. Now, during a seemingly endless series of MRIs, she was again in absolute agony. She was also claustrophobic, and she hated that awful thumping sound.

But when she could separate herself from the pain and the noise, she kept seeing in her mind's eye the woman she'd met up with in the ER—the cop with the uniform and the badge, the one with her mother's face—with Isobel's face. Hannah had heard the cop's name, but she couldn't remember it. Still she had to be one of Eddie's offspring, one who had taken after Hannah's side of the family—the Andersons rather than the Gilchrists. Whoever she was, she'd been at the funeral and she'd come to the hospital after the crash. What was it she'd said earlier about wanting to keep Hannah safe?

"We're done now," the attendant said. "Let's get you moved to your room."

As soon as they rolled Hannah's gurney out into the waiting room, the cop with Isobel's face appeared next to her, walking beside the gurney as it traversed two different sets of elevators and several long corridors.

No matter how hard Hannah tried, she couldn't quite summon the name.

"Who are you again?" she asked finally, as they rolled along.

The woman nodded. "My name is Lieutenant Crystal Manning. I'm with LAPD."

"And you're one of Eddie's." It was a statement, not a question, and Crystal nodded a second time. "You look just like my mother," Hannah continued. "Her name was Isobel. I never liked her much."

Crystal smiled grimly. "We're even there," she muttered. "I never liked my mother either, and my father wasn't much better."

That was a surprising admission. Hannah had always assumed that the people who'd come to Eddie's clinic and successfully conceived a child would have turned out to be perfect parents. Evidently that wasn't true.

While riding upstairs in an elevator filled with several other people, both women remained silent. As they started down another long corridor, Hannah spoke again. "What about Marco Gregory, my driver? Is he okay?"

Crystal nodded. "My understanding is he was brought here, too, but he was treated and released."

"Good," Hannah said. "And why are you here?"

"Someone tried to kill you, Mrs. Gilchrist. You already knew that, because you told my friend Ali Reynolds as much before they managed to cut you loose from the wreckage. She also said you know who's responsible. Now I'm hoping you'll tell me."

In reply Hannah zipped her lips and turned her head away.

They rolled her into a room while Crystal waited outside in the corridor. When the attendant and a pair of nurses transferred her from the gurney to the bed, Hannah managed to keep quiet during the shift, but it hurt so much she could barely stand it. Afterward one of the nurses stayed around long enough to take Hannah's vitals. As soon as he left, though, Crystal reappeared and settled into a visitor's chair.

"Am I under arrest?" Hannah asked.

"No," Crystal answered, "not at all."

"Then I don't have to talk to you."

"That's correct," Crystal agreed, "but there's something you need to know."

"What's that?"

"Gloria Reece showed up here at the hospital a little while ago. She came armed with a handgun and claiming to be your granddaughter. Based on what you told Ali earlier, I instructed them not to let her inside."

Neither woman spoke for the better part of a minute. "Where is Gloria now?" Hannah asked at last.

"In an interview room at Valley Station for the time being, waiting for me to come and talk to her," Crystal answered. "She was carrying a gun with no sign of a concealed-carry permit. That's why she was taken into custody—on a weapons charge."

"But she came to the hospital looking for me and armed with a weapon?"

"That's correct," Crystal replied. "Now, why do you suppose she would do something like that?"

Hannah said nothing, so Crystal continued. "Back at the crash scene, you told my friend Ali that three people had turned on you, and you named names—your son, Edward; Luis Ochoa; and Gloria Reece. While you were undergoing your scans, I made a few phone calls. I've learned that Edward Gilchrist and Luis Ochoa are both lifers at Folsom State Prison. And I also learned that Gloria Ochoa Reece is the daughter of Luis's late brother, Antonio.

"From what I saw this afternoon, what happened in the street in front of the funeral home was an organized hit, done with malice aforethought. So what do those three individuals have against you, Mrs. Gilchrist? Ali told me you disobeyed some kind of directive, and the three of them turned on you. Why would they be so determined to take you out? Why would your own son want you dead?"

Just then two white-coated men appeared in the doorway of Hannah's room. Hannah recognized the first one, Dr. Pennington, but the second was a complete stranger. It was the ER doc who actually entered the room.

"Ms. Gilchrist, I'm afraid we have some very bad news for you," he said gravely. "The MRI revealed—"

"I already know about the cancer, if that's what you mean," Hannah interrupted. "According to the biopsy, it's a recurrence of breast cancer that has already metastasized to at least three separate organs. It was diagnosed about two weeks ago. I could already see the dollar signs in my oncologist's eyes. He was ready to go all out in terms of cancer-care warfare—surgery, chemo, radiation, the full-meal deal—but I put my foot down. I told him that at my age I'm prepared to let things run their course. I'm not in pain from the cancer, at least not so far, and when that happens, I'll deal with it. What I want to know right now is can you fix my hip?"

The second man entered the room. "I'm Dr. Donald Fairfield," he said. "I'm an orthopedic surgeon. Yes, I can replace your damaged hip. However, we're talking invasive surgery with a painful, long-term recovery, and given your prognosis—"

"The recovery can't be any more painful than what I'm dealing with right now," Hannah snapped back at him. "My oncologist gave me six months to a year, if that. I want my hip fixed for however long I have. If you won't do it, I'll find someone who will."

Hannah could tell from the startled expression on the man's face that she'd caught him off guard, and that made her feel a little better. She had seemed to lose some of her gumption over time, and right now she was glad to have it back.

"Very well," he agreed. "When did you eat last?"

"I had brunch around eleven," she answered, "just before I left the hotel."

He checked his watch. "Because of the danger of aspirating food particles into your lungs while you're under anesthesia, we need to wait several more hours before we can schedule the surgery."

"Thank you," she said. "I'm looking forward to it."

"You should probably try to rest now."

"No," Hannah said. "Before I worry about getting some rest, I need to speak to Lieutenant Manning here. There are a number of things we need to discuss."

60

The room was silent for some time after the two doctors left. When Hannah spoke again, it was with a question. "Do you have one of those phones that can do videos?"

"Yes, why?"

"Because I think you're going to want to record what I have to say, and you should probably start by reading me my rights. I'm prepared to plead guilty to everything I've done. Since I'm in no condition to write out a confession, recording it will have to do."

It took some maneuvering on Crystal's part to position the phone, propping it up on the tray on Hannah's bed in a way that captured both their faces on the screen. Although Hannah was sure the officer knew the cautioning words by heart, she pulled a small laminated card out of her jacket pocket and read the contents word for word.

Once her rights had been read and the names of those present for the recording session stated, Hannah wasted no time in coming to the heart of the matter. "After my son went to prison for murdering Dawn, his second wife, he made a list—his A List, as he likes to call it. In it he listed all the people he held responsible for his destruction, and he vowed to get even with every one of them."

"He wrote it out?" Crystal asked.

"He didn't actually write it—he tattooed it on his arm, and not the full names either. Just the first letter of each of their names—*D* for Dawn, *L* for Leo Aurelio, *K* for Kaitlyn Todd, *A* for Alexandra Munsey, and *A* for Ali Reynolds. He called it his A List—*A* for annihilation. He was determined to take them all down. Each time one of them was dealt with, Eddie adjusted the tattoo by x-ing out that person's initial, starting with Dawn, even though she was already dead long before he went to prison. But when it came to dealing with the others, I agreed to help him."

"Why?" Crystal asked.

Hannah shrugged. "Because he was my son," she answered simply, "and because he was all I had left."

"How many of the individuals on that tattooed list are dead?"

"Four—Dawn, Leo, Kaitlyn, and Alexandra."

"And why is Ali's name on the list?"

"Because she was the one who brought the media into play. Without that none of it would have happened."

"I take it you weren't the actual triggerman in any of those cases?"

"No, I provided the funding. Eddie chose his preferred target, Luis had the necessary contacts and connections, Gloria made the hiring arrangements and handled payments to the various contractors."

"So you're saying it was all four of you together?"

"That's how it was to begin with," Hannah answered, "but over time things changed. I paid for all the hits in advance. Once they had my money, Gloria began to think she could boss me around. She and Eddie both started ignoring my wishes and shutting me out of the conversation. They treated me like I was nothing more than a walking, talking ATM. And when Eddie and Gloria both forbade me to come to Alexandra Munsey's funeral, that was the last straw."

"Why was coming to the funeral so important?" Crystal asked.

"Wait," Hannah said suddenly. "What happened to my purse?"

"It's probably still with the wreckage. Why?"

"I came for a trophy," Hannah replied. "I wanted a trophy, and I had it in my purse."

"A trophy?"

"I have Leo Aurelio's ashes back home in Folsom, along with a copy of Kaitlyn Todd Holmes's death certificate. This time I wanted a printed program from Alexandra Munsey's funeral, and I came here in person to get it. First Eddie told me I shouldn't come, and then Gloria stopped by and told me the same thing. We had words."

"And you came to the funeral anyway?"

"Yes."

"Maybe Gloria decided to come after you on her own."

"No, Gloria is not an independent operator. She takes her orders from Luis."

"Ali claims you saw Gloria at the coffee shop across the street just before the crash occurred?"

"That's right, she was sitting there just as pretty as you please, waiting and watching, expecting to see me die. But I've got news for Gloria and for the rest of them as well. If I'm going out, I'll do it on my terms, not on theirs."

"You said Luis has the contacts. That makes it sound

as though he's central to this operation. How does it work?"

"It's too hard to smuggle money in and out of the prison. People pay for the various services he provides, but Gloria handles all the monetary transactions."

"What about communications?" Crystal asked.

"He's got a cell phone," Hannah answered.

"In his cell in prison?" Crystal asked.

"You'd better believe it. Gloria let that slip sometime ago when she came by to do one of my manicures. She probably thought I wasn't paying attention, but I was."

"If you were not involved in the actual homicides, do you have any way of proving that any of this is true?"

"I have the account records."

"What kind of records?"

"Luis operates on a cash-only basis. There's a garage refrigerator at my place in Folsom. That's where I keep my cash—hard, cold cash, as it were. It's also where I keep my ledger. I've been blessed with having a good deal of money in my life, but that doesn't mean I'm not careful with it. I've always kept track of exactly how much I had, of where it went, and why."

"So the ledger is still there?"

Hannah nodded. "Along with a little over two hundred thousand dollars in cash."

"What can you tell me about those other deaths?"

"Leo Aurelio was found hanging in his prison cell and was presumed to have committed suicide. Kaitlyn died in a one-car automobile accident when she plunged off a snowy highway. And Alexandra Munsey? She was gunned down in her home."

"But you don't know any of the individuals actually involved as the doers in those incidents?"

"No, I operated strictly behind the scenes," Hannah answered, "but I'm getting tired now. Is that all you need?"

"I believe you've given me enough probable cause to go for warrants, and I'll be doing so. I'll also be placing you under arrest on suspicion of conspiracy to commit homicide. I'll be making arrangements for a uniformed officer to be stationed outside your door both before and after your surgery."

"To protect me or to keep me from running away?" Hannah asked.

"Tell me this," Crystal said. "Are you prepared to turn state's evidence and testify in a court of law against the others—against your son, Luis Ochoa, and Gloria Reece?"

"I am."

"Why?"

"Years ago, when Eddie first went to prison, he told me about his list. When I offered to help him with it, he said that two people with nothing to lose going up against four people with everything to lose gave us pretty good odds. He was in prison, and I'd already survived one bout with cancer. Now my cancer is back, and I'll probably die of it, but the same holds true. Someone with nothing to lose going up against three people with everything to lose can win hands down. Eddie, Luis, and Gloria all think nothing will ever touch them. I want to prove them wrong."

"All right, then," Crystal said, "in that case the guard will be here primarily for your safety and protection."

"I'm not certain I take too much comfort in that," Hannah said. "I have it on good authority that guards can be bribed on occasion."

"These won't be," Crystal Manning replied. "I'll see to it."

There was a soft tap on the door, and a young woman entered the room. She wore a lanyard with photo ID and carried a clipboard. "I'm from admissions," she said. "Even though Ms. Doe is being admitted to the hospital under a pseudonym, we need to straighten out her insurance coverage and next-of-kin arrangements before she undergoes surgery."

"You can do that while still keeping her identity off the books?" Crystal asked.

"Yes, ma'am."

"I'll step out into the hall, then," Crystal said, turning, collecting her phone, and switching off the recording. "I have some calls to make, but I'll be right outside if you need me."

"She seems nice," the admissions clerk said once the door swung shut.

Hannah nodded. "She is. She's also my granddaughter. When you get to the part about next of kin, you can fill in her name—Crystal Manning."

The clerk had already taken a seat and was putting pen to paper. "What's her phone number?" she asked with her pen poised above the applicable box on the form.

"I don't know," Hannah answered. "You'll have to get that from her. She may be my granddaughter, but we've only just now met."

An hour later, as they rolled Hannah's bed through the hallways toward the OR, she was thinking about Crystal Manning and that ginger-haired boy named Rory Davis Munsey. Eddie hadn't wanted her to go to the funeral because he was afraid people would recognize her—and that they'd all end up being caught. What he hadn't anticipated and what he should have feared was the idea that if she actually met any of those people in the flesh—the ones who were Eddie's presumed enemies—they'd turn into people in their own right.

But she had and they had, and that made all the difference.

61

On that Sunday afternoon, California Bureau of Investigations Agent Bob Owens was having his best golf game ever! On the front nine, he'd made two birdies and an eagle. On the back nine, he'd birdied the par three. As he waited his turn to tee off on the fifteenth hole, he was six under and cleaning everybody's clock, but that's when his phone rang. It didn't actually ring, because out of respect for his fellow golfers he had silenced the damned ringer, but when it buzzed in his pocket, he dragged it out and looked at the screen. Seeing his boss's photo appear in the caller-ID window, he went ahead and answered.

"What's up?" he asked.

"I need you to come in," Agent in Charge Samantha Jacobs told him. "I've got search warrants on one of the unsolved cases you and Mansfield worked years ago, and they need to be executed immediately."

"Which case?" he asked. Unfortunately, there were several to choose from.

"A guy named Leo Aurelio," Samantha answered. "He was a lifer at Corcoran who supposedly committed suicide."

"I remember," Owens said. "The one who was later found to be plugged full of fentanyl."

"Yup, that's the one."

"Where are we searching?"

"According to Lieutenant Manning from the LAPD, the warrants list four separate locations—two are cells at Folsom Prison, one is a residence in a Folsom area retirement community called Arbor Crest, and the last one, also in Folsom, is on Rugosa Drive. Lieutenant Manning says that Leo Aurelio was the hired hit man who killed the wife of a guy named Edward Gilchrist. After Leo was arrested, he turned state's evidence and testified against the guy who hired him, a guy who is currently serving life without at Folsom. Now, according to Gilchrist's mother, she's been underwriting her son's vendetta against a number of people whom Gilchrist regards as responsible for his fall from grace. At least four of those individuals are dead, and all of this has been accomplished with the help of another lifer at Folsom, Luis Ochoa, and his niece, someone named Gloria Reece. The residence on Rugosa belongs to her."

"And the Arbor Crest residence belongs to the old lady," Owens added. "I remember her. She's the one who offered to pay Leo's final expenses. Have you called Danny?"

Danny was Danielle Harper, Bob Owens's current partner.

"Did," Sam answered. "She doesn't live too far from here, so she's stopping by the office to pick up the warrants and check out a vehicle from the motor pool. Where are you?"

"On the fifteenth hole at the Ancil Hoffman Golf Course in Carmichael."

"Sorry about that," Samantha said.

"Tell me about it," Owens grumbled.

"Do you want to ride with her, or do you want to take your own vehicle?"

"I'm already halfway to Folsom as it is," Owens told her. "Have her meet me at the prison. Has anyone advised the people in charge that we're coming their way?"

"That would be negative," Sam replied. "According to Manning, there's a good possibility that some prison personnel may be involved in this whole business. It'll be better all around if we spring the warrants on them at the last minute—less chance of a cover-up that way."

"Hey, Bobby," one of Owens's fellow golfers called impatiently. "Are you going to stand around gabbing on the phone all day or are you going to play golf?"

"Okay," Owens said into his phone. "Tell Danny I'm on my way."

"Sorry about your golf game," Samantha said.

"You have no idea."

With that, Owens returned his phone to his pocket and dropped his driver back into his bag.

"Wait a minute," another of the foursome demanded as Owens reached for his club cover. "Does that mean you're calling it quits?"

"Got to," Owens answered. "I've got warrants to execute in a cold case," he said, unstrapping his bag from the golf cart and hefting it onto his shoulder. "I'll have to pay up what's owing at the nineteenth hole some other time."

The other guys were all professional law-enforcement officers, too—Johnny Richards was a captain with the California Highway Patrol, Cuzzy Arwine was an assistant chief of police with the Sacramento PD, and Gabe Ortega was the chief deputy for the Sacramento County Sheriff's Department. All three of them knew the drill. They knew that Owens had to go, but that didn't keep them from razzing the hell out of him as he went.

After walking off the course and dropping his golf bag into the trunk of his Camaro, he thought about going back to his place to change clothes but decided against it. There'd been an urgency in Sam's voice that put speed over decorum. He had his badge along, and that's the only thing he really needed. The people at Folsom would have to take him as is, golf shorts and all.

As Owens headed for Highway 50, he wished he could call Bill Mansfield and let him know what was up, but there was no point. The last time he'd stopped by Bill's "memory home" to see his old partner, the poor guy had slipped so far into dementia that he'd had no idea who Bob was. And that was one of the reasons the two of them had left a number of unsolved cases behind, including this one—Leo Aurelio's. That had more or less marked the beginning of it. Bob Owens had been the new kid on the block back then, though when things started going haywire with Bill, Owens couldn't help but notice. Reports didn't get filed in a timely manner. Leads didn't get followed up on. When Bill was called into court to testify, he blew his testimony more than once, forgetting key details. As a result several people walked who never should have.

At first Owens had let things go and simply chalked it up to the fact that Bill was absentminded. But then one day Bill got hopelessly lost trying to get back to the office from an interview. That's when Owens had finally blown the whistle to the agent in charge. Within a matter of weeks, Agent Bill Mansfield was medically retired from the CBI and Bob Owens was in the market for a new partner.

As Owens headed out, he checked the GPS, which told him that going to US-50 would be slightly faster, so that's the way he went. Once on the highway, he called Danny. She had headed out slightly before he did, so she was only about five minutes behind him.

"Sam called me off a golf course," he told her, "so I'm not exactly dressed for the part. You'll need to take lead."

"No problem," Danny said, "but what can you tell me about the case?"

"Leo Aurelio died in prison," Bob explained. "When he turned up dead in his cell, hanging from a rope, the death was presumed to be suicide. Later on, he was found to have a fatal dose of fentanyl in his system. His manner of death was ruled to be undetermined, but since he was in prison and had no relatives to keep the investigation on course, the investigation went cold in a hurry and stayed that way."

Owens didn't bother to go into the details of how much Bill Mansfield's worsening condition had contributed to that.

"What about the two cells we're supposed to search?"

"One belongs to a lifer named Eddie Gilchrist, the guy who hired Aurelio to murder his wife. The other belongs to Luis Ochoa, another lifer, who's been aiding and abetting. The Arbor Crest residence belongs to Gilchrist's mother, and the Rugosa Drive residence belongs to Luis Ochoa's niece, Gloria Reece. Both of them are presumed to be participants in a program of revenge against Edward Gilchrist's enemies."

"Sounds like fun," Danny Harper told him. "I can hardly wait."

Call-waiting buzzed. "I've got another call coming in. See you at the main gate in a couple," Owens told his partner. Then he switched over to the other call. "Hello."

"Agent Owens?"

"Yes."

"Lieutenant Manning with LAPD here—the detective who obtained the warrants. Are you at Folsom yet?"

"I'm just pulling in to the parking lot," he answered, "but thanks for calling. I'm glad to have a chance to talk to you. What exactly are we looking for?"

"My cooperating witness says Ochoa has a cell phone. At the moment I've got Gloria Reece confined to an interview room. Once she asks for a lawyer, she'll make one call and any incriminating evidence will disappear. So call me back on this number as soon as you execute those two in-prison warrants."

"Will do," he said. "Anything in particular we should be looking for?"

"I believe Luis has access to a cell phone. Finding that would be a real prize, but be aware it's likely that some of the prison staff may be involved in all this, so play your cards close to the vest. If there's any advance warning of the search, crucial evidence is bound to disappear. And one more thing: Before you leave the prison, I need you to take a photo of the tattoo on Edward Gilchrist's forearm."

"What kind of tattoo?"

"It's a series of mostly crossed-out letters—initials," Crystal told him. "According to his mother, it's Gilchrist's kill list."

"Okay," Owens said. "We're on it, and since my partner just pulled up beside me, we'd best get with the program."

He and Danielle did a quick strategy session in the parking lot before approaching the entrance. Agent Harper was designated to do most of the talking, with the proviso of keeping knowledge about the reason for their visit limited to the fewest number of people possible. Which wasn't easy.

Danielle offered her badge and credentials to the clerk at the front desk and then asked to see the warden.

"Purpose of your visit," the clerk demanded.

"I'm afraid I'm not at liberty to say."

The female clerk, a surly old bat who was at least twice as old as Danielle, was not the least bit amused. "It's Sunday, so the warden isn't in. If you want to speak to Assistant Warden Masterson, I'll need to know the purpose of your visit."

Danielle didn't back down. "This is confidential police business, so either let us in or put me in touch with your supervisor."

The threat of involving a supervisor worked. Moments later Harper and Owens were issued visitor passes, told to stow their weapons, and then escorted through a grim corridor into the office of the assistant warden. Obviously he had been warned in advance, because he was more than ready for them.

"This is highly irregular," he told them. "You have no business barging in here like this without providing any reason for your visit."

"Here's the reason," Danielle said, dropping the warrants on his desk. "We're here to execute these."

Bob Owens had been trained to observe changes in facial features. As Assistant Warden Masterson read through the verbiage of the warrants, the CBI agent observed the involuntary tightening of the man's jawline and the deepening furrows in his forehead. What Masterson was seeing on the pages was causing some concern, and that bothered Agent Owens. Folsom was a big place. A phone call from inside the prison could disappear evidence as easily as one from outside.

"We're hoping you'll accompany us as we execute the warrants," Agent Owens said, speaking for the first time.

"Why would I do that?" Masterson wanted to know.

"I know the prison has been under attack by both the feds and by outside activists due to suspicions about prison personnel violating inmates' human rights. I'd like to have you along with us to avoid any allegations of impropriety on our part or on yours."

Masterson gave Owens a long look. Sitting there in his brightly colored Hawaiian shirt and his chartreuse shorts, the CBI agent might have seemed harmless enough, but Masterson's stiff silence testified to his growing anxiety. Owens understood what was going on. He had just dropped the words "outside investigations" into the conversation, and that was usually enough to make the blood of any self-respecting middle manager run cold. It worked this time, too.

"Very well," Masterson agreed finally, pushing away from his desk and rising to his feet. "Let's get this done. Where do you want to start?"

"Thank you for your assistance," a beaming Danielle said brightly. "If you don't mind, I believe we should probably start with Mr. Ochoa's cell."

Luis was upset when he was shown the search warrant and ordered to vacate his cell. He stood fuming in the corridor, stationed between a cellblock guard and the assistant warden while Agents Owens and Harper conducted their search. When Ochoa realized Danielle was conducting a systematic search of each CMU in the cell, he became even more agitated. At last one of the blocks gave way under Danielle's probing fingers, and the inmate was forced to look on in helpless fury while the CBI agents removed each of his treasures from the cubbyhole and entered them into inventory and evidence bags—a cell phone, a small iPad, a charger, a vicious-looking knife, tattoo equipment, several bottles of ink, and a number of clear plastic bags, some laden with pills and others containing supplies of white powder. In addition there was a supply of cash that amounted to almost twelve hundred bucks.

At last the search ended and Ochoa was returned to his cell. As the two agents and Assistant Warden Masterson headed toward Edward Gilchrist's cell, Bob Owens pulled out his phone and dialed the most recent number. "Where are you?" he asked when Crystal Manning answered.

"Interview room. Why?"

"I wanted to let you know we have Ochoa's phone in our possession."

"Good," Crystal said. "I'll be right out."

The remark puzzled Owens for a moment. Then, less than a minute later, the cell phone stowed in one of the glassine evidence bags began to vibrate. Owens held the bag up to the light so he could see the caller-ID screen. Once he saw the number, he grinned at his partner.

"No need to answer," he told the others. "Crystal Manning must have left her phone in the interview room as bait. Praise be to God, not only did Gloria Reece take it, the interview room will have it all on tape."

Edward Gilchrist was almost as outraged by the search warrant as Luis Ochoa had been. "What's this all about?" he wanted to know. "What's going on?"

"We have reason to believe that you and your friend Mr. Ochoa are involved in a criminal conspiracy," Danielle told him sweetly. "We're here looking for evidence."

"You're not going to find it," Gilchrist fumed.

But it turned out they did find something. Stored behind the loose CMU under Edward Gilchrist's washbasin, Danielle Harper located a whole pack of cigarettes, along with seven hundred dollars in cash, and some envelopes filled with a white powder that would most likely turn out to be either cocaine or heroin. They were about to walk away when Owens remembered the tattoo.

"I'll need to photograph the tattoo on your left arm," he said.

"Why?"

"According to your mother, I believe it's what's known as a kill list."

For the first time, Edward Gilchrist's confidence faltered. "My mother told you that?" he demanded.

"She did," Owens replied. "Since the three of you tried to kill her, she's a little pissed at the moment."

"Wait," Gilchrist said. "Someone tried to have my mother killed? Who?"

"Apparently you and your partners in crime," Owens told him.

Gilchrist seemed genuinely surprised by that statement. His surprise seemed so real that Bob was forced to conclude that although Gilchrist had no doubt been involved with the other deaths, it seemed likely that he'd had nothing to do with the attack on his mother.

"That's something a judge and jury will have to determine," Owens said, "a judge and jury and a court of law."

The CBI agents left Folsom State Prison with the satisfaction of knowing that both Luis Ochoa and Edward Gilchrist had been moved into the hole, with each of them placed in solitary confinement. Owens and Harper then enlisted the help of the Folsom Police Department in executing the two remaining warrants, starting with the one for Gloria Reece's place on Rugosa Drive. When they surveyed the contents of Gloria's faux wine cellar, they finally began to see how big Luis Ochoa's operation really was. It took hours to collect, inventory, and load the contents from the cellar. Just in terms of packets of cash, they were looking at more than $2 million.

It was almost midnight when they arrived at Arbor Crest. A sleepy-eyed receptionist took them to Hannah Gilchrist's unit and let them inside. At Crystal's suggestion they started with the garage fridge, coming away with more than two hundred thousand in cash and Hannah's promised ledger.

"What else?" Danielle asked when they finally finished in the garage.

They went through the rest of the house but found nothing. It was only as they were about to leave that Agent Owens went over to the urn. "We need to take this," he said.

"Why?"

"It's Leo Aurelio's cremains," he said.

"The guy she paid to have killed?" Danielle asked.

Bob Owens nodded.

"But why would she have them?"

"I'm pretty sure she wanted gloating rights," he answered. "In the world of serial killers I believe the urn and Aurelio's ashes count as trophies."

62

When Hannah finally awakened, it was hours later and there were two people in the room with her—Crystal Manning and Ali Reynolds, both of whom seemed to be dozing in visitors' chairs. It was odd—surreal, almost—to be in the presence of someone who was undeniably her own granddaughter and someone else whom she'd sworn to murder. Ali Reynolds, the woman who'd stayed with her and comforted her in the wreckage—who'd done her best to stanch the flow of blood—was someone who might have been Eddie's next victim—Hannah's next victim.

Hannah waited quietly until a few minutes later, when one of them stirred. "Do I have a new hip?" she asked.

They had intubated her during the procedure, and her voice was scratchy and hoarse.

Crystal was the one who answered. "Yes, you do."

"It doesn't hurt at all."

"You're on drugs right now," Crystal said. "The hurt will be later."

"What about Eddie and the others?"

"We served our search warrants and found what we needed," Crystal answered. "As long as you testify against them, they're all three going down. That won't make much difference for Luis Ochoa and your son, but it will for Gloria Reece."

"Good," Hannah said. "I hope I live long enough to do just that."

"So do I," Crystal said.

"Is there a guard stationed outside my door?"

"Yes," Crystal answered, "two of them, in fact. When we searched Gloria's vehicle, the GPS led us to a very bad guy named Tank Rowland who has long been suspected of criminal behavior. We served warrants on several of his places of business and discovered two vehicles—a box truck and a motorcycle—that are suspected of having been used in the attack on you. Now that we know what we're looking for, we'll be able to find all three vehicles involved—those two and the Suburban as well—on traffic cameras near the scene. Tank is currently in custody, but he's a very dangerous man with plenty of equally dangerous friends. That's why I've called for two guards. Once you leave the hospital . . ."

"I'll be in jail, won't I?" Hannah asked.

Crystal nodded. "Considering the severity of the charges, you most likely won't be allowed to make bail."

"That's fine, then," Hannah said, "because I'll be under guard there as well."

With that, Hannah turned her attention to Ali Reynolds. "Thank you for staying with me in the car yesterday. It was yesterday, wasn't it? I believe I've lost track of time."

"You're welcome," Ali said with a nod, "and, yes, it was yesterday."

"I seem to remember that you had blood all over you—my blood."

"Yes," Ali said again, "from the cut on your head. I was finally able to go back to the hotel and change clothes."

"Did you know you were supposed to be our next victim?" Hannah asked.

"I do now."

"I'm glad you're the one who got away."

"That makes two of us."

Hannah glanced up at the clock on the wall. It said five minutes to six. "Do you suppose one of you could figure out how to order some breakfast? I'm starved."

It was more of a command than a request, and Hannah smiled as Ali went looking for a nurse to order breakfast. There was no telling how long it would last, but, for now at least, the old Hannah Gilchrist was not only back, she was in charge, and that meant that things were exactly as they were supposed to be.

63

It was noontime on Tuesday. The whole crew was gathered in the break room at High Noon Enterprises, celebrating Ali's return from California with a generous round of pizza.

"So Frigg really did save the day," Stu marveled.

"In every way possible," Ali replied. "Her ability to penetrate those security-camera systems both at the scene of the crash and later at the hospital was critical. Without that there's a good chance Gloria could have gotten to Hannah Gilchrist and finished her off. As it is, she's alive if not exactly well, but she's still willing and able to testify against the others."

"So maybe I shouldn't disable Fido after all."

"Who's Fido?" Ali asked.

"It's Frigg's new work-around program."

"A work-around for what?" Ali asked.

"A work-around for me," Stu said despairingly. "I told her that she'd been using one of her illegal pet programs, so when she created a new one, she named it Fido."

"Frigg's the one who made that revised threat-level assessment," Ali said, "and without that, Hannah Gilchrist would be dead and maybe I would be, too. So all in favor of keeping Frigg and Fido, raise your right hand."

In the end it was unanimous. Frigg stayed on, and so did Fido.

64

It was almost a month later, a perfect day toward the end of June, when Ali Reynolds held her garden party in honor of both current and past recipients of Amelia Dougherty Askins scholarships. The party was held in the English garden that Leland Brooks had designed, which was in full glorious bloom for the event.

The party was catered by Raphael Fuentes, the first-ever male Askins recipient. He'd been given a full-ride scholarship to the Cordon Bleu branch in Scottsdale. For the party he had produced a full-bore Cornish cream tea that Leland would have loved. As the young people chatted together, talking hopes and dreams as only the very young can do, Ali gravitated toward her other two honored guests—Sister Anselm and her new copilot, Sister Cecelia. Sister Anselm had been invited because she'd always adored Leland's formal teas, and Sister Cecelia came along because these days she was Sister Anselm's constant companion. Ali was relieved to see that despite Sister Anselm's initial misgivings, a genuine affection had already sprung up between the two nuns.

Ali was about to sit down to visit when her phone rang. Seeing Crystal Manning's name in the caller-ID screen, she excused herself and moved away from the party.

"Hannah's gone," Crystal said, when Ali answered. "When?"

"Yesterday afternoon," Crystal said.

"What got her?" Ali asked.

"It was the cancer, of course," Crystal replied. "According to the ME, it was the tumor on her pancreas that took her out. It's got to be one of the shortest life sentences ever. She went to court and pled guilty only a week ago Friday, so her sentence lasted exactly a week and one day. The Munseys were there for the plea deal, of course—Evan, his dad, and his stepmother. So was Kaitlyn Todd Holmes's husband. Her father was too ill with lung cancer to travel. Hannah addressed each of those people individually, asking their forgiveness. And I think she really meant it. The woman may have been a killer at heart, but she was also one classy lady."

Ali was used to listening to people, and she caught the undertone in Crystal's voice. "One way or the other, Hannah Gilchrist was also your grandmother," Ali observed, "so how are you doing?"

"Not well," Crystal admitted with a slight catch in her voice. "For some strange reason, this whole thing has hit me really hard. She gave me a picture of her mother, Isobel, one that was taken years ago when her mother was having tea with Mamie Eisenhower. The thing that's really spooky is that except for the color of my hair I look exactly like Isobel Anderson."

"It sounds like you grew close to her in the last few weeks."

"I did," Crystal admitted, "because she didn't have anyone else. I helped her get her will rewritten and her final arrangements in order. She left everything to the guy who was driving the limo that day—a guy named Marco Gregory and his wife, Bettina. I've met them both. They're nice people who had apparently worked for

Hannah for years before she moved to Folsom. They'll be coming into at least a million dollars that they never expected to have. And so will Rory Munsey."

"She left something to him, too?"

"She did. A million dollars to be held in trust until he's twenty-one. She said that he's the great-grandson she never had, and she wanted him to have it."

There was a break in the conversation and a slight hiccup in Crystal's voice before she continued. "She left something to me, too—her grandmother's cameo brooch—my great-great-grandmother's brooch. I never expected to feel this way, but you're right, Ali. Hannah Gilchrist was the grandmother I never had, and now I'm sorry she's gone."

"And I'm sorry for your loss," Ali said.

"Thank you for understanding," Crystal murmured. "I'm not sure anyone else will get it."

Ali returned to the party, but some of the brightness had gone out of the day. It was only later, after everyone else had left, that she shared the whole story with Sister Anselm and with Sister Cecelia, too.

"That's what happens sometimes," Sister Anselm told Ali afterward as the two sisters were loading up to return to the convent in Jerome. "Where Edward Gilchrist sowed hatred and deceit, God sowed love, and Hannah and Crystal found it. We'll pray for them both tonight when we get home."

"Thank you," Ali told her. "Thank you for the prayers, and thank you for being my friend."

"That cuts both ways, Ali, my dear," Sister Anselm said. "It certainly cuts both ways."

Keep reading for an excerpt of

CREDIBLE THREAT

The newest mystery featuring Ali Reynolds

Available soon from Gallery Books

Prologue

On a mid-March afternoon as the sun drifted down over Piestewa Peak to the west, Rachel Higgins wrapped her sweater a little closer around her body and took another sip of her vodka tonic. Snowbirds might be running around dressed in Bermuda shorts, Hawaiian shirts, flip-flops, and sandals, but for Rachel—a Phoenix native and true desert dweller—mid-March still counted as winter. Even so, she wasn't ready to go inside, not just yet. For one thing, there was nothing to go in for other than another evening of mindless viewing of whatever empty-headed crap happened to be on TV. No, she was better off staying outside for a while longer, savoring the luscious perfume of orange blossoms from her neighbor's trees, an aroma that seemed to intensify each day as afternoon turned to evening.

Rachel had long since become immune to the rumble of rush hour traffic on State Route 51 and Highway 101 in the near distance. When Rachel and her husband, Rich, had bought the place on Menadota Drive, the mountain formerly known as Squaw Peak had not yet been renamed Piestewa Peak in honor of Lori Piestewa. Lori was the young Hopi woman who had become the first Native American woman ever to die in combat, back when her convoy was ambushed in 2003 during the Iraq War. At the time Rachel and Rich had moved to the neighborhood, both Loop 101 and Route 51 had barely been a gleam in the eye of some crazed highway engineer. Now the name Squaw Peak was no more, and what had once been a serenely quiet desert landscape was overwhelmed by the unrelenting roar of 24/7 traffic.

This had been their dream home back then—one of the first houses to be built in a new subdivision. The new house was a far cry from the modest bungalow off 7th Avenue and Indian School that had been their first home. No, this one was spacious inside and out. Rich had told her at the time that this lot on a corner of the cul-de-sac would be plenty big enough for a pool, and five years later they had one. At the time it had seemed as though their family life was coming to order at last. Rich had just been given an amazing promotion as an engineer at the Salt River Project that had made their purchase of the new place financially feasible. As for Rachel? At age twenty-five, after years of trying, she had managed to get pregnant. On the day they moved into their new house, their son David had been a babe in arms.

Rachel had been ecstatic with the way things were turning out. She'd never wanted to be anything other than a housewife and mother. That's why she'd majored in Home-Ec in college. *Was that major even an option these days?* she wondered. Rachel didn't know, but that's exactly what Rich had wanted back then—a stay-at-home housewife and mother—and Rachel had settled into the job with enthusiasm.

Rachel's father, Max, had been an accountant—a mousy little man with a propensity for letting people walk all over him. Her mother had been glad to spend his CPA earnings, all the while calling him a milquetoast behind his back. Naturally Rachel had gone looking for something different from that, and Rich Higgins had turned out to be her father's polar opposite. He had been a big, burly "my way or the highway" kind of guy. Which may have worked all right to begin with, but what happens when the guy calling the shots loses his way? What are you supposed to do then?

In their family, Rich had always been the sole bread-winner, and he hadn't bothered consulting her when he'd accepted an employer-offered buy-out at age sixty. Starting his pension then meant it was far less than they had counted on. And because his leaving was considered a voluntary separation, he didn't qualify for unemploy-ment benefits, either.

Realizing how tight money was becoming, Rachel had offered to try getting a job, but Rich nixed that idea completely. It was fine for Rachel to volunteer here and there, but no wife of his was going to work outside the home. They would survive on the money he brought home come hell or high water. It was the way it had always been, and that was the way it would be in the future.

And what had Rachel done about that? Absolutely nothing. At age fifty she had morphed into a female version of her father. She had let Rich have his way and had gone along with that edict. Besides, when it came to entering the workforce at her age, what could she do? Office work? Hardly. She was no typist. She could manage their home computer well enough to find things on the Internet when she needed to and to send out occasional e-mail, but she was definitely not computer literate. And when it came to typing, she was of the hunt-and-peck variety. She could have looked for a job as a sales clerk, she supposed, but she couldn't imagine standing behind a cash register for eight hours a day scanning other people's groceries at Safeway or A.J. Bayless.

In the end, it had been far easier to be complicit and simply go with the flow. She and Rich had made their bed together, and now they were lying in it. Except that wasn't entirely true. They slept in separate bedrooms now. Rachel had the master, and Rich slept down the hall in the room that had once been David's. They woke at different times and went to sleep at different times. The meals they ate together were generally eaten in silence. They were more like roommates now than they were husband and wife. Was Rich as unhappy as Rachel was? Maybe, but it wasn't something they talked about because they mostly didn't talk.

At this point, Rachel was bored. She'd had a few flirtations here and there, but the relationships had never gone beyond that. Dealing with one man was quite enough, thank you very much! Had she thought about getting a divorce? Not really. For one thing, despite the fact that neither she nor Rich had attended Mass in years, she still regarded herself as a Catholic, meaning that divorce was out of the question. She would do the same thing her mother had done, which is to say, she would stick it out to the bitter end.

Once Rich's Social Security income started coming in, that too was lower than it would have been had he started collecting benefits later. As they gradually depleted their savings and their financial situation deteriorated, they were forced to cut one corner after another, and that's when Rachel's resentment about that early buy-out began to simmer beneath the surface. She looked after the house, read the books she dragged home from the library each week, read her on-line newspapers, watched TV, and otherwise lived the life of a hermit—or at least the life of a hermit's wife.

The shabby cars they drove—her aging Mercedes and his Cadillac Escalade—were ten and fifteen years old respectively but at least they still worked. Years of being parked in full sunlight out in the driveway meant that their exterior paint jobs had faded away to powder, and the interiors were ragged with drooping head rests and sun-damaged upholstery. Buying a new car for either one of them was simply out of the question.

As the mandatory belt-tightening continued, things Rachel had always taken for granted as part of her social life simply went away—restaurant meals, golf outings, gatherings with friends, going to movies, standing appointments at her favorite nail salon. It had been a real blow to her when she'd been forced to let her long-time cleaning lady go. They still had a yard man and a pool guy, but only because the homeowner's association would have come after them if they'd let those items slide, and Rich simply refused to do the work himself. He was too busy—making bird houses!

With mourning doves cooing in the background, Rachel thought about how things had been back at the beginning when they had first moved here as opposed to how things were now. Their house had been among the first ones built when the new development had been carved out of open desert. Once they moved in, Rachel soon discovered that the creatures who had been the original inhabitants of the area were none too happy about ceding their territory to these infringing interlopers.

As a little one, David had never been allowed to play outside alone without having his eagle-eyed mother watching over him. Rachel had been forced to use a hoe to dispatch more than one rattlesnake that had somehow managed to slither into their yard. There had always been a plethora of centipedes and scorpions hanging around as well, but Rachel had signed on to protect her child from all comers, and that's exactly what she did.

When it came time for David to go to school, she had cheerfully donned her chauffeur's hat and driven him back and forth to a small, newly established parochial school at St. Bartholomew's Church on Shea Boulevard several miles to the south. She'd driven him everywhere he needed to go—to Boy Scout meetings and Little League games and swim lessons because that's what she'd signed up for—to raise her son; to take care of him; to see that he thrived. And then . . . She shook her head. How on earth could it all have gone so terribly wrong?

The doorbell rang just then. Later Rachel would think of that sound as something her high school drama coach, Miss Reavis, would have referred to as a "knocking within." At a critical point in a play, someone from offstage announces his arrival with a sound of some kind. Once that character appears, he brings with him some bit of compelling information that will propel the drama to its final conclusion. Eventually Rachel would come to realize that's exactly what that doorbell had been—the tipping point that had turned everything in her life upside down, but at the time it was nothing more than an unwelcome intrusion on her solitary afternoon cocktail.

There was no question about Rich emerging from his workshop to answer the door. Even if he'd heard the bell, he wouldn't have bestirred himself from behind his workbench to bother. And that was Rachel's initial reaction, too—that she would simply ignore the ringing bell until this unwelcome visitor gave up and went away. After all, how important could it be?

In the old days, a caller this late in the afternoon might have been a paperboy out collecting from customers on his route, but Rich had stopped subscribing to paper-and-ink newspapers long ago. Since this was March, it might be one of the Brownies from up the street, peddling Girl Scout cookies. Or it might even be some political hack out canvassing the neighborhood, looking for votes in an upcoming municipal election.

The doorbell rang again, but still Rachel didn't move. After a minute or so, it rang a third time. Obviously whoever was at the door wasn't giving up and going away. They probably assumed that, with two cars parked in the driveway, someone had to be home. Only then did Rachel finally go inside to answer. In the front entryway, she paused long enough to use the peephole. What she saw was a heavily tattooed young woman wearing jeans and a T-shirt and holding a banker's box. She looked to be twenty-something, so she was most definitely not hawking Girl Scout cookies.

Once Rachel unlatched the deadbolt and security chain, she swung the door open. "Yes?"

"Are you Mrs. Higgins?"

"I am," Rachel responded.

"David Higgins's mother?"

"Yes," Rachel replied. "I'm David's mother. Who are you and what do you want?"

"My name's Tonya Bounds," the young woman said. "My dad was John Bounds, and I came to give you this."

She held out the box, but Rachel made no move to accept it.

"Who's John Bounds?" she asked.

"After my folks divorced, my father took in boarders for a while," Tonya answered. "I'm guessing your son must have rented a room from him at one time or another. My father died a couple of months ago. My boyfriend and I have been helping my mom get the house ready to sell. The place was a mess. We found this box in a corner of the garage with your son's name on it. Inside was a copy of his obituary. I found your address, but the phone had been disconnected."

"Yes," Rachel said, "we gave up having a landline years ago."

"I didn't know if you still lived at the same address, but since it's on my way home, I decided to take a chance and try dropping by to give it to you."

"What's in it?" Rachel asked.

Tonya shrugged. "Not much, just random stuff David left behind, and I'm not even sure why my dad bothered saving it. There's a comb and brush, some clothing, and a pair of shoes, along with some odds and ends—a class ring, a pin from Disneyland, a school yearbook, and a little notebook that looks like he used as a journal or diary."

Relenting, Rachel reached out and took the box. When she did so, she found it to be a lot lighter than she'd expected.

"Thank you for going to the trouble of tracking us down to deliver it."

"You're welcome," Tonya said with a smile. "Like I said. Your address was on my way. I live just south of the Scottsdale city limits in Tempe."

"If you don't mind my asking, what did your father die of?"

Tonya's smile faded and she shrugged. "An overdose," she answered bleakly. "What else? That's what caused Mom and Dad to split up in the first place. Dad was in and out of treatment time and again. He lasted longer than anyone thought he would, but still . . ." She paused for a moment before adding, "But then I guess you know that drill."

Rachel nodded. She had tried getting David into treatment several times, too, always to no avail. "I guess I do," she agreed, "and it's no fun. So sorry for your loss."

Tonya turned to go. Rachel remained on the front porch long enough to watch the young woman drive away, before going back inside, closing and bolting the door behind her. Initially Rachel started toward the kitchen with the box before changing her mind and heading for her bedroom instead.

David's untimely death was what had plunged Rich into his pit of despair, and to this day, even the mention of his son's name was often enough to provoke a relapse. Rather than leaving the box out in the open, Rachel tucked it away in a corner of her closet and shut the door. When she returned to the kitchen, she was surprised to find Rich there, making himself a bologna sandwich.

The way things were those days, Rachel no longer bothered with cooking nutritious meals. Chances were, Rich wouldn't be interested in eating them anyway. Instead, they subsisted on a steady diet of cold cereal and sandwiches. Rachel's natural metabolism was still serving her in good stead. Rich's was not. In the past seven years he had gained at least fifty pounds, probably more. She hadn't said anything about it. If he didn't care, why should she?

"Who was that at the door?" he asked.

She wanted to say, *why didn't you answer the damned door yourself*, but she didn't. "Magazine salesman," she replied, lying to him without the slightest hesitation. "I told him we didn't want any."

"Good," he said. "We sure as hell don't."

With that he collected his sandwich and a bottle of Bud Light and returned to the garage without bothering to clean up his mess. Rachel did so because that's what she always did—cleaned up after him. And then, rather than make herself a sandwich, she poured another vodka tonic. Before she would be able to face the contents of David's box, she'd need some of what her mother had always referred to as "Dutch courage."

It wasn't until much later that night, after Rich had retreated to his room without a word to Rachel and after his TV set was blaring behind his closed door, when Rachel, more than slightly drunk, finally meandered down the hall to her own room where she closed the door, pulled the banker's box out of the closet, and moved it to her bed.

When she removed the lid, the first thing she saw, of course, was the obituary along with the printed program from the funeral home—the one that had been handed out to people attending the service. That meant that Tonya's father had been enough of a friend that he had gone to the funeral, but Rachel had been in so much pain at the time that she had no real recollection of that day—not of the service itself or of the people who had bothered showing up. John Bounds may have lived and died a druggie, but he had been kind enough to preserve David's paltry collection of belongings, and Rachel was grateful to him for that.

Just under the yellowed newspaper clipping and funeral program was David's moth-eaten letterman's jacket from Scottsdale's St. Francis of Assisi High School. David had been an outstanding athlete. He had lettered in basketball and swimming all four years. He'd played point guard on both the JV and Varsity basketball teams and had been captain of the swim team his senior year when St. Francis had walked away with the state championship. He'd been smart, too. He should have gone on to school, but he hadn't. Rachel had never understood why he had simply turned his back on the idea of going to college, but he had. The night when he had told his parents that he had no intention of going on to college, father and son had gotten into a terrible row.

"Do you have any idea what you're doing?" a livid Rich had demanded. "Don't you care anything about your future?"

"No," David had replied. "I don't."

He had packed up his things that very night and moved out of the house. He had never gone on to school. He had held a series of menial jobs, but mostly he had hung out and done drugs, drifting deeper and deeper into that world until there was no turning back. A heart-broken Rachel had tried reaching out to him from time to time, to no avail. Rich had not. Once David was dead, Rachel had the advantage of having already processed some of her grief. Rich, on the other hand, had been utterly grief stricken. Paralyzed with guilt and unable to cope at work or at home, he had fallen into a downward spiral and had been stuck there ever since.

Rachel unfolded the jacket and held it up to her face, hoping that some trace of David's scent had lingered in the material. It had not. All she smelled was dust with just a hint of motor oil in the background. Laying the jacket aside, she returned to the box. Next up were a few shirts, two worn pairs of Levis, and a broken-down pair of Nike's. At the bottom of the box she found the odds and ends Tonya had mentioned—the pin and the class ring as well as a copy of the St. Francis High School yearbook for 2001, the *Clarion*.

Two thousand and one had been David's senior year, and the swim team had been the center of his existence. Since St. Francis had walked off with the state swimming competition title that year, it was hardly surprising that when she put it in her lap, the book opened almost of its own accord to the sports section near the back and to a page that featured the swim team. The shock of what she saw there took Rachel's breath away. The page featured a full-page photo of the ten members of the team along with their coach, Father Paul Needham. The boys, grinning for the camera, all wore their swim suits. As for the priest? He was fully dressed, but above his white dog collar, every feature of his face had been blacked out with a Sharpie.

In that instant and despite all the vodka she'd consumed, Rachel found herself stone-cold sober because, for the first time in all these years, she finally had some inkling of the reality of what had happened to her son. And that's when the tears came. She and Rich had wanted only the best for David. That was why he had attended parochial schools. That was why they had coughed up the tuition so he could attend St. Francis High, and yet all their good intentions had backfired on them. In wanting to give David everything, they had given him worse than nothing. Rich and Rachel had failed their son, and the Catholic church had failed the whole family.

The storm of tears that followed rocked Rachel to her core. At last, spent with weeping, she dried her tears, repacked the banker's box with David's things, and then steeled herself for the grim task ahead. One way or another she would have her revenge. Someone needed to be held responsible, and if God wouldn't smite them, she would.

Chapter 1

On a bright Monday morning in late June, Ali Reynolds and her husband, B. Simpson, sat drinking coffee on the patio outside the master bedroom of their Sedona home.

"Okay," he said. "The party's over, so time's up. Are you coming to London with me or not?"

The party in question had been a garden-party homecoming event for current and past recipients of Amelia Dougherty Askins scholarships. As a high school senior at Cottonwood High, Ali had been one of the first students to be awarded one of the Verde Valley–based scholarships, and it had enabled her to do something she might not otherwise have been able to do—attend college. She'd gotten a degree in journalism that had allowed her to pursue an award-winning career as a television newscaster. When that had fallen apart, she had returned home to Sedona to regroup. Sometime later, she had found herself in charge of the scholarship program from which she herself had once benefited.

Yesterday's afternoon tea had been in the works long before Alexandra Munsey, one of Ali's good friends from her news anchor days in L.A., had been brutally murdered in her home outside San Bernardino. In the aftermath of Alex's death, Ali, along with several members of B.'s cyber security firm, High Noon Enterprises, had been sucked into the vortex of a homicide investigation.

Alex and Ali had both led complicated past lives. Maybe that was part of what had created such a strong bond between them. Both of their lives had crashed and burned at about the same time and they had both reinvented themselves afterward. At the time of her death, Alex had been on the cusp of a blossoming literary career. The novel that had been published within days of her death had been a huge success and had hit the *New York Times* Best Seller list several weeks in a row. That was one of the reasons her homicide had hit Ali so hard. Alex's death had forever denied her the critical and literary accolades she had so richly deserved.

As for Alex's killers? Hannah Gilchrist, one of the people responsible, was dead of natural causes. The other conspirators were either already incarcerated on other charges or in jail awaiting trial, but Ali knew that it would take years of court proceedings before justice was finally served—if ever. Even so, there would be no eye for an eye here. No matter what the final outcome was in some California courtroom, nothing would ever bring Alex Munsey back. She would never live to see her precious grandson grow up, graduate from high school, go off to college, marry, or have a child of his own. She would never have the opportunity to write and publish another book. No, her untimely death had destroyed all those potential outcomes, and the unbearable finality of that was wearing Ali down.

Weeks earlier she had risen to the challenge, traveled to L.A., and stood up to speak at Alex's funeral, but back home it had been all she could do to go through with the party. The food had been catered by one of the scholarship fund's food science graduates, and B.'s and Ali's new majordomo, Alonzo Rivera, had sorted out most of the physical details. Still, it had taken real effort on Ali's part to simply dress up, put on a happy face, and go forth to welcome her guests. Once the party had ended, late in the afternoon, she had been ready to collapse.

B. was due to attend an international cybersecurity conference in London at the end of the week, and days earlier, he had invited Ali to come along with the added incentive that they'd be able to see a play or two in the West End and maybe spend a couple of days hiking in the Cotswolds once the conference ended.

"Come on," he had said. "It'll be good for what ails you. We've got a full team on board to look after things in your absence."

If B. had expected an enthusiastic affirmative, it wasn't forthcoming. "Maybe," she had said. "Let me get through the garden party first."

"I just checked with BA," B. added. "There are still a couple of first class seats on my flight. Shall I book one for you?"

Ali had stalled him on the subject earlier, but now with the party in the rearview mirror, it was time for her to give him a final answer.

"All right," she agreed reluctantly. "I'll come along, but I'm not sure I'll be very good company. When do we leave?"

"Wednesday," he replied, "Wednesday afternoon."

"Sorry," she said after a thoughtful pause. "I guess I'm acting like an ungrateful, spoiled brat."

"You are," B. agreed with a smile while reaching

across the table to take her hand. "But at least you're my spoiled brat, and one who's been through one hell of an ordeal."

"Thank you," she said. "And maybe a trip is exactly what's needed."

Chapter 2

On a Monday morning in late June, Francis Gillespie, Archbishop of the Phoenix Archdiocese, fled the air-conditioned chill of his study for the welcome warmth of his shaded outdoor patio. The perimeter of the property was lined by an impenetrable wall of oleanders that had grown to be twenty feet tall. Beyond the wall to the back, the craggy red expanse of Camelback Mountain loomed large against a hazy blue sky. To the front, the hedge shielded the property from the roar of city traffic rushing past on Lincoln Drive East. Inside that green barrier, the manicured grounds of his residence constituted a whole other world.

The archbishop loved sitting here on the patio, surveying his lush domain. Because the residence had its own private well, water was not an issue. There was grass, plenty of hearty, thick-bladed grass. There were raised flower beds scattered here and there, all of them alive with riots of vivid color from blooming petunias and snapdragons. Most of the palm trees in the city and on neighboring properties had been stripped of their skirts, but that wasn't the case here. Every year the gardener came to him begging to be allowed to strip off the palm trees' masses of hanging dead limbs, and each year the archbishop overruled him. Those dead leaves provided habitats for any number of flying creatures—a flicker or two, a woodpecker, and squadrons of bats. Several rock doves resided there along with a pair of house finches that migrated back and forth between the trees and the bubbling fountain at the foot of the patio.

The archbishop had taken his old bones outside to warm them in the summer heat, and he had brought his work with him. His Holiness at the Vatican may have taken strong positions on things like climate change and reducing carbon footprints, but Archbishop Gillespie had seen no reduction in the amount of tree-based paperwork that flowed like a gigantic river in and out of the Holy See. After being sidelined by ill health for the better part of two months, the archbishop regarded the incoming missives as more of a flood than a river.

In late March, something the archbishop had tried to pass off as a minor cold had soon morphed into a full-blown case of bronchial pneumonia. He had spent close to three weeks in the ICU at the Mayo Clinic Hospital and another four weeks confined to their rehab facility. The doctors had warned him that at his age—closer to eighty-eight than to eighty-seven—he was lucky to still be "on the right side of the grass." As an exceedingly young doctor had told him, his recovery would be a "long, slow process."

That was certainly proving to be true. To his dismay, Francis was still having to depend on a walker to get around, and the previous night, while trying to push his way through another pile of paperwork, he'd fallen asleep at his desk and had awakened a full three hours later. He was making better progress in the paperwork department now, but with a noontime appointment looming, he wasn't going to come close to getting to the bottom of the pile.

At that moment the patio slider opened and Father Daniel McCray, Archbishop Gillespie's private secretary for the past fifteen years, stepped outside.

"Excuse me, Your Grace, but one of your luncheon guests has arrived early and would like a word."

Father McCray and Archbishop Gillespie had worked together on a daily basis for a decade and a half. Although the archbishop might have welcomed a bit of informality between them, Father McCray was careful to maintain the proper amount of distance and decorum.

Archbishop Gillespie removed his reading glasses and set his paperwork aside. Back when he'd been a parish priest, his flock had been his parishioners. Once he was appointed Archbishop of the Phoenix Diocese, his flock had become the priests and nuns who did the hands-on work of spreading the gospel. Some archbishops tended to isolate themselves and stay far above the fray. That was not Archbishop Gillespie's *modus operandi*.

He understood the essential loneliness of living a godly life. A shepherd is there to guide and protect his sheep, not to befriend them, so priests were always set apart from their parishioners. As both a bishop and archbishop, Francis Gillespie had loved the camaraderie of meeting with others of his own ilk—men who knew both the joys and burdens of doing God's work. As a young priest he had formed close friendships with several of the men he'd met at church gatherings, one of whom was now a cardinal.

Francis wasn't a political animal. At the time of his appointment, there had been two warring factions inside the Phoenix Archdiocese. Considered to be a natural outsider, he had been promoted from within for that exact reason—because he wasn't a member of either clique. He had risen through the priesthood by dint of being both smart and direct. If he saw a problem, he didn't care to sit around endlessly jawing about it; he wanted to fix it. As a consequence, early in his tenure as archbishop he had made himself available to his flock by hosting monthly luncheons for the priests in his diocese. The gatherings, held in his residence, were certainly not mandatory but they were always widely attended, as much for the delicious food provided by Father Andrew, the arch-bishop's cook, as for the fellowship provided by simply being together.

The archbishop's luncheons were customarily held on the last Monday of the month—Mondays being the one day of the week when priests might reasonably take a day off. The luncheons allowed his far-flung clerics to socialize and come to know one another. For Francis Gillespie, the gatherings allowed him to keep his finger on the pulse of his flock. Since the previous two luncheons had been scrapped due to his illness, the expectation was that this one would be especially well attended, and Father Andrew had been cooking up a storm for days.

"Which priest?" Archbishop Gillespie asked.

"Father Winston from Prescott," was the reply.

Father Jonathan Winston was one of the newer priests in Archbishop Gillespie's fold. He was an Iraq War veteran who had gone to seminary and joined the priesthood after three separate deployments to the Middle East. In addition to serving as the priest at St. Mary's in Prescott, Father Winston did a good deal of chaplaincy work at his local VA Hospital. He and the archbishop had carried on many long conversations on how best to serve veterans dealing with PTSD.

"Have Father Winston come out here then," Francis told Father McCray. "Once I've had a chance to hear what's on his mind, the two of us will go in to the luncheon together."

"Very well," Father McCray replied, nodding his assent. He disappeared through the slider and returned a few moments later with Father Winston following on his heels. Once he had delivered the newcomer into Archbishop Gillespie's presence, Father McCray disappeared inside.

With the exception of his white collar, Father Winston was dressed all in black, and it occurred to the archbishop that perhaps the younger man wouldn't find the outside heat nearly as comfortable as Francis did.

"Your Grace," Father Winston said, holding out his hand, "it's good to see that you're on the mend."

"Mending, but not altogether one hundred percent at this point," the archbishop replied, waving in the general direction of his much-despised walker. "I'm still having to use that confounded thing."

"We've missed you," Father Winston said.

"Thank you," the archbishop said. "I've missed you, too. Have a seat," he added, "and tell me what's on your mind."

Seating himself at the round patio table, Father Winston withdrew something from his pocket and handed it over. Looking down, Father Gillespie saw a standard offertory envelope. There were places where parishioners could write in their names, addresses, and phone numbers along with the amount of their offering. Those lines had all been left blank.

"What's this?" Archbishop Gillespie asked.

"It showed up in the collection plate yesterday when the deacon in charge was sorting the banking deposit. Take a look inside."

Archbishop Gillespie opened the envelope and pulled out a folded three-by-five card. On it, handwritten in ink, was the following message:

HEY HEY, HO HO.

ARCHBISHOP GILLESPIE HAS TO GO!

Looking up from the message, the archbishop smiled. "I'm sure this reflects the feelings of any number of folks around here who are of the opinion that I'm well past my sell-by date."

Father Winston didn't smile in return. "It sounds like a threat to me," he said. "And the fact that it was anonymous . . ."

"I doubt it's as serious as all that," Archbishop Gillespie advised. "What is it they call people like that—the ones who post all kinds of awful things on the Internet under the mask of anonymity?"

"You mean trolls?" Father Winston asked.

"That's it exactly—trolls. Trolls used to hide out under bridges. Now they hide behind computer screens or, as in this case, behind an offertory envelope, where they can be totally anonymous and feel perfectly free to say all kinds of appalling things. Hidden behind a curtain like that, they can spit out all kinds of nonsense that they'd never have gumption enough to say directly to someone's face. If I were you, Father Winston, I wouldn't give this message another moment's thought."

With that, the archbishop returned the card to the envelope and slipped it into his pocket. Then he gathered his papers and rose to his feet. "It's getting hot out here. What say we go inside and see what Father Andrew has been up to. He told me at breakfast that he's outdone himself today."

For the remainder of the day, Archbishop Gillespie followed his own advice and didn't give the handwritten missive another thought. It wasn't until he was emptying his pockets in preparation for going to bed that evening when he came across the envelope again. He studied it for a moment before slipping it, unopened, into the top drawer of his dresser.

Father Winston was a priest who'd had firsthand experience with war. He'd been in combat. He'd done tough things and seen worse. No wonder he was suspicious and maybe even a bit paranoid. But that wasn't Francis Gillespie's worldview.

"It's nothing," he said aloud, closing the dresser drawer with a thump. "It's nothing at all."

Unfortunately, he was wrong about that. The message that had been dropped into the collection plate at St. Mary's in Prescott was anything but nothing. It may have been the first threat Archbishop Gillespie received, but it was certainly not the last. Although the wording would be different, they would all be similar in nature and dropped off in collection plates in churches scattered all over the archdiocese. And each time Francis Gillespie added a new one to the growing collection in his dresser drawer, he was forced to draw one simple conclusion. Someone was after him, and whoever it was wouldn't quit until he was gone.